The
Secret Book
of Kings

The
Secret Book
of Kings

Yochi Brandes

Translated by
Yardenne Greenspan

St. Martin's Press
New York

THE SECRET BOOK OF KINGS. Copyright © 2008 by Yochi Brandes. English translation copyright © 2016 by Yardenne Greenspan. All rights reserved. Printed in the United States of America. For information, address St. Martin's Press, 175 Fifth Avenue, New York, N.Y. 10010.

www.stmartins.com

Designed by Kathryn Parise

The Library of Congress Cataloging-in-Publication Data is available upon request.

ISBN 978-1-250-07698-4 (hardcover)
ISBN 978-1-4668-8889-0 (e-book)

Our books may be purchased in bulk for promotional, educational, or business use. Please contact your local bookseller or the Macmillan Corporate and Premium Sales Department at 1-800-221-7945, extension 5442, or by e-mail at MacmillanSpecialMarkets@macmillan.com.

First U.S. Edition: August 2016

Originally published in 2008 in Israel by Kinneret Zmora-Bitan Dvir Publishing House, Ltd., under the title *Kings III*.

10 9 8 7 6 5 4 3 2 1

The Secret Book of Kings *is lovingly dedicated to*
my many Bible teachers
who taught me to read the Bible
to love the Bible
and to carry it with me everywhere I go.

Acknowledgments

When I was eight years old, I learned in school that the ancient nation of Israel had split into two rival kingdoms—the great Kingdom of Israel of the ten tribes, and the smaller Kingdom of Judah of the tribe of Judah. Only then, for the first time in my life, did I realize that we, the Jews, are all descendants of the Kingdom of Judah, while the people of the Kingdom of Israel became assimilated and are no more. This realization saddened me greatly. Throughout all the years of my childhood, I yearned for a miracle that would return the Ten Lost Tribes to the Land of Israel. I so wanted them to live in the State of Israel together with us, the people of the Kingdom of Judah.

Nearly forty years had to pass before my love for the people of the Kingdom of Israel turned into a book. The idea occurred to me in the wake of an essay I published on the Biblical princess Michal. The excited reactions to my essay made me realize that most people are unaware that hiding within the pages of the Bible are several storytelling traditions claiming that David methodically and purposefully annihilated the House of Saul. I decided to write a novel about Michal that would describe her life from the unfamiliar point of view of the scribes of the House of Saul, and not from the familiar point of view of the scribes of the House of David. But even at the beginning of my research, I realized that a historical novel about the destruction of the House of Saul at the hands of David could not make do with a single protagonist, as had the other novels I had written up to that point. Rather, the novel would have to be written from the perspectives of two main characters—Michal daughter of Saul, whose passionate love for David brought terrible calamities upon her and upon her family; and also Jeroboam son of Nebat, who avenged her two generations later by persuading the ten tribes to split off from the kingdom of the House of David and establish a separate kingdom for themselves under his leadership.

The Secret Book of Kings was published in 2008, and I was overjoyed when it quickly became one of the best-selling novels ever in Israel. Since then, I have been asked again and again when it would finally be translated into other languages, but I wondered whether a Biblical novel written in Hebrew would be successful outside Israel.

That was what I asked Daniel Libenson, the founder of the Institute for the Next Jewish Future in the United States, when he visited me about two years ago and asked my permission to search for an American publisher for an English edition of *The Secret Book of Kings*. Daniel confidently declared that the book would succeed in English-speaking countries precisely because I was an Israeli writer, and one with a rather unique background at that. While many readers of English are generally familiar with the major stories and characters of the Bible, he said, most are not intimately familiar with the details of those stories, and even fewer are likely to have noticed the secret stories of the scribes of the House of Saul. Only a person like me, who has studied Judaism through both the traditional approach and the academic approach, and who reads the Bible in the original, could draw out its hidden stories and weave them into a subversive novel like this one.

I don't need to tell you the rest. The fact that you are holding the English edition of *The Secret Book of Kings* in your hands says it all. Thank you, Daniel Libenson, for initiating the connection with St. Martin's Press, and thank you so very much for your exceptional editing, which has made *The Secret Book of Kings* read as though it were originally written in English. You labored for two full months, day after day, from morning until night. Even the passing of your mother, of blessed memory, didn't stop you from completing the difficult and important task that you took upon yourself and that only you could have accomplished.

Thank you, Anya Lichtenstein, for reading *The Secret Book of Kings* in Hebrew and recommending with faith and confidence that your company publish it. And thank you, leaders and managers of St. Martin's Press, for accepting her enthusiastic recommendation. How pleased I feel that my book has found a home in your outstanding publishing house.

Thank you, Yardenne Greenspan, for translating the book with complete fidelity to the source and giving it life in English.

And thank you, Silissa Kenney and Sylvan Creekmore. When Anya took a new position outside the press, I was very concerned. But when I began working with you, I realized right away that I had no cause for concern. You have ushered the book through every stage of its editing and production with unending dedication and with attentive and sensitive understanding.

Thank you, Yuval Horowitz, my dedicated agent from Kneller Artists Agency, who has been helping me for many years in all my activities and creative endeavors. You believed that *The Secret Book of Kings* would be published by a major American publishing house, and you persisted in your faith despite all the delays.

Special thanks to you, Ofer, my husband and my love. You contribute to my creativity with your wide-ranging talents at every stage of the research, the writing, and the editing, but this time your help was greater and more significant than ever. You went over Daniel's excellent editing and checked every quote, every verse, every sentence, every word, and every letter. Your meticulous thoroughness and your broad knowledge of the Bible gave *The Secret Book of Kings* what I should have given it had I known English. . . . Thanks to you, I am certain of the quality of the book that I present here to my new readers in English.

Yochi Brandes
Israel 2016

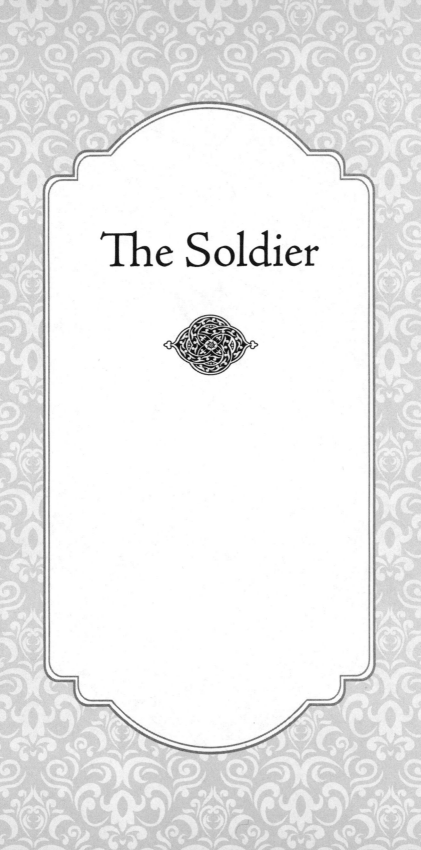

The Soldier

One

Mother took me to the lepers' cave for the first time on the fifteenth day of the eighth month. I remember the date because of the Festival of Rain, which turned me into the most famous boy in Zeredah. The story spread quickly throughout the entire land of Ephraim. Everyone wanted to hear about the little boy who had managed to fool the king's soldiers and save his townspeople.

It began with the first rainfall, which brought crowds of revelers out into the streets and scuttled our plan to sneak out of Zeredah at dawn, before people wake up. Mother didn't want anyone to see us in the wagon together for fear that if they realized I was going with her to the cave, they would try to scare me with horror stories about healthy people who only glimpsed the lepers from afar and instantly lost their hair and nails, holes gaping in the middle of their faces where their noses used to be. Mother is the only person in Zeredah who isn't afraid of lepers. Every month, when the moon is full, she heads to the cave with food and medicines for them, and she speaks with them intimately, the way one speaks with friends. She believes that the God of Israel loves the lepers and favors those who help them. And indeed, our house is truly blessed. Many other families in Zeredah barely survive under the weight of the taxes. Their little children must go out to work in the fields and vineyards, while I get to stay home with my tutors, who teach me arithmetic, reading, writing, and even Egyptian. My parents will also hire tutors for my sister, Elisheba, when she grows up, even though she's a girl.

⮞⮜

I sat on the wagon and tried to hide my trembling hands under my knees. I'd been begging Father a long time before he agreed to let me join Mother at the cave. That's the way wishes are. You pine for them and look forward, but when they finally do come true, you'd rather be somewhere else.

Suddenly, it started to rain. Mother hesitated. She didn't want to delay, but the rain grew harder, and we were drenched from head to toe. There was no choice but to go back home and install the wagon cover. It was still early, and we thought we'd be able to get everything done quickly and be on our way again before anyone noticed us, but before we even knew what was happening, we were surrounded.

Mother dropped the reins and gripped my shoulder.

I peeked out of the wagon and saw dozens of people skipping and dancing in the rain. They were raising their hands to the sky and calling out, "Happy holiday! Happy holiday!"

Crowds always make me uneasy. Our house is at the edge of town, concealed by a dense thicket, and I am used to having only my sister and parents for company. I grabbed Mother's leg and buried my head in her lap. Her fingers gripped my shoulder harder.

Hazy figures began mounting the wagon from behind. I could hear their words but couldn't decipher their meaning.

"The first rainfall waited for the day of our festival."

"It's an omen for a blessed winter for Ephraim."

"It's an omen for a blessed winter for all of Israel."

I don't know why, but this meaningless chatter filled me with terror. I burst into tears. All the air left my lungs. I felt like I was suffocating.

All of a sudden, I heard Mother laughing. I looked at her, stunned. Her face was beaming.

"Happy holiday, Shelomoam." She stood up and held out her hands. "Come, let's join the festivities. The lepers' cave isn't going anywhere."

⮞⮜

Father stepped outside with Elisheba, whom Mother took into her arms, jumping around with her to the sounds of the drums and the harps. Elisheba caught raindrops in her little fingers and licked them voraciously. Father tried to persuade me to return home with him. I generally obey him, but these festivities were interesting, so I told him angrily that this time I wasn't willing to miss out.

Mother took my side, reminding him that the king's soldiers had already been to Zeredah that month and there was no chance they would come back again. He finally agreed, on the condition that I stayed by his side at all times. But I ventured off on purpose, mixing in with a group of children. I thought I'd gotten away from him when I felt his strong hands seize my waist and raise me up onto his shoulders.

I felt strong and confident, a head taller than anyone else. The children watched me from below, barely able to contain their envy. I waved at them as if I were the king. No child in Zeredah has a father as young as mine. Some kids' fathers are practically old men, older than even Grandfather, who is so old that sometimes when Father comes to see him, he doesn't remember who Father is. Mother says that's what happens when an elderly man decides to take a second or third wife—he has children the same age as his grandchildren or even his great-grandchildren, and instead of him caring for them, they have to care for him. Six months ago I went out to the fields with my family for the Festival of Harvest, and someone told Father he looked like my older brother. I thought it was funny, but he didn't. His eyes were panicked. As if the king's soldiers would care how old he was when he had me!

⚘

I recalled the strange things the people on the wagon had said and wanted to ask Father why we didn't celebrate like this last year or the year before, why it was that this year the first rainfall signified a blessed winter in Ephraim and possibly all of Israel. But I knew he didn't like it when I asked about our tribe's special customs, so I decided I'd ask Mother on the way to the cave. Then I realized that we might not make it out that day, for the celebrations would probably go on until the evening. I saw women bringing out wine and food and spreading green cloths over long tables. Green is also the color of the dancing girls. They raise the hems of their green dresses up above their ankles and twist like snakes in front of the boys, who stop dancing and watch.

Father also stops bouncing around with me in the rain and turns to look at them. I can't blame him. If I were his age, I would also watch the pretty girls. But it angers me to see Mother notice him looking and glumly join the women setting the table. I know that she worries Father might take another wife who would threaten her position in the family, the way Grandfather did, taking no fewer than four wives, each one younger than the one before. With each new decade in his life, he took a new wife to rekindle his youth, neglecting his previous wives, turning them bitter. Father once told me, in a rare moment of candor, that he would never forgive his father for the way he'd wronged his mother, which was the only reason she had died brokenhearted and young.

Father keeps promising Mother that he will never bring home a rival wife. He only watches the young girls from afar, but he goes to bed with Mother every night. "You are my Rebecca," he told her just a week ago, having returned from the wedding of an old miller who had taken a third wife.

"Mother's name is Bilhah, not Rebecca," I corrected him.

Father laughed and said he meant that Mother would be his only wife forever, just like Rebecca of old. "A son mustn't always follow in his father's footsteps, just as Isaac didn't follow in the footsteps of Abraham. Abraham had three wives—Sarah, Hagar, and Keturah—while Isaac remained faithful to the love of his youth."

I lingered over Father's words and finally told him that, in that case, I would have to follow in Grandfather's footsteps, just as Jacob followed in Abraham's, by taking several women.

Father went quiet. I could tell I had surprised him. But Mother answered instantly, without even pausing to think, that the case of Jacob proves that sometimes a son ought to follow in his father's footsteps rather than his grandfather's. "Had Jacob done as Isaac did and spent his entire life only with his beloved Rachel, his sons wouldn't have hated each other, and all of us—the three tribes of Rachel—would have lived peacefully together in the land of our fathers." She paused and then whispered, "And the king would have been one of our own, a son of Rachel, just like Joseph, the father of Ephraim, the great ruler of Egypt, or like Joshua the Conqueror, Deborah the Judge, or Samuel the Priest—all children of Ephraim. Or perhaps our king would have been a son of Benjamin, like Ehud the Hero and S—"

Mother couldn't finish because Father slapped her back hard. She looked at him, shocked. He had never raised a hand to her before. She hissed angrily that the king's soldiers weren't in Zeredah that day and that she was allowed to express her longing for the mighty leaders of the line of Rachel.

Father walked to the window, pale-faced, and looked outside in all directions. Then he told me to go out and play in the thicket. I preferred to stay home and talk some more about our ancestors, but his tone and expression told me I'd best not argue.

⚘

The rain dances lasted for hours, and we only paused to eat around noon. I was impressed with the tables heaped with delicacies that the women had prepared for us without prior notice. Just last night the sky had been copper, and the earth had been iron, and no one could have foreseen the coming of the first rainfall. I pounced on the food, stuffing myself. Father signaled for me to mind my manners, but I pretended not to notice. I tasted everything. My favorites were the crispy honey pastry and the raisin and fig cake.

Though I was busy eating, I didn't take my eyes off my sister. I could see that Mother was busy serving and that Father was in the middle of a conversation, and neither of them noticed her on her tiptoes, trying to reach the sweet oat porridge. I pulled the pit out of a ripe date and put the fruit in her mouth, but she spat it out disgustedly and demanded porridge.

Suddenly I felt the table jiggling and the ground shaking beneath us. Mother and Father had told me that the earth was angry at human beings for conquering and enslaving it. Most days it submitted, granting us its fruits, but once every generation or two it fought back and destroyed our homes. It must have been especially angry this day over our festivities celebrating the first rainfall. Instead of thanking the earth for its yield, we were giving thanks to the sky. The earth was trying to knock us down to our knees so that we would have to crawl, bent and submissive, and beg for its mercy.

I fell to the ground and laid my head in the moist dirt. I was sure that everyone else was doing as I had done, but the silence had a strange tinge to it. I looked up and saw them all standing, frozen, their eyes fixed on a point behind me. I didn't dare get up and went on lying in the mud until I could feel that the tables were no longer shaking.

Only then did I see them. It was the biggest group of soldiers I had ever witnessed in my life. No wonder the hooves of their horses had made the tables shake. There were at least a hundred soldiers out there.

I wondered why they had sent so many. Ever since the Rebellion of the Temples, we have all been paying our taxes without resistance. Mother told me that the rebellion had started after the king took the throne and announced a new tax to fund the construction of a great temple in Jerusalem, the most fabulous edifice in all the world. The Judeans had been eager for a new temple that could attract visitors from every land and make their capital an important, central destination. But the other tribes resented it, asking why they should be forced to invest their money in a Judean temple and not their own. In spite of their rage, the taxes were nonetheless paid in full. No one wanted trouble with the authorities. But the Decree of the Temples shattered that peace. At first, people refused to believe that the king would order the destruction of their temples and the dismissal of their priests. How is it possible to live without temples? How can we pray to God? Make requests of Him? Offer sacrifices?

Emergency delegations headed for Jerusalem to determine whether the rumors were true, and the king replied that sacrifices would now be permitted only in Jerusalem, at the Tabernacle for the time being. Later, when the temple was ready, the Tabernacle would be destroyed, as well, and all of Israel would make pilgrimage only to his magnificent temple, which would be the only one in the land.

The stunned messengers tried to explain to the king that Jerusalem was far away and that the Israelites wanted God by their side, but the king wouldn't relent, and the new decree was written in the Book of Laws. The first rebels were of course from the tribe of Benjamin, the wolves of Israel, and the people of Ephraim and Manasseh soon followed. But the rebellion was not limited to the tribes of Rachel. "We have no share in Judah, no part in Jerusalem. Every man to his temple, Israel!"—this was the rallying cry of the rebellion, and warriors of every tribe stopped paying their taxes and went out to defend their temples.

"So much blood was shed," Mother sighs whenever she recalls those days, "especially in the lands of Benjamin and Ephraim."

Ever since, for seven consecutive years, all the tribes of Israel have paid their taxes. Delegations from every corner of the land arrived at the inauguration of the new temple in Jerusalem six months ago. Each month, a convoy of soldiers enters Zeredah, riding confidently on horseback and waving to us in greeting. The adults hurry to the house of administration with their taxes, while the children run after the soldiers, trying to keep up. The soldiers don't get mad. On the contrary, they smile warmly, sometimes even tossing raisins and almonds to the kids.

One time, I left the house without permission and crossed the thicket alone. When I arrived on the main road, I saw the children running after the horses and decided to join in. The commander, riding in front, pulled up and invited me to hop on. He must have noticed that it was my first time running after them. All the other children gathered around, watching me with envy.

Father seethed when he heard about this and warned me never to leave the thicket alone or go near any soldier.

"But why?" I tried to protest.

"They are not our friends," Mother answered for him.

⁂

I watched the large company quietly, unmoving, just like everyone else. The only thing I could think of was that a war had started and that the soldiers were drafting all the young men of Zeredah. I was afraid they would draft Father, but then I recalled that there were no more wars. The previous king had conquered the entire land, and no other nation dares threaten us now.

Suddenly, I recognized the commander who had let me ride with him. I wanted to ask him why they had decided to come with so many soldiers today. We were paying our taxes as required. But I knew that if I tried to approach him, Father would panic and get angry, so I continued to watch the commander from afar, hoping he would eventually recognize me and give me a wave and that everyone would calm down and realize that nothing bad was going to happen. Perhaps the soldiers had only come to taste of our delicacies. Let them feast! Why not? Our tables are full. There is enough for everybody.

But the soldiers didn't move toward the tables. Instead, they remained on their horses, watching their commander intently, waiting for a go-ahead. The commander looked over us through narrowed eyes, though the sun wasn't even bright. Then, slowly, with a long, accentuated motion, he turned to face the soldiers and gave a nod. I could see his expression. It was so menacing that I squeezed my eyes shut in fear. I opened them only when I heard the horses galloping. I grabbed Elisheba and jumped aside at the very last moment. My leg must have twisted, because rather than continuing with the others, I found myself on the muddy ground again, my sister in my arms. She wasn't crying.

The shock was too great. I stood up slowly with her, careful not to slip, and I saw the green tablecloths strewn about on the ground and the tasty food trampled by the horses' hooves.

"What is this holiday to you?" the commander shouted.

People tried to run away, but the soldiers surrounded them. The commander repeated his question. I felt relieved when I heard my mother behind me:

"We are celebrating the first rainfall, my lord."

I was so proud of her courage. Among all the people of Zeredah, she was the only one who dared to speak to the commander. But he wasn't satisfied. Mother's explanation must have angered him further, and he raised his whip in her direction.

One of the soldiers rode forward and pulled up at the commander's side. I recognized him. He was the only soldier Mother liked. With my own eyes, I once saw her smiling and nodding at him in greeting when he rode past our thicket. I had asked her why she was allowed to greet soldiers while I wasn't, and she had answered firmly that she hadn't given him any sort of greeting, that I was only imagining it. I didn't believe her.

"This is Bilhah, the wife of Benaiah the vine grower," the soldier introduced Mother with exaggerated formality. "They own many vineyards in Zeredah, and their taxes are always paid in full."

The commander lowered his eyes to examine Mother. "Where is your husband?" he finally spat mockingly. "Why does he hide behind your back rather than talk to me himself? Is this the famous heroism of Ephraim?"

Father shuffled meekly out of the crowd and stood before the commander. I could tell that he was trying to hide his nervousness, but his sweat dripped for all to see. I was ashamed of him.

The commander shot him a quick look. "Are you Benaiah the vine grower?"

Father nodded with tight lips.

"Your wife tells me you are celebrating the first rainfall. Why does it make you so happy this year in particular?"

Father said nothing. I gritted my teeth and held back my tears.

"Because of the drought," Mother answered for him. "Last year it hardly rained at all, and our crops were meager."

The commander furrowed his brow with scorn. "Is your man a mute?"

I balled my hands into fists when I heard the soldiers laughing.

Father opened his mouth, but instead of speaking, he just exhaled heavily.

I walked over and took his hand. I wanted him to feel ashamed that his little boy was braver than he was. Maybe then he'd stop burbling like a frightened baby and start speaking like a man.

The commander stared at me intently, trying to remember how he knew me. Then he smiled. "Shelomoam," he said my name affectionately, or so I thought.

I smiled back at him, hoping it would relieve the tense atmosphere and make Father stand up straight.

"Tell me, Shelomoam, which holiday did you celebrate this year before the Festival of Booths?" he asked, his voice soft, almost beseeching.

I wondered why he was asking me such a simple question. The Festival of Harvest is my favorite holiday, the only time Father allows me to go out to the fields with everyone else. We wear white clothes, adorn our heads with green wreaths, and celebrate the first wheat stalks of the season. The priests sacrifice the gift of the first fruits in the fields and thank God for His abundance. Mother told me that, before the Decree of the Temples, the priests used to sacrifice the harvest in our beautiful temple, whose remnants can still be found in the center of Zeredah. Its walls were made of wood and lined with a velvet curtain. What she missed most of all was the stone bull in front, the symbol of our patriarch Joseph. The soldiers had shattered it, leaving nothing behind.

"The Festival of *Ingathering*," Mother whispered.

"Silence, woman!" The commander resumed his frightful expression.

I suddenly remembered that I had heard of such a holiday before. Mother had once muttered angrily that the king forced us to celebrate Judah's Festival of Ingathering and commanded us to forget our own holiday. I had asked her how our holiday was observed, but Father cut her off and wouldn't let her answer me.

"The last holiday we celebrated in Zeredah this year before the Festival of Booths was the Festival of Ingathering." I said this confidently, and a sigh of relief sounded behind me, as if everyone had just exhaled at the same time.

The commander ordered me to come closer and describe exactly how we celebrated it. Without thinking, I told him about dancing in the fields around large piles of gathered harvest, and about the wonderful feast we had. I don't know where these descriptions came from, but the commander's expression told me that I sounded convincing.

"And how did you thank our God?" he asked slowly. "Did you offer animal sacrifices, or did you make do with a sacrifice of the gathering?"

I was confused and unsure what to say. I glanced at Mother and saw her turning pale. Then I looked back up at the man and said, "Sacrifices? In Zeredah? God forbid! We only offer sacrifices at the new temple in Jerusalem!"

❧

The people of Ephraim would recount this story for a long time, marveling at the little boy who had managed to trick armed soldiers and save the people of Zeredah.

Mother was also impressed. She waited for the military convoy to disappear into the mountains, then called me back up to the wagon to accompany her to the lepers' cave. But I had had enough for one day and suggested we wait till morning.

"Don't be lazy," she urged me. "I can't wait to tell the lepers what happened to us today. I want them to know what a clever son I've got."

"It's *my* story," I said proudly. "*I* want to tell it."

"You?" She chuckled. "You'd better not. The story is interesting enough without your embellishments."

Two

Mother had never told me what the cave looked like on the inside. Lepers were one of her favorite topics, second only to her hatred of soldiers, but she spoke mostly of our ancestors who had suffered from leprosy, not of the lepers she met in the cave.

My favorite was the story of Miriam the Prophetess, the older sister of Moses and Aaron. Miriam had contracted leprosy during the years of wandering in the wilderness and was lovingly cared for by the Israelites. Miriam was Mother's role model, even more than Joseph, the father of our line. In her opinion, Miriam should have been the one to redeem the Israelites from the Egyptians and to bring the Torah down from the heavens, and the role had been taken away from her and given to her younger brother only because she was a woman. Father once told me that when Elisheba was born, Mother wanted to call her Miriam but eventually decided the name was common enough, while Elisheba, the wife of Aaron the Priest, had been forgotten. That's how my sister got her name.

"Too bad you didn't name me Aaron," I told him. "She and I could have been like husband and wife."

I could tell that Father was troubled by this comment, but I didn't understand why. I hadn't said anything wrong. No soldier would arrest me for wanting to be named after the first priest of Israel.

When I was old enough to argue with Mother, I told her that I admired only the leaders of the tribes of Rachel's line, and that Miriam, a Levite, belonged to Leah. She responded with a long lecture about the deep camaraderie of the tribe of Levi and the tribes of Joseph. To make her point, she gave the examples of Moses, who had appointed Joshua of Ephraim as his successor, and Aaron, who, of all the symbols of Israel, had chosen to place the symbol of Joseph in the doorway of the Tabernacle.

"A bull stood in the doorway of the Tabernacle in the wilderness?" I asked, excited. I realized she was telling me things that were not to be discussed and was proud to have gained her trust and to be included.

"Not just any bull," Mother declared. "A golden calf. Its mere presence was a proclamation that Joseph was the chosen son of Israel."

I considered this and told her that I didn't understand why the king had ordered the destruction of the bull at the Zeredah temple if Aaron the Priest himself had set our symbol inside the Tabernacle.

That kind of question would have had Father running anxiously to the window, but he was in the vineyard at the time, and Mother could speak freely, describing the ancient rivalry between Judah and Joseph. "The Judeans refuse to accept the superiority and leadership of the tribe of Joseph. Sometimes they use force against us, like when Caleb son of Jephunneh tried to rebel against Joshua, and at other times they use stories."

"Stories?" I asked with wonder. "But stories aren't weapons."

Mother answered with a grave expression on her face that stories are more dangerous than swords. Swords can only harm those standing right in front of them, while stories determine who will live and who will die in future generations.

I didn't understand. I asked what any of this had to do with our bull that the king had destroyed.

"The Judeans' story is that Aaron betrayed the God of Israel," Mother said disgustedly. "In order to defile our symbols, they spread vicious slanders about the distinguished priest of Israel. I can't even bring myself to repeat what they say."

I knew Mother wanted me to insist, and so I immediately began to beg. She finally consented, whispering with a shudder that the Judeans claimed that Aaron had said of the golden calf, **"These are your gods, Israel, who brought you up out of Egypt,"** and ordered the people to make sacrifices to it.

I was so shocked that I couldn't speak.

Even during the journey, Mother still would not describe the cave. "Be patient," she rebuked me. "We'll be there soon." She held on to the reins confidently and appeared consumed by the road ahead. By the time we reached the foot of the mountain, night had fallen. The clouds completely blocked the light of the full moon, and the horses climbed up the muddy path. It felt as though we were about to slip down the slope.

"It's going to be all right," Mother calmed me. "The horses are used to this road."

When we reached the top of the mountain, I hopped off the wagon. Mother took my hand and led me into the cave.

It was different from how I'd imagined it. I had expected a dark, moldy place with moist, collapsing walls. I was surprised to find myself inside a spacious hall lit with dozens of small torches spreading the lovely smell of incense. It was as if I'd left the maddening, threatening world outside, a world where soldiers might appear at any moment to shatter holiday tables, and arrived at the kingdom of tranquility. I must have been smiling to myself, because Mother said I looked happy again.

I breathed in the incense with obvious pleasure. "I like it here."

She looked at me with wonder. "Not everyone feels that way."

I examined the colorful rugs on the floor and walls, then stepped out of the main hall into a wide corridor with dozens of small cells carved into its sides, each hidden behind a curtain. I wanted to pull one of the curtains aside and peek in, but Mother stopped me. "They're asleep right now," she whispered.

"I told you we shouldn't have come so late."

"I thought maybe they—"

"You promised to tell them how I tricked the king's soldiers."

I saw in her eyes that she knew I was right. I love being right and love it even more when my parents admit it. I usually forgive them generously, but occasionally I like to play up a little how insulted I feel. I know this isn't a good quality, but it's hard to change.

"I had to come today."

"Why?"

"They know I bring them food in the middle of every month."

Her answer angered me. "They'll only see the food tomorrow anyway."

"You're right, Shelomoam." She said the words I'd been waiting for with an effort. "I'm sorry, but . . . ," she trailed off.

I looked at her intently. "But what?"

"There's a woman here who wants to meet you. She's been expecting you. I promised I'd bring you to her today."

"Why does she care so much about me?"

"She's a good friend of mine and is curious to meet my children."

"Then why didn't you bring Elisheba?"

"I'll bring her when she's older."

I made a quick calculation. I was eight and a half, but Father would let Elisheba come to the cave far earlier than that, when she would be only five or six. I'm the only one he watches over so anxiously, as if I were made of glass and could shatter at any moment. When I get annoyed at his excessive protectiveness, he explains with tears in his eyes that I am both his eldest and his only son, and that he won't let me end up like Joseph, who grew tired of Jacob's overprotectiveness and persuaded him to let him go out on the road alone. I try to explain to Father that it isn't the same—Joseph was hated by his brothers, but no one hates me—but he refuses to hear it.

Mother took my hand and led me into one of the cells. In the torchlight, I could see a figure sitting on a bed. Her body was wrapped from head to toe in a gray cloak, her face covered by a rough fabric that resembled a mask, with two small eyeholes and one large hole at the mouth. I knew that the lepers covered their bodies—Mother had told me this—but I couldn't have imagined how terrifying their masks were. I didn't want this woman, who had been so looking forward to meeting me, to notice my revulsion, so I let go of Mother's hand and walked over to her.

"Hello, my lady." I tried to speak loud and clear. "I've come to visit you."

I looked at her directly and could see her eyes watching me from behind the mask. Suddenly she began to shake. I could see her entire body trembling under her cloak. Everything shook—her arms, her legs, even her face.

"Hello, Zeruah," Mother said, trying to sound chipper. "I've kept my promise."

Her name startled me even more than the mask and the shaking. *Zeruah*—a leper.

"Shelomoam." She said my name in a whisper. I could barely hear her.

Before I knew what was happening, I felt her covered hands trembling along my cheeks. Her fingers explored my face thoroughly, studying my every feature. Had I not seen her alert eyes, I might have thought she was blind. I tried to stay put.

Mother saw my distress and rushed to my aid. She took the leper's hands and gently pulled them away. "It's late," she said. "We need to unload the food."

When we went back out to the wagon, I asked Mother if all lepers shook like Zeruah. She looked away and said pointedly that Zeruah hadn't been shaking, that I'd only imagined it. I helped her unload the food without a word. We put the sacks of flour and the jugs of oil in a deep nook inside the large hall and placed the bags of figs and raisins on a high shelf.

We got back into the wagon silently. I had so many questions, but I could tell that Mother was concentrating on the difficult descent from the mountain, and I didn't want to distract her. When we had reached flat ground, I stated emphatically that I wouldn't visit Zeruah ever again. Her name disgusted me, and she did too shake.

I thought Mother would chastise me, but she said nothing. Her silence angered me even more. I repeated myself and asked mockingly if all lepers liked to name themselves after their disgusting disease.

That was too harsh a statement to go unanswered. Mother finally opened her mouth and said, with restraint and without anger, that most lepers kept their real names, all that remained from their previous lives, but that Zeruah had decided to conceal her identity for the sake of her family's honor. No one knows who she is, where she came from, what tribe she was born into. She appeared in the cave almost ten years ago, covered from head to toe, and said she had terrible lesions all over her body. She had decided not to reveal her disgrace to her family but rather to run away instead, so that her little sister could marry. Years had gone by, her sister was already married, but Zeruah continued to conceal her identity.

I asked myself whether I would consider my sister's happiness if something bad happened to me, and I felt ashamed of the harsh things I'd said about Zeruah. As penance, I quoted everything I'd learned from Mother about how God sends leprosy as a test for society, which is why the righteous are the ones plagued by it, because they are the only ones who are able to accept misery with love, like Miriam, the older sister of Moses and Aaron, who contracted the disease in the wilderness. Only after the Israelites showed concern for her and took care of her did God know that they were worthy of entering the Promised Land.

I couldn't see Mother's face in the dark, but I knew she was smiling. I rested my head against her shoulder and felt the warmth of her cheek on my head.

"You'll be taller than me soon. You're practically a giant."

Every year when I arrive at the field for the Festival of Harvest, people look at me with wonder and say that I'm the tallest boy in Ephraim. It makes Mother happy, but Father looks around with worry, as if the soldiers have nothing better to do than to capture tall children.

⤞✦⤝

We got home after midnight. I waited patiently to hear Mother's rhythmic breathing coming from the next room and then woke up Elisheba. She mumbled that it was still dark outside, but I knew she wasn't mad at me. She knows that I have to tell her about my day before I can go to sleep.

I started the practice the moment I first saw her. I vividly remember the day she was born, not only because I have a good memory. No one forgets the day he nearly lost his mother.

I remember waking up to the sound of moaning, the strangest sound I'd ever heard. Father tried to reassure me. He said Mother would soon bring me a little brother, but Father looked even more scared and helpless than I was. I think that was when I first realized that it was better to live in a little shack within the bustling city, with neighbors all around, than in a huge, isolated house. Here, no one could hear us scream. But Father didn't scream for help. Instead, he showed me how to place moist towels on Mother's forehead and how much water to rub on her lips, then he harnessed the wagon and went out to get the midwife.

Mother tried to smile at me, but her forced smiles often turned into long, frightful howls. When Father got back he found me in tears. The midwife asked in horror where the women of the family were and whispered to her assistant, a pretty girl with long braids and bright eyes, that only an irresponsible husband would leave a woman in labor alone with a little boy.

Father blushed and started to explain that we had no female slaves or servants, nor any other women in the family. His wife had lost her parents when she was young, and he had only an elderly father who lived with his wives near

Bethel, but the midwife cut him off impatiently and said that instead of rambling he'd best get the little boy out of the room, because, judging by the screaming, the baby could be born at any moment, and there would be no time to get her to the birthing stones. Mother would have to give birth on the floor.

We left the room, and Father told me to go play in the thicket. That's when the pretty girl stepped out and said sadly that Mother's womb was completely blocked. Her contractions were painful, but otherwise without strength. The midwife had decided to take her to the birthing stones on foot, rather than in the wagon, to help the contractions along. Father rushed back to the room and tried to convince the midwife not to take Mother on a hike midlabor, but she ignored him and walked Mother out without another word.

I stayed home with Father. Though I was worried, I couldn't stop thinking about how rudely the midwife had disrespected Father. I thought sadly that she would have treated him with more respect if he had had a big family, and consoled myself with the thought that he'd soon have another boy, and I would have a little brother and wouldn't be alone anymore.

The hours passed slowly, and Father just stared silently out the window the whole time. At first I thought he'd take a break from his silence at noon to make us lunch, but he kept on staring and barely moved at all. I was hungry, but I didn't want to bother him, so I ate the remnants of the bread that Mother had made the previous day. In the evening, he finally broke his silence, saying that he was going to the birthing stones. I reminded him that men weren't allowed there, and he whispered in a choked voice that the labor was taking too long, and he had to check on Mother and bring her some herbs that could strengthen her contractions. The tears I had held back all day almost burst out, but I managed to hold them back and promised him I wouldn't open the door to anyone.

I was almost asleep when a loud banging on the door startled me. Someone was calling out my name. I tried to ignore it, covering my head with the blanket, but then I recognized the familiar voice of Gera, Father's loyal worker, and went to open the door.

Gera apologized for the late hour, saying shamefacedly that he knew we didn't want anyone coming in, but that he was going mad with worry for the lady. All of Zeredah was talking about the difficult labor. It was good that the master had gone to the birthing stones, Gera said. They might need him to go to the fields to gather fresh herbs. Gera said I should go back to sleep and that he would sit with me until Father got back.

I was glad he was staying and slipped easily back to sleep. When I woke up the next morning, Father was home. I asked him if I had a little brother already, and he put his trembling arms around me and shook his head. I went outside to play and kept thinking of Rachel, who had died giving birth to Benjamin, Joseph's younger brother, and about my grandmother, who had died giving birth to Mother. I didn't want to eat or drink, but in the evening hunger got the better of me, and I went home to ask Father to heat up the lentil stew Mother had cooked two days earlier. He looked at me as if for the first time and said that was an excellent idea, but before he could even light the fire, the pretty midwife's assistant burst in and stood before us with her head hanging low. Father dropped the candle. He gaped at her, barely breathing. I knew something awful had happened, but I couldn't cry.

The assistant whispered that she was sorry, but it was a girl. At first, Father just stared at her, but then he exploded with laughter and ran out to the stable with long strides, as if dancing in the fields at the Festival of Harvest. I ran to follow him, but he told the girl to take me home and keep an eye on me. I was glad to stay with her, so I didn't protest. I sat on the mat wordlessly, hoping she would figure out that I was hungry and heat up the lentils. It worked: she asked if we had anything to eat and suggested that we eat the stew cold because she was afraid of starting a fire.

At first we ate in silence, but toward the end of the meal she smiled and said I could call her Tirzah, then added bashfully that I was a handsome boy and that she would tell me everything about Mother's labor as long as I didn't tell anybody, especially not Father. I was flattered to have a pretty, older girl talking to me as if I were her own age, and I told her that Mother had already explained to me how I was born, so it was no secret. Tirzah was surprised and said that Mother must be the only woman in the world who tells her young son such things, and in that case she really could tell me everything about the labor. But she suggested I tell her what I'd learned from Mother first, so no one could accuse her of teaching me things I wasn't supposed to know.

I enjoyed astonishing her with descriptions of Mother's swift labor, how she gave birth to me all alone in a wagon on the side of the road, on her way back from her monthly visit to the lepers' cave; how she tore the cord with her teeth and pulled the afterbirth from her body. Only after it was all over had two people walked by, noticed the lone wagon, and peeked in curiously only to find, to their amazement, a woman sitting on the floor of the wagon cradling a bloody baby. They couldn't believe that a woman could look so healthy and happy, having just given birth all by herself, with no help, to such a big baby.

Tirzah's bright eyes widened. She'd never heard a five-year-old talking about cords and afterbirths as if they were things he saw every day. She also couldn't believe that a woman who had such an easy first birth would have such trouble with her second. I was glad to be able to astound such an experienced, mature girl, and I explained to her that the second birth isn't always easier. Rachel had died giving birth to Benjamin, while her eldest, Joseph, had been born without a hitch.

Tirzah laughed and said I spoke like a little man. No one would ever guess that I wasn't even five years old yet, she said, considering my height and the way I spoke. I laughed, too, but when she began telling me about poor Mother's difficult birth, about how she had almost died, just like Rachel, my laughter gave way to tears, and everything I'd been holding back for the past two days erupted all at once. Tirzah was alarmed. Suddenly, without any warning, I felt her warm lips against my ears. She whispered softly that Mother wasn't unlucky at all. On the contrary, she was unbelievably fortunate to have such a smart and handsome boy who understood everything, and a young, kind husband who wasn't disappointed to have a daughter.

I was so lost in her pleasant touch that I didn't even hear the wagon. Then, suddenly I saw Father and the irritable midwife walking inside, carrying a large plank and laying it carefully on the bed.

"Come here, Shelomoam!" I could barely hear Mother calling me from the plank. "Come meet your sister."

I looked at Mother from a distance. She seemed like a stranger. Suddenly I noticed that she was holding a bundle in her hands. I walked over to her hesitantly. The sight was disappointing. The tiny face between the sheets was scrunched up and blue. I'd never seen such an ugly creature before. I wanted to look away from this ugly baby, but all of a sudden the feeling came over me that I loved her more than anyone else in the world—more than Tirzah, more than Father, even more than Mother. I leaned in and ran my lips over her face. My cheeks burned with love. I held on to her tight fist and told her what had happened to me that day. Mother watched us silently. She had an odd look in her eyes, as if she was trying to solve some sort of riddle.

⋅≫∘≪⋅

Now Elisheba twisted her black curls in that soft, indulgent gesture I love so much. I knew she was widening her eyes with curiosity, trying to see me through the dark, and that she had no anger or frustration over the sweet sleep I'd just ruined. I told her everything in order—from the moment I'd gotten onto the wagon with Mother to the moment we'd returned home. At first I tried to stick to the facts, barely embellishing at all, but when I reached the part where we rode up the steep mountain, I couldn't resist any longer. She gasped at the detailed descriptions of the rickety wagon slipping down the muddy incline, and of the howling of wolves that accompanied us on our climb. I knew that I was scaring her, but I didn't stop.

My writing tutor once admiringly told my parents that I had a great gift for storytelling and that he thought I had a bright future ahead of me as scribe of the chronicles of the tribe of Ephraim, and perhaps of all Israel, as long as I stopped embellishing and learned to describe reality as it really was. Mother welcomed his opinion and remarked with a thin smile that embellishments like mine guaranteed my future as the king's own scribe. The teacher gave a belly laugh and tried to say something witty about the cushy lives of court scribes, but Father cut him off and rushed to the window. In spite of Mother's teasing, I knew that embellishments were bad, almost like lying, but I couldn't suppress my need to spice up my tales with large helpings of imagination, because whenever I tried to stick to the facts, everything seemed routine and dull.

Even now, rather than soothe my little sister with stories of the cave as a pleasant and peaceful place, I made up all sorts of things. I described the lepers' cave to her as I'd imagined it all these years and not as I had actually experienced it. The longer I went on, the more I embellished, and the story turned into a nightmare.

Elisheba clung to me in terror. "How can they breathe in those narrow burrows?" Recalling her innocent questions makes me even more ashamed of my selfishness. She was only four years old.

"They wheeze."

"What's wheeze?"

"It's like . . . the sound he-goats make when you slaughter them."

"And then they die?"

"No, but their entire body shakes under the cover."

"Even their faces?"

"Especially their faces. Their masks bounce around because they shake so much, and when they try to speak all that comes out is crow screeches."

"But you said they only wheeze."

"They're able to wheeze or screech, but they can't talk."

"Then how does Mother talk to them?"

"She's learned how to speak in the language of screeching and wheezing. She's the only one who can understand them."

❧❧❧

After the visits that followed, I managed to restrain myself and tell Elisheba the truth: the lepers can talk just like healthy people and don't shake at all. Only Zeruah shook the first time we met, but now her body was steady and strong, and her voice soft and pleasant. "She loves me more than all the other lepers do, and she always begs me to stay in her cell until the end of the visit and tell her all about everything I've experienced over the past month. She wants to know everything: the new Egyptian words I learned, the new game I invented with Mother in the thicket, how I helped Father pick grapes, and what I told my sister each night."

Elisheba was very glad to hear that Zeruah took an interest in her and wanted to know everything about my monthly visits to the cave, but she refused to join us there. The horror story I had told her after my first visit still frightened her, and no subsequent reassurances could counter that terrifying first impression.

Three

After the Festival of Rain, Father was certain that his anxiety had finally rubbed off on me and that from now on I would stay away from men in uniform. He was right at first. The soldiers really did scare me, and I tried to avoid them, but I soon changed course completely and looked for any opportunity to get close to them. I told him that if a little boy like me had managed to trick so many soldiers, it meant that they were pathetic and that there was nothing to be afraid of. Or perhaps I was trying to deal with the fear head-on and prove to myself that the monster wasn't so terrible. When I was ten years old, I decided to go to the house of administration by myself and pay the taxes for Father. I knew that I shouldn't, but I wanted to prove to him that I could handle the soldiers and didn't need to be hidden from them all the time. Looking back, I know that this was no innocent act. It was a harbinger of my rebellion against my upbringing. Even back then, I understood that no child in Zeredah had been brought up like I had been.

I was beaten badly for disobeying, but I gritted my teeth and didn't cry out.

"Promise me you'll stay away from soldiers. No, a promise is no longer enough. Swear to me!"

Had Mother not come to my aid, he might have injured me, he was so furious. Eventually, I forgave him. His expression looked to me like he was in such agony that I felt that he was the one who needed comforting. He held me tight, and his salty tears streamed down my cheeks and wet my lips.

"I'm sorry, Shelomoam. My love for you gets in the way of my sense of proportion. Forgive me, beloved son."

He never hit me again. For my part, I stayed away from soldiers and went back to my routine at home and in the thicket. But three years later, I firmly informed him that I was now old enough to go along with him every summer on his weekly market excursions. He tried to change my mind with his usual arguments and reminded me that I hated crowded places. I replied angrily that if they had gotten me used to the company of other people, I would have enjoyed crowds like everybody else.

That night I heard him arguing with Mother and told Elisheba that Mother was probably trying to convince him to give me more freedom. And indeed, the next day she announced that from then on, I would be allowed to go out to the fields not only during the Festival of Harvest, but also during the Festival of Love.

"The Festival of Love?" Elisheba railed. "But he's still little."

"He might be too little to snatch up girls"—Mother laughed—"but not too little to enjoy their dancing."

I could see that my sister didn't like this idea, and I immediately informed my parents that I had no interest in the girls' dancing, nor in the celebrations, but that I actually was very interested in the market. And as long as I was kept away from there, I would declare a full retreat from my studies since, in my opinion, being a member of society was more important than learning to speak Egyptian and improving my writing.

This uprising achieved victory, and in the beginning of summer I found myself unloading grapes in the market square. At first I felt stifled and dizzy and almost confessed these feelings to Father, but within a few weeks, I had made friends with other boys my age who worked in the market, and I joined them in watching the coquettish sauntering of the merchant girls, who pointedly ignored us and had eyes only for the older boys.

Market days eclipsed my monthly visits to the cave. I loved the spicy smells, the vibrant colors, even the crowdedness. In the evenings, Mother and Elisheba would join us, and we would go to have dinner in the shack of Necho the Egyptian, whose cooking was famous all over Mount Ephraim. I gorged myself on hot pita and lamb and raisin stew, but even more so on the flowing conversation with the owner, who didn't miss any opportunity to talk with a Hebrew boy who spoke Egyptian. One time, Mother started to explain to him that the tribes of Joseph didn't hate the Egyptians like the other Israelites did because Asenath, our matriarch, the wife of Joseph, had been an Egyptian. But, for Father, this topic was on the list of dangerous topics, and he gestured for her to keep quiet.

We continued our tradition of eating at Necho's place on market days until a strange encounter with the king's soldiers, which startled not only fearful Father but also brave Mother. After this incident, she made me swear to stay away from Necho's shack so that I wouldn't run into any more curious soldiers who might further investigate my accent.

We were sitting as usual on the mat, soaking up the leftover sweet sauce from the lamb stew with our pita bread, when three soldiers walked in. They greeted everyone politely and sat down next to us. I felt no hostility toward them, nor fear of them, but only attraction and curiosity. Father's anxiety and Mother's resentment made me yearn for their company all the more. They must have noticed that I was interested in them, unlike the rest of my family, and they smiled at me. I smiled back and tried to start a conversation, but Mother stood up and said that it was late and that we had to get going. I stood up, too, but before I could leave the shack, one of the soldiers asked me if we were going back to the land of Benjamin that night.

"Benjamin?" I asked in puzzlement. "I'm from Zeredah."

The three soldiers looked me up and down. "Say Shibboleth," said one of them.

I knew what they were doing, and it amused me. I did everything I could to emphasize our particular whistling *sh* sound as I said, "Sibboleth."

The soldier burst out laughing. "What do you say about that?" he asked his friends. "The voice is the voice of Ephraim, but the height is the height of Benjamin."

Only when we got outside could I see how pale my parents' faces had become. I whispered to Mother that it disappointed me to see that she was scared of soldiers, too. I wanted to ask her if all Benjaminites were as tall as I was, but I decided it was best not to bring it up.

Four

Elisheba persisted in her refusal to visit the lepers' cave. Each month she came up with a different excuse, but I knew that she just couldn't put out of her mind the scary stories I had told her after that first visit. The guilt I initially felt turned into puzzlement, then anger, and finally resentment. My little sister was and remained my closest confidante, but her stubborn refusal cast a shadow upon our special connection. The monthly visit to the cave had become a most significant part of my life, and I knew that if she didn't take part in it, a rift was liable to form between us. Eventually, I got my chance, but it led to the family's good and obedient child having her first conflict with our parents.

That day, I was sitting in Zeruah's cell as usual, reporting everything I had been up to since our last meeting. Since I had already turned sixteen, my stories about playing in the thicket and about new Egyptian words had been replaced with racy descriptions of the pretty girls I saw on market days. I knew Zeruah was even more afraid of the king's soldiers than Father was, so I didn't tell her about the other expeditions I'm able to accomplish thanks to the excellent excuses of my faithful sister, who backs me up and enables me to enjoy some freedom every once in a while. Zeruah wanted to know who the most beautiful girl in Zeredah was, and I answered without even a moment of thought that it was Elisheba, though she wasn't yet twelve. I added with enthusiasm that no other girl had curls as abundant as hers, almond eyes as bright, or a body as lithe. Zeruah studied me with interest from behind her mask, but I wasn't embarrassed.

At some point, I got up to set the table. When I came to visit, Zeruah liked to eat with me in her cell, rather than in the big hall with everyone else. She didn't want to miss a moment of my company. I carefully ladled Mother's lentil stew and tore off the fragrant bread she had baked early in the morning before we had headed to the cave. Zeruah got up from her bed and went to the table, but when she tried to sit down on the mat her long cloak got caught between her legs and pulled up all the way to her elbow. I looked at the bare arm and couldn't believe what I was seeing: the skin was smooth and healthy.

Zeruah quickly covered up and then embarked on an unusually long series of questions. I realized that she was trying to hide her feelings and pretend that everything was normal. I wanted to go along with her charade and carry on our conversation as if nothing had happened, but my food got stuck in my throat.

On the way back, I didn't tell Mother what I had seen. When we got home, I reluctantly sat down to supper and couldn't wait for it to end. Elisheba sensed that something was wrong and tried to find out what it was. I signaled for her to be patient. But Father chose that night to give us a long, boring description of the low-quality vines his competitor had grown this year and the fine profit we could look forward to. When he saw that I wasn't listening, he took offense and muttered that it was time I showed some interest in his business, since, as their only son, I was the one who would carry on this fine family tradition. I replied that the occupation of a single generation was hardly a fine family tradition. His own father had worked as a hired servant his entire life, barely able to feed his many wives and children. Mother intervened, saying angrily that if tradition was what we cared about, then we might consider the fact that Father and Grandfather had both been married by my age. She said that the time had come to find me a wife, too, and that only marriage would be able to bridle my raging youth and tamp down my rude behavior.

I wanted to kick the table and run out with Elisheba, but I held back and apologized for what I had said. Lately, fighting with my parents has become a daily occurrence. Father's fear of the soldiers is driving me crazy. As a child, I saw it as an expression of love, but now I feel isolated and trapped. Marriage could be my way out, but I'm not ready to live with a woman. The pretty girls in the market excite me, but at night, when I pleasure myself in bed, I am not thinking of them.

The unpleasant dinner was finally over, and my parents retired to their bedroom. I went out to the thicket with Elisheba, nearly at a run.

"Why do you always fight with them? When will you learn to restrain yourself?"

"I'm hotheaded."

"Tell me what happened today. I'm dying to know."

"Talk about restraint!" I said, making her wait a little longer. "What could possibly happen to lepers who spend their entire lives in a cave?"

"Come on, Shelomoam. I'm begging you."

I tried to tell her everything exactly as it had happened, the way I did every night, but I was so excited that I couldn't find the words and mumbled something about Zeruah's cloak getting caught between her legs. Elisheba didn't understand a thing. I started over again, from the beginning, but I was so excited that I jumped right back to the end again.

"So what do you think?" I asked. "Can you explain it?"

Elisheba was at a loss. "An unblemished arm?" she finally asked. "Are you sure?"

"I'm positive."

"It can't be. Did you ask Mother about it?"

"She'll say I only imagined it, just like she did years ago when I saw Zeruah shaking."

Then I had a bold idea, and though I knew it was a wicked one, I could think of nothing else. Elisheba noticed the glint in my eye and demanded an explanation. I laid out my plan with enthusiasm, but when I saw how shocked she was, I knew that I had no partner.

"Have you lost your mind?"

"I need your help. I can't do it alone."

"I can't."

I knew that I mustn't give up. "We don't have a choice," I told her. "We have to find out the truth."

⌘

A month later, Elisheba was sitting beside me in the wagon. Mother was absolutely overjoyed and talked the whole way there about the surprise we had in store for Zeruah, who had been waiting for so long to meet the little girl who had now grown so big and so beautiful.

"I'm not big at all," Elisheba protested. "My head barely reaches Shelomoam's waist."

To distract Mother from our nervousness, I chatted cheerily about my height, telling her proudly that everyone looked short next to me, and that when I came to the market with Father people whispered about how unbelievable it was that little Benaiah was the father of such a giant. I had hoped that Mother would laugh, like she had in the old days, but instead she pursed her lips and said nothing more the rest of the journey.

When we got to the cave, I was afraid that Elisheba would change her mind and refuse to get off the wagon. I already had a plan for persuading her behind Mother's back, but she jumped off without hesitation and gave me her hand.

"Take me to Zeruah," she said.

Mother's face testified to her utter astonishment. "Wait a moment. Let's unload the food first."

"We'll help you later, Mama. Please. I can't wait to meet her."

I admired the tone of entitlement that Elisheba uses when she wants something from our parents. It is so different from my aggressive attitude, which never achieves anything and only confirms my status as the rebel of the family.

The desired outcome soon followed. It was demonstrated once again that Mother is powerless to withstand her daughter's sweet talk. "Fine. Go meet Zeruah, but don't be too long. She'll have a flood of questions for you and will want you to stay with her until we leave. Tell her you have to help me unload the wagon first."

"Don't worry, Mama. We'll be right back."

Elisheba bounded confidently into the main hall, as if she knew the place. Not a muscle in her face so much as twitched as she sped past the covered-up lepers who watched her with clear interest from behind their masks. I recalled how frightened I had been the first time I saw Zeruah's mask and was proud of my brave little sister. But when I thought of what we were about to do, I felt my knees buckle and had a hard time keeping up with her as she moved down the long hallway. When she paused in front of the correct cell, I nodded. She drew the curtain aside and walked in.

Zeruah was sitting on the bed. She turned to face us.

"I promised you I would get my sister here one day."

I thought that her body would begin to shake beneath her cloak, the way it had the first time she saw me, but she watched Elisheba with calm curiosity.

We walked over together. I stood behind Zeruah and pulled my knife out from its hiding place, while Elisheba stood in front of her and leaned forward, as if she were about to kiss her.

Zeruah recoiled, and then, in perfect synchrony, I made a quick slit in the cloak, from the top of the head down to the neck, while Elisheba pulled the mask off Zeruah's face.

It all happened so quickly that we met no resistance. She didn't even cry out.

One look was enough.

The woman sitting before us was no leper.

Five

Instead of protesting our act of violence and making us apologize, Mother looked in all directions with horror, the way Father always did, and made us swear not to tell anyone what we had seen. Then she ordered us to get back on the wagon, and she drove the horses wildly down the mountain. Elisheba and I tried to remind her that we hadn't unloaded the food yet, but she ignored us and went on with her flight.

When we got home, I said to Elisheba that we could no longer pretend to be a normal family. I had often tried to convince her that our parents were hiding something from us. I told her that they had chosen to live in our huge house not only because they were wealthy enough to purchase a thicket of wasteful trees that bore no fruit, but also in order to seclude themselves from the world and hide their mysterious secrets among those trees. That's why all the rich people in Zeredah have slaves, while we don't even have hired servants, but just the workers who help Father in the vineyards and who never enter our house.

Now I didn't have to convince her anymore. I told Elisheba my plan for the rebellion, and she promised to stick to it until our parents revealed all their secrets.

We didn't speak with them for over a week. We spent almost all the hours of the days and the nights in the thicket, among the oaks and the terebinths, and we came inside only for sustenance. There were a few moments where

Elisheba came close to breaking. She missed her soft bed, hot meals, and, most of all, Mother, but I was able to strengthen her resolve and give her hope that our nightmare would end soon.

Maybe it was only my imagination, but I could swear that our parents weren't mad at me. Their contorted faces showed signs of confusion and distress, but not anger. I was surprised. I couldn't comprehend why Mother would send fleeting tender glances in my direction when she knew that I was inciting Elisheba against her, or how Father could stop himself from beating me over my open rebellion against him. I was taller and stronger than him, but fathers are allowed to beat their sons even after they grow up.

Sleeping outside wasn't good for Elisheba. For my part, I actually enjoyed lying by her side on the moist dirt and watching the stars beyond the treetops, but I knew that I was putting her health at risk. Her bright eyes were sullied by a burning redness, and her coughing fits became ever more frequent. Still, I wouldn't end my rebellion. "It's now or never," I kept telling her. "There won't be another chance." I was willing to do anything to uncover our family secrets.

Our rebellion lasted eight days. On the ninth night, Mother stepped outside quietly and woke us up with gentle caresses. I don't know what would have happened if she hadn't declared her surrender. It scares me to think how far I would have gone.

"Be quiet," she whispered. "Father won't let me tell you the secrets, but I know that they are ruining our family life and disrupting the most important thing in my life: my relationship with my children. I'm sorry I hurt you, but now you will hear the story and understand that I had no other choice."

Mother's confession went on till morning, and when she had finished, I knew that what she had told us was only part of the mystery and that it would be my fate to go on living in the dark.

⤜⟡⤏

As soon as she began, Mother surprised us by saying that she and Father had been born in Bethel, the large, important city on the border between the lands of Benjamin and Ephraim.

I was eager for Mother to skip to the end of the story so that I could find out what our parents had been hiding from us all these years and what it all had to do with Zeruah, but Elisheba kept interrupting her with annoying questions, and Mother couldn't keep going. I realized that my sister, who after all was still a child, was reveling in the very fact of this conversation and wasn't as eager as I was to solve the mystery, but I decided not to stop her. She had paid a heavy toll on my behalf. Her resilient body would recover from the cough and from the burning eyes, but the battle with our parents might come at the cost of her comfortable position as the good girl of the family.

"Then why did you always tell us you were born in Zeredah?"

"We didn't want you to make a connection between us and the events that occurred in Bethel."

"What events?"

"That's what I'm trying to tell you."

"Sorry, Mama, please go on."

"The God of Israel, the maker of matches, the One who brought Rebecca to Isaac and Jacob to Rachel, brought me and your father together in the home of a small family."

"Small like ours?"

"Much smaller. That family only had a father and a daughter."

"Poor things."

"Don't feel too bad for them. They owned many fields that yielded the best oats on Mount Ephraim, and they had a fine pedigree as well."

"What pedigree?"

"The father was a direct descendant of Rahab the Canaanite and Joshua son of Nun the Ephrathite, the great leader and conqueror."

"How did you and Father come to know such an important man?"

"We were his servants."

Elisheba gave a huff, as if she was having trouble breathing. I couldn't see her face in the dark, but I knew it had turned pale from the affront.

"That can't be. It's true that Grandfather was a hired servant, but Father studied the art of growing vines, bought some land, and became an independent grower. And you received a large inheritance after you were orphaned at a young age. That's what you've always told us."

"We've told you lots of things." Mother sighed.

"So, you were servants?" Elisheba asked, unable to process this new information.

"Well, Father was a hired servant, while I . . . I was . . . a slave."

This time I caught my breath as well. Our strong and independent mother, who always stood her ground and feared no one, had been a sl . . . I couldn't even repeat that wretched word in my mind. Mother's warm hand searched for mine, as if trying to tell me that she was the same woman I knew. I didn't respond to her touch. I felt like this revelation had turned me into somebody else, as well.

"What kind of slave were you?" Elisheba asked. We all knew what she meant.

"Officially, I was the personal slave to the master's daughter." I was relieved to hear this. "But in reality, I was her closest confidante."

Elisheba gave a sigh of relief. "Were you the same age?"

"She was six years older."

"But you were friends anyway?"

"Much more than that. I would have given my life for her."

"That close?"

"Without her, I would have remained a slave forever, or worse. I was born into a poor family with no land, in a small tent at the edge of Bethel. My mother died while giving birth to me. She was only fourteen. Five years later, my father was killed accidentally by a scythe while he was in the fields collecting abandoned grain for us. I was alone and impoverished, with no relation or redeemer. While the town elders were discussing what should be done with me, a venerable gentleman brought them documents proving that my father had borrowed money from him and had died before he could repay his debt. The elders quickly gave me over to the debt collector, to be sold in exchange for the balance owed. I was considered fine goods. Many would have been glad to purchase a young girl and make her the shared property of all the men in the family. Who knows what my life would have looked like if I hadn't been bought by a decent, kind man, who never even considered using the body of a helpless child and intended me only for housework. The ear-piercing ceremony of a new slave was supposed to have taken place within a few days, but God heard my pleas and sent me a savior. The master's daughter, who looked like an angel, was eleven when I was brought into their home. She was old enough to know what was in store for the little girl who spent all night sobbing in the slave wing, but also young enough to still have a pure heart, not yet hardened by the years. I think that the fact that she had also lost her mother at birth made her feel a special affinity toward me, and she asked her father for permission to take me under her wing and treat me as her little sister. Her father, of course, refused to even consider this strange idea, but after a few long arguments, they reached a compromise that put off the piercing ceremony for the time being while I became the daughter's personal slave. Needless to say, the training she gave me was unusual. Instead of training me to subsume my own personality and demur to others, a requirement for any slave and especially a female one, she taught me to believe in freedom and be prepared to fight for it. Each night before I fell asleep she told me about our ancestors who had been freed from slavery in Egypt, and about the God of Israel who created us as free people and forbade us from enslaving ourselves to mere mortals."

"And then, when you grew up, she set you free," Elisheba completed the story gleefully.

"That was the plan, but things don't always go according to plan. Sometimes outside forces take us off course and lead us to places we never imagined. For nine years, I lived happily with my beloved mistress, until the terrible rebellion came and shook up our lives."

"Do you mean the Rebellion of the Temples?" This time I was the one to interrupt. The timing of what she was describing seemed off, and I was trying to make sense of things.

"No, Shelomoam. The Rebellion of the Temples was fifteen years ago, while the one I'm talking about took place two years earlier, at the end of the previous king's reign. The people of Benjamin decided to take advantage of his old age and weakness and tried to reclaim the throne. They had some successes at first: the soldiers retreated, and the leader of the rebellion, Sheba son of Bikri, declared victory. There was a new spirit in our land. The adults had been schooled by bitter past experience and worried that the uprising would fail, just as the ones before had failed, but young people flocked to join the rebel army. I was so worried when I heard that my mistress was planning on joining, too."

"I've never heard of this rebellion."

"It was part of the secret that Father and I have been keeping all these years."

I couldn't understand why a rebellion would have become a family secret, and I understood even less what Zeruah had to do with it. Then I had an idea, and as usual, I could think of nothing else.

"What was her name?" I asked, cutting Mother off midsentence.

"Whose name?"

Instead of chiding her for trying to evade the question, I smiled with satisfaction. Apparently, she realized that I had found the key to the mystery.

"Your mistress's name."

Her silence told me that I was on the right track.

"What was the name of the angel-faced girl who joined the rebels?" I repeated the question, demanding details.

I thought that I would have to badger her for more information in order to fit the pieces of the puzzle together. I never imagined that one short answer, spoken in a hoarse whisper, almost a grunt, would suffice.

"Zeruiah."

❦

Elisheba rolled the name around in her mouth, feeling its texture, tasting it, connecting its pretty, clear sounds with that other, sadder name. "Zeruiah. Zeru-i-aaah. Zeru-aaah." Then she grew silent and did not interrupt Mother again until the story had ended. I didn't interrupt her, either. I tried hard to recall the frightened face I had seen for just a brief moment. I had to employ every bit of my powers of imagination to reconcile that face with the pretty girl who had saved Mother from a life of slavery and joined the rebel army.

❦

"Zeruiah ran away from home and bore weapons at the age when most young women are nursing babies. She told me where the rebels' cave was located and warned me never to go there unless something out of the ordinary happened. I didn't understand what she meant, but I swore to obey her. Her grief-stricken father became withdrawn, his cheeks sunken, his eyes red, his beard wild like that of a mourner. We tiptoed around him, anxious and aching, trying to gather bits of information about the fate of our mistress. One moment we were jumping for joy over a reliable rumor about another town conquered by the rebels, and the next moment we were weeping with despair when a different rumor, from a source no less reputable, described the victory marches of the Judean soldiers in cities reconquered by the king. We swung between hope and despair, alternately crying and laughing. Then, still in those dark days, when my heart was practically bursting with my longing for her, love bloomed between me and Benaiah. I had seen him every day since I was brought to the house at the age of five. Sometimes I could feel his eyes following me around, but I never gave him much thought. My love for Zeruiah filled my entire heart, and only when we were forced to be apart could it make room for a new love. I needed someone to talk to, a shoulder to lean on, and when I tossed and turned at night, I knew he would soon come to ease my pain. We planned for a life together in the house of our beloved master, never guessing what the future would soon bring. Who could have imagined that the most solid house in Bethel would crumble into ruins.

"The rebellion was suppressed with cruelty the likes of which our land had never seen before. Most rebels weren't as lucky as their leader, Sheba son of Bikri, who was killed before he could be delivered into the hands of his enemies. When he saw that the rebellion was failing, he fled north to Beth Maakah. The people of the tribe of Asher did not believe that the king's army would follow him so far north and agreed to give him shelter. By the time they realized their mistake, it was already too late. The king's soldiers closed in on their city, set on utter destruction. One clever woman, who knew that the king had a special fondness for the speeches of clever women, decided to find out if the same magic also worked on his soldiers. She called over the wall to the commander of the army and gave him a long, detailed speech about the mark of disgrace that would plague anyone who destroyed a major city of Israel. The commander told her that he was willing to forego the destruction of the city, on the condition that she surrendered Sheba son of Bikri to him. The woman took pity on the leader of the rebellion and decided to kill him before turning him over. His severed head was tossed over the wall, and the commander blew his trumpet and lifted the siege.

"The soldiers who burst into our home killed our master at the sword and threatened to torture us with some of the king's favorite instruments—saws, iron picks, iron axes, and brick kilns—if we didn't disclose Zeruiah's hiding place. That was when I first realized that she was no ordinary rebel, but rather the leader of the rebel forces of Ephraim. I don't know who drew the sketch of her face, which was passed around by the soldiers, but it was incredibly accurate.

"That night, I escaped the house with Benaiah, and we ran to the rebels' cave as fast as we could. I warned Zeruiah that the king's soldiers were about to find them and had the means to identify her. She covered her body and face with a gray cloak and told us to follow her. We felt our way slowly through the dark until we reached a well with a wide opening. We decided to lower ourselves down the well, but before we could make our move, we came face to face with three armed soldiers. One of them grabbed Zeruiah while the other two approached Benaiah and me. I felt cold air on the back of my neck and suddenly heard myself shouting, 'She's a leper!'

"The soldier let go and recoiled. 'You're lying,' he said, trying to sound confident. 'Let's see who's hiding under this cloak.'

"'Go ahead,' I said. 'Take it off.'

"He looked at his friends hesitantly.

"'Go on,' I urged him. 'I can't wait to see what happens to someone who touches a leper. I've heard that the hair falls out first, then the nails, then the eyes and ears, until finally all that's left is a black hole in the middle of the face. Take off her cloak! What are you waiting for?'

"Zeruiah was taken to Zeredah that very night. The soldiers ordered us into their chariot and dropped us off outside the lepers' cave. 'Don't you dare take her to crowded places again,' they warned us. 'Remember the law: lepers leave the cave at their own peril.'"

⚬⚬⚬

"Seventeen years have gone by since then. Father and I started a family, bought some land, and had a boy and a girl, while Zeruiah remains buried alive in the lepers' cave, never seeing the light of day. She mustn't ever show her well-known face. She will probably stay in that cave until the day she dies.

"Now do you see why Father is so afraid of soldiers? He wakes up drenched in sweat every night. Some memories cannot be forgotten with time.

"Why do we live in seclusion? Because the large thicket gives him a sense of security. He doesn't want to see soldiers.

"Why don't we have slaves? By now, you can probably understand. A person who once was a slave could never enslave others.

"How could we afford this huge house, the trees, and the vineyards? Zeruiah gave them to us. Did you really believe that we got all this from hard work? The king's taxes don't leave enough money to make a decent living, not to mention educate children.

"Where did Zeruiah get the money? Her father's possessions were confiscated by the king. That's the law when it comes to dead traitors. But she knew where he had buried a large treasure of gold that he had inherited from his ancestors, and she decided to give most of it to us. We are the only ray of light in the darkness of her life. That's why she loves you so much, Shelomoam. That's why she wants to know you, Elisheba. Go visit her, my dear children. She will forgive you. I'm certain of it."

Six

Elisheba pounced on Mother, hugging her and thanking her for her brave confession, telling her enthusiastically that not only were we not ashamed of her lowly beginnings, but also we admired her even more than we had before. Only a noble and benevolent woman would have remained loyal for so long to her old mistress, who had grown up a princess and was then sentenced to a miserable life in hiding.

I wanted to explain to my little sister that Mother's *brave* confession was nothing but a sophisticated camouflage designed to reveal a little so as to conceal even more, that the essence of her secret remained locked up, but I got a terrible headache and felt like I was about to be sick. The pain was so awful that I didn't even realize I was being brought back home. When I woke up, I felt a dull pulsing in my temples, and Mother was by my side. She tried to smile amiably, but the obvious strain that this gesture required of her revealed her true emotions.

"It's night already. You've slept almost an entire day. I'm sorry I told you everything all at once. I should have broken it up into small bits and given you time to process the information in between. It isn't easy for a son to hear about his mother's difficult childhood, not to mention her lowly past as a slave. Forgive me, Shelomoam. Are you feeling better?"

I propped my weakened body up on my elbows and looked up at her. I meant to speak softly and was surprised by how bitter I sounded.

"Your story is so very moving," I said with scorn. "No wonder it made Elisheba melt. I would have melted, too, if I had believed you."

Mother looked as if she'd been punched in the stomach. "You think I lied?"

"I think you held back the important part."

Her face paled with hurt, or perhaps anger. "How can you not trust me after I put the fate of the woman who is dearer to me than anyone into your hands and into your sister's? I admit that I wouldn't have done so if you hadn't forced me. I didn't want to place such a heavy burden on your young shoulders. Father and I wanted you to live in the paradise of a happy and innocent childhood. That's why we built a protective wall around you, so as to keep out the dangerous and wicked world. But now that you're in on the secret, you are our partners. Partners, Shelomoam, not rivals. It's time you stopped fighting us."

The pulsing in my temples grew stronger, threatening to bring back last night's monstrous headache. I wanted to look away and sink back into a restorative sleep, but I knew that what I didn't say now might never be said at all, and so I mustered what was left of my strength and declared that the battle between us would go on for as long as they held back the essence of the secret.

"I've told you everything!" Mother muttered in despair.

"Everything?" I shouted. "Then why don't you tell me what all this has to do with me?"

"Every member of our household is involved in this, Shelomoam. Father's and my past threatens not only Zeruiah, but all of us, even you and your sister. Father is protecting you from the soldiers because the danger has yet to pass. The king continues to persecute everyone who rebelled against his father."

"Then why is Father's anxiety mostly about me?" I interrupted her.

"Because you are his eldest and only son."

"I'm sixteen and a half already." I was really begging now. "These excuses aren't good enough anymore. It's time you told me the truth."

"I have nothing more to tell you, Shelomoam."

My elbows could no longer support my limp body. My head landed back on the bed with a thump.

⁓

The months that followed were unbearable, and there wasn't a soul with whom I could share my agony. I no longer came to visit my sister's bed at night to tell her about my days. I explained it away, telling myself that an immature little girl was unworthy of being my conversation partner, but deep down I knew there was something else standing between us, something dangerous and dark that I mustn't even think about, let alone speak of. I stayed as far away from her as I could, even skipping dinner with the family.

At first Elisheba tried to understand what had happened between us and asked me, clearly feeling insulted, why I was avoiding her. She said she missed talking to me, that she couldn't fall asleep without our conversations. Her desperation made me want to fall upon her neck with kisses, but thinking about how sweet it would feel to be close to her paralyzed me with fear. I answered, with a nasty coldness, that friends my own age interested me much more than she did. My cruelty shocked her, and she stayed away. Only the pained look in her eyes, which followed me around silently, attested to her misery. Sometimes I felt as though I would be torn apart by my feelings of compassion and longing, but I held strong. My parents, too, stopped bothering me, and they let me come and go as I pleased. For the first few weeks following her confession, Mother begged me to visit Zeruiah, who had been asking about me and missed me and felt no anger toward me. But when I persisted in refusing to go, she dropped the subject and took only Elisheba along on her monthly visits.

My house became nothing but an inn to me. I spent most hours of the day riding on the handsome horse that Father had bought me for my seventeenth birthday, hoping that the gift, which epitomized the freedom now so lavishly granted to me, would compensate for the deficit of freedom in my past. I felt like a former slave, newly freed from bondage, and I swore to make the most of it. For the first time in my life, I visited all the towns in Ephraim, traveling all the way to Shechem. But instead of enjoying the outdoors that I had yearned to experience for so long, I sank deeper into myself. I tried not to let the burden of the past ruin my life in the present, but my imagination kept taking me to the moment I was desperately hoping for: the moment when Mother would step into my room at night, kneel at my bedside, ask for my forgiveness, and make a second confession, that, as opposed to the half-measure of the first one, would fully reveal everything that had been kept from me all these years and would allow me to turn over a new leaf with my parents.

But as the days went by, I came to realize that the moment would never arrive. And rather than daydreaming about a reconciliation with my parents, I'd be better off enjoying what was left of my youth with the boys at the Zeredah market. But, ironically, just when I finally had the freedom to build true friendships with them, I could feel the unwelcome sense that I was a stranger, which had plagued me all my life, welling up inside me more powerfully than it ever had before. While I was no longer anxious in a crowd, I couldn't feel like a part of one either. Despite my inability to conceal my sense that I wasn't one of them, I was surprised to discover that people seemed attracted to me as though they were spellbound. I didn't understand what they saw in me. True, I'm tall and handsome—I could feel my good looks in the stares of the girls walking by me in the market and on the streets—as well as wealthy and educated, but can't people see that I'm a stranger in their midst? I know how to read and write, I speak fluent Egyptian, and I'm capable of complex calculations, but all this gives me no satisfaction as long as I see the freewheeling behavior of other boys my age and know with excruciating certainty that I will never be like them.

"Why don't you join us at the prostitutes' tent?" the boys asked me. "A boy becomes a man only after he has known a woman."

My silence led to all sorts of conjecturing. Some argued that I must prefer to sleep with men, like the Egyptians, while others were willing to swear that my towering height and broad shoulders hid the body of a prepubescent boy. I made no comment. What could I tell them? I couldn't even admit to myself the true reason I kept away from women.

Ultimately, I decided that the company of the boys in the market wasn't enough for me. They spent their days working like dogs, while I didn't have to work for a living; in spite of the rift between us, my parents continued to support me generously. I sought the company of young people like me, who could afford to be carefree.

I found my new associates by chance, and though they weren't what I had been expecting, they met my needs perfectly. It happened one day as I was strolling alone in the market of Shiloh and paused by a stall selling cakes. I was fishing out my coin purse when a short, skinny boy passed by, snatched it away from me, and disappeared. I gave chase and finally caught him outside the market, at the foot of a desolate hill. I knocked him to the ground with a punch to the face that left him writhing in pain. I took back my coin purse and turned to return to the market to get Aner, my beloved horse, who had remained by the cake stall. I made it perhaps thirty steps, no more, when I noticed a group of boys emerging as a single unit from the other side of the hill. They approached me confidently, and before I knew what was happening I was surrounded. I politely asked them to let me pass, and they responded by shoving me into the hillside. The pain I felt knocked the breath out of me. My knees buckled. I slipped down to the ground, my back against the hill. I tried to crawl, but they kicked me all over my entire body. The pain and helplessness gave me a power I didn't know I had in me. I have no idea how I got up; all I could remember later were the desperate punches I threw until I finally sank into darkness.

When I regained consciousness, they were all sitting around me, cheerful and content. I thought they were waiting for me to wake up so that they could torture me to death, but instead of cutting me open, they handed me a jug of wine and watched, clearly impressed, as I sucked it down. "We need a giant like you in our group," one of them said. I could tell that he was the leader, seeing as everyone else quieted down respectfully when he spoke.

Thoughts swirled through my mind. I knew I had to avoid doing something stupid. "Fine," I said. "I'm going to get my horse, and I'll be right back."

Their laughter was sincere. "Your horse is here," the leader said, pointing behind me. "We don't leave horses roaming freely around the market. They don't much like being alone."

I looked back and saw Aner drinking calmly out of a large trough.

"You're free to go, if that's what you want," the leader went on. "I'm sure you'll figure out how to find us."

I got back in the saddle quickly and rode away as fast as I could. Midway back to Zeredah, by the Land of Tappuah, I turned around and rode back to Shiloh.

Seven

Within a few days, I was already one of them. I tried not to discuss my family, but I couldn't hide the fact that, in contrast to them, I was educated. They had been born to poor families and, having spent their childhoods at hard labor, were completely illiterate. Only the leader was a member of a landowning family and so had some education, but he, too, had been left with nothing after his mother was caught in an adulterous act. His father had killed her and sent her children away, no longer believing they were his. The leader's two younger brothers had been sold into slavery, while he himself had wandered the roads and made his living as a thief until he formed this group and made himself its leader.

"It's hard to be poor," I said, sighing at his sad story.

"It's much worse not knowing who your father is," he replied.

❧

I was so swept up by this new way of life that I almost managed not to think about my family. We spent enjoyable evenings training in mock battles, got mind-numbingly drunk at night, and had exhilarating adventures as thieves in the markets during the daytime. Our main thief was the skinny fellow who had snatched my coin purse in Shiloh—he had quick hands and was a great runner. I was appointed the guard who would follow him around on foot, while the other members of the group kept watch on horseback so that they could look in all directions and warn him about approaching soldiers. They had an easy job because the king's soldiers focused on tax collection and didn't waste their time with small matters like thievery.

I also didn't have to work my muscles very hard to stop people who spotted the pickpocket making off with their coin purses. My mere presence was deterrent enough. The infuriated victims would look me up and down and stand frozen in place. But every once in a while, when a person wasn't persuaded just by the look of me, I knew how to stop him. I preferred not to use violence unless there was no other choice. The beatings helped me release my suppressed rage, and they energized me, but I didn't like the sight of the bruises and blood they caused. It made me feel sick.

My new friends teased me for my weakness, but it didn't seem to diminish their adoration. Once more, I marveled at my mysterious appeal, which causes people to crave my company despite my standoffishness. I don't know how it happened, but within a few weeks I found myself the leader of the group. The previous leader didn't try to fight me, but rather vacated the position acceptingly, almost willingly.

My parents knew that I slept somewhere else most nights and only came home to get money and clean clothes. I didn't need their money anymore since joining the gang, but I still came to see them in the first few months. Father and Elisheba didn't speak to me, but Mother tried to ask about my life, persisting even after I rudely rejected her queries. I thought with contempt that she had grown old all of a sudden. I couldn't believe she was only thirty-one. Her hair was still jet-black, the way it had been in my childhood, but I guessed that it would turn gray overnight when she learned of my plan to join the army.

The idea had seeped in slowly. The first time my friends told me about their dreams of joining the army, I was appalled.

"You want to become the king's soldiers?" I shouted. "But you are sons of Rachel."

They looked at me like I was mad. "So? The army is open to any able-bodied man, no matter which tribe he is from. The king knows it's best to station native-born soldiers in each tribe's land. No one wants to harm someone from their own tribe, even if that person is collecting their taxes. This king is much wiser than his father. There are no rebellions against him."

I couldn't believe my ears. I told my ignorant friends about the Rebellion of the Temples that had taken place at the start of the king's reign, and of how despised he was not only by the tribes of Rachel, but also by the entire nation of Israel, except for Judah. "How can you aspire to join the army of the man who destroyed our temples and banished our priests?" I yelled excitedly. "How is it possible for young men of Ephraim to come to admire the person who trampled the symbol of Joseph and who shattered our statues of bulls?"

They listened with astonishment and said that they had never heard of such a rebellion, but that even if I was right, it proved nothing. The king had been young and inexperienced at the time, and he had made a demonstration of power for all to see. Today, he is full of confidence and isn't afraid to draft soldiers from other tribes. The military salaries are exempt from taxes and include an Egyptian horse, a plot of land, and two slaves. And if you become a commander, you can take the prettiest girl in the area for yourself without any resistance whatsoever. No father would dare turn down a commander from the king's guard who wanted his daughter.

At first, I was appalled by what they were saying, but the more I thought about it, the more the idea appealed to me. I realized that Mother had successfully brainwashed me with her burning hatred of the king, and I was merely quoting what she had said like a baby. It was time I formed my own opinions and stopped mumbling her slogans. So, he banished our priests? Destroyed our temples? Shattered our symbols? I didn't actually care about any of this.

I liked the idea of declaring my independence and becoming a soldier—the one thing Mother hated most and Father was most afraid of. I took pleasure imagining the looks on their faces when I would come in uniform to visit them in Zeredah. They would be begging to reveal their stupid secrets to me then, but I wouldn't care to listen.

When I asked my friends how one joined the army, they said they were glad that I was interested and explained that potential recruits were examined in Jerusalem. A two-year training process followed for those who were accepted, and if I made it through that, I would become a soldier in the king's army. We were extremely enthusiastic and decided to leave for Jerusalem right away because we had all grown tired of being petty thieves in the markets. Ultimately, though, I decided to delay our departure and announced that we would go through a challenging training program of our own to ensure that we were prepared to meet the entrance requirements.

My friends regularly visited prostitutes, but they were surprisingly accepting of my celibacy. Once in a while, however, over some bottles of wine, they tried to get to the bottom of it. Our conversations always began the same way, with the fellow sitting next to me in the circle mischievously refusing to pass the jug.

"Give it over," I would say in rebuke.

"First you have to answer the question we've asked you dozens of times."

"Which question?"

"Why are you celibate?"

"I don't like prostitutes."

"What *do* you like?"

"Lovers."

General laughter.

"Then go find yourself some lovers. It would be nothing to you. Women swallow you up with their eyes already."

"I will. Now give me the wine."

What my friends' efforts at persuasion could not accomplish one woman at the market did. I thought that I had encountered her before, but she looked like every other woman, so I didn't give her a second look until I heard her name and occupation.

"Hello, Tirzah the Midwife," the wool merchant greeted her. "I saved you some especially soft diapers from Kush. They say that even the sons of the Queen of Sheba used ones just like them."

I wanted to jump off Aner's back and go to her, but my legs froze like pillars of salt. It took a long time before I could get hold of myself, and by the time I did, she was gone. I began searching between the stalls like a madman. All I could remember was the blue headdress she had been wearing, but many other women wore those, too. I returned to my friends and instructed them to roam the streets of Shiloh and find out where Tirzah the Midwife lived.

"Someone has finally captured your heart!" they cheered. "Don't worry. We'll bring her to you on a golden platter, and you'll be able to do with her as you please."

"Don't you dare touch her," I warned them. "She's an older woman, and

I'm not attracted to her. I met her many years ago, when I was a little boy, and I'd like to see her again, that's all."

"As you wish," they said, shrugging their shoulders, and were on their way. The mission was easier than I had expected, and I quickly received the information I had requested about Tirzah the Midwife, the wife of Ramiah son of Perez, the sycamore fig gatherer.

When we arrived at her home, I asked my friends to leave. I knocked on the door with trembling fingers. I was so excited that I felt as though my feet were about to give out.

A little girl stood in the doorway. She was normal-looking. Nothing about her appearance reminded me of the beautiful girl I'd remembered.

"Call your mother," I told her.

My heart seized with disappointment at the sight of the withered woman who approached me.

"Are you the midwife?" I asked.

"Is your wife about to give birth?"

"Yes."

"I'll get Tirzah."

I leaned my head against the door, breathing heavily. I heard the sound of her footsteps but didn't dare look up.

"Greetings, my lord." Her voice still retained traces of its old clear sound.

I looked up. Her pretty face remained almost untouched, but her waist had thickened and her breasts had grown fuller.

She examined me intently. "Are you from this area?"

"Yes, madam."

"And where is your wife in labor?"

"I left her in a safe spot in the big forest. We were on the way to visit her family in the land of Manasseh when she suddenly started having contractions. I wasn't prepared. She's only eight months pregnant. I tried to—"

"There's no time to talk. I'll have them get the wagon ready. We must reach her quickly."

"We can take my horse."

She hesitated for a moment, then gave me her hand. I helped her climb into the saddle, got on behind her, and headed out of town at a gallop. I felt her warm body against my stomach and between my legs, and I could feel the sweet sensation of my body melting away.

Only after we reached the middle of the forest did I tell her that there was no woman in labor expecting us. She cried for help and tried to jump from the saddle. I held her from behind and told her who I was.

"I don't remember you." The rage that mingled with her fear afforded her a wild beauty. "So what if I helped your mother give birth to your sister? Is that any reason to abduct me?"

"You're right," I whispered. "I only meant to look at you from up close, but suddenly I wanted to be alone with you. Forgive me, Tirzah. I don't know what came over me. I'll get you home right away."

She turned to look at me and examined my face with wonder. I could feel her breath against my lips.

"How could I not remember a giant like you?"

"I was only five years old."

A gentle smile lit up her pretty face. "You can take me home later. I'm in no rush."

We sat together in the shade of the trees. I described in great detail the special encounter we'd had thirteen years before, trying to jog her memory. And indeed, after a short while, her eyes sparkled as she joyfully told me that no one could forget the cold but tasty lentil stew we had eaten together while sitting on the mat or the interesting things I had told her. "To this day, I have never met a boy as well-versed in childbirth," she chuckled.

Time passed quickly, and before we parted on the street leading to her home, I asked to see her again. Our next meeting spawned more meetings, and within a few weeks my friends could declare with satisfaction that Shelomoam was finally rid of his virginity. True, his lover was an older married woman and not a single girl, but to each his own.

Tirzah's work gave her the freedom to come and go as she pleased without raising her husband's suspicions. He himself spent his days among the sycamore fig trees and his nights in the embraces of his three wives.

"The woman who came to the door isn't my mother," Tirzah explained. "She is his first wife."

"Why did you agree to be a second wife?"

"Such is the way of the world." She had made her peace and accepted her status submissively, and I couldn't help but picture my proud and confident mother, who had managed to remain my father's one and only wife. "My father gave me away to the highest bidder. I thought Ramiah would be satisfied with two wives, but after I bore him a child, my body thickened, and he wasted no time before marrying a third one. This won't be the end of it, either. His third wife, not yet nineteen, is in the first months of pregnancy, and he's already saving money for another bride price." She pulled me on top of her naked body and writhed passionately beneath me. "He can take another ten wives as far as I'm concerned. My poor sister-wives can pleasure themselves with his pathetic body all they want. I have you."

In those moments I would have been ready to swear to love this woman forever. Only years later, when I had known the love of my life, did I realize that Tirzah had been a substitute for the family I had lost. I had met her when I was five, in the midst of a momentous family event, and this had turned her into a family member in my eyes, a kind of older sister one could have desire for without guilt. The fact that she was married didn't make me feel like a sinner. To this day, when I think back on the look of gratitude in her eyes each time we drank deeply of love, I know that the act will not be listed among my transgressions in the book of judgment of the God of Israel.

"How did a sweet, gentle boy become such a savage, the leader of a gang of thugs who rob people in the markets?" On Tirzah's tongue, this sounded almost like a compliment.

"Would you have wanted me had I stayed sweet and gentle?"

The question remained unanswered, as we were already entwined in a not especially gentle activity. She loved me fiercely and with abandon, and only after she was sated could I cuddle in her arms and relax my body. Then, as I lay in her lap like a baby, she would launch into a series of probing questions, forcing me to open the wounds I had been trying to forget.

"How long has it been since you've seen your family?"

"More than half a year."

"Do your parents know about your gang?"

"No."

"Do they know how you live?"

"No."

"Do you love them?"

"No."

"Why not?"

"I don't want to talk about it."

Had Tirzah accepted my refusals, we would have stayed together for many more years. She couldn't have imagined that a casual comment, made one day almost offhandedly, would put me on a path of no return and change the course of my life.

I didn't understand its significance at first. I was enraptured in that fuzzy postcoital languor, and her statement didn't register in my mind. By the time I returned to my senses and asked her to repeat it, she had already gone on to other topics and had difficulty recalling the words she had spoken only moments before.

"What did you say?"

"I said it's a shame you don't visit your parents. They must—"

"No, what did you say about the labor?"

"What labor?"

"My mother's labor."

"I said it was the most difficult one I had even seen before and is still one of the most difficult ones I've ever worked on."

"And . . ."

"And?"

"And you can't believe that . . ."

"And . . . oh yes, and I can't believe it was her second one."

"I don't understand."

"Her opening was narrow and smooth like a young girl's. I've never seen a woman who had an easy first birth that didn't even leave a scar be nearly ripped to shreds by the second."

It took a few moments before I could respond. "It's exactly what happened to our matriarch Rachel," I whispered, mostly trying to convince myself. "She gave birth to Joseph easily, but bled to death giving birth to her second child, Benjamin."

She scoffed. "I wasn't present at the birth of Benjamin, so I can't say what happened there, but I was present at the birth of your sister, and I remember that even the midwife, who was older and more experienced, said despairingly that the poor woman was about to die from her difficult first labor."

At this point, Tirzah still hadn't recognized the degree of my horror and tried to distract me with the tales of our ancestors that I loved so much. "Who knows, Shelomoam," she said, making an obvious effort to laugh. "Maybe your mother found you in a basket floating on the river? You told me you admire

Aaron the Priest, but perhaps your story is more like that of his younger brother? Moses grew up as a prince, believing that Princess Bithiah was his mother and that the Pharaoh was his grandfather, and only when he got older did he learn that his birth parents were miserable slaves from the Land of Goshen."

Eight

I spent the next ten days lying almost perfectly still on the mat. This time, I wasn't suffering from debilitating headaches. On the contrary, my mind was more lucid than ever. I felt as though my eighteen years of life were passing before my eyes with cruel clarity, forcing me to examine them from the outside, as if they belonged to someone else. I kept asking myself how I could have been so blind. The answer had been right there in front of me all the time. How could I have missed it?

Tirzah wouldn't give my worried friends any details, only saying blandly that I'd discovered important information about my family and that they had best give me a chance to process it so that I could get on with my life.

Get on with my life? I almost cried when I heard her say that. I didn't know what to do yet, but I already realized, deep inside, that nothing would ever be the same again.

A week and a half later, I managed to get back up on my feet and walked over to my beloved Aner, who was waiting patiently outside the tent. I was barely able to mount him. He seemed to have grown taller since I'd last ridden him. I inhaled the crisp morning air of early winter and rode away without saying farewell to my friends.

My muscles ached as if I had been performing some sort of vigorous physical activity. My entire body had been placed in the service of my mission.

I came to see that it took less energy to move my muscles than to stop them from moving. Emotions seem to come upon us when we need them least and impair our judgment. I mustn't let them in if I want to reach my objective. I need to carry on like a lifeless statue, to freeze even more deeply the part of me that began turning to ice so long ago, when I left my home and my family and went out to search for a different life, far from the mystery that was driving me mad.

Onward, Shelomoam, onward. Go back to your country, your people. Go forth to that familiar place. Only there will you be able to find what you have been searching for your entire life. Do not allow your longing to break your determination. Do not give a foothold to compassion. Keep riding up that mountain and ignore those old sights and smells. You did not come here to reminisce about your childhood.

Here is the cave you first set eyes on ten years ago. Just like then, it is wet from the first rains of winter. It hasn't changed at all—the same wide threshold, the same spacious hall, the same little torches dripping incense, the same colorful rugs on the floor and walls, the same long corridor leading to the small cell, the one you could not take your mind off these past few days.

Only the woman in the cloak is not the same. This woman alone, of all the cave dwellers, changes the face behind her mask from time to time. First she was a leper, then she was healthy, and now she holds the answer to the riddle of your existence.

And just like then, she is sitting in the torchlight. Her body is wrapped, her face covered. Her two eyes blaze at me from behind the mask.

"Greetings, Zeruiah."

I grind her name, foreign and strange, between my teeth with a tone of distant coldness. Her name evokes no feelings in me.

Her body shakes beneath the cloak. Her arms, her legs, even her face. Just like then.

"Take off your mask, Zeruiah."

She says nothing in reply.

"Take it off. I have some questions for you, and I want to see your eyes so I can make sure you aren't lying."

She remains silent.

I bend toward her and reach for the mask.

She flinches and grabs it with her covered hands.

"Did you bring a knife?" she asks scornfully, teasing me.

The wall I'd built around my emotions collapses like a sand castle. I am gripped by uncontrollable rage.

"I can rip that mask off your face without a knife."

"Indeed, you have enough strength and savagery to get the job done. Nor do you seem short on cruelty. Go on, Shelomoam—tear it off!"

I want to shake her, to roar my pain into her ears, to hurl the bitter suffering she has caused me back at her. But I am able to restrain myself. I mustn't allow an outburst of emotion to disrupt my plan. My need for revenge will find its outlet some other time.

"Is that what you think of me?" I soften my voice and lend it an almost ingratiating tone. "On what do you base such a judgment?"

"On what do I base it?" Her mockery turns to accusation. "I base it on what you've done to your family—to your mother, to your father, even to your little sister."

"You know they aren't my family."

She is silent.

"What are you waiting for?" I ask, no longer able to hold my bitterness at bay. "I can't wait to hear more of the imaginary tales I've been told ever since I was a little boy, especially that well-known legend of the difficult labor that Moth—" I stop myself before uttering that false word again—"that Bilhah had." The name, barely coaxed from my mouth, rolls over my lips with an odd sensation of foreignness. "It's been a long time since I've had the pleasure of hearing those thrilling descriptions of the blood running between her legs and the cord she cut with her sharp teeth. And most important, you mustn't forget to note that the birth occurred in a wagon on the side of the road after the usual monthly visit of the heroine to the lepers' cave. Without that information, the story isn't complete."

She breathes heavily under her cloak. "All right, Shelomoam." She speaks my name softly. "You've discovered what we've been trying to hide from you. Now what?"

"Why did you do it to me?"

"The king's soldiers were searching for me everywhere. The cave was the only place in the world where I could feel safe. There was nothing I wanted more than to nurse you and hold you in my arms. Even right now, when you are grown and bitter and angry, I long to hold you, to lay your head in my lap and to caress your face. I felt such uncontrollable longing every time you came to visit me."

Her despicable outpouring goes in one ear and out the other. I spit questions at her in rapid succession: "Why didn't you tell me the truth? Didn't you trust me? Were you afraid I would betray you? Why did you give me up?"

"I put you in the best possible hands." She is almost in tears now. "Benaiah and Bilhah devotedly raised you and gave you—"

"Lies," I complete her sentence. "That's what they gave me."

"How can you be so ungrateful?" How easily apology turns to accusation. "They love you like a son. Only because they loved you so much did you sense that something was wrong. Had Benaiah been a little less protective, the secret would not have been uncovered."

"Why did he need to protect me? *You* rebelled against the king, not me."

"The king . . ." She hesitates. "The king took revenge not only on the rebels, but also against their families. He . . ."

"The king you rebelled against is long dead. Why did Benaiah continue to protect me all these years?"

"Bilhah and I begged him to let you grow up naturally, with freedom like other children have, but his concern for you drove him mad. He loves you too much. That is his only sin."

"That is his *only* sin?" The stifled cry erupts from me in a roar. "Because of his anxiety, I wasted my childhood in a secluded thicket, and you did nothing. Your own safety was more important to you than I was. And your own fears are as baseless as his. You've been hiding in this desolate cave for nearly twenty years. Twenty years. As if the king has nothing better to do than search for an old woman who participated in some forgotten rebellion against his dead father ages ago."

She exhales heavily. "What do you want, Shelomoam?" I can barely hear her quiet voice. "Tell me what you want."

"I want to know who my father is."

⌘

I'd said it. All my hopes and dreams in those six words.

"To know who my father is."

The silence that followed proved to me that the information I sought wouldn't come easy. I realized that I had been wrong to explode with anger.

I tried to think quickly about how I might repair the damage I had done and persuade her to reveal the one missing piece.

"The three of you made a mistake by allowing your exaggerated and unfounded fears to control you." I chose my words carefully. "We've all paid a hefty price for that mistake. You are buried alive in a cave. Benaiah and Bilhah are grieving over my escape, and I wasted my childhood and my youth. But that's all in the past. Now that I have found out what you have been hiding, we can begin to rebuild our relationship. Tell me who my father is, and I promise to come home and stop fighting with my . . . adoptive parents. I'm willing to still call them Father and Mother, if that's what you want. You can take off that cloak and come live with us, or you can remain in the cave. Either way, I will stay in touch with you, and I won't hold a grudge. Just tell me who my father is."

I spoke almost ceaselessly for the next hour, stopping from time to time to see if I'd managed to soften her up, and when she kept silent I started talking again.

"I will only find peace if I know who my father is. Tell me who he is, and I'll no longer be a wanderer. A person who doesn't know his roots walks the world detached and anonymous. I have to know who my father is."

At some point I began to rock in place. My head was spinning. I couldn't feel my arms and legs. I felt as if my body were starting to float in the air.

Suddenly, without warning, she removed her mask. I looked away. I felt unable to look at her. Not now.

"Look at me, Shelomoam."

When I had torn the mask off her two years before, the only thing I wanted to know was whether or not she was a leper. Now I truly saw her for the first time, and what I saw was too painful. I couldn't help but notice the resemblance between us. It was so strong that for a moment I wondered if that was why she continued to hide her face.

Only our sizes didn't match. Even through her cloak, I could see the contours of her skinny body. My great stature didn't come from her.

"Look carefully, Shelomoam. Commit me to your memory. I'm the only root you have. You have no roots but me."

I gazed at her through expressionless eyes.

"Is my father dead?"

She sighed softly.

I wanted to cry, but my throat choked up. I couldn't produce more than a stifled whisper. I don't know where I found the strength to go on, but I knew I couldn't give up.

"Tell me everything about him. What was his name? Who were his parents? What tribe did he belong to? People sometimes think I'm from the tribe of Benjamin. Was he one of them?"

When I heard her answer, I lost my footing. I had never been so shocked in my life.

"I don't know."

"What . . . what do you mean?"

"I don't know who your father is."

"I don't understand."

"You're a grown man now, Shelomoam; it's time you understood such things. Life doesn't always follow the customary patterns. It was a different time. We lived in the rebels' cave. Just imagine: hundreds of young men and a few girls spending a great deal of time together in a crowded cave. They eat together, train together, bathe together, and sleep together. I was with many men; I can't even remember how many. Was he from the tribe of Benjamin? Perhaps. Most of the men in the cave were from Ephraim and Benjamin, but there were others, too. The fact that you're tall and handsome means nothing. Most of them were big and strong. That's how it goes; thin, weak men prefer to live quietly and not get involved with rebellions. I remember one giant from the tribe of Dan. We called him Samson the Hero, after the ancient giant from the same tribe who fought against the Philistines. There was another giant of a man, let me try to remember . . . he was from Gilead. Did you know that the men of Manasseh are also tall and handsome? But they say the most impressive men come from—"

I don't know whether I screamed or held my tongue. I plugged my ears to stop her words from continuing to cut into my body. I had no idea where I was. I tried to flee, but my feet got caught on the rug.

She got up from the bed and reached out her hands. I shoved her, and she fell on her back.

I grabbed the wall and walked toward the doorway. Before I left I turned to face her one last time.

"Whore," I stretched out the one syllable, spewing it out like vomit. "Whoooore! I won't let you touch me with those impure hands."

Nine

Once again, I was alone in the world. But as opposed to when I first left my family and felt like I was suffocating, this time I felt no need of the company of others. I wanted to be alone, which seemed to be my natural state. The whole ride, I was lost in thoughts of rage toward the woman who birthed me, toward my adoptive parents, and even toward Elisheba. Now that I had discovered that she wasn't really my sister, I actually felt even deeper embarrassment over my feelings for her. I tried not to think of the friends I had left behind either. They should feel indebted to me for everything they learned from me, and I owe them nothing more. Only Tirzah still aroused searing guilt and agonizing longing in me, but pleasant thoughts about the army dulled the pain.

A few hours later, I reached Gibeah, the capital of the land of Benjamin. Continuing on to Jerusalem in the dark would be difficult, so I decided to stop for the night. I wasn't deterred by the frightening stories spread about the city by the Judeans. Bilhah, the woman who raised me, told me those stories throughout my childhood so that I would learn not to believe them. She was especially angered by the story that depicted the dwellers of Gibeah as bloodthirsty wolves who once demanded that a kindhearted man from Ephraim surrender to them a pair of guests who had taken shelter in his house. The man did his best to protect his guests, but the wolves of Benjamin grabbed the woman, a Judean woman, and tortured her all night long, until she finally died.

"Stories are more dangerous than swords." Bilhah repeated this statement every chance she got. "Swords can only harm those standing right in front of them, while stories determine who will live and who will die in future generations. The Judeans want us to loathe Benjamin and think of Gibeah as Sodom so that we'll stop longing for our first king."

I was angry with myself for failing to wipe away these memories from my childhood. I need to look ahead and stop dwelling on the past. Tomorrow I will be standing at the gates of Jerusalem, opening a promising new chapter in my life as a strong, independent, formidable man, and my troubled childhood will disappear like a fleeting dream.

⁂

The first guesthouse I saw at the entrance to Gibeah looked fairly derelict, but I decided I shouldn't be picky. All I needed was some feed for Aner, a warm meal for myself, and a bed for the night. I greeted the owners, an elderly couple, and asked them to set their price in advance. I didn't want any surprises. I negotiated aggressively and only after we reached an agreement did I tell them to take Aner into the barn. The year and a half I'd spent with the gang had made me a suspicious and assertive man, someone that nobody would dare cheat. I liked that about myself.

"I thought you were a local," the woman said, trying to make conversation as she served me my dinner. "Until I heard your *sh*."

I chewed in silence. I didn't feel like being friendly to anyone.

My bed was comfortable and clean. I fell asleep instantly. When I woke up, the sun was already in the middle of the sky, but I didn't care. I'd needed that rest. I would be in Jerusalem in just a few hours presenting myself for the army examinations, and I needed to be at full strength.

When I entered the barn, I saw that Aner wasn't where I had left him. At first, I wasn't concerned, assuming that the elderly couple had decided on their own to let him out for some fresh air and to graze in the grass that had sprouted following the first rain. Only when I ventured outside did I realize that I was in trouble. Four young men were surrounding my beloved horse, holding on to his reins. Aner was trying to free himself, but they wouldn't let him move.

My fury filled me with strength. I recalled the first time I had met the gang, when they had come to take revenge for the punch in the face I had given their friend. I had been one against many, but I'd been able to hold my own anyway. Eventually I had fallen, but I am much stronger now.

I looked them over quickly, trying to assess their strength. They are tall and broadly built, but I am taller and no less broad. They can't imagine that my innocent-looking left boot hides a sharp, serrated knife. I can easily take on these four miserable thugs who think they've found easy prey in the form of a frightened guest who believes the horror stories about them. They don't know who they're dealing with.

They surrounded me before I had a chance to reach for my knife.

"Give us your money." Their knives were longer and sharper than mine. "It would be a shame to damage that beautiful body."

I leapt over them in a single bound. I had intended to hop onto Aner's back and gallop away, but I was knocked out by a kick in the head. I felt as if my body were on fire and collapsed to the ground, my head spinning with nausea. I was trying to sit up when I felt a deep stab in my leg. I ran my hand over it, writhing in pain, and felt the familiar warm liquid on my fingers. My leg was covered in so much blood that I was certain it had been chopped clean off.

They took my satchel, and there was nothing I could do about it. I remained on the ground helplessly, even as I heard Aner being dragged away. I must have screamed because one of them came back and kicked me in the head again.

"You should be thankful you're still alive!" I heard him shouting as if from far away, like an echo. Then that familiar darkness enveloped me once again.

⁊⧟⧟

I was awakened by a sharp pain in my leg. The flickering light in my eyes made it difficult to identify the large figure sitting at my side, but I could feel its nails against my flesh. It took me a few seconds to realize that I had fallen into the hands of some fat man who was taking advantage of my unconscious state and torturing me. He was poking my wound with a sharp object and pinching my skin. I girded all the strength in my aching muscles and tried to fight him, but he pinned me down with one hand, almost effortlessly.

"Save your attacks for another time, kid." It wasn't hard to recognize his Edomite accent. "By the look of your leg, I'd say this is no time for jumping around."

My feeling of helplessness hurt more than the physical torture. Ever since I had joined the gang, I'd felt invincible. I could easily overpower the few people who even considered threatening me. My fists of steel were infamous in every market in Ephraim. But here, in the land of Benjamin, they're able to defeat me again and again. First, thugs make off with my beloved horse and steal my money, and now a mad Edomite is abusing me. It was a mistake to travel alone to Jerusalem. Had I taken the gang with me, no one would have dared attack us. But what's done is done. I must be cold and calculating as I plan my next steps or the Edomite may yet cut me into twelve pieces, just as the Levite husband of that poor woman from Judah did after she was raped and murdered here in Gibeah. The stories Judeans tell about Benjamin apparently aren't the fantasies produced by the raging minds of the king's scribes. This tribe really is mad. All the good things Bilhah told me about it were just as false as the other fabrications I was force-fed throughout my childhood. Nothing I'd learned was the truth. Even the legends of Ephraim had been lies. So what if we spawned a few leaders? That doesn't make us the chosen tribe. It was time I stopped thinking of Ephraim in the first person plural. I don't know what tribe I belong to, and I actually don't care. Bilhah can continue to fill Elisheba's mind with ridiculous slogans about the wondrous tribes of Rachel, whose members were destined for royalty, but I have more important things to do. I have to find Aner and get out of the awful land of Benjamin.

"Get your filthy hands off me!" I said, lowering my voice as much as I could. "If you touch me one more time, I'll have your head rolling like a gourd."

The Edomite looked at me and burst into a powerful laughter, jiggling his many rolls of fat. "Well done, kid." His mocking tone ignited my rage once more. "I admire your attempt to sound threatening despite your rather dire condition, but let's see you get up and learn to walk before you start trying to impress me with your threats."

He examined my leg up close and rubbed his hands with satisfaction. "A good job. The wound is sutured well. Now just don't move your leg, and let time do the rest."

"You sutured my wound?" I could barely talk, I was so shocked.

"What did you think I was doing? I have better things to do than poke around in the wounds of a foolish boy looking for trouble and getting into a fight with a gang of thugs from the most savage tribe in Israel."

I started to like him. His origin also had something to do with it. I noticed a long time ago that the sense of not belonging I have when interacting with other people makes me partial to foreigners, especially those from nations despised by Israelites—Ammonites, Moabites, and Edomites. The only ones I like better are the Egyptians, perhaps because I am fluent in their language, or maybe because of our matriarch Asenath, the wife of Joseph.

Once again, I am thinking of Ephraim in the first person. I have to erase this tribal way of thinking from my mind. I am about to become a soldier in the king's army, and that is the only identity I care about.

"I'm not scared of Benjaminite thugs. If I'd been focused on the fight and not trying to save my horse, I could have beaten them, easy."

"Sure, kid," he said, squeezing my arm affectionately. "But before you try, you could use a good trainer."

Had anyone else dared talk to me like that, they would have gotten a taste of my wrath as proof that I was no kid. But coming from this big Edomite, "kid" sounded like a compliment. I couldn't figure out why I cared what he thought about me. I was usually the one that people worked to please, not the other way around.

"They'll train me well in Jerusalem. I'm going to join the king's army."

"If you can convince me that you're serious, I'll train you myself. I can teach you how to incapacitate a rival on the spot."

"I need weapons training. I know how to throw a punch."

"That you manage to rob innocent people in the markets and maybe throw a few punches every once in a while doesn't make you a warrior."

I was confused as to how he'd learned this information about me. He must be a sorcerer, I thought. The Edomites and the Egyptians are the best sorcerers in the world. When I was six, Bilhah took me to a magic show at the Zeredah market. The magician spat fire and turned wooden sticks into live snakes, just like Moses. I cheered for him, practically squealing with excitement, but when he placed a young woman in a box and sliced her in two, I burst into tears. A few moments later, the woman stepped out, unharmed and with a smile on her face, and took me in her arms. She fed me honeyed nuts and spoke in a language I didn't understand. On the way home Bilhah explained that the woman had been speaking Edomite, adding with admiration that only the Edomites and the Egyptians knew how to do real magic. I walked around all day dizzy with joy, and even the quarrel that broke out at home couldn't spoil my mood. Benaiah yelled at Bilhah about how irresponsible it was of her to bring me to crowded places, but Bilhah was unfazed by his yelling, insisting that the boy deserved to have fun once in a while, especially when the Edomites were putting on a magic show, which was something you didn't see every day.

"Who are you?" I tried to push out of my mind those accursed memories from my childhood that wouldn't leave me alone, and turn my attention back to the mysterious man at my side.

"Hadad the Edomite. And who are you?"

"Shelomoam."

"That's it?"

"Shelomoam the . . . Hebrew."

He laughed. "If you want to hide your tribal identity, find a name that doesn't have a *sh* sound." I felt as though he were uncovering my innermost thoughts.

"Are you a sorcerer?"

He laughed harder. "No, and neither was my father. I just know how to read people. That's an essential quality for a warrior. If you choose to train with me, you'll learn how to do it, too. Reading people is much more important than wielding swords. But we'd best put aside any discussion of our future together. Your body needs rest."

"Why are you caring for me?" Although I liked him, I wasn't so stupid as to fall for his strange solicitude. The past year and a half had taught me that everything comes at a price.

"I need soldiers like you."

"What for?"

"I'm the commander of the army of the Palace of Candles." He said the words with great ceremony, as if he were standing on a high stage, announcing his rank to a cheering crowd.

"I've never heard of such an army. Is it in Edom?"

"What are you talking about, kid?" he said, his giant belly jiggling with laughter. "The Palace of Candles is in Jerusalem."

My body trembled with excitement. I had been left without money, without a horse, and almost without a leg, but I still felt lucky. Of all the people in the world, it had been my good fortune to fall into the hands of a senior commander from Jerusalem, who was offering to train me without examinations.

"Does your army belong to the king?" I wanted to be sure I wasn't deluding myself.

He looked around quickly and then leaned close and whispered into my ear, "Have you heard of the Mad Princess?"

Ten

Hadad helped me up onto his magnificent chariot and ordered the coachman to proceed with care so that the bumpy road wouldn't cause my sutures to come undone. I asked him if it was far to Jerusalem, and he exclaimed in surprise that I was the first Hebrew boy he'd met in his fifteen years in Israel who had never been there. I didn't want to explain the bizarre circumstances of my childhood. Even if I had told him, I think he would have found it hard to believe that the people who raised me were afraid to expose me to the outside world just because my birth mother had taken part in some silly rebellion against the previous king twenty years ago.

I tried to fall asleep, but hunger ate away at my belly. The satchel that the thugs had stolen had carried not only my money, but also a fine breakfast that the innkeeper had prepared for me.

"When was the last time you ate?"

I can't say that all my suspicions disappeared at once, but it was the first time in a long time that I felt I could trust somebody. I must have been smiling to myself, because he asked what was so funny.

"Your questions are. Why do you bother asking? You know everything about me anyway."

"Not everything, but you can't hide how hungry you are. It's bothering you even more than your leg. We'll be at the Palace of Candles soon, and you'll be fed like a king. The Mad Princess employs the best cooks in Jerusalem, though she barely eats a thing."

He looked me over with his piercing eyes. "But I can tell that you can't wait. We'll stop at the food stalls by the city gate. We don't want you arriving at the palace unconscious."

The coachman jumped off the chariot and returned with three steaming pastries. The fresh aroma drove me nearly crazy. I gobbled them down, one after another, hardly taking a breath in between. "Thank you, Hadad."

"You're welcome. You may call me by my name for now, but once we get to the palace you must call me Commander. Understood?"

"Completely understood, Commander. I know the rules. I wouldn't dare call you by your name, just as I wouldn't dare call the princess mad to her face."

He blew out a sigh. "Well, to be honest, you can call her anything you want. She can't understand it anyway."

"Then why did you whisper her name in my ear and look to make sure no one was around?"

"Nice, kid, good attention to detail. That's one of the most important qualities in a warrior. I didn't want anyone from Benjamin to hear what I call her. She is one of them, and they're not the kind of people you want to have trouble with."

"You're telling me! That tribe is deranged. The stories the Judeans tell about them are true. Violent thugs, that's what they are."

He narrowed his eyes, giving me an amused look. "And I understand that you, personally, frown upon thuggish behavior."

My cheeks burned.

"Makes no difference to me, kid, I understand you. A man has got to eat, and not everyone has a plot of land to call his own. I've done some things in my lifetime that I'd rather forget. But ever since coming to Jerusalem, I've been innocent as a lamb."

"Why did you come here?"

"Because of my wife, the lady Eno. Have you heard of her?"

"Why would I have?"

"She is the sister of Tahpenes, wife of the Pharaoh Siamun."

I couldn't believe my ears. "Do you mean to tell me that your wife is a princess?"

He laughed jovially. "I'm a prince, too."

My mind was spinning with amazement. "An Egyptian prince?"

"I told you I was an Edomite. Can't you hear my accent? I come from the royal family of Edom."

At that moment, I realized that I was stuck in the chariot of an impressive, charming man who was no less mad than the Mad Princess. Only a person who couldn't tell the difference between reality and imagination could make up such a far-fetched story. I began to consider plans for escape, but, of course, he read my mind. Expressing no alarm, he warned me apathetically that I should think twice before I jumped off a speeding chariot with an already severely injured leg.

"You don't believe a word I say?" he asked almost proudly. "I suppose I wouldn't have believed such a story either. I wonder what you'll say when I tell you that my wife is not only the sister of Lady Tahpenes, but also the aunt of the king's wife."

"What king?"

"Your king, naturally."

"How can an Egyptian princess be a Hebrew queen?" I mumbled desperately. I was so confused that I didn't care about understanding anything anymore.

He looked at me with pity. "Say, kid, what have they been teaching you over there in Zeredah? Don't you know that one of your king's many wives is Pharaoh's daughter? When Princess Hatshepsut traveled from Egypt to Jerusalem to marry the King of Israel, Pharaoh Siamun asked me to join her so that she wouldn't feel all alone in that foreign country. I agreed. Why not? What did I care? I was a stranger in Egypt, so why not be a stranger in Israel? I took Eno, my wife, and our son, Genubath, and we joined Hatshepsut in Jerusalem."

"I still can't understand how an Edomite managed to marry the Pharaoh's wife's sister." The free and easy way he spoke made me believe him, but I still suspected his story might have been made up, or at least wildly exaggerated. I was actually an expert on the subject of embellishments; I used to make them up all the time as a child. I loved peppering any experience, even meaningless little events, with imaginary details. Bilhah nicknamed me the Dreamer and complained that even though Joseph had been a great man, not all of his qualities were worth mimicking.

"An Edomite prince is certainly a worthy match for an Egyptian princess," Hadad said. He wasn't insulted by the disrespectful tone I had taken when referring to Edomites. "Especially if he's also a celebrated military commander. The Pharaoh appreciated my talents, unlike your king. In Egypt, I trained warriors whose praises were sung throughout the country, but here, in that strange Palace of Candles I've been stuck in, I'm wasting my talents on spoiled brats parading around in their uniforms as if they were evening gowns, playing make-believe with pointless roll calls and marches. I know that the king had no choice because the Mad Princess demanded me for herself, and he didn't want to get into a fight with her, but who would have thought that in the land of the heroic Hebrews I would be wasting away with toy soldiers? I really miss the position I had in Egypt. I would go back today if it wasn't for Tahpenes. Whenever she hears about us planning a return to Egypt, she writes us distraught letters begging us not to leave her daughter alone. And I, like an idiot, relent. Inside this big body hides a very soft heart."

I didn't know whether or not to believe his story, but I realized that it didn't really matter. The situation was as bad as it could be. He himself admitted that military service in the Palace of Candles was merely symbolic, while I stupidly had thought that I could use the experience to train to become a soldier in the king's army. Life had taught me that there was no such thing as a free lunch. Why would some stranger I had never met before offer me a shortcut and turn me into a warrior? I'd been misled again. When would I finally learn to trust no one?

"Are you disappointed by what I told you?" I should have known he would read my mind again. "But that's just it—that's why I need you."

He watched me expectantly, hoping I would ask him the meaning of that enigmatic statement. I pursed my lips and looked the other way to stop him from reading my mind and figuring out my plan of escape. It didn't work. He commented calmly that I was free to go whenever I wished, but that he first wanted to explain how I fit into his plans.

"Do you think I just happened to help you out? Forget it. With me there's no such thing as a free lunch." Now I was feeling truly scared by his ability to quote my thoughts, word for word. "For years, I have been asking the king to permit me to train the soldiers biding their time in the service of the Mad Princess, so that when the time came they could leave the Palace of Candles and join his own army. So far, my requests have fallen on deaf ears. The king doesn't believe that toy soldiers can be turned into warriors. But at our last meeting, he must have gotten tired of my pleading, and he agreed to give me a chance to prove myself. I need one clear success in order to demonstrate my skills. I'm looking for a young man who can withstand my training program and successfully pass the tests of skill that the army officers will arrange for him. If I can prove that I have managed to turn a toy soldier into a warrior, the king will appoint him a senior commander in his army and permit me to train more like him. I cannot fail. I am not willing to continue to waste my time on ridiculous parades. Now do you see why I need you? As soon as I saw you fighting off those thugs from Benjamin, I thanked my god Qos for placing you in my path. You were defeated, but at least you gave the fight everything you had. If they hadn't ripped your leg apart, you would have kept fighting until your last breath. With your body and my training skills, you'll become the greatest warrior in the land. Give me a year, and I'll make you invincible, a new and improved version of Samson, the hero from the tribe of Dan. And, unlike him, you won't be defeated by a woman. Trust me. My fighters work to improve themselves in every way, not just muscles and flexibility, but brains and personality as well. But if you want to become a true warrior, you must promise me you'll follow me blindly and do whatever I order you to do, without question or doubt. That's all. I've said my piece. The choice is yours."

"The thought of following you blindly scares me. I know so little about you," I mumbled as my resistance crumbled.

His confident smile proved that he was already inside my head, knowing I would follow him anywhere. "You know a great deal about me, more than you need to."

"To make this decision, I need to understand more about this place." I tried to maintain the appearance of a person who still had a choice.

"About the Palace of Candles?"

"And the Mad Princess."

His sigh of compassion sounded familiar, and I realized he sounded it whenever the Mad Princess was mentioned. "You don't need me for that. Just take a walk around Jerusalem, stop the first man you see on the street, and ask him about her. Everyone knows the stories."

"I want to hear them from you."

"I'm tired, and you aren't well. Your stomach has only received a small advance on what it's owed, and the swelling in your leg is getting worse. We'll eat a good meal, sleep for a few hours, and then we'll have more energy for stories. But if you enter the Palace of Candles, you will be required to stay for at least a year. That is the law. Only servants and soldiers may enter."

"I'm not about to commit to spending a year in a place I know nothing about," I said, taking pleasure in regaining control.

"All right, you've convinced me." I was no longer angry at myself for relishing his faint praise. "We'll let the coachman go inside, and we'll stay in the chariot telling stories of the Mad Princess. Did you know that she was the first wife of the previous king and the daughter of the first king? Of course you didn't; you hadn't even heard a thing about her before today. All right, kid, I'll tell you everything from the beginning."

⊸≎⊷

My last day in Gibeah had made me detest the entire tribe of Benjamin, but I was still saddened to hear about the bitter fate of Israel's first princess. Hadad spoke animatedly of her legendary beauty. It was said that she was one of the five people who were formed in the twilight of creation. When He created the world, God also decided to create several great wonders, including five people—two men and three women—who would be the most beautiful in all the world. All of them were descendants of Rachel and all were royalty, with the exception of Rachel herself, the matriarch of the line. The first was Rachel, beloved wife of Jacob, the father of Israel. The second was her eldest son, the great ruler of Egypt. The third was the first Hebrew king, a Benjaminite. The fourth was his daughter, the first Princess of Israel. And the fifth, also a daughter of Benjamin, is yet to be born. Legend has it that she will be named for the goddess Ishtar, will marry the king of the great empire, and will save her people from a terrible calamity that a descendant of the nation of Amalek will try to bring upon them.

The beautiful princess had been given in marriage to a young warrior of Judah as a prize for the killing of a giant Philistine who'd been terrorizing the tribes of Israel. Her passionate love for her husband was also the stuff of legend. Love has always been considered a mighty force that helps men chose their mates, but here was a young woman, practically a girl, who had proven that women could also follow their hearts and choose their own husbands.

But the beautiful princess's great love could not save her marriage. Her father, the king, who was haunted by his demons, was jealous of his son-in-law and wanted to kill him, and the young man was forced to abandon her when he fled the palace. Only years later, after the king was dead, could she finally return to the arms of her beloved, and yet she bore no children. Her husband was crowned king and succeeded in all that he did, while she slowly faded away into bitterness, living her life in an isolated wing of the palace and taking no part in its society. Twenty years ago, shortly before her husband's death, she lost her mind all at once at the height of a great celebration of the rain that had brought salvation from three hard years of drought. Following that attack of madness, she lost her ability to speak and began screaming at the top of her lungs and lighting candles in every corner of the palace. Her sanity has never returned. In the daytime she sits still as a statue, and at night, after sunset, she comes alive and fills the palace with hundreds of candles, screaming unintelligibly all the while. The most beautiful princess in the world thus became the Mad Princess, and the isolated wing where she lives became known as the Palace of Candles.

When I was a child, every little thing made me burst into tears, but for the last three years, ever since my first fight with Bilhah, I have shed tears for no one, not even for myself. Even that morning, when those Benjaminite thugs tore open my leg and stole my horse, I didn't cry. I mustn't cry. It's the most foolish thing I could do. Someone who is impressed with my manliness will not appreciate my tears and is liable to regret choosing me.

"Go ahead, cry," he reassured me. "I cried, too, the first time I heard this story. Cry now, while you still have tears for the beautiful princess who lost her mind. If you decide to come with me, your tears will turn into contempt, then anger, and finally resentment. Her candles make the nights unbearable; her screaming can be heard throughout Jerusalem, and it haunts the sleep of little children. It's no great honor to serve in the Palace of Candles. Soon, when the people of Jerusalem marvel at your fine uniform and ask you where you are stationed, you'll find yourself evading the question, mumbling a few platitudes and avoiding any details. So, what do you say, kid? Do you want to go home?"

"I have no home," I said. "I'm coming with you."

"Good decision," he said, pretending I had a choice in the matter. "Now, before we bring the chariot into the stable, take a peek outside and have a look at the Temple. You've never seen anything like it."

That was the last thing I wanted to do at that moment, but I knew I had to show some degree of interest. I drew the curtain and glanced out the window. What I saw so astounded me that I couldn't look away.

"Your temple is beautiful," Hadad said, unable to hide his envy. "Much nicer than the great temple in Edom that we built for our god Qos."

The rage instilled in me by Bilhah returned full force, and I couldn't suppress it. "It is not *our* temple."

"Not yours?" Hadad's eyebrows rose in surprise.

I gazed at the proud lion etched into its chiseled stones. I tried not to think about the ox that had played such a major role in the stories of my childhood, but the words burst out of their own accord: "Our temple was destroyed."

Then, a moment later, against my will: "This is the temple of Judah."

Eleven

My arrival at the Palace of Candles did not go as I had expected. Instead of getting to meet the Mad Princess and her soldiers and receiving the meal and bed I'd been promised, I found myself inside gigantic dark tunnels. I looked out the window of the racing chariot and saw a ghost town complete with houses and stables, barns and horses, wells and mills, even racetracks. Only two things were missing: sunshine and people.

"Welcome to your new home," Hadad announced festively, as if he were showing off a splendid hall.

"This is the Palace of Candles?"

"This is your own private training facility. The palace is right above us."

"I won't be training with everyone else?"

"You'll be here by yourself."

I could barely drag my leg down the steps of the chariot. Hadad didn't offer any help.

"For how long?"

"Until I say otherwise."

"Let me see the Mad Princess first."

"There's nothing to see. Her decrepit body is nothing but an empty shell. Rather than wanting what you don't need, you'd best focus all your energy on your training. We'll give you some time to recover from your injury, and then we'll get to work."

In a matter of days, I lost my sense of self and put my body and soul into the hands of a man who tortured me in every possible way. Until not long before, I'd taken pride in my mysterious ability to make people follow me and do as I said, but now I blindly obeyed his every order. I would have jumped to my death without hesitation had he ordered me to do so.

"I'm going to bury you alive."

Even outrageous statements like that merely floated past me calmly.

"Now climb down to the bottom of the pit and stand absolutely still." I could tell that even he was surprised by my indifference. "The servants are going to bury you up to your chest. You'll only be able to move your arms."

"And if I refuse?" I said, only because I knew that he expected me to protest.

"Whether or not you agree, you'll be standing in that hole in just another moment."

For the first hours, I felt only a bone-chilling cold and a sense of numbness in my feet. The true horror began after a day.

When I got out, my legs couldn't carry me, but I knew I had defeated fear.

Tortures were heaped upon me one after another, ceaselessly, each torment worse than the one before. I don't know how I held on. I felt as though my body was no longer a part of me and that I was watching it from the outside. I drank bull urine, I was thrown off a galloping horse, I spent two days tied to the top of a tall pole, and worst of all, I was left locked in a barn with an enchanting foal who captured my heart and made me miss Aner even more deeply than I already did. I managed to resist hunger for almost a week before it took over my body and drove me mad. I crushed the foal's skull with a rock and ate his hot flesh raw. I felt nothing other than satiation.

My willpower didn't come from bravery or ambition, nor from a thirst for revenge or a wish to visit my hometown as a soldier in the king's army. I felt as though I were being reborn out of my own body, not bound to any womb by some eternal cord, without parents smothering me with their worries and oppressively demanding that I feel gratitude toward them, and, especially, without a distant sister who had until not long ago plagued my dreams and filled me with painful yearning. When I found out that she wasn't my true sister, I stood naked before my forbidden desire, which had, in an instant, become a possibility and therefore ever more frightening. Only now, inside Hadad's torture chamber, did I finally feel released of the menacing weight of it. My body no longer sent any pain signals, and my heart was emptied of all feeling. I didn't long for any person or any thing, not even for Tirzah or Aner. Eating the flesh of that foal had erased whatever shards of personality were still left in me. It had made me feel powerful, but I took no joy in the feeling, as my emotions were gone completely.

The days went by; I cannot say how many. Inside the dark tunnels I lost all track of time. Sowing and reaping, cold and heat, summer and winter, night and day—all at once, the pulsations that had been part of my life's blood were gone, and I didn't even feel their absence. I knew that up above, in the Palace of Candles, the people were leisurely going about their business: the Mad Princess sits still all day and lights her candles at night, the dolled-up soldiers wear their elegant uniforms and play at their pointless formations and parades, and the skillful cooks prepare fine meals for all the denizens of the palace. But nothing of what was going on up above ever reached my ears. I couldn't even hear the princess screaming.

"Why don't you ask me when all this is going to end?" Hadad asked me in a resentful tone after his servants had spent several hours whipping my naked back, never getting so much as a grunt out of me.

"You can keep torturing me for the rest of my life."

"Is that what you call my training?"

"Training includes fighting methods, hand-to-hand combat, and weapons instruction. But if you would rather call this torture 'training,' then so be it. Call it whatever you want."

"Soon we'll be able to move to the next phase, and I'll teach you all the things you've just listed."

"I don't care what you teach me. As far as I'm concerned, we can keep playing this game until I breathe my last or you do, whichever comes first."

"What game are you talking about?"

"The game you chose: you command, I obey."

"And if I commanded you to slaughter Aner?"

"Send your servants to find him in the Land of Benjamin. Within five minutes of giving him back to me, you'll have his head on a platter."

"And your lover?"

My heart beat wildly for a moment, just as it had in my previous life, but I got ahold of myself and regained my composure. "Who?"

"The pretty midwife from Shiloh. Don't feign ignorance. You know that I know everything about you."

"I'm not feigning ignorance; the word 'lover' sounds so foreign to me that I forgot for a moment who it could be. Would I be able to slaughter Tirzah? I already told you: you command, I obey. Those are the rules of the game."

⚘

One night I woke up, groggy and confused, to the sounds of shouting. I was lying on my bunk as usual, and I didn't know what to think. Since arriving in the tunnels, I hadn't encountered anyone but Hadad and his three servants, who'd spoken very little, and that only softly. I tried to connect the unusual sounds to things I knew from my previous life, but before I could reach any conclusions, dozens of young men stormed inside, calling out excitedly. In the pale light of the oil lamp I could see their stunned expressions as they spotted me watching them from my bunk. I asked myself whether I was surprised and discovered that the feeling of surprise had been lost along with the rest of my emotions.

"Who are you?"

"Soldiers of the Palace of Candles. And you?"

"Ask your commander."

"What are you doing here?"

"Ask your commander."

"Don't you know how to talk?"

"I actually do know how to talk, but I don't know how to answer questions."

"Judging by the looks of you, you'd best not get too smart. It looks like you've taken quite a few beatings already."

I turned to face the soldier who had said that. I liked his red curls and the bright eyes that looked me over with curiosity. In my previous life, I would have been prepared to admit that he was the kind of person I would get along with, but at that moment I felt nothing but boredom.

"You see this scar?" I asked, pulling up my gown to reveal my ankle. "It only recently healed. You're welcome to start there. That way you won't have to work so hard before you see blood."

"Thank you for bringing it to my attention," he said with an amused smile.

"I'll use that crucial piece of information in due time. But for now, I'd rather take you up to the palace with your leg in one piece. Can you walk by yourself, or should we drag you?"

"I have no will of my own. How hard is it for you to fathom something so simple?"

The boys chuckled. All at once, as if at some invisible command, they raised my bunk to their shoulders and walked at a slow march through the dark tunnels. I lay on my back, looking up at the ceiling, and tried to relax my body and go back to my interrupted sleep, but before I had time to shut my eyes, I could see flickers of sunlight ahead of me.

They put me down on the ground. I stared at the sun with my eyes wide open. It hurt badly, but I'd been through worse.

"I've already gathered that you don't mind injuring yourself," the redheaded soldier said, standing in front of me and blocking out the sun. "But you'd be better off doing it gradually. If you start by going blind, what will be left for the end?"

"What end?"

"My name is Ithiel. Why don't you tell us yours?"

"Shelomoam," I muttered. "Shelomoam, and that's it. You had better not ask whose son and which tribe because I'll give you no further answers. Now go see your commander and tell him you've found me. He won't be too enthusiastic about your rescue mission."

But Hadad actually *was* enthusiastic. Or, more precisely, he burst into uproarious laughter that shook his fat body. I realized that I hadn't seen him laugh like that since we had ridden together to Jerusalem, ages ago.

"Well done, soldiers. I didn't believe you'd be able to find the tunnels."

I got the feeling that he was putting on an act, playing at some sort of strange game, but what kind of game it was remained a mystery to me. I stayed on my bunk, lying in the sun, and watched them from down below. I was having trouble seeing them clearly, but I could hear everything they said.

"Go to noon formation without me. I have to take care of this fellow you saved."

"This time, let's skip formation, Commander," Ithiel said firmly. "We want to hear who this man is and why you've been hiding him in the tunnels."

"Go to formation!" Hadad said, but his decisive tone couldn't quite mask a curious hesitancy. Now I was certain that he was just putting on an act.

The soldiers, too, must have sensed their commander's hesitation, and they immediately joined Ithiel in his protest, demanding an explanation for my puzzling presence. They argued that there would be no harm in putting off the formation or even canceling it in light of the situation. The Mad Princess wouldn't notice anyway. The derogatory nickname was spoken naturally, without a hint of embarrassment, as if they were saying, "Her Royal Highness the Princess."

Eventually, Hadad had to use all the power of his authority to send his soldiers to their formation, but not before promising to tell them everything about me in the next few days.

Only after their departure did he allow the muscles of his face to relax. I asked him if we would be going back down now, and he replied that I could have used another six months in the tunnels, but now that everything was out in the open we had no choice but to continue my training in the palace. I was surprised to learn that it had been only half a year since the torture that Hadad euphemistically called training had begun.

The three servants led me into an elegant washroom, its walls made of shiny ceramic blocks and adorned with silken sheets. They scrubbed my skin with tiny grains of sand, washed me with warm water, and anointed me with lotions. I realized that I hadn't felt the luxurious sensation of warm water on my body for two years already, ever since I had permanently left the home of the couple who raised me and joined the gang in Shiloh. I stood there, stiff as a statue, and thought to myself that they could just as easily have bathed me in melted ice or boiling water—I'd lost all feeling anyway.

It was only when they combed my beard that I paid attention to the fact it had been short and stubbly when I'd first entered the tunnels, while now it was thick and full, dark brown in color, just like my long hair, which flowed past my shoulders. When, for the first time in my life, I donned the uniform I'd so craved to wear in the past, a flicker of excitement ran through me, but I knew it was nothing more than a pale shadow of my wild emotions from the old days.

Hadad stared at me, wide-eyed. I thought I was going to get a compliment, but instead he walked over and felt my arm like a cattle merchant examining the goods. "Too thin," he declared.

"For someone who's spent the past half year eating only grass and bread, and sometimes, as a special treat, a young foal, I think I look pretty good."

"From now on, you'll eat like a king and put some meat on those bones." He tried to laugh but instead said something I wasn't expecting: "You're the most handsome man I've ever seen."

When we'd first met, I would have been willing to give up half my beauty in exchange for a compliment from him, but now I was indifferent to it.

About an hour later, his three servants walked in to announce that the Mad Princess was ready. I realized that I was finally going to meet her and tried to muster up a little curiosity, but what I felt was more like anger.

"What's the rush? I've barely gotten used to daylight, and you're already taking me to her?"

Only later, after my emotions returned, did I identify that moment as the turning point. I hadn't yet realized at that time that it was my anger, more than a clean body or an elegant uniform, that heralded my return to the family of man.

"A rule is a rule, Shelomoam. Anyone who comes here must present himself before the lady of the palace."

His voice was soft, so different from the commanding tone I was used to. It was strange to hear him call me by name. He'd called me kid before we got to the tunnels, and while he was torturing me he called me nothing.

"I've been here for half a year," I said bitterly. "Now you remember?"

He hushed me sharply. "No one needs to know how long we were down there."

"You promised the soldiers you'd tell them everything."

He twisted his face in contempt. "The only soldier here is you. The others are nothing but toy soldiers."

"Toy soldiers or not, they were able to uncover your tunnels, and now they're expecting an explanation."

"Don't you dare tell them anything."

"But—"

"Stop stalling. The Mad Princess is waiting for us."

Twelve

The old woman who sat across from me had a skinny neck and an unbent spine, and she wore her white hair in a tight bun. Her slim body was wrapped in a blue silk dress, and a delicate golden crown adorned her head. She was missing one thing, though: a sparkle in her eyes.

But in spite of her hollow gaze, the remnants of her beauty were still apparent. The woman who had once been considered one of the five wonders of the world remained noble and impressive in spite of her age and insanity.

I stood at attention, hypnotized by her vacant eyes. I waited for Hadad to introduce me, but he stood behind me and didn't open his mouth. I turned to look at him and signaled for him to say something. His expression seemed odd to me, as if he were undergoing an exciting experience. He nodded and said nothing.

I turned back to the Mad Princess and knelt before her. "Your Highness," I said, searching for the right words. "I am Shelomoam, your faithful and devoted servant."

"Stop that nonsense," Hadad grunted from behind me. "She can't understand a thing."

"Then why did you bring me to her?"

"Rules are rules. Now let's give you a tour of the palace. Your new friends will be surprised to discover what a handsome fellow was hiding behind those rags."

I felt a strange affinity for her, perhaps because of the remnants of her legendary beauty that were still apparent on her face, or maybe it was the way she held her neck. But that same night, as her horrifying screams echoed through the palace, my affinity transformed into revulsion. I buried my head in the blanket and tried not to listen to the insistent pleading of Ithiel, the redhead with the striking eyes who had led the group of soldiers that found me in the tunnels and brought me up to the palace:

"Come on out! You've never seen anything like it."

"She doesn't interest me."

"You cannot live in this palace and not experience the spectacle."

I knew what I was about to see, but it shocked me anyway. When Hadad had told me about the candles, I'd been sure he was exaggerating. I never imagined that one shriveled old woman could possibly light thousands of candles by herself, and I couldn't comprehend how such a tiny body was able to produce screams like that.

"Why does she light them in groups of seven?" I asked, trying to shout over the deafening noise.

Ithiel shrugged. "Who can say what goes through the sick mind of a mad old woman."

In spite of my feeling of revulsion, there was something captivating about her. I felt as though I was participating in some kind of terrifying ritual being performed by a witch who had risen from the underworld and was threatening to incinerate us all.

⟞⟝

My days in the Palace of Candles passed pleasantly, though I didn't like the training exercises we performed for the hollow-eyed Mad Princess every morning. Sometimes I felt like her gaze was focused on me, but when I looked back at her, I could see only a vacant stare. In general, I actually enjoyed the training even though I worked harder than most of the other soldiers. They were perfectly satisfied with silly drills and waving fancy weapons around in a theatrical manner, but Hadad trained me in actual combat, which often came along with some deep cuts. Only then did I begin to see the value in his torture. I found that I had complete control over my body, as well as my soul, and I was able to will myself into a state of icy calm. One moment I was a normal person—living, breathing, feeling—and a moment later I was an insensate statue. My sparring partners lost their heads anytime a sword pierced their skin, while I would watch my blood trickling out of me and calmly fight on.

The only challenging partner I had was Ithiel. Hadad was chilly toward him and held him at a distance, but he had to admit that, compared to the pathetic toys all around us, this fellow was the closest thing to a soldier one could find in the Palace of Candles. His impressive abilities did not stem from natural talent alone. Most of the soldiers came here having grown up as peasants and never saw a sword up close before they were inducted into the army, but swords were commonplace for Ithiel. As a member of the royal family— the grandson of the previous king and nephew of the current king—he had received military training and learned to use all kinds of weapons. When I first found this out, I wasn't sure what impressed me more—the fact that he was a prince or the fact that he was from Judah, the tribe I had been brought up to fear.

"Should I bow to you?" I asked the question in all seriousness, without a hint of irony.

"Of course," he said, giving me his enchanting smile. "And preferably with your head all the way to the ground, like a slave."

I later asked Hadad why he was put off by Ithiel. There was nothing to fear; just because he was the king's nephew didn't mean he was an informant. Hadad seemed shocked by the question and insisted firmly that he had nothing to hide from the king. Everything in the Palace of Candles occurred with his knowledge. Besides, he feared only his god Qos and nothing else, certainly not a subordinate soldier, no matter what his lineage.

I knew Hadad was lying, but I preferred to pretend that I believed him. And contrary to his explicit counsel, I deepened my friendship with Ithiel. I had never had a friend before. I wasn't truly close even with the members of my gang in Shiloh, whom I had called friends. They viewed me as their leader, not their equal. Ithiel had a power of attraction of his own. He didn't need someone to look up to and to tell him what to do. For the first time in my life, I was able to form a bond of love and affection with a young man like me, and this made me happy and gave me a sense of confidence. I gave him much of the credit for the relatively rapid recovery of my spirits from my tribulations in the tunnels.

Nonetheless, there were things I kept buried deep inside. I told him honestly about leaving Zeredah, meeting Tirzah, and the shameful acts I'd performed as the leader of the gang of thieves in Shiloh. I didn't even conceal my stinging defeat at the hands of the thugs at Gibeah. But his questions about my family ran into a wall of silence.

For his part, he kept nothing from me. I inhaled his vivid descriptions of life in the palace. Again and again, I asked to hear about the royal visits and glamorous balls. I especially enjoyed his amusing story about the visit of the wise Queen of Kush, who had tried to embarrass the king by presenting him with difficult questions and riddles designed to trip him up, but in the end she had declared that there was no one wiser in all the world.

My friendship with Ithiel filled me with pride. There I was, the helpless little boy who'd spent his life hiding in a thicket out of fear of the king and his soldiers, walking confidently through the king's own palace and building a close bond with his nephew. I liked to imagine the faces of Bilhah and Benaiah when they found out where I was and with whom I was fraternizing. It wouldn't be long before I would have a chance to see their horror up close, when I would visit them in uniform.

The love I felt for my new friend deepened when he told me about his parents. I asked him why he was wasting his military skills in the Palace of Candles, and he replied painfully that he wasn't permitted to serve in the army like the rest of the princes because, prior to his mother's death, the king had promised to protect his life at all costs. He'd been only a month old when his father was murdered at the altar by one of the priests, having come to the Tabernacle to offer a sacrifice to his God. The murderer was executed that very day, but that didn't make things any easier for the young widow. Though the generous king had offered her a comfortable life in his palace, her grief for her husband had been more powerful than wealth, and within only a few months her agonized soul was returned to her Creator. Ithiel was less than a year old when he became an orphan.

When I heard his story, I felt both sorry for him and jealous of him at the same time. I was sorry for his orphanhood and his pain, but I couldn't help but think about the sense of security that can be felt only by a person who understands his roots and knows where he belongs. I wanted to tell him how jealous I was in order to lift his spirits, but I realized that a too-hasty confession might prompt investigations and inquiries that would force me to pick at my wounds and reveal my secrets. I also didn't know how he would react to the shameful revelation that the two people who'd given birth to me had participated in a foolish rebellion against his deceased grandfather. As a result, I had to make do with a tight hug and a few standard words of consolation and act as though this latest story meant nothing more to me than the rest of the stories of his life in the palace.

Thirteen

I thiel invited me to join him and spend our time off together celebrating the Festival of Freedom in the king's palace. The thought of personally meeting members of the royal family was so exciting that I could barely wait for the moment to arrive. But Hadad found out about the plan and forbade me from accepting the invitation. He argued vehemently that I mustn't meet the king before I was ready for the examinations, and that if I tried to take shortcuts I might end up out of the army. Thus, instead of enjoying a dinner of unleavened bread and roasted meats at the king's table, I found myself in the crush of a crowd, standing with Ithiel in the Temple courtyard. Whenever I caught sight of the Temple, the splendor of it pained me just as it had the first time I'd seen it, even though I knew the brainwashing I'd gone through as a child was a disease. I was surprised to hear that Ithiel was under the impression that the laws of the king were obeyed throughout the land, and that all tribes took care to offer sacrifices only in Jerusalem. Amused, I described the speed with which the tribal priests would dismantle their altars before the king's soldiers arrived and reassemble them when they left. When I saw that Ithiel was entertained by my description, I told him that the people of Ephraim did not celebrate the Festival of Ingathering.

"Why not?" he asked in shock.

"Because it's a Judean holiday. Each tribe has its own special holiday."

"And when is the holiday of Ephraim?"

"On the fifteenth day of the eighth month."

"What holiday is that?"

"The Festival of Rain."

"Sounds nice. How do you celebrate?"

I was about to correct his use of pronouns and point out that I wasn't a member of the tribe of Ephraim, but I suddenly felt my false tribal identity returning to take hold of me and speak for me. At that point, I realized that if the conversation went on any further, we might arrive at the one subject I didn't want to discuss with Ithiel or with anyone else, not even myself. But instead of being evasive, which was my specialty, I allowed myself to be pulled into reminiscences from childhood. In the blink of an eye, I was once again that little boy dancing in the fields on his father's shoulders, feeling totally secure in his sense of belonging.

"We aren't allowed to celebrate the Festival of Rain," I said, surprised by the bitter tone in my voice. "Your uncle has banned the unique holidays of each and every one of the tribes of Israel."

"He wants the nation of Israel to become a unified people," Ithiel said, as if quoting a slogan that he himself didn't believe.

I laughed with open contempt. "He wants the nation of Israel to become the nation of Judah. That's what he wants."

Within a few hours, Hadad had heard about our conversation. Grave faced, he led me into his room and ordered me to sit down opposite him. I could tell that I was about to be given a long lecture. And indeed, he started with an insulting rebuke over my lack of self-control and demanded that I stop chattering about my childhood and keep my tribal opinions to myself. I was getting tired of his patronizing attitude and goaded him further by declaring that Ithiel was my good friend and that I intended to discuss anything I wanted with him.

"Not good," muttered Hadad as he glanced quickly around, as if someone could hear us in the closed room. "I thought you were smarter than that. Just a little more chatter and all our work will be as good as gone. Instead of the army, you'll find yourself in prison. Do you think the king will appoint an army commander who bad-mouths his laws and reminisces publicly about the holidays of Ephraim? Promise me that from now on you will keep your big mouth shut and stop yourself from pouring your heart out to anyone else."

"I don't want to make that promise. I like pouring my heart out."

"Then eliminate that pleasure from your life. I've given you a special power that only a chosen few can ever experience. You have complete control over your body, over your desires, over your thoughts, and even over your pleasures."

"Ithiel is the only person I can trust. Before I met him, I never had a true friend in the world. Everyone I ever trusted betrayed me. Everything I ever believed was a lie. Even you weren't honest with me. You promised to take me to the Palace of Candles, but instead you buried me in the tunnels. Had it not been for Ithiel, I'd still be there today. I won't give up our friendship."

His high forehead was covered with perspiration. His fingers were trembling. He held his head in his hands and said nothing. All of a sudden he got up, walked over to me, and brought both his hands up. I thought he was about to squeeze my face between his hands, like he used to do in the tunnels. I was preparing my body to go into its frozen state when I felt a tender touch, not intense pressure, against my cheeks. The only thought that went through my mind at that moment had to do with the strange sense of security I felt when I was around him. Even at our worst times, in the initial days of the torture, before I'd learned how to freeze my body, even then, I never doubted his love for a moment.

"Can I go?" I asked, breaking the silence.

He stayed cupping my cheeks in his hands. Finally, he emitted a deep grunt. "Maybe the time has come," he mumbled, as if to himself.

I waited for him to explain, but he walked out without another word.

⟡

The pleasant hours I spent in the company of Ithiel almost made me forget the awkward incident with Hadad. I only thought of it sporadically, wondering to myself what he'd meant about the time having come, but I had more interesting things to think about. Although the training became more demanding day by day, I got through it easily and enjoyed it. I even had free time, most of which I spent with Ithiel, and a bit of which I spent with the other soldiers. They didn't hide their envy of the special treatment the commander gave me, but at the same time they were drawn to me and even admired me. They tried to fulfill my every wish.

"You have the personality of a king," Ithiel explained. "Believe me, I know about such things."

"Being a king is not a matter of personality. It's a matter of lineage."

"There are two hundred princes in the palace, maybe more; I've lost count. But only a few of them have it."

"Have what?"

"It's hard to explain. If you have it, people go quiet when you speak and hold their breath when you enter a room. When you ask for something, everyone rushes to serve you. If you don't have it, no lineage will help you, nor will study and training. Either you have it or you don't." He paused for a moment and then whispered, "And our crown prince doesn't have it."

I was surprised by his candor. "Does the king know?"

"He believes that good training can provide him what God has withheld."

"How old is he?"

"The king?"

"The crown prince."

"Our age. Around twenty."

"Perhaps the king is right," I tried to console Ithiel. "At our age, a person can still change."

Ithiel shook his head sadly. "He's a lost cause."

"What about you?" I dared ask.

"Me?"

"You have it, and you're a prince. Maybe you'll become crown prince?"

I knew him well enough to recognize the hint of yearning behind his laugh. "In order to be king, I'd have to kill at least two hundred princes. That's a little much for me."

⁓

As fate would have it, only two months went by before I had the chance to prove to Ithiel that my personality wasn't quite as well-suited to royalty as he might have thought. It was also when I heard Hadad for the second time say that strange thing about the time having come.

On Friday night, following the Sabbath meal, I sat with the other soldiers in the palace garden, passing the hours in conversation and laughter. Friday nights were our only nights off, for the Mad Princess refrained from lighting her candles on the Sabbath, allowing us to enjoy the quiet and gather our strength for the next six nights. A few of the fellows got themselves ready for a visit to the whorehouse near the army camp, across the way from the king's palace. Though we weren't considered full-fledged members of the army, we were permitted to enjoy the places of pleasure that served the king's soldiers. The whorehouse was the most popular of them all, and hundreds of soldiers visited it every Sabbath.

When the soldiers were in high spirits from drinking wine, one of them, a cheerful, short soldier named Uzziah, announced a contest for the title "King of the Fornicators," which would include a prize.

"Well done!" people cheered from all directions. "What's the prize?"

Flattered by the enthusiasm over his suggestion, Uzziah announced that he would forego his wages for the week and give the money on Sunday to an expert goldsmith who would create a golden medallion for the greatest fornicator of all.

Within moments everyone was busy planning the contest. A wild argument ensued over whether or not the winner should be determined by the length of intercourse, but it was eventually concluded that the number of sexual acts would be the deciding factor. When I noticed that even Ithiel was taking an interest in the contest and was actively involved in planning it, I decided to retire to my room and spend the rest of the evening reading. Among the treasures of the Mad Princess were dozens of Egyptian papyrus scrolls that were of interest to no one. Hadad had given me permission to read them as long as I did so alone, in order to keep them safe.

I was already on my way out of the garden when I heard Uzziah say, "Shelomoam has to participate in the contest. I want to know if what people say about the poor sexual skills of tall men is true."

I meant to smile and say something funny in response, but Uzziah didn't give me a chance. He shouted passionately that the contest would have no value unless we determined once and for all whether tall men or short men had the advantage.

Before I knew what was happening, I found myself pinned to the ground by several soldiers. "You have to participate!" they cried gleefully. "Let's see who wins."

"The short men will win," I said, shaking them off and getting back to my feet. "Now let me go read! Your whores don't interest me."

"What *does* interest you?" Uzziah cried, stomping his feet angrily. "So what if you grew up rich and learned to read? Just because you don't sleep with whores doesn't make you better than us."

I didn't get overly excited by his reaction. The cold distance I exuded actually caused people to be subconsciously eager to please me, but on occasion it also inspired aggression. I'd learned that a warm apology was the most effective avenue of appeasement. I was beginning to arrange my features into the requisite expression of contrition when, before I could open my mouth, another soldier called out, "Better than us? Don't make me laugh. He doesn't like to visit the whores because he's like an Egyptian. That's why he likes their papyri so much, if you catch my meaning."

The bursts of laughter all around me made my cheeks flush. I wanted to throw a few punches, but instead I used what I'd learned from Hadad and froze my emotions.

"Fine," I said apathetically. "I like to sleep with men, so be it."

They all stared back and forth at Ithiel and at me. He hung his head, ashen-faced, and said not a word.

I turned my back to them and began walking in the direction of the palace. Suddenly I heard Uzziah shouting behind me, "Shelomoam doesn't sleep with whores because his mother is a whore!"

Then, a moment later, "Tell us how your whore of a mother spreads her legs—"

He didn't finish. I pounced on him and knocked him to the ground. He let out a weak cry and pulled something shiny from his belt. It was a knife. I saw the glint of the blade. A moment later, it was in my hand. I thrust it at him with all my might.

Suddenly I felt someone grab my arm from behind, stopping its motion. I waved the knife around, trying to shake off my unseen opponent, but he wouldn't let go. I don't know how it happened, but in our struggle the knife flew out of my hand and lodged in his foot. By the time I saw what was happening, it was already too late.

First I saw the blood, followed by the legs collapsing to the ground, and only then did I see his face, twisted in pain.

It was Ithiel.

⌘

That night, as I sat by his side on the bed, dripping oil onto the white bandage wrapped around his foot, he woke up and gave me a wide-eyed stare. I wanted to hug him, but I didn't dare move.

"So that's your secret. . . ."

He spoke so softly that at first I thought I'd imagined it. I stroked his red curls and felt my heart about to break with guilt. "Sleep," I whispered. "That will make the pain go away."

His bright eyes shone at me from the darkness with that glint of amusement that I liked so much. "Honestly? I was expecting your secret to be something much worse. Jephthah of Gilead, one of our greatest heroes, was the son of a whore, so I think you have a fine future ahead of you."

But on Saturday night, when Hadad finally heard about what had happened, he didn't appear especially amused. In truth, I had never seen him more upset. I tried to apologize and explained that my heart had gotten the better of my head, but that only made him more angry. He screamed at me, telling me that he had no other choice but to send me back for another round of torture in the tunnels, because the fact that I could lose control over some stupid remark meant that apparently I had not sufficiently internalized the ability to detach myself. His roaring carried on all night, but no one other than me heard any of it. The screams of the Mad Princess were louder.

Only with the dawn, when the princess became still once again, was Hadad forced to lower his voice and return to his routine. I was about to leave so I could get ready for the morning formation when he suddenly reached out his hand and ran it softly against my cheek.

"The time has come," he said, the pain in his voice even more puzzling than the words. "Now the time has truly come."

Fourteen

Not only did my violent outburst not hurt my social standing; it seemed to have increased the aura that surrounded me. Even Uzziah, whose small body I had nearly ripped to shreds, insisted on flattering me to the point of obsequiousness, and he wouldn't stop apologizing for the thoughtless things he'd said to me. I felt secure enough to declare magnanimously that I was the one who owed him an apology and that the incident was now behind us. Ithiel's swift recovery strengthened my sense that the event was in the past and had not taken any toll on me.

Only the cold shoulder Hadad gave me marred this perfect image. He stopped training me and avoided all interaction with me, positive or negative. Though I'd lost a father once before, I felt especially hurt this time. I now came to appreciate how dear and meaningful Hadad's love had become to me. The torture I had experienced in the tunnels was nothing but a slight nuisance compared to the excruciating feeling of being an orphan again due to his abandonment of me. I would have preferred many times over to take a beating from him than to be ignored by him. I was afraid that he'd given up on me and decided to find another soldier to fulfill his dreams and stand for the king's examinations. I was alone again in an empty and meaningless world. Only Ithiel, my faithful and devoted friend, remained by my side in these hard times.

When I was urgently summoned to Hadad's room one morning, I was so upset I could barely put one foot in front of the other.

"Are you ready?"

The air emptied out of my lungs in a sigh of relief. He wants to punish me, that's all. "You are my commander; I will accept any punishment you see fit to impose on me."

"I was asking if you were ready for the examinations."

I was so stunned that my voice came out strangled. "What examinations?"

"The king's examinations."

I stood there flustered and gave him a blank stare.

"Do you not understand when people are talking to you?" Oh, how I had missed his impatience. "The decisive examinations that will determine both your fate and mine."

"Is that what you meant when you said that the time had come?"

A cloud passed over his face. "My intentions are not the subject of this conversation. We have ten days before the examinations, and there are a few more things we need to get done before you go."

"Such as?"

"Leave that to me. The servants will come fetch you in two hours."

"And where will they take me?"

"That's all you need to know."

"Do I need to pack anything?"

"Some clothes. No more."

⁂

Instead of sharing my joy, Ithiel begged me not to go with Hadad unless he revealed where he planned on taking me. I tried to explain that nothing bad could happen in ten days of secret training. At worst, he would take me back to the tunnels for another round of torture. The most important thing was that I would finally be able to stand before the king for the examinations that would determine my fate. Ithiel wasn't convinced, and he tried to instill his unreasonable fears in me as well. I realized that he was worried that the end of our friendship was approaching. After all, upon passing the examinations, I would be appointed as a commander and stationed in some far-off place, perhaps in the land of Ephraim, while he would remain in Jerusalem.

"I promise to take you with me." The idea came to me all at once, un-planned.

He shook his head in despair. "The king swore to my mother on her death-bed not to appoint me to any dangerous position."

"I'll keep you safe."

"He will never agree. No place is more dangerous for a Judean soldier than the towns of the tribes of Rachel." He paused for a moment, smiling at me with affection. "You hate us even more than you hate the Philistines."

"Naturally," I said, hugging him hard and doing everything I could to stop the tears. "At least we learned to work with iron from the Philistines. What could we possibly learn from you Judeans?"

"We can teach you how to steal the throne." His arms nearly crushed me with love. "You have to admit, we're experts at that."

⁓

I was certain that Hadad's servants would take me back down to the tunnels, and I was already preparing myself for the sickly smell of mildew and for the flood of bad memories. But, to my surprise, they led me first to the garden and then outside the palace walls. Hadad's chariot was waiting at the gate.

"Get in!"

I took the vacant seat and looked out the window. My fellow soldiers were standing on the parade ground watching me with wonder.

"Draw the curtain."

"I want to see the view." It bothered me that Hadad's previously tight-lipped servants had now taken on their master's commanding tone. "How long is the ride?"

Instead of getting an answer, the curtain was snapped shut in my face.

I sat in the darkness, trying to get into Hadad's head and guess where he was taking me. One completely absurd possibility occurred to me, but I liked it. Perhaps he had decided to take me back to Gibeah to see if this time I could defeat the thugs who had robbed me. I pictured the delightful battle and the moment when I would take back the captive Aner, but before this sweet vi-sion could reach its conclusion, the chariot arrived at its destination and the servants ordered me to get out.

The smell of mildew left no room for doubt. The long journey had been meant to confuse me and distract me from the thought of another round of torture. No matter, I consoled myself. I could go into my frozen state whenever I wanted.

I asked the servants why we had ridden for so long only to return to the tunnels below the Palace of Candles, but I received no answer. To my surprise, instead of being lowered down into the depths as I had been two years before, I was taken up an unfamiliar flight of stairs that ended in a long, twisting hallway I'd never seen before. I tried to guess which wing I was in. The place was completely foreign to me. I was taken into a dark, windowless room. The total blackness kept me rooted in place. I opened my eyes wide and spread my arms out helplessly, but I couldn't see a thing.

Then, all at once, the darkness disappeared, and a tiny flame illuminated the room. The servants placed a burning torch into my outstretched hand and seconds later left the room, locking the door behind them.

My torch lit up the room, and I looked it over with curiosity. Suddenly I noticed a chair in one corner, and on it was sitting a figure like that of a person. I approached it with cautious steps. The figure did not move. I stood in front of it and moved my torch to shed light on its face.

It was the Mad Princess.

❧

A minute passes before I understand.

Her eyes.

They're alive.

She sits before me in regal splendor, her back and neck straight, devouring me with hungry eyes. I have no other way to describe her expression.

I stare at her.

"Shelomoam."

The clarity of her voice shocks me even more than the life in her eyes.

Dark shadows dance before me. An uncontrollable shivering takes hold of my body. Hadad's betrayal punches me in the gut. My breathing is heavy; I am paralyzed with helplessness. Why, Hadad? Why did you lie to me? Why are you in league with those who have done me evil? My betrayers stand in a line before me, laughing at my pain, mocking me for my innocence. Here is the woman who raised me, the one whose waist I used to cling to back in the long ago days of my childhood, the one in whose lap I would bury my head, the one I called Mother. At her side stands her husband, the man whose hands I held and upon whose shoulders I felt safe and secure. And here stands their daughter, my soul sister, the closest person I had in the world. And far behind them, wrapped in a gray cloak, the woman who gave birth to me covers her face.

You too, Hadad?

I followed you blindly. I was willing to accept any torture you brought upon me—being buried alive, being burnt, freezing nearly to death, starving, being tied to a pillory, even being forced to devour a young foal.

You were my surrogate father, Hadad. I believed you. I loved you. And you betrayed me.

Just like everyone else.

⁂

"You aren't mad," I say, struggling to form each word.

She cackles. I want to lunge at her, to squeeze my fingers around her dainty neck, to crush her skinny body with my bare hands, but a voice inside me whispers: Another falsehood, what's the big deal? Haven't you grown used to it by now?

"Liar," I say, getting hold of myself and turning my back on her with blatant contempt. "You don't deserve my anger."

In a few long strides, my feet carry me to the doorway. I hold up my torch to try to see the way out in the darkness.

"The door is locked, Shelomoam," she says matter-of-factly.

"I can break through anything that stands in my way."

"Not this door, Shelomoam."

"Stop saying my name! If you don't open this door, I'll call for my friends. They'll find me. I can depend on them."

"No one will hear you, Shelomoam. This room is completely sealed off."

"You're not the only one who can scream. My vocal cords are just as strong as yours."

"Sit with me, Shelomoam. I want to tell you the story of my life."

Just then, the headache I had known so well in childhood returns. It must have something to do with lies. Whenever I encounter lies, my skull begins to pound.

"I'm not interested in your stories."

"You will become more interested than you can imagine."

"I've heard enough lies in my life."

"I swear I will tell you only the truth."

"Why should I believe the oaths of a liar who pretends to be mad?"

She does not lower her eyes. "You are welcome to ask me anything you want, Shelomoam, and you'll receive a truthful answer. Try me, Shelomoam; you'll see I'm not lying."

"I've got nothing to ask you."

"Ask me the questions that have been with you all your life and that have been driving you mad. Ask me the questions that keep you up at night."

A cold gust of wind sends chills down my back. I lean against the wall. "You're the last person in the world I want to discuss my life with."

"If you don't want to talk about your life, ask me about mine."

"Fine," I growl. "Why do you pretend to be mad? That's my question. Are you happy now?"

She smiles with satisfaction, as if she's defeated me in a game whose rules I had no part in setting. "I learned it from my husband, the previous king."

"Was he mad as well?"

"It's a long story, Shelomoam. Why don't you sit here on the rug, and I'll tell you everything, from beginning to end."

"I told you I have no interest in your stories."

"You asked a question, Shelomoam."

"An answer that is short and to the point will do."

"So be it." She is silent for a moment, scrunching up her forehead, biting her lip, and shaking her head slowly. "Many years ago, the previous king escaped his pursuers in Israel and took refuge with the Philistines. His true identity was quickly discovered, and he was brought to trial before the king of Gath. And then, instead of falling to his knees and begging for his life, he started drooling all over his beard and making incoherent noises. The king of Gath watched him with revulsion and rebuked his servants: 'Am I so short of madmen that you have to bring this fellow here to carry on like this in front of me?'"

"Nice story," I say with scorn. "But I didn't ask about the previous king's madness. I asked about yours."

She looks at me with those same hungry eyes. "People who are mad threaten no one, Shelomoam. They see but are not seen. That is the source of the power of the miserable: the fools, the lunatics, and the lepers."

The word "lepers" makes my skin crawl. The blood rushes out of my face. I race to the exit and beat on the door with my fists. "Let me out!" I scream. "Get me out of here!"

"Shelomoam," she calls, practically begging now. "Don't be so stubborn. You need to hear my story."

I run back toward her and hurl my torch at the rug beneath her feet, but before the flames can spread, Hadad's three servants appear from out of the shadows and put the fire out calmly, as if it were something they did every day. Afterwards, they go around and light all the lamps in the room.

Hadad's familiar arms of steel seize me from behind. It feels like an animal has taken control of him. "You see who we're dealing with here?" he asks her. He shoves me down onto the partially scorched rug and grimaces in an expression of despair. "Don't say I didn't warn you. And this is after six months in the tunnels. Just imagine what he was like before."

A smile of satisfaction lights up her face, as if she had just heard a piece of good news. "A wolf." She stretches out the word with evident pleasure.

"A wild animal," Hadad confirms.

"I tried to do it nicely, Shelomoam"—she speaks my name again softly—"but your suspicion and bitterness are an impassable barrier. So now you'll listen to my story by force. We will not permit you to refuse; it's the reason we brought you to the Palace of Candles."

"Another lie," I interrupt her. "I came by my own free will. I chose to join Hadad so that he could train me to be a soldier in the king's army."

Hadad huffs. "Your will wasn't so free after those Benjaminite thugs left you with no money and a shattered leg."

"Those Benjaminite boys are savages," she says, chuckling.

"You're from Benjamin, too," I mutter angrily.

"It was no accident that Jacob bestowed that symbol upon you on his deathbed," chuckles Hadad. "'Benjamin is a ravenous wolf; in the morning he devours the prey, in the evening he divides the plunder.'" He quotes Jacob's well-known testament with obvious pleasure while she nods with approval, as if they had orchestrated it all in advance.

Suddenly there is a ruckus behind me, and four musclebound brutes walk through the door. They are practically giants. I look at them with surprise, reassessing my circumstances and realizing that I've seen them before. I look at them again, and there can be no more doubt. It's been almost two years, but I'm certain.

"How's your leg?" one of them asks amiably. "We went a bit too far. We had planned something more gentle, but things got out of hand. It didn't occur to us that you might be able to fly over our heads! You almost slipped through our fingers, so what else could we do? You tell us, what choice did we have?"

❧

As my body remains in perfect stillness upon the rug, I hover above it and view my life from the outside, and once again, just like two years ago, I cannot understand how I could have been so blind. How did I not put two and two together? How did I fail to see it? Why didn't I see how all the pieces fit together?

"Ask me, Shelomoam."

I don't want to ask. I don't want to know. I don't want to understand. I don't want to feel. What I want is to go into a frozen state. It's the state that suits me best. It's the only thing that can give me peace. Instead of suffering further betrayal and deception in a world of falsehood, I'll remain frozen for the rest of my life.

"You are twenty years old, Shelomoam," she whispers. "The time has come for you to get real answers to your questions. All of them. Even the ones you haven't dared to ask."

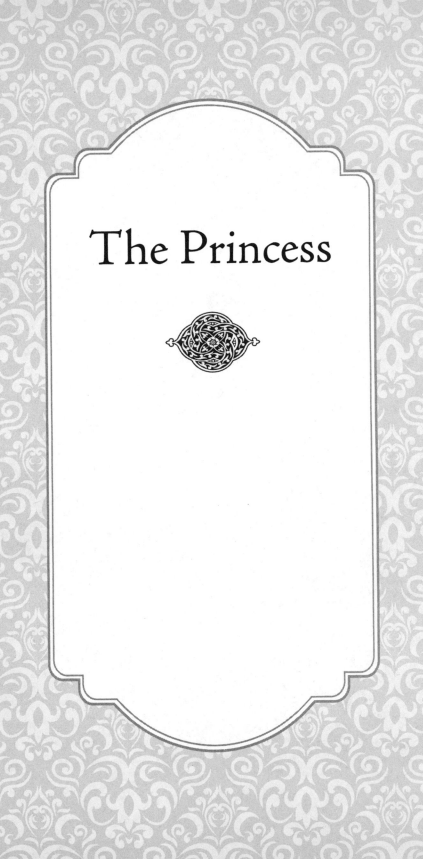

The Princess

One

Still staring at me with that same angry helplessness, my wild wolf. Clinging to the mat as if it were the last plank from a sinking ship. You have nothing else left to hang on to. Everything around you has collapsed, disappeared, faded away. Nothing is as you thought it was. Every time you dug into a dark hole in your life, you found another underneath it, darker still.

My story is all you have left now. I've been preserving it for many long years, guarding its details inside me. Day after day, hour after hour, nothing is erased: the shreds of conversation, the colors, the smells, the touches, the laughter, the tears, the screams.

The memories flash before me. They are for you. Only for you. They have been waiting for you, for this time, for this moment. Even before you were born I knew you would draw them out of me, that you would grab hold of me with clenched fists and put me to your mouth, suckling every whisper that's been seared into me in the passing of the years. I've been waiting for you for twenty years, turning my heart to ice in the daytime, lighting the candles at night, waiting for you to grow up.

I always thought that when the time came you would come to me willingly. I never imagined I would have to lock you up, tie you down, and force you to listen to my story. At first, I refused to believe the rumors that a wild animal had burst forth from out of that handsome boy, who might doom us all to go down in flames. They must be exaggerating, I thought to myself. It cannot be. That charming boy has become a violent thug who robs other people? That delightful child now beats down anything standing in his way? How did that happen? Yes, his childhood was complicated, but so what? He was given so much love, how could he simply run roughshod over it? What demon told him to crush and uproot every flower in his life? Where did this disordered soul come from?

Slowly but surely, though, I began to like what I was hearing. This is just the kind of man we need, I told Hadad. The violence, the cruelty, even the ingratitude—we need these traits. Only the fits of rage are undesirable. That tendency is so familiar to me, and I understand so clearly where he got it, but it is simply too dangerous for us. We must teach him complete control of his body, and, more important, of his soul.

Hadad was actually optimistic. "Give me a year, or two at the most, and I will cook up the perfect wolf. The ancient Edomite training secrets, passed on from father to son, will turn him into someone else."

"But I don't want someone else," I told him. "I prayed for *this* child."

"The wildness and the cruelty will remain untouched," Hadad promised. "I will excise only the rage."

What choice did I have? If I had left you as you were, I wouldn't have been able to entrust the story to you, and that was something I would not accept. How could I? That was the only reason I had stayed alive.

Hadad's faithful servants dug the tunnels in complete secrecy, and we were certain that no one up above had any idea of what was going on right under their noses. But we underestimated the redheaded fox that was sniffing around while maintaining the innocent face of an angel. We never imagined that viper would uncover not only the existence of the tunnels, but you as well. And we certainly didn't believe that you would fall under his spell. Looking back, I'm embarrassed not to have foreseen that you would be attracted to him. I've seen it before, that same deep, wild, uncontrollable attraction. Many years ago I saw two other young men, one handsome and tall just like you, but unlike you in his innocence and noble spirit, and the other with beautiful eyes and full of charm. Oh, what charm. No one could resist his bewitching charm.

I really should thank your redheaded friend. Had it not been for the danger, Hadad would have kept putting off our meeting, and I would have gone on peeking at you surreptitiously from behind the mask of my madness, all the while my icy heart burning with a stifled flame and crumbling into shards of longing. "The time is not yet ripe," Hadad would tell me whenever I demanded that he bring you to me. "I have not been able to tame him. He walls himself off with a fortification of stone. I cannot reach him to quiet his tormented soul. Everything they told us about him is true. In fact, things are worse than we thought."

And now here you are, sitting before me on the mat, watching me with the angry eyes of a wolf. Do I detect a budding curiosity? Am I seeing a glimmer of the feelings you were hiding beneath the cover of your thuggishness?

I've been telling you this story for twenty years, working hard to retain every fragment of memory, rehearsing every word, every smell, every flavor. I've been waiting for you for twenty years, and now that you're sitting before me I don't know how to start.

If only I could begin at the end, holding that giant body close, kissing that menacing face, burying my head in that wild tangle of hair. But you won't be able to bear the ending without hearing the story in order. I must tell you everything from the beginning.

And when I finish the story, my beloved boy, nothing in your life will ever again be as it was, and then we will know if I've pushed too far and too fast, as Hadad suspects, or if I've chosen just the right moment.

Two

I was born to my mother, Ahinoam daughter of Ahimaaz, and to my father, Saul son of Kish. My three older siblings, Jonathan, Malkishua, and Merab, were born when my father was still a simple peasant, while I and my two younger brothers, Abinadab and Ishvi, were royalty from birth. My father was crowned king over all the tribes of Israel while I was still in my mother's belly, but it would be another six years before he agreed to move into the palace built for him in his hometown of Gibeah, which had become the capital of Benjamin. Had it been up to him, we would have stayed in our little house, but the Israelites, after yearning for a king for so many years, wanted their royal family in a palace. At first, my father ignored the people's wishes and continued raising his cattle and plowing his fields. He claimed that working in nature sharpened his mind and helped him better run the affairs of the young kingdom. It was only thanks to Abner, his cousin and commander of the army, that he finally agreed to sit on a silver throne, wear a golden crown, and ride in an eight-horse chariot.

But he demanded that his children, especially his daughters, live lives of modesty and simplicity. "I have no choice," he spat angrily whenever he saw our fine dresses. "Neither does Jonathan. People expect the king and the crown prince to wear finery. That's what the people want. But you? There's no reason for you to waste your brief childhoods in victory marches, choked by silk gowns and precious gems, instead of playing in comfortable linens like other girls."

Father's tasteful opinion made sense, but it could not compete with the seductions of regal splendor. Mother, who had a better understanding of human desires than he did, continued to take us to the parades held in honor of his military victories, seating us on the dais of honor in all our glory, so that the people of Israel could burst with pride at the sight of their beautiful princesses.

They especially loved me. The first Hebrew princess, that's what they called me. And before I even turned ten, I had acquired a second title: the Most Beautiful Princess in the World. Poems were composed and stories were told about the young daughter of the first Hebrew king, who was born a princess and had inherited his incredible beauty. But while my beauty was always described as nothing but a pure gift of God, Father's beauty became a weapon in the hands of his opponents. His critics maliciously claimed that the Israelites, after yearning for a king for so long, could not resist the handsome face, the broad shoulders, and the terrific height of the young peasant from Benjamin and forced Samuel to anoint him. These nasty stories led Father to demand even more vehemently that we deemphasize the family's good looks. But Mother, who couldn't hide the pleasure she took at the awestruck gasps of the crowd every time I walked onto the dais, continued to adorn my fair hair with pearl tiaras, to rub rose oil into my lips, and to dress me in silk gowns embroidered with gold.

Merab took pride in me as well. Only when I grew older could I appreciate the magnanimity required of a young girl, herself very pretty, who constantly hears people praising the beauty of her little sister and reacts by glowing with pride rather than wallowing in jealousy. My admiration for her only increased when I came to know the sad story of Rachel and Leah, the sisters who became enemies due to their increasingly vicious rivalry over the love of the man that they shared. I didn't know yet that our love would also be put to the test over a man who would want my sister and receive me instead. But let us not get ahead of ourselves. At this point in the story Merab and I were still cheerful, careless princesses, over whose love no shadow had yet been cast.

Father believed that the truth had a power of its own, and that everyone would eventually remember that his anointment as king followed his incredible victory over Nahash the Ammonite, which had restored the deterrent force the Israelites lost in the failed battle at Ebenezer. The stinging defeat at the hands of Philistines had been seared into the nation's memory as if by fire and had turned them into a desperate and despondent nation. Thirty thousand soldiers had fallen in that war, among them the two sons of Eli, the old priest of the Shiloh temple, who fell out of his chair and broke his neck when he received the bitter news that the Holy Ark had fallen into the hands of uncircumcised foreigners. Samuel the Prophet, who inherited the priesthood from Eli and became the leader, served his people with rectitude and devotion but led them in not a single battle, and the enemies of Israel came to understand that the brave Hebrews of the days of Joshua had become nothing more than a collection of miserable tribes that dared not even defend themselves and could be stomped upon at will. Indeed, when the King of Ammon demanded that the people of Jabesh Gilead become his slaves, everyone assumed they would submit quickly, offering no resistance, as had happened on every previous occasion. But Nahash the Ammonite was not satisfied merely piercing the ears of his new slaves; he demanded that their right eyes be put out as well. The poor Gileadites begged for help, but, as was to be expected, the tribes of Israel clucked their tongues, sighed deeply, and went on plowing their fields and pruning their vines. Only the people of Benjamin, the wolves of Israel, answered the call. Their wild nature wouldn't allow them to sit idly by and watch as that evil snake disgraced their brothers. They left their fields and their homes, and banded together, preparing to cross the Jordan River, though they knew well that their chances of defeating the Ammonite army were slim. At that point Father stood before the tribal elders and asked for the opportunity to try to recruit fighters from all the tribes of Israel and create a strong, united army, just like in the days of Joshua. The skeptical elders told him that one could not all of a sudden inject a fighting spirit into the weak hearts of the Hebrews. Even the great Joshua needed forty years to turn a nation of slaves into mighty warriors who could take possession of a land. Instead of giving a response, Father selected a prime bull from his herd and cut it into twelve pieces as the stunned elders of Benjamin looked on. That very day, twelve messengers set out for the twelve regions of Israel, each one carrying a blood-soaked bundle and a message: thus will be done to the cattle of any person who refuses to join Saul's army. This unusual call-up order worked better than expected. The Israelites knew better than to cross the wolves of Benjamin, and they hurried to send their bravest sons to Gibeah.

Father recruited three hundred thirty thousand fighters into his army, which became the region's largest force. The complacent Ammonites, so certain of their victory, suffered a crushing surprise attack, proving to all the surrounding nations that the Hebrews were defending themselves once more.

"Samson has slain his thousands, and Saul his tens of thousands," sang the dancing girls in the thanksgiving parade, and the joyful masses joined their singing with choked voices, cheering the tall and handsome young man of Benjamin who had assembled the united army of Israel and led them to victory. Father was embarrassed by all this and tried to hide among the supplies, but Samuel the Prophet dragged him by his cloak up to the dais. Everyone understood that two hundred years of division had ended and that the united Kingdom of Israel had risen, and a suitable king had been found to stand at its head. Father's resistance was futile. The old prophet made him kneel so that he could anoint his forehead with oil. "Long live Saul son of Kish, King of Israel!" the crowd roared, and jubilation spread throughout the tribes of Israel.

Even then, in that sublime moment, people were already telling wicked stories of the young king's great beauty and stature, behind which, they claimed, hid a weak, insecure leader. The stories were spread mostly by the Judeans, who had trouble accepting the crowning of a king from the tribes of Rachel. "Leah was the eldest," they whispered bitterly, "and Judah was her favorite son. The king should come from *our* tribe, not from Benjamin, the youngest of Jacob's sons."

Father paid no attention to these stories. "Let them talk," he said dismissively. "The Judeans have always tried to undermine leaders from the line of Rachel. They even tried to question Joshua's position by spreading false tales about Moses appointing the head of their tribe, Caleb son of Jephunneh, to be his successor. Little good it did them. The stories of Caleb turned to dust in his own lifetime, while all the tribes still to this day tell the stories of the heroic Joshua, conqueror of the land."

But Samuel knew that stories were powerful weapons, and he wasted no time in assembling the detractors in Hebron, which was the capital of Judah at the time, before the founding of Jerusalem. "The nation of Israel has always opposed the twisted idea of primogeniture!" thundered the old prophet. "It has always been thus. Isaac overtook Ishmael, Jacob defeated Esau, Joseph ruled over his older brothers, and Ephraim rose above Manasseh. So too Rachel, the younger sister, was the chosen wife, Jacob's most beloved. She is the matriarch of our greatest leaders: Joshua, Ehud, Deborah, Barak, Gideon, Jephthah, and even me. That's the way it always has been, and that's the way it always will be."

The Judeans, thus chastised, tried to bring up Moses, a descendant of Leah, but Samuel replied with scorn that Moses was a Levite, and the Levites, as everyone knew, stood outside the tribal divisions. Moreover, Moses was further proof of Samuel's point—he was the youngest child in his family and was chosen to be the leader over Aaron and Miriam.

"You're a firstborn son!" someone in the crowd shouted. "Why did God choose you?"

"I am a priest," came the decisive reply. "Priests are required to be firstborns. That is the sacred law of the temples."

"Kings must also be firstborns," boldly protested the tribal elder who believed himself to be entitled to the throne.

Samuel's face darkened with fury. "Judah was not the firstborn," he thundered.

"But he was the son of the older sister," replied the tribal elder. "Jacob cursed his three oldest sons, but he called our forefather a lion cub and granted him eternal rule."

"Only a prideful tribe calls itself a lion," said Samuel. "The God of Israel prefers humility. That is why He dispossesses firstborns and chooses their younger siblings over them. Go home, children of Judah, and accept the yoke of the new king. He may be from Benjamin, the youngest of the tribes, but there is no one on earth as good."

And indeed, Father turned out to be a brave and wise king, leaving no doubt that his humility was a result not of weakness or insecurity, but of a pure heart. Under his leadership, the divided tribes of Israel became a strong, united nation that cast its shadow over every other people in the land, with the exception of the Philistines, who relied upon the iron weapons they had brought with them from the lands of the sea. Even so, the Judeans were not impressed by the young king's startling success and went on spreading their false tales with persistence and determination. Abner wanted to make laws banning such slander and to hunt down their sources, but Father preferred to ignore them and keep working for the good of the nation. "Reality will make these stories turn into dust," he said confidently. "That's the way it is—the truth always wins out."

Many years passed before he realized his error and came to understand that stories are more powerful than truth. Many more years passed before I, the last remaining descendent of the House of Saul, realized that this war was a war like any other, and that the stories of Judah could be fought only with counter-stories of our own.

Three

I fell in love at first sight with the two men of my life. To this day I have never deciphered that mysterious force that, in a single fleeting glance, transforms a stranger into an object of longing and yearning.

The first time I fell in love, it was at a parade to honor my brother Jonathan. The crowds had gathered in Gibeah from all over the country to show their gratitude for the great victory at Mikmash and to hear the master storytellers describe how the brave-hearted prince had invaded the Philistine camp with the aid only of his shield bearer. The people couldn't get enough of the hilarious depictions of the panicked soldiers of the apparently invincible army, fooled into believing that thousands of fighters had invaded their camp, fleeing for their lives in a wild stampede and leaving their legendary iron weapons behind. Not since the war against Nahash the Ammonite had the army of Israel won such a glorious victory.

Merab and I sat to either side of Mother on the dais and waved to the enthralled masses. For the occasion, the seamstresses had made each of us a silk dress in a different color, and the goldsmiths had cast exquisite golden crowns with matching gemstones. My dress and crown were sky blue, and I felt more beautiful than I ever had before. The cheering of the crowd when I appeared on the dais proved that I had made the right decision in taking my sister's advice. That morning, when the dress had been brought to my room,

I'd been dazzled by its beauty but declared that I would wear something less glamorous. I was afraid that when the parade was over Father would admonish me for my ostentatiousness, but Merab convinced me that we were dressing up to honor Jonathan and that even a modest man like Father would understand that this time it was the right thing for the women of the palace to appear in all their splendor so as to delight the people on the great day of their beloved crown prince.

"Saul has slain his thousands, and Jonathan his tens of thousands," sang the dancing girls, as they beat their drums and twisted their lithe young bodies. Abner tried to silence the girls, but Father glowed with joy. He stood proud, a head taller than anyone else, and joined in the song with giddy laughter.

"Saul has slain his thousands, and Jonathan his tens of thousands," the crowd sang with hoarse voices, cheering enthusiastically for the crown prince, who was leading the parade.

I looked up to wave at him, but the sun blinded me, so I shifted my gaze to the other end of the parade. That's where I saw him, sitting erect on his horse.

The sunlight etched thin shadows across his face, accentuating his cheekbones. A spring breeze toyed with his long hair, which swayed gently from side to side as if in a dance of seduction. I felt my heart pounding, as though it were trying to burst out of my blue dress. And just as would happen to me a year later when I fell in love again, I was overcome by the scent of lilies.

"What's wrong?" Merab asked in surprise.

"Nothing." I wiped my forehead with my trembling hand and looked back toward Jonathan.

In the weeks that followed I had visions of him during the day and dreams of his caresses at night. I decided that it made no difference who his father was, what pedigree he had, or what tribe he belonged to—I wanted him, and I would have him. I would never give up my right to love the nameless soldier, even if it turned out he came from a lowly tribe, a descendant of Bilhah or Zilpah. I swore to myself that I would follow my heart despite the fact that I'm a girl. I don't care that I might shock the people. Let them stop singing their praises of my beauty. Let them turn me into a cautionary tale about a woman who crosses the line and doesn't know her place. Love is not the exclusive domain of men. Granted, the ancient Hebrew stories passed down from father to son describe only the love of our patriarchs, but we women tell different stories. Not only Isaac and Jacob knew love. Rebecca and Rachel knew it as well, and even Leah.

Many weeks went by before I dared confess my love to Merab. I was worried that she would be appalled and would try to convince me to let go of this puppy love and wait patiently for our father to give me away, as was the custom. To my surprise, she fell upon my neck with kisses and confessed her own secret love for a young officer named Adriel the Meholathite, whom she first had seen, in a very similar fashion, in one of the victory marches. They had been meeting in secret, with the help of our older brother, ever since.

"So Jonathan knows?" I asked, amazed.

"Knows?" Merab laughed. "Without his help, we would never be able to meet. He isn't only our messenger; he also makes up creative cover stories for us. A month ago, for example, he convinced Mother to let me ride with him to the battlefield to boost the spirits of the soldiers before the battle."

"I remember that," I interrupted. "I asked her to let me go with you and she—"

"Said you were too young," Merab finished my sentence. "That's what Jonathan told her. But the truth is that we were worried about your powers of detection."

"How presumptuous," I muttered.

"It was thanks to that presumptuousness that I was able to spend time alone with my Adriel," Merab said with delight.

"Do you think that Jonathan would be willing to help me, too?" I asked with trepidation.

"Why not?"

"Your beloved is a Meholathite, of the tribe of Manasseh. I don't know how Jonathan would react if he found out that my beloved is not from one of the tribes of Rachel."

"You're getting ahead of yourself. Let's find out who he is first, and then we'll see if his tribe is an issue."

"How do we do that?"

"You can count on Adriel. He knows almost all the soldiers. Tell me exactly where the young horseman who stole your heart was riding and I'm sure we can track him down for you."

And sure enough, in a matter of days I received the information I'd been pining for: Paltiel son of Laish, from the town of Gallim in the land of

Benjamin, a warrior of great renown who had even received a commendation for bravery from our father. Could the news be any better?

"Now let's see if he will have you," Merab teased me affectionately. "Just because you're the Most Beautiful Princess in the World doesn't necessarily mean that absolutely any man would fall for you. Adriel is willing to be your matchmaker, just as Jonathan was mine."

"I don't need a matchmaker."

"Then how . . ."

"Did Rachel need a matchmaker to get Jacob to kiss her by the well?"

Merab furrowed her brow in confusion. "What are you planning to do?"

"To bring him to me at the well."

Her eyes widened. "How?"

"I'm sure he can read." I tried to maintain a jaunty tone. "Do you think Adriel would be willing to pass him a letter from me?"

⊰⊱

Ever since I first heard the stories of our matriarchs, I had decided that my own first meeting with my beloved would take place by the well. I yearned to be like our matriarch Rachel, who had gone to the well simply to water her sheep and was kissed by the mysterious wanderer who then worked fourteen years to have her. Or like Zipporah the Midianite, who girded herself up to fight for the right to draw water from the well but received unexpected help from an Egyptian man, who was then invited to dine at her father's table and asked him for her hand. And even like Rebecca, the most assertive of our matriarchs, who was cunning enough to figure out how to impress the servant by the well so much that he brought her back with him to the man who would become her husband in Canaan.

I composed a tempestuous letter that vividly described that special moment at the victory march and the feelings that had been stirring within me ever since. At first I liked the letter, but when I read it a second time I decided it was unbecoming of an independent, boundary-breaking princess who was daring enough to follow her own heart, so I replaced it with a concise letter instructing him to meet me the next night by the old well at the edge of the fig orchard.

The next day, I hurried to the well with my heart racing but was disappointed to find only Adriel the Meholathite there. Without a word, he handed me a sealed letter. I broke the wax seal with trembling fingers. The short message slowly came into focus: "As a soldier in the king's army, I am obligated to follow his orders and his alone."

Adriel crossed his arms and smirked. "If you want to demonstrate your royal power, you'd be better off finding someone else. I don't know Paltiel personally, but he doesn't seem like the type to get excited by an attempt to court him that's phrased like an order to a servant."

"Who gave you permission to read my letter?"

"I didn't need to read it. It was enough to see Paltiel's expression to know what it said."

I knew that any further conversation would betray the turmoil I was in, so I pursed my lips and ran back to the palace. Merab understood right away that something had gone awry at the meeting at the well. I told her everything. Rather than mocking my stupidity, she tried to explain how a soldier in the king's army would feel upon receiving an unexpected letter from the king's daughter trying to court him.

"Men like to feel important. If you decide to fall in love with a commoner, you are going to have to give up your regal airs."

She grabbed my hand and dragged me back to the well. Adriel was still there. He took her in his arms. I watched them silently. I was happy for my sister, but I couldn't help but envy her sure and solid love.

"I'll be your matchmaker," Adriel told me.

"I don't need a matchmaker," I replied in a fit of rage.

"Even our matriarch Rebecca had one."

"I want to be like Rachel." I tried to smile through my tears.

"You don't want that," Merab said, laughing. "Rebecca had a much easier life."

"I still want to be like Rachel."

But when I received the happy news a few days later, I didn't think anymore of the matriarchs, only of the chiseled face of the man I believed would be my one and only love.

❦

The fig trees give off the perfume of early summer. I sit upon the lip of the well and await him. So young, I'm only fourteen years old, but I know that this waiting is making me a woman.

The sound of the crunching of leaves marks his approach. I close my eyes. This is the moment. No turning back. I sit up straight, waves of nausea cutting through my stomach, the ground burning beneath my feet.

He does not bow.

"Greetings."

His clear voice makes me shudder. My entire being contracts in his presence.

I open my eyes. His beauty pains me. His hair runs down his shoulders; his cheekbones stand out from his face. His soft velvety eyes glint with a teasing shyness, serious and amused all at once.

"I am Paltiel son of Laish."

His direct gaze pierces my heart. Tears sting my eyes.

"And I am Michal daughter of Saul."

Four

My second love came upon me a year later. One look, chills down my neck, a cold sweat, heart fluttering, dry mouth, the scent of lilies—and I was lovesick once again.

Merab recognized the scale of the disaster right away. "You like him," she lamented.

I tried to deny it, but she regarded my moist forehead sadly and looked down at my trembling hands. "Poor Paltiel." She sighed. "He loves you so much."

But Jonathan glowed with joy. "He's irresistible. Everyone who sees him falls in love with him. Even Father."

"*I* haven't," said Merab.

"You don't feel his charm?" Jonathan asked in astonishment.

"I do," she said, "and it scares me."

⌇

Paltiel was off training for the upcoming great battle against the Philistines and would send me heart-wrenching letters from the field. I read them vacantly, trying to recapture the passion I had felt for him until recently. I managed to get my body to tremble, my stomach to tighten, and my breath to catch, but I knew that it all was but a pale shadow of the storm that threatened to consume me now. I tried to fight the strange attraction with all my might. Let me go! I cried out to it. I love Paltiel, only Paltiel. One cannot love two men. But it merely laughed at my defeat. *Can't you?* It felt like a taunt. *Can't you? Then why can a man love more than one woman? Who decided that a woman can only love one man?*

I couldn't stop thinking about his fingers plucking the strings of his harp, his erect posture, the firm line of his jaw, which stood in stark contrast to the youthful roundness of his red cheeks, his curly hair shot through with licks of fire, and, most of all, the look in his eyes. I'd never seen such eyes before.

I did everything I could to avoid him, but again and again I found myself wandering around the entrance to the throne room when I knew he would be coming to see Father. He would bow to me with a proud confidence that made me feel as if I were bowing to him. I would give him a chilly nod and feel my blood boiling in my veins. Through the locked door I would hear the enchanting sounds produced by his skilled fingers. I didn't want to pull away, but I knew that I mustn't be seen like this. I would go to my room, lie in my bed, and feel my flesh languishing in pain. My ribs would tighten below my breasts and chew away at my heart. I knew I'd been defeated.

"You have to talk to Paltiel," Merab said, as she caressed my forehead with concern.

"It's just a passing condition," I mumbled. "I'll get over it."

"I'm going to tell Jonathan to find another musician for Father. No player is worth losing a man like Paltiel."

"If you send him away from the palace he'll continue to haunt me for as long as I live. I must encounter him as often as possible, one encounter after another, until I grow weary of him. His charms are only effective at the beginning, before you get to know him."

"How do you know how his charms work?"

"It's my only chance. I don't want to lose Paltiel."

❧

Jonathan was excited by my request to arrange a meeting with the young musician who'd stolen his heart, but was willing to do so only on the condition that he received permission from our father.

"Too bad you didn't ask for his permission last time," Merab muttered.

"That encounter wasn't planned," Jonathan apologized. "He just happened to walk by as we were sitting in the palace garden. This time I'll introduce you formally, according to protocol. Father will agree; I'm sure of it. You should see the way he looks at him."

And indeed, our father agreed wholeheartedly and even suggested broadening the meeting by inviting the entire family to a musical dinner. Mother rejoiced at the idea and ordered the cooks to prepare a special meal in the guest's honor.

"The king's servants have told us he plays the harp wonderfully," said the cooks.

"Not only the harp," said Mother enthusiastically. "After dinner he will play the eight-string, the flute, the pipe, and even the lyre!"

The cooks' eyes sparkled with admiration, and Mother, whose reputation as the most generous queen in the world was well deserved, invited them to come listen to the performance.

In the hours before the event I tried on all my dresses, one after another, but I felt awkward in all of them. Merab came in, glanced at the pile of dresses on the floor, and turned right around and left. Eventually I chose the sky blue silk dress I had worn at the victory march a year earlier, when I had seen Paltiel for the first time. This choice further deepened my guilt, but I could see that betrayal looked good on me.

When I walked into the hall, Mother's eyes widened in wonder. Even Father looked at me with pleasure. I took my place on the dais and felt my bones crumble with expectation.

⟞⟝

He walked in, erect and proud, bowed to Father, and gave Merab a long look. I tried to take comfort by telling myself that it must have stung his eyes to see how beautiful I was and that it was easier for him to look at the less glamorous sister.

My throat was dry. I wanted to moisten my lips with my tongue, but I worried about the shiny rose oil coming off.

Jonathan stepped down from the dais, embraced his beloved friend, and introduced us, one by one:

Queen Ahinoam.

Prince Malkishua.

Princess Merab.

Princess Michal.

Prince Abinadab.

Prince Ishvi.

He bowed to each of us. We were paralyzed by his charm. Even little Ishvi caught his breath. Only Merab looked at him with open hostility.

He stood before us and fixed his eyes on her. "And I am your loyal servant, David son of Jesse."

Five

The way his eyes sparkled when he looked at my sister made the truth slap me in the face without mercy.

"Are you out of your mind?" Merab spat out the words in disgust. "Even someone as arrogant as he is, so certain that everyone in the whole world is swooning over him, can't help but notice how deeply I loathe him."

I was only fifteen, but even then, in a flash of insight, I could see that her loathing was the very reason he wanted her, the only member of the royal family who wasn't blinded by his charms.

Evil winds blew through the palace, but outwardly we continued to go about our business. I continued to receive letters from Paltiel, Merab continued to daydream about Adriel, and only David changed course, shifting his gaze from her to me.

My woman's intuition wasn't fooled by his tricks. "He wants to make you jealous of me."

Merab's eyes flashed with contempt. "His desires are of no consequence to anyone."

I tried not to think about him, but his mysterious disappearance was driving me mad. In vain I desperately listened for sounds of music coming from the throne room—but none came. I couldn't understand why he had stopped playing now, of all times, in these wearying days of waiting, as war with the

Philistines threatened to break out at any moment. Father is with his soldiers in the Valley of Elah, and when he comes back to the palace every few days, he needs soothing music more than ever.

"Where is David?" I fought to conceal the concern in my voice.

Merab's face clouded over. "You promised to take no more interest in him. You said yourself that he didn't love you."

"I want to know where he is."

She sighed dejectedly. "Abinadab gave him leave to visit his old father in Bethlehem."

"Since when does Abinadab give leave to Father's musicians?"

"If you noticed anything that was going on around you, you would know that when Jonathan and Malkishua are in the Valley of Elah, Abinadab is in charge of palace affairs."

"How could Father agree to give up his most talented musician now, when he needs music more than ever?"

She shrugged disdainfully. "Anyone can be replaced, even the son of Jesse."

"David." The way the name felt on my tongue made me shiver. "His name is David."

"Old Jesse has eight sons and three grandsons, and they were all drafted into the army, all except for the dainty youngest son who would rather not taint his delicate hands with a sword. But someone has to take care of the untended herd in Bethlehem."

"He'll be back," I said confidently.

"Back to the herd," she said, her face twisting with scorn. "They say he used to be an excellent shepherd. Sheep and goats appreciate good music, too."

"He'll be back," I repeated the words of consolation aloud, then again silently, over and over, like a prayer: He'll be back. He'll be back. He'll be back.

⌖

I felt like I was going mad with yearning. There wasn't a soul in the entire palace with whom to share my suffering. The person who had been my soul sister had warned me not to mention him in her presence; her nerves were already shot with worry for the safety of her beloved and of our brothers—the rumors reaching us from the battlefield do not bode well. Our soldiers are eager to start the war, but our father is putting it off, trying to draft more fighters. And those accursed Philistines are taking their time as well. Rumor has it they are expecting a giant warrior from the city of Gath, who will supposedly join their forces at the Valley of Elah and win the battle decisively for them.

I tried to feign interest in what she was saying. She looked me over icily, her face hardening with that disapproving expression I hated so much. "Even the fate of the nation doesn't interest you anymore. Your head is only in Bethlehem."

"What do you want from me, Merab?" My cry echoed throughout the palace.

"I want you to take an interest in something other than him. That's what I want. I'm waiting for you to ask me to read you the letter I received from Adriel this morning. Actually, I don't even need to read it; I've memorized it."

I turned my head away and said nothing.

Her eyes filled with tears. "It's nice out," she whispered. "Let's take a walk in the garden and chat like we used to. I miss those days so much. It seems like an eternity ago. I can hardly believe that, until just recently, our entire lives revolved around the men we loved. We would show each other the letters, talk about the secret encounters, and take pleasure in the memories of their tongues upon our lips."

"Those days will never return." Sorrow pinched my throat. I was silent for a moment, then said slowly and emphatically, as if making a promise, "But nothing can spoil our love for one another."

"I'm not so sure."

"Don't talk that way, Merab. We'll never be like Rachel and Leah, who allowed a stranger to burst into their lives and turn their love for one another into poisonous envy. We'll keep loving each other until death."

"Until death?" Merab's voice caught in her throat, but then her hoarseness turned into a roar: "We're so young. Why are you talking about death? When you loved Paltiel, life seemed so promising to you. Look at what the spell of the son of Jesse has done to you!"

The voices of the servants outside interrupted us. They shouted through the door that the king was summoning Merab to the throne room. I wondered why he was calling for her and not me. Until recently, the two of us would sit with him every once in a while and have a relaxed talk over wine and fruit. Once, little Ishvi complained that Father only indulged the girls this way, and Father explained patiently that he spent many hours with the boys discussing work, and that if he didn't set aside time for his daughters he would only see them at victory marches. It's been weeks since the last time we were invited to the throne room. Father is preoccupied with the war in the Valley of Elah and can't make time for family. Odd that he is suddenly available, and odder still that he chooses to see only Merab. For a moment I was afraid that he had sensed the change in me and decided to question her about it, but then I rebuked myself for my selfishness. Merab is right; I really am unable to think of anything but my love. Even now, as my sister is being summoned for a mysterious talk with Father, I can think only of myself.

I lay in bed and tried to keep my thoughts on her, but they kept calling me back to the fields of Bethlehem. I felt like a court jester walking a tightrope and taking care not to look down at the abyss beneath his feet. I don't know how long I slept. I woke up suddenly to the sound of crying. I leapt out of bed in alarm and hurried toward the sound. Merab was lying on her bed with her face buried in the blanket, her hair wild, and her body convulsed with panicked breathing.

"What happened?"

She raised her head. I was startled by the terror in her eyes. "Father has declared that I am to be a prize."

"What kind of prize?"

"A prize for the warrior who kills the giant from Gath."

"It can't be!" I cried. "Father loves you."

"He has no choice." I heard an attitude of acceptance behind her tears. "The Philistines have managed to gather an enormous army and forge thousands of iron swords."

"We also have iron swords, the ones we pillaged in the war at Mikmash."

"Only a few. They have iron chariots, too."

"Iron isn't everything. In the days of the Judges, when the people of Israel were scattered and divided, that weapon was decisive in battle. But today we have a big, strong army. The Philistines' iron didn't help them in the last war."

"Things are different now," Merab whispered in fear. "Father is desperate."

I felt terror crawl up my back and grip my throat. "The God of Israel will come to our aid," I said, trying to cheer myself up.

"We can't rely on Him. The prophet Samuel has acknowledged that it has been a long time since God revealed Himself to him. That's a very bad sign."

"Then what's going to happen?" I had trouble wiping the cold sweat off my forehead with my trembling hands.

"Father has consulted with his best fighters, as well as with Jonathan and Malkishua, and everyone agrees: the Philistines are certain of their power and have no fear. They would have started the war long ago if they hadn't been waiting for Goliath the giant, who is making his way from Gath to the Valley of Elah. He is their most revered symbol. Perhaps if they saw his severed head with their own eyes, the balance of power could change. A stampede is a powerful weapon that has defeated many a great army before. It's our only chance."

"Sounds like a great plan," I said admiringly. "That's how Jonathan settled the battle of Mikmash."

"But at Mikmash the target was clear and stationary, while here we're dealing with a stealthy monster who wanders the roads alone, never sitting still. Even the Philistines don't know where their giant is."

"Our soldiers will find him," I said confidently. "The Judeans know the area like the backs of their hands."

"Father needs his soldiers on the front lines. He can't disperse the army. His messengers have roamed the land, asking for volunteers to assist with the search, but the response has been meager. Anyone willing to help has already been drafted, and the people at home prefer to stay among the sheep pens to hear the whistling for the flocks. That's why Father must offer a tempting prize for whoever brings him the head of the Philistine monster."

"And that prize is you," I whispered in horror.

"He has no choice," she sobbed.

For a moment, I was truly convinced that Merab had to make this sacrifice for her people. She wasn't being asked to give up her life like the daughter of Jephthah, nor to put it at risk like Jonathan and Malkishua, but rather only to give up her love. But then I felt the rage stirring in my blood and coursing through my veins.

I jumped up and ran as fast as I could to the throne room. The servants tried to stop me, but I pushed them away and raced to Father. He looked down at me from his great throne, appalled.

"One does not come to see the king without being summoned," he said. His deep voice always terrified me. "You are no longer a little girl; it's time you learned the rules."

In the past, I would have begged his forgiveness in the sweet childish voice that never failed me, but this time I stood up straight and looked him in the eye. "You are just like the wicked Laban," I told him.

He recoiled with surprise. I took another step toward him and hurled the words that burned within me directly into his ears. "You treat your daughter like an object, selling her to the highest bidder. It makes no difference whether the price is paid in coin or in military victory. When Jacob asked Rachel and Leah to flee their father with him, Rachel said that Laban wasn't even her father. 'Does he not regard us as foreigners?' our brave matriarch said. 'Not only has he sold us, but he has used up what was paid for us.' Rachel knew that she had found a loving husband thanks to God alone. If it had been up to her father, she may well have found herself in the hands of a scoundrel. You are like Laban, Father. Exactly like Laban. You have no idea who will kill the giant Philistine, yet nevertheless you have promised your daughter to that man."

Just then, Merab walked in, mumbling in a frightened whisper, "I didn't send her," and she began to wail.

Father descended from his throne, lowered his head, and kissed her wet cheeks. "Michal is right," he said.

The servants watched us with amazement. I felt not gladness, but rather a twinge of sorrow. Since when does a father admit that his daughter is right? All the more so a king, who is never wrong? As it is, Father is criticized so harshly for his extreme modesty and humility. He needs to be careful not to give up his honor so easily. Our people want a strong king who demonstrates his power. If this event becomes known to the public, it is liable to diminish him in their eyes, and they might go back to telling those wicked Judean tales about the great beauty and stature concealing insecurity and weakness.

"She is more righteous than I," Father said, gesturing toward me. "I'm proud to be like Amram, who admitted that his daughter was right. Miriam dared to confront her father over his decision to abstain from lying with her mother after the decree that sons born to Israelites would be put to death. 'You are worse than Pharaoh,' Miriam told him. 'Pharaoh's decree was against only male children, while your decree is against females as well.' Instead of spanking the child for her impudence, Amram admitted that she was right and went back to his wife, Jochebed. Thanks to a brave young daughter, who dared to stand up to her father, Moses was born to take us out of Egypt and bring down the Torah from heaven."

The servants stood rooted in place and listened to this unexpected sermon in tense silence. I waited for Father to go on and announce that the offer of the prize had been canceled, but he only stroked his beard in silence. I loved him so much at that moment.

"Everyone get out and leave me alone with my daughters," Father ordered the servants.

I never took my eyes off him. He smiled at me and pulled me into an embrace. "My child," he whispered. "I promise not to give your sister to a scoundrel."

"But you cannot know who will kill Goliath," Merab dared to whisper.

Father laughed. "The prize doesn't cancel out the requirement of a bride price."

"I don't understand. . . ."

An impish glint shone in his eyes. I hadn't seen him in such high spirits since before the days of waiting in the Valley of Elah had begun. "My dear daughters," he savored the words with pleasure, as if enjoying a fine wine. "Let's wait and see who kills the Philistine, and only then will we determine the bride price. If I don't like him, I'll set a price so high no man could meet it. Then no one could complain. That's life: a person has to pay to get a princess."

Six

Father was absolutely certain that his daughters were leaving the throne room reassured and in good spirits. He wouldn't have believed that his older daughter was, in fact, in her bed weeping, her face buried in her sheets, while his younger daughter was sitting beside her, unable to offer solace.

"All is lost," Merab sobbed. "I probably won't marry a scoundrel, but I've lost the love of my life."

It seemed silly to try to cheer her up by suggesting that perhaps no one would be able to kill the Philistine. What kind of comfort could she draw from the knowledge that we would all soon die or be taken captive? Even a loveless marriage would be better than becoming a slave to Philistine masters, who would be all the more excited to discover that their pretty Israelite captive was the king's daughter.

"We must pray that God gives Goliath into the hands of a scoundrel." In spite of the situation, I was still able to laugh at the ironic conclusion. "The worse he is, the higher the bride price, and with it your chances of remaining free."

She looked up at me. I was startled by the dark circles under her eyes. "If we're praying, I'd rather pray that God gives Goliath into the hands of Adriel."

"That's a brilliant idea," I said, impressed. "You must write to him immediately and tell him about the prize."

"You think he hasn't heard about it already? My brave Adriel is at the front line and isn't allowed to leave his duties to run around between Gath and the Valley of Elah. Only the good-for-nothings who haven't joined the army can spend their time that way."

⤙⤚

Over the next few weeks, I was so immersed in my sister's grief that I took no notice of the obvious distress of another member of our family. Mother wasn't a demanding person, and so it was easy for us to disregard her worries and turn a blind eye to her anguish. Even when the servants summoned us to see her, we assumed it was just for a routine visit. Only when we saw her lying motionless in her bed did we realize what our self-absorption had done to her during these difficult days. My first reaction was paralysis; that's how I've always responded to sudden stress. But Merab, ever the practical one, came to her senses quickly. She massaged Mother's temples, blew air into her mouth, and called for help. By the time the doctors arrived Mother had already opened her eyes, and all that was left was to give her a strengthening elixir and instruct her to rest. We sat beside her in silence. What could we say? How can one cheer up a mother whose two sons are on the front lines? What words can one say to a wife whose nation's destiny rests on the shoulders of her husband?

"The one who saved our ancestors from the Egyptians will save us from the Philistines," I finally muttered.

Merab gestured for me to shut up. I, too, felt that such hackneyed slogans only made the feeling of despair worse, and I hung my head in shame. But suddenly we heard a sharp scream, followed by a deafening ruckus. Before we had a chance to go out to see what had happened, Mother's servant burst inside and fell upon her with kisses. Everyone knew that Mother was a warm and gracious queen, who didn't put on airs, but kisses from the servants were still unusual. We stared at her in astonishment and awaited an explanation.

"We won! We won!" the servant cried. "Our soldiers are chasing down the Philistines, killing them in their own cities. They say that we've reached all the way to the gates of Ekron."

Merab and I traded stunned looks. Our joy over the sudden salvation was mixed with anxiety over what was still unknown, and our complicated emotions left us frozen in our tracks. Mother, who had heard nothing of Father's prize, shook her head dismissively and ordered the servant out. "The war hasn't even started yet," she declared. "I forbid you to spread false rumors."

In spite of the queen's orders, the rumors continued to arrive at the palace all day long, each one more positive than the one before, and by evening everyone in Benjamin had heard them. The people gathered around the palace, cheering, dancing, and celebrating, and they shouted in unison, "Long live the king! Long live the army of Israel!"

Mother felt she deserved to rest after the difficult day she'd had, and she tried to bury her head in her blankets, but the screaming grew louder. "It's impossible to sleep in this palace," she groused. "Those Benjaminites are wild animals—wolves, simply wolves."

At the height of her despair, she ordered the servants to summon her daughters back, so that she would have someone with whom to pass the sleepless night.

"They are not in their room," the servant reported.

"They are curious girls." Mother sighed affectionately. "Especially Michal. Whenever something is happening outside, she feels the need to climb up to the highest room in the palace to look out the window. She loves windows, my little one."

Had Mother known where we actually were at that late hour, she would have fainted a second time. Had she known where my love of windows would lead me in the future, she would have begged for death. But let's not get ahead of ourselves. Windows will return to my story later on, but at this moment I was sitting on the back of a galloping horse, clinging on to Merab from behind. We'd never been out on the roads by ourselves before, let alone at such a late hour, but my concern for my sister's fate had given me courage. I wasn't afraid of runaway slaves, outlaws, or scoundrels. Only one thing made me shiver: the thought of Father's expression when he found out where his two sheltered princesses had strayed.

"He will never know," Merab reassured me as she confidently pointed the horse toward a dark ravine.

"They'll recognize us right away at the camp. Many of the soldiers know our faces. We always appear on the dais during the parades."

"No one will pay any attention to two girls dressed in rags. They only recognize us in our gowns and our crowns."

I tried not to think of the menacing darkness and asked Merab how she had learned the way to Judah.

"We traveled to Hebron two years ago, don't you remember?"

Of course I remembered. As princesses, we spent most of our days within the confines of the palace, allowed to go outside only on rare occasions, and then only within the land of Benjamin. But one year Father took us to celebrate Ephraim's Festival of Rain at the Shiloh temple. The Judeans protested the royal visit, claiming that our father favored the tribes of Rachel. To appease them, the following year we celebrated Judah's Festival of Ingathering at the Hebron temple.

The realization that we would be passing near Bethlehem made me shudder. I focused my thoughts on my beloved and was alarmed to find that I couldn't conjure up his face, as if a malevolent hand had wiped the memory of him from my mind. But I remembered well the way his face beamed and the sparkle in his eyes, and those images accompanied me throughout the journey.

"The God of Israel was at our side," I said with relief when we arrived safely at the Valley of Elah.

"Let's hope He stays at our side." I couldn't see her face in the dark, but I detected the bitterness in her voice.

"I'm sure that we defeated the Philistines without killing the giant." I tried to express my optimism in a decisive tone of voice. "No hero will receive you as his prize."

"Let it be so," she said through her tears. "Please, let it be so."

I had imagined a large, well-organized camp with polished soldiers marching in straight lines, as they did in the victory marches, but to my disappointment we found ourselves in a crowded and dirty tent area, in the midst of a boisterous crowd, just like the one that had surrounded our palace the night before. Large torches burned everywhere, inside and outside the tents, and in their light we could see that most of the people were not soldiers, but civilians—men, women, and even a few children—who had heard about the great victory and hurried down to the Valley of Elah. I was relieved to find that Merab had been right. No one gave us a second look. We looked just like the other sweaty women filling the camp.

"How did we achieve the victory?" Merab asked one of the girls.

"A panicked retreat," she said, her eyes alight. "Just like in Mikmash."

"Who caused them to flee?"

"The God of Israel, of course."

"But how?" my sister angrily demanded.

The girl shrugged and walked away, her wooden clogs clacking against the rocky ground and the bells around her ankles softly ringing. When she was already behind us, she turned back. "We killed their giant!" she called. "A heroic warrior brought the king his severed head."

⁂

Merab's weeping continued until morning, when the crier announced the king's victory speech.

"We have to hide," I said, tugging her arm. "Father might notice us."

She gave me a vacant stare but let herself be dragged into the bushes at the edge of the camp.

It took a long time before we finally heard the sounds of trumpets announcing the arrival of the king. The crowds stood quietly and looked toward the west. A convoy approached from the hills. I assumed it was being led by Abner son of Ner, guarding Father, who would be riding just behind him. The Philistines had been defeated, but past experience had taught us that a lone Philistine soldier might well be lurking about, ready to try to assassinate Father with an arrow or a spear. I waited for the convoy to get closer, but it stopped far away, on top of a rocky hill. This was the sign for the crowd, which had been waiting quietly, to begin cheering rhythmically, "Long live the king! Long live the army of Israel!"

The herald climbed to the hill and hushed the crowd. Then, behind him, I saw Father. I couldn't see his face, but the rays of sunlight coming from the east glinted upon his golden crown, giving him a breathtaking appearance.

"My brave soldiers," Father's powerful voice boomed, making its way from the hilltop all the way to the camp. "After our great victory at Mikmash, we removed the Philistine yoke from our necks, and we warned them not to try to conquer our land. They failed to heed our warnings and invaded the land of our Judean brothers. In the days of the judges, our enemies knew that when they attacked a tribe, or even imposed tribute, the other tribes would ignore their brothers' plight and carry on with their lives."

The huge crowd held its collective breath. Silent and spellbound, the masses watched Father, committing his every word to memory, knowing that they would recount this sublime moment to their children and grandchildren for the rest of their days.

"Never again!" Father cried. "Never again! Now every tribe comes to the aid of its brothers. Now we all stand united against our enemies. Now we have a single army. The Philistines failed to take our unity into account. They have made a grave mistake."

"And they will pay for their mistake!" someone yelled out.

Relieved laughter accompanied the comment. I laughed, too, until I felt Merab's fingernails digging into my flesh.

"Oh, they will most certainly pay!" Father responded, joining in the laughter. "We've chased the Philistines all the way to the gates of Ekron and killed the best of their fighters. The Judeans have been freed from the yoke of occupation. Long live the liberated land of Judah!"

"Long live the liberated land of Judah!" the crowd screamed. "Long live the king! Long live the army of Israel!"

"Long live the God of Israel!" our father called.

"Love live our God, blessed be His name forever!" the crowd answered.

Father turned his head to the side and signaled to a rider sitting erect on horseback and holding aloft a long spike. From where I was positioned, I couldn't see what the spike had pierced, but just the thought of it made me squeeze my eyes shut with revulsion.

"Give thanks to the brave hero who killed Goliath the Philistine and led us to victory!" Father cried joyfully.

"He likes him," I whispered to Merab sadly. "He likes him very much."

"I've promised my eldest daughter to the victor," Father continued. "But the question remains whether he will be able to pay my bride price."

Silence returned and enveloped the crowd once again. Everyone awaited the king's verdict. He paused before continuing, giddily drawing out the suspense, then he suddenly raised his voice: "One hundred Philistine foreskins." Father laughed. "That is the bride price that the prospective groom must pay."

The laughter of the crowd drowned out my sister's keening. The people in the crowd practically fell over laughing. The young victor joined in, his body rocking forward and backward with glee. He waved the spike from side to side and rode down the hill. The crowd split apart to let him through amid a chorus of cheers.

Merab's wails grew louder. I turned to look at her. She was staring at the man, and all of a sudden her face twisted in horror, as if she were seeing a demon rising up from the underworld.

"No!" she screamed at the top of her lungs. "No! No!"

I looked back to the man. He was standing right across from me. The light enveloped him with a blinding aura, as usual.

"All hail the king's son-in-law," Father's voice echoed from the top of the hill. "All hail David son of Jesse from the tribe of Judah!"

"Long live the king's son-in-law!" the people called. "Long live David son of Jesse!"

Seven

The idea that we would switch places, as our matriarchs Rachel and Leah once did, floated in the air all the time, but neither of us dared speak of it out loud. I said nothing because I knew that David wanted her and not me, while Merab wasn't willing to ask me to sacrifice my life on her behalf. She viewed my love for David as nothing but a young girl's passing fancy, not the considered decision of an adult.

The silence of Adriel the Meholathite only exacerbated her suffering. In her heart of hearts, she hoped that he would beg her to escape with him to Mount Carmel or some other remote location, but she soon came to understand that his unconditional loyalty to his king was greater than his love for her. She never considered that the reason for her beloved's silent acceptance was his veneration for the young victor who had won her. As the only person not enchanted by David's charms, Merab had trouble seeing the signs that others had fallen under his spell.

I knew it was wrong of me to tell her what I'd seen, but my out-of-control jealousy had poisoned my feelings for her. The thought of that red head buried in her lap and those rosy lips suckling her breasts had driven me mad.

"It isn't possible." Her grief-stricken eyes gaped at me in amazement.

"You know I wouldn't make up something like this."

"Jonathan gave him his coat?" she repeated what I'd told her incredulously.

"Not only his coat, but also his tunic, his sword, his bow, and his belt."

"And Adriel saw them and did nothing?" she cried.

"He stood guard so that they wouldn't be interrupted. When he noticed me, he immediately signaled for them to stop, but it was too late. Jonathan's entire body turned red, and he hung his head in shame, but David fixed his serene eyes upon me and welcomed me with a confident smile, as if nothing at all had happened."

The next day, Jonathan came to see us and pleaded for me to switch places with Merab. "You love David," he told me. "I saw the way you were looking at him yesterday, while Merab is in love with Adriel."

"Michal is in love, too," Merab whispered.

"With David, the son of Jesse," Jonathan declared.

"With Paltiel, the son of Laish."

He tried to process this new information. His high forehead furrowed in concentration, and he fixed his eyes on me, wonder mixed with anger. "Is this true?"

I nodded silently.

"How long has this been going on?"

"Over a year."

"Does Father know?"

"Leave Michal alone, Jonathan." Merab's broken voice tore through my heart. "I'm the prize, not her. It's my fate, not hers. The daughter of Jephthah also sacrificed her life for her people."

⤝⤞

The tribes of Israel rejoiced over the approaching wedding, especially the tribe of Judah, which had finally achieved its ambition of putting one of its own in the palace. Songs were composed and stories written about the young shepherd from Bethlehem who had become the king's personal musician, and who scampered alone through the valleys of the Land of Judah during the exhausting period before the war began, carrying neither sword nor shield, but only a staff and a slingshot in his soft artistic hands. When he saw the giant Philistine in the distance, he didn't run for help. Instead, he quickly gathered five smooth stones and shot them at the monster's forehead, making him fall backwards with a mighty crash. And then, instead of running for his life, he bent over the terrifying body, pulled out its sword, and chopped off its head. With the insight of a brilliant strategist, he saw right away that victory was in his hands, and without another thought he mounted the severed head on a spike and dragged it to the enemy camp. And indeed, when the Philistines saw that their hero was dead they retreated in panic, and the Israelites chased them all the way to Ekron and won the battle.

"The *youngest* of Jesse's sons," the people of Judah laughed. "Just the way Samuel likes it."

The stories and songs spread quickly throughout the land and reached the ears of Abner, who demanded that Father put an end to them. "The Judeans are taking credit for the victory," he seethed. "You were the one who planned the Philistines' stampede. The victory is yours." But Father, as usual, just shrugged his shoulders and went about his business. Many years would pass before I, his youngest daughter, went out to do battle against the stories of Judah. The king's scribes sit securely in the palace, never imagining that, like a mole burrowing from the inside, I have planted my own scribes in their ranks, and that they are inserting subversive voices into the official stories so that future generations may know the truth. But I'm getting ahead of myself again. We'll get to the war of stories later on. At this point, my miserable sister is trying on her wedding dress, as the grief on her face tears my heart to pieces with an impossible combination of compassion and envy.

The white silken dress emphasized her slender body and afforded her noble face an angelic quality. The maids whistled appreciatively and whispered to each other about all the leaders of the region that were expected to attend the wedding. Even the great Egypt would be sending a royal delegation, led by Pharaoh's Minister of Wheat. The young Kingdom of Israel would surely burst with pride when these honored guests caught sight of our bride and agreed that no other kingdom had a princess more beautiful than she.

What the maids were saying momentarily alleviated my distress. I was glad people were finally talking about Merab's beauty, too, not just mine. But when I pictured those long skilled fingers taking her hand from Father the following week, the poisonous fire began to lick at my throat once again.

"What a beautiful bride," said the people of the palace.

"What a regal bride," said the people of Judah.

"What a lucky bride," said the young women of Israel, as they held final rehearsals for their breathtaking dance performance.

Only Mother, who still remembered how her own eyes sparkled on the eve of her wedding, could see that something was wrong. "Look at our daughter," she said to Father with concern. "It's as if she is going to a funeral."

But Father calmed her, telling her it was all in her head. "That's just how brides are," he chuckled. "Have you forgotten what you were like before our wedding?"

And Jonathan, our eldest brother, kept badgering me, day and night: "Why shouldn't both of you marry the men you love? Merab loves Adriel, and you love David. Don't deny it. You don't love Paltiel anymore. I know you too well, Sister. Switch places with Merab. Don't sentence yourselves to two unhappy marriages. It's up to you alone. Switch places with her!"

It wasn't Jonathan's efforts at persuasion that made me change my mind, but rather the humiliating realization—which penetrated slowly, through nights mad with longing—that I could live without his love, but I couldn't live without him.

Then, three days before the wedding, I shared my feelings with Merab. I kept nothing from her. I even described the jealousy that ate away at me in all of its ugliness.

She shut her eyes and said nothing.

"Say something," I begged her.

"What's there to say? You're mistaken."

"Mistaken in what way?"

"Do you really think that David loves me? Look in his eyes. Can't you see it?"

"I see incomparable eyes like I've never seen on anyone else before."

"The eyes of a person who doesn't know what love is. David doesn't love me, Michal. You're attributing feelings to him from your own naïve heart. David has never loved, doesn't love, and never will. He wants me only because I'm a princess, and he prefers me over you because I'm the older sister. Samuel the Prophet can make as many fiery speeches as he wants against primogeniture, but David knows the truth. Being a firstborn *does* count, especially in the royal family. I'm just a ladder for him to climb on his path to royalty. You see, Sister? That's what David needs—a ladder, not a love."

⁓

Now, I tell myself when Merab finishes talking. Now, before it's too late. And right away, without pausing even for a moment, I call for Jonathan and tell him to summon David to meet me at the old well at the edge of the fig grove. And I give him one more instruction, whispering it into his ear so that Merab will not hear it and try to stop it.

Jonathan is delighted with my decision but tries to persuade me to tell Father the truth and not go behind his back. I remind him that it would take at least a week for Father's rage to subside, and by that time Merab would have been given to David already. He knows that I'm right, but he is paralyzed by fear. I promise him that once Father calms down, he'll appreciate what we've done and will be glad to have a crown prince who is bold enough to choose his own path. It'll be just like after the battle of Mikmash—at first he was enraged over what he called a reckless invasion of the enemy camp, but once he calmed down, he openly admitted that it had been the reason for our victory.

What I've said gives my brother the courage to act, and he heads out to summon David to the well, and Adriel and Merab to the apple tree. And when the surprised David gets to me, I stand before him with my back erect, and I look him in the eye. "Merab hates you," I tell him.

He fixes his serene eyes upon me. They show no surprise. There is silence all around us, except for the sound of crickets chirping that rises from the well.

"David," my lips whisper. "I love you. Have me instead of her. I know you don't love me, and I am willing to be your Leah."

"It's not up to me," says David. "Your father chose to give me Merab. One cannot overrule the king."

"One can," I say. "Jonathan is doing so as we speak."

His pretty eyes narrow. "Jonathan would never contravene the king's decision."

"Merab will marry Adriel," I whisper. Then louder: "And I will marry you."

A wisp of tension, nearly invisible, passes like a dark cloud over his serene expression and etches a tiny wrinkle of worry between his wine-colored eyebrows. "I'll marry both of you," he declares, "just like our patriarch, Jacob."

The bitterness of my laughter deepens the furrow in his brow. "At this moment," I tell him, "at this very moment, Adriel is paying the bride price to Jonathan—a real bride price, not the foreskins of Philistines."

"Jonathan would never violate the king's command!" he cries.

"At this moment," I repeat, "at this very moment, Adriel the Meholathite is taking the hand of his beloved from her brother and leading her to the apple tree. She is clinging to him and letting him drink of her love."

"The king will kill him." Beads of sweat well up above his upper lip. "He'll kill them both."

"Father won't kill his son-in-law." My confident smile makes his eyelids tremble. "And he certainly won't kill his son. He'll get mad. Father is good at getting mad. But his rage will soon subside, and he will accept Adriel. The glow of his daughter's face will cool his anger, and then he'll summon you, ask for your forgiveness, and offer you his younger daughter as compensation. That's what Father will do. I know him."

His thick lashes flutter nervously, as if trying to keep out the bitter news. I step closer, standing right in front of him and taking in his breath. "Take me, David; you have no other princess. I do not demand your love, only that I be your one and only wife. Promise me that you will never take another."

A long moment passes. "I promise," he says at last.

I close my eyes. Darkness envelops me. I feel nothing. "I always thought I was Rachel," the words escape me involuntarily. "Now I know that I'm Leah."

With a quick shake of his head he tosses his red curls off his forehead. His skilled fingers stroke my bare arms, climb to my face, caress my cheeks, and slide down my neck.

"You aren't Leah, Michal," he whispers. "You are Rachel. You will always be my Rachel."

Eight

The roars of rage that emerged from the throne room terrified the palace servants. Yet only two days later, everyone breathed a sigh of relief at the sight of the smile that lit up the king's face when, upon leaving his rooms, he saw the joy in both his daughters' eyes and realized that Jonathan had done the right thing. While it ought to be unthinkable for a son to violate his father's command and help his sisters choose their own husbands, isn't that precisely the quality an heir to the throne requires? Isn't it far better that he be bold and independent than weak and complacent?

When, on my wedding day, I walked into Father's chamber wearing my sister's dress in order to receive his blessing, he let out an appreciative gasp and kissed the fair hair that flowed down my shoulders under a pearl tiara. He gave me the same blessing that was given to Rebecca before she left Haran: "May you increase to thousands upon thousands; may your offspring possess the cities of their haters."

"We have no more haters, Father." I tried to conceal the lump in my throat. "The Philistines have been vanquished, and they will not dare to attack us in the foreseeable future."

"Haters and enemies are not the same," Abner interposed himself into this private moment between father and daughter. "Enemies come from the outside, while haters rise up out of your own people."

"We have no haters, either," I said, laughing. "The nation of Israel loves Father and will be grateful to him and to his descendants forever."

And I truly had no hater on my wedding day. Even Paltiel son of Laish demonstrated astonishing magnanimity and came to the palace to tell me that he did not hold a grudge against me.

Not a muscle moved in his chiseled face, but his velvety eyes revealed the agony raging inside him. I looked into those eyes, which could melt my heart not so long ago, and I yearned for that other pair of eyes, the ones that would soon be looking at me with their special light, and for those long skilled fingers that would take my hand from Father.

"I'm sorry." I looked at the ground.

"I know you did it for your sister."

I was about to correct him, but then I saw that it would be better to sacrifice honesty for the sake of compassion.

"Thank you, Paltiel." I said his name softly, almost the way I used to. "I thought you'd hate me."

"I love you, Michal," he choked. "No one in the world can take that away from me."

The voices of the crowd that had gathered in Gibeah from all across the land filtered in through the palace windows, asking in amazement: *Merab was given to Adriel?*

And a moment later, in shock: *Michal loves David?*

And then, with anxiety: *Is this now the custom here? Our own daughters might follow suit and choose their own mates, and then how could we get rid of our disgrace?*

And finally, with acceptance: *The king approves of Michal's love. At least our hero is marrying the prettier of the two princesses.*

Only the commotion caused by the uninvited guest from Judah threatened to put a damper on my joy. He arrived at the palace gates mere hours before the wedding ceremony and demanded to see the bride right away. The guards tried to explain that members of the royal family did not make it their practice to meet with just anyone, and certainly not on this day, but he grabbed hold of the stones of the gate and screamed at the top of his lungs that Merab could not possibly fathom whom she was about to marry.

"Merab was given to Adriel the Meholathite three days ago in a modest family ceremony," the guards corrected him patiently. "The one who's about to get married with all the pomp and circumstance is Michal, the younger princess."

"She is whoever she is," he cried, " but I have to warn her before it's too late!"

One of the maids overheard this exchange and rushed to give me the worrisome news of the madman standing at the palace gate and defaming my beloved. I did what I could to calm her down, assuring her that the guards knew how to handle these sorts of cases, but she persisted, telling me that he was an especially compelling speaker and that people were gathering around and listening attentively to what he had to say. I was angry at the guards for failing to fulfill their duties and decided to go myself to make sure they sent away the man who would dare make a scene on the happiest day of my life. But, on second thought, I realized that being banished by the royal bride for all to see might turn this madman into a hero and only make people listen to him even more intently.

"Tell the guards to let him in, and bring him to the palace garden," I instructed the bewildered maid.

I sat on my favorite bench, in the shadow of the pomegranate tree and the olive tree, and considered the situation. In just about an hour, the crowd will be gathering at the foot of the stage, enthralled, as the marriage ceremony unfolds. Nothing will be able to distract them then. As such, I have to convince this madman that I am interested in what he has to say so that he will tell his story at length until the ceremony begins.

The maid returned moments later with a powerful-looking young man. I had to admit that the look in his eyes was not at all mad.

"Who are you?"

He bowed quickly. "Elhanan son of Jair, of Bethlehem."

"What do you want?"

He surveyed my dress in wonder, then he looked into my eyes and said nothing. His handsome face expressed sadness. "The things I am about to tell you will make you miserable," he said at last. "But silence is even worse."

"Speak!"

⤙⤚

What astounded me most of all was how carried away I got by his story. At first he jumped around from one thing to another, moving back and forth between past and present, between love and hate, between laughter and rage, but eventually he started to put his ideas in order. "It's all true," he repeated. "You must believe me. You must not marry this man."

With warmth and enthusiasm, he described his father, Jair, a weaver from Bethlehem, who had passed away many years earlier, leaving four young orphans behind. If it hadn't been for the generosity of their neighbor, Jesse, they would have starved to death, along with their widowed mother, or been sold as slaves. At around the same time, Jesse lost his wife and was left on his own with ten orphans, two girls and eight boys. Zeruiah, his eldest daughter, herself already a mother of three, took over the upbringing of her siblings and cared for them with great devotion. She took special care of little David, who had been only three when his mother died. Jesse and Zeruiah decided to invite Elhanan, the youngest of Jair's sons, to live with them so that David wouldn't feel so lonely. The two boys were raised as brothers and were practically soul mates. When they got older, they watched over Jesse's many herds of sheep together.

I was pleased to hear about my beloved as a small child and as part of a family, and even more pleased to learn of the kindness of my father-in-law, Jesse, but I also knew the story was about to move in another direction and turn into malicious slander.

Elhanan admiringly described the musical talent of the young son of Jesse, who built wonderful instruments out of reeds, goat skins, antlers, and even hollow stones, and who was able to make them produce captivating melodies that he composed himself. The proud father was delighted with his young son's extraordinary talent, not to mention his handsome features, but his seven brothers and the three sons of his sister Zeruiah would admonish him for his childish wasting of time. They would scornfully proclaim that Jesse's family had ten strong men who would soon be warriors in the king's army and one little boy who squandered away his life on frivolous musical games.

The seven sons of Jesse and the three sons of Zeruiah truly did make the journey to the land of Benjamin to enlist in the army, while David continued to frolic in the fields of Bethlehem. But, contrary to what his brothers believed, David was also planning on becoming a warrior, and to get himself ready, he carved swords out of flint for himself and for Elhanan, and they would engage in mock battles with each other. When they turned seventeen, the two ambitious boys abandoned the sheep and set out for Gibeah intending to join the king's army. Abner son of Ner held out little hope for the two shepherds but agreed to let them undergo the usual examinations. Eventually, he decided to accept only the powerful Elhanan and sent the other shepherd home. The disappointed David tried to convince Abner that, though his arms didn't ripple with muscles and he wasn't especially tall, he was a quick-witted warrior; that he had once pummeled to death a bear that had threatened his father's herd; and that he had even chased down a lion that had stolen one of his sheep, managing to free the poor animal from the lion's maw. But Abner replied that lions and bears didn't have iron weapons and suggested that the eager boy return home to Bethlehem and go on chasing wild animals away from his father's herds. But David was not one to give up so easily. He pounded on the palace doors, seeking to join the king's troupe of musicians. His skilled fingers worked their magic, quickly making him the king's personal player. But this was not enough for him. He continued to dream of a great future as a mighty hero. When he met Elhanan from time to time outside the camp, he would always tell his friend that he, the youngest of Jesse's sons, would yet become a senior officer in the king's army, and that he would show those ten strongmen which son was truly the most worthy.

Elhanan had assumed these visions of grandeur would find their outlet in music, but then the war broke out in the Valley of Elah and proved how wrong he was. During the long period of waiting before the fighting began, when he was encamped on the battlefield with the other soldiers, he was surprised one night to find David at his bedside. At first, he'd assumed that the king had summoned his favorite musician in an attempt to get some relief from the stress he was under, but David explained in hushed tones that Prince Abinadab had given him special leave so he could tend to his father's herd since all the other shepherds had joined the army. While wandering the fields of Bethlehem, he had heard rumors of the prize that was to be given to whoever killed Goliath, and he immediately abandoned the herd and rushed to the camp to persuade his friend to join him. Elhanan was reluctant to leave his post and reminded David of the punishment for desertion, especially in wartime. But David declared confidently that the hero who killed Goliath would receive no punishment. Elhanan was forced to admit that David's argument made sense, as long as his desertion actually did lead to the desired result, something that was not at all certain, for even if the God of their ancestors was at their side and put Goliath in their path, it was doubtful that they would be able to cut off his head. Rumor had it that his plated armor weighed no less than five thousand copper coins and that only an iron sword could cut through it. They had neither an iron sword, nor anything else made of iron for that matter. The Philistines guarded the secret of iron well, and not a black-smith could be found in the whole land of Israel.

David listened patiently to these reasonable objections and then answered each one in turn. He explained to his worried friend that Goliath would have to pass through Judah on his way from Gath to the Valley of Elah, and that only experienced shepherds like them, who knew every nook and cranny, could track him down. They would wait patiently for him to fall asleep, then tiptoe over, silent as tigers, and cut off his head with the iron weaver's beam that was used years ago by the late Jair. Those kinds of beams had once been common, but now that the Philistines no longer sold iron to Israel, they had become rare.

Elhanan understood that the beam was an essential element in the plan to kill Goliath and that it was the reason David had come to see him. With a smile, Elhanan noted that it would be difficult to cut the princess in half and share the prize, but David reminded him that the reward had two com-ponents: the hand of the princess and a lifelong exemption from taxes. He proposed that whichever one of them located Goliath would get the princess, and the other would settle for the tax exemption.

That very night, Elhanan deserted the army and returned with David to Bethlehem. They picked up Jair's old beam, got on their horses, and set out to track down the giant. During the day they left the heavy beam hidden in a cave in Azekah and wandered around separately in order to cover more ground, and at night they returned to sleep in the cave. One night, when David got back to the cave after another day of fruitless searching, Elhanan fell on him, squealing with excitement, and announced that God had come to his aid and placed Goliath the Philistine in his path. The shaken David wanted to take the beam and go out together at once to the monster's hiding place, but Elhanan gave an enigmatic grin and stood serenely in place. Then, ever so slowly, he bent down, reached into a niche in the cave wall, and pulled out the monster's head.

That entire night Elhanan dreamed sweet dreams of his princess, but when he awoke in the morning, he realized that the man who had been like a brother to him had stolen her away. The severed head was gone, and so were the two horses. Two full days passed before he managed to find another horse and ride to the Valley of Elah. It was too late. The king had already publicly introduced his new son-in-law, and all of Israel was singing the praises of the young musician from Judah who had taken down the Philistine giant and given them victory.

⊰⊱

The painful blows I've absorbed slowly dissipate. I raise my head up again. I find the strength to stand up straight.

"Go," I tell him.

Elhanan looks at me, his mouth agape, and tries to say something.

"Go!" I repeat in a commanding voice. "My wedding is about to begin. Now no one will listen to you defame my groom."

"You have to believe me!" he cries. "David didn't kill Goliath!"

"Get out of here," I growl, and a moment later, as the guards drag him out, I call after him soundlessly: What do I care who killed or didn't kill the Philistine giant? I'm not marrying David because he defeated Goliath. I'm marrying him because I love him.

⊰⊱

Many years would pass before I would order my scribal moles to insert a short, inscrutable sentence into the Chronicles of the Kings of Judah about some unknown boy named Elhanan son of Jair of Bethlehem who killed Goliath the Philistine with a weaver's beam.

The scribes, who thought they'd heard it all, would be paralyzed with shock.

"David didn't kill Goliath?" they'd ask in amazement. "Are you sure?"

"No," I would tell them. "I'm not sure. But I want future generations to be not sure as well."

Nine

When the guests were gone and the two of us entered the bedchamber, I had to pinch myself to be sure I wasn't dreaming, and I was certain that I would never again ask for another thing. I needed nothing more.

My love stunned me with its intensity. It seemed to me that no woman could have ever loved like this before. I loved all of him: the mysterious look in his eyes, the ruddy roundness of his cheeks, his firm jaw, the confidence in his step. I loved his lips, too, and the taste of his tongue in my mouth, and the skilled fingers that played astounding unexpected melodies on my body. "I love you, David!" I said, again and again, quietly, out loud, in a cry. "I love you! I so love you!"

Only in the morning, when his distant look made me momentarily ill at ease, did I ask in a hesitant whisper, "And you, David, do you love me?"

The sweetness of his words spread through my blood, and I melted. "My princess, the loveliest of women. You'll always be my Rachel."

I prayed to God that life would go on like this forever, but my prayers were not answered. On the morning of the eighth day, after the seven days of feasting, I heard him telling the coachmen to get his chariot ready.

"Where are you going?" I asked in shock.

"To the army."

"The army? You're a musician, not a man of war."

He looked at me fondly. "My princess, being the king's son-in-law is a duty, not a privilege."

"According to the law of Moses, you are required to stay home with me and to give me pleasure for a full year," I said in the girlish voice that seemed appropriate for a young bride. "Merab told me that Abner gives leave to any soldier who gets married. Her Adriel is planning to take her on a long visit to his parents' home in Abel Meholah, far away from the palace and its concerns. She asked me what you were planning to do to please me in our first year of marriage."

David said nothing for a long time, and then, in a low voice, as if speaking to himself, he grumbled that Merab's was no innocent question and that she would do anything to turn me against him. "Your sister won't rest until I am out of the family." He was on the verge of tears. "She's gone mad with hatred. Jonathan warned me about her from the start, but I viewed her as a challenge and couldn't get her out of my head. I like challenges. I'm not interested in things that come too easily. My lust for the conquest blinded me and made me prefer her over you. I can't imagine what would have happened if it hadn't been for your determination, my brave princess. Instead of being in the bosom of a loving wife, I would have found myself in the arms of a crafty enemy planning to cast me into a pit, just like Potiphar's wife did, or to hand me over to my enemies, like Delilah did."

I was astounded by what he was saying. The unusual circumstances of our marriage threatened to cast a dark shadow over our life together, and I was glad to hear him speaking about it all so candidly, which could only help build a foundation of openness and trust for our relationship. But presenting my sister as a villain pleased me far less, and I firmly declared that Merab had never meant him any harm.

"Hatred impairs common sense." David sighed with melancholy.

"So does love," I said, smiling. "Merab loves me. She wouldn't hurt my man."

David decided to put off his trip so that we could continue our honest conversation. That was when I heard for the first time that his seven brothers were having a hard time accepting his dizzying rise and were now trying to get in his way, just as Jacob's sons once did to their younger brother Joseph. "Your sister isn't the only one who's jealous of me," he said and couldn't quite hide the bitterness in his laugh. "So are my brothers."

I tried to convince him that Merab's hatred had nothing to do with jealousy. People envy those of equal or lesser status who suddenly rise to greatness and surpass them. "You haven't surpassed Merab," I teased. "She is a princess in her own right, while you only have your lofty status thanks to me."

David gave me a long look and finally sighed as he quoted the proverb, "Jealousy is as unyielding as the grave," adding that it wasn't possible to explain the destructive emotion rationally because it was completely unpredictable.

It seemed that our conversation, which had started off with such beneficial candor, was now becoming tense, so I decided to change the subject to his family by suggesting that he give his brothers titles of nobility in order to ameliorate their jealousy. "That's what Father did in his first days on the throne. It's an excellent way to turn an enemy into a friend."

David expressed interest and asked me to tell him more about it. In the few days we'd been married, I had already learned that the best way to pique his interest and get him excited was to tell him stories of palace intrigue, so I told him about the time early in Father's reign when he learned that a relative of his was envious and that it wasn't the kind of jealousy that would quickly pass, but rather something menacing, destructive, and long-lasting.

"Who was it?" he asked, his face reddening with impatience, like a little boy who can't restrain himself at the sight of candy. I couldn't help but compare the way my husband's face flushed to the way my father's did. Father's face gets red when he is ashamed or angry. Shame sends him into silence, while anger sends him into loud fits of rage that frighten and intimidate everyone around him. But my David never gets angry. His firm jaw shows steadiness and restraint even in the most stressful of situations, and only the flush of his round cheeks hints at the storm inside.

"Abner son of Ner."

His eyes widened. "Our renowned army commander got his position because of jealousy?"

"Father would never have appointed someone unworthy to the most important military position in Israel, but he had many candidates—all of them warriors, all heroes, all having proven themselves in past battles. Mother told me that he had been planning to choose a decorated warrior from Ephraim to become commander of the united army of Israel, but then he started to hear troubling rumors about Abner son of Ner, brother of his father, Kish. People said he was defaming him, spreading nasty lies, presenting him as a weak, insecure, and unsuitable king. Father never pays much attention to stories and believes with all his heart that the truth always wins out, but at that time he was still new in his position, and Samuel was demanding that he punish the slanderer to the fullest extent of the law, lest his connection to the royal family lend credence to his wicked tales. But rather than execute Abner, as Samuel expected him to do, Father decided to take care of him in a different way. He invited Abner to join him for a meal in his modest home, reminded him of the camaraderie they'd shared in their youth, praised him for the heroism he'd displayed back when they'd herded their grandfather Abiel's sheep together, and declared that no one else was better suited than he was for the position of commander of the army of Israel. Father's unusual strategy proved itself over and above what anyone expected. There is no one more loyal and devoted to us than Abner. He values the lives of the members of the royal family more than he values his own, and there is no doubt that he would die for us."

David was fascinated by the story. When I finished, he told me that he was surprised to hear that the slander against my father did not come only from Judah, but even from within Benjamin itself. I was glad to hear him speaking openly about the hostility between the tribe of Judah and the tribes of Rachel, and I replied teasingly that it was no wonder his older brothers were unwilling to accept his impressive rise to royalty, for Judeans were well known for being jealous of their younger brothers. That's the way it always has been, and that's the way it always will be.

David wasn't offended. He said cheerfully that our marriage was a blessing not only for us but for the entire people of Israel, and that our holy union presaged a reunification of the tribes of Judah and Benjamin, just like in ancient times, when Judah told Joseph he was willing to rot in prison in the place of his younger brother Benjamin.

I could tell that he was trying to insinuate that Judeans didn't always envy the sons of Rachel, so I reminded him that Judah's devotion to Benjamin came only after Judah sold Joseph to the Ishmaelites. With a playful wink, I added that the best way to help jealous family members get over their resentments was to give them jobs and gifts, as Joseph himself had done, granting his older brothers the land of Goshen and providing for all their needs.

David nodded in agreement and said sadly that only a king could hand out benefits and titles to his relations. Then he leaned in, kissed my eyes, and said in a passionate whisper that I was a wise woman. I felt myself bursting with pride, and to cover my embarrassment, I made a teasing comment about how men usually gave their wives compliments about their beauty, not their brains.

"I like pretty women," he said, as that special sparkle returned to his eyes. "But wise women are much more attractive to me."

After we made love, he played the harp and lyre for me until morning. I lay beside him, overcome with joy, and prayed for our lives to go on like this, every day, every month, every year, until the end of my days.

But the very next morning, before I even had a chance to press my lips to his, I heard the sounds of the coachmen outside and realized that his travel plans hadn't changed.

"I'd hoped that the special closeness we had last night would keep you here with me," I said, my disappointment taking me to the brink of tears.

"There's nothing I'd like more, but the soldiers are expecting me to make a royal visit."

"Why you? There are other princes in this family."

"Jonathan appointed me to this role."

"Which role?"

"Making appearances before soldiers."

"Does Father know?"

"It was his idea. When I rode with him in his chariot before our wedding, the crowds began to sing, 'Saul has slain his thousands, and David his tens of thousands.' At first, I was afraid and was about to signal Abner that he should shut them up so as not to inspire jealousy in my father-in-law, but—"

"My father isn't a jealous man," I cut him off. "Merab and your brothers—maybe you can attribute jealousy to them. But the King?"

"Kings get jealous, too, sometimes, but you're right—your father envies no man. The emotion is completely foreign to him. He listened to their singing with pleasure and calmly told me that I seemed to be able to charm the people effortlessly and that we needed to use my talent for the good of the kingdom. He himself was too busy with affairs of state, Jonathan had to remain by his side so that he would be prepared to inherit the crown one day, and the other princes, including Merab's Adriel, weren't gifted with my powers of attraction. It was time the army of Israel had a member of the royal family making appearances before them. And indeed, two days later, while the second ban-quiet was still going on, Jonathan called me into a side room and officially appointed me."

"Why didn't you tell me?"

"I didn't want to spoil our marital bliss."

I felt utterly exhausted, as if I hadn't just awoken from a long, blissful sleep. Life now seemed gloomy and dark. David looked miserable, too. He bent over me, wrapped his arms around my waist, and looked at me sadly. His pretty eyes filled with tears.

"Come with me," he suddenly said.

"Where?"

"To the army."

It seemed impossible. I didn't know what to say. I thought he might be joking to lighten the gloomy mood, but in an instant he had a list of persuasive arguments that made the odd idea sound entirely rational. He left out any selfish arguments, focusing only on the good of the army.

"Your visit will improve morale," he declared. "Your father and Jonathan think soldiers only want to see heroic warriors at their sides. They're wrong. Soldiers are first and foremost young men, and a pretty princess like you could imbue them with more fighting spirit than any warrior. When they see you, that vague concept of 'The Kingdom of Israel' becomes tangible, and no words are needed to make them understand that some things are worth dying for."

I was flattered and had no desire to remain alone in the palace, but I was worried about the bumpy roads. Years ago, Mother explained to me that when a young woman wishes to conceive, it's best for her to maintain a regimen of complete rest. Rather than admit how much I yearned to bear his child and ask whether he, too, was passionate about becoming a parent, I bickered with him childishly, trying to refute his arguments and undermine his self-confidence. The most hurtful moment in our argument came when I asked him in a mocking tone how he would know what effect a pretty princess had on fighters, having never gone to war. He'd killed Goliath by himself and had collected the hundred Philistine foreskins—my bride price—without a battle.

"Two hundred," he corrected me, trying without success to conceal how offended he was.

"Let it be two hundred. What difference does it make? You collected them off the battlefield."

The edges of his lips trembled, but he quickly regained his composure, and explained coolly that one didn't need to serve in the army to know how soldiers would feel when a beautiful princess visited them. It was necessary only to understand human nature.

"I can't come with you," I mumbled in despair.

"Why?"

"A princess must stay in the palace, not roam about on the roads." I don't know why I couldn't just tell him the truth. "That's the law."

He gracefully tossed the red curls off his face. "Is that the law, my obedient princess?" My entire being ached for that glint in his eyes. "An obedient daughter waits patiently for her father to give her to the man of his choosing. She doesn't take the man she desires on her own."

"If I hadn't taken you, I would have had nothing to live for," I whispered, spent.

"Then come with me. Together, we'll make an irresistible duo. The soldiers will be beside themselves with adoration."

⁂

Indeed, the soldiers surrounded the royal chariot with shouts of joy, as if we were returning victorious from the battlefield. They almost passed out with excitement as we stepped out to greet them. They moaned at the sight of my dress and jewelry and stared at my face in wonder. But the main attraction was my husband. They devoured him with love. I tried to decipher the secret of his charms. I thought about shy Father's power of attraction—how embarrassed he feels among the crowds, how he can never change the way his face turns to crimson at the sounds of their cheering. Father's shyness makes him seem cold and distant, which makes people yearn to get closer to him. I've often seen how people react when he speaks to them. They glow with pride, as though they've overcome a challenging obstacle that only a few can ever surpass. David, on the other hand, walks through the crowd with confident ease, seeming to enjoy every moment. His hands reach out with a natural calm, his fingers touching all who want to be touched. When someone tries to speak with him, he stops in his tracks, stands very close, and gives his full attention and the feeling that he has all the time in the world and that he has never before heard such words of wisdom.

In spite of my efforts, I couldn't adjust to my new life. Nothing was left of the past. Even my precious jewelry, the last vestige of my previous life, had changed beyond recognition. I wore jewels only occasionally in my father's house, mostly in victory parades, but now they had become routine accessories. David beseeched me to join him at the army encampments dressed in fabulous gowns, adorned in golden jewelry, and wearing a crown on my head. He himself traveled in simple clothing, like a commoner, but he wanted me at his side in full regalia. It took me less than two months to discover that, in spite of my well-known fondness for gowns and victory marches, I'd inherited my father's introverted personality. The trips became torture for me, and not only because of the difficult roads. Sleeping in tents and squeezing into the chariot bothered me much less than the extended mingling with the crowds. At times, I felt like the forced smiles were tearing my lips apart and worried that I might scream or burst into tears at any moment. But the time spent with my beloved gave me the strength to go on. I saw how proud he was as I descended from the chariot before the thunderstruck soldiers, and I swore to myself that I'd remain at his side for as long as he wanted.

On one journey, we met Abner son of Ner, and I asked him to tell me exactly how many army bases there were in our kingdom. When I heard the number I felt like a prisoner granted a pardon, and hurried to tell my husband that we would soon be able to return home and be alone together.

"We've got much more work to do," David answered sadly.

"You're wrong. We've only got three bases left."

"Our success has increased the scope of our duties."

"Meaning?"

"We will now begin making appearances before the entire people."

"Where?"

"In all the tribal lands. We'll even have to cross the Jordan River."

It took me a few attempts to finally swallow the lump in my throat. "Does Father know?"

He wiped away my tears and whispered softly, so that no one would hear, "He will."

Ten

No woman dreams of married life with a third wheel, even if that wheel is the nation itself. That wasn't why I'd followed my heart and publicly broken the rules that required me to marry the man my father would choose for me. All I wanted was a small house on the palace grounds, two or three children, and my husband by my side. I hoped to share a bed with him every night, to wake up with him each morning for another quiet day, and to know there were only two kinds of people in the world: us and them—"us" meaning the two of us, and "them" being everyone else. I didn't think it was too much to ask or that I wanted too much out of life, but I quickly learned that my husband also divided the world into "us" and "them," but my "them" was his "us"—nothing was more important to him than the nation.

I knew I couldn't live without him, so I gritted my teeth and resigned myself to playing the symbolic role he'd cast upon me.

But a year later, when I realized that he would never give me his seed as long as we were still on the road, I made a decision.

"I'm going back to Gibeah," I told him.

"For a family visit?"

"For good."

The last time I'd visited my family had been six months earlier, for the Festival of Freedom. He'd assumed that I was planning another short visit this time, and when he heard my answer he gave me a heart-wrenching look and asked me not to leave him.

"You've got the people; what do you need me for?" The hard year had made me a bitter woman.

"There's nothing I like more than staying home with you and playing the harp and lyre for you, but your father has given me the task of making appearances before the people, and I obey the king's commands as I would obey the commands of God."

"How long are you going to carry on like this?"

He shrugged in despair.

"I can't play the glamorous princess any longer, smiling at people from morning till night."

"Patience, my wife." Now he was begging. "Sooner or later, your father will call me back to the palace, and then I'll make up for everything I've put you through."

I shook my head. "I can't."

His eyes narrowed. "But living without me is something you can do?"

◆◆◆

I couldn't live without him, but I had a plan for getting him back to the palace, and I believed it could work.

I set out the very same day, accompanied by two coachmen and a maid, and it took us less than two days to reach the land of Benjamin. The horses sped like lightning over the familiar landscape, and for a few hours I felt happy.

The guards at the palace gate welcomed me with cheers and asked how long I was planning to stay.

"This isn't a visit," I answered. "I've come home."

"And your husband?"

"Continuing to fulfill his duty."

They hurried to share the sensational news with my family, leaving me alone. I decided to walk through the palace garden that I loved so much and to take a quick look at the fig trees. I ran my hands over the curve of the old stone well, and when I realized it was making me sad, I looked up at the figs overhead, still ripe even in late summer. I wanted to sit on the bench and close my eyes for a few minutes, but I heard the servants looking for me and knew I had to appear before my family at once.

I hugged my mother, kissed my little brothers, and embraced the older ones. I gasped at the sight of Elhanan, my sister's baby, and I fell into her arms, weeping.

"Where is Father?" I asked her.

She evaded the question and wouldn't look me in the eye. I was hoping it was just that she was overwhelmed by intense emotions, and her eyes were stinging from the tears, but I couldn't help thinking about her old resentment.

My longing for my husband ate away at me, and I couldn't enjoy the hearty meal that the cooks had been able to put together for me on short notice. I thought my family would sit with me for hours, that we would tell one another about everything that had come to pass since the last time we were together, but Mother, who appeared ill and weak, announced that everyone was tired and declared that it was time for bed. I was surprised by the firm tone of voice that was so unlike her, and I was even more perplexed when I saw how quickly my brothers and sisters obeyed her and left the room. I ordered the servants to get my bed ready in the house that had been given to David and me after we got married, adding with a smile that I had missed it more than any other thing in the palace.

They gave each other awkward looks and explained meekly that Abner son of Ner was now living there with his family. I was appalled to learn that my property had been bequeathed to others while I still lived, but I took on a calm expression and announced confidently that Father would surely soon offer Abner a different home. For the time being, I could stay in my old room.

But when I got there, I knew I wouldn't be able to fall asleep, so I decided to go be with my sister. Adriel was in the army, and she would no doubt be glad to have the chance to chat with me through the night, just like old times. The stone-faced servants opened the door to her house and told me that Merab needed rest and that I'd best come back the next day. I ordered them to call her at once, all the while pained at the thought that only a year ago the palace had been my home, but now everyone was treating me so coldly, as if I were a stranger.

Merab arrived, cradling little Elhanan in her arms, her expression one of embarrassment. I tried to look at ease, announcing cheerfully that the disagreements of our youth were all in the past and that I was certain that we could go back to being the soul sisters we once were. She made an effort to engage in conversation with me, but she seemed restrained and preoccupied.

As we spoke, I caressed her small belly, which had already begun sprouting new life, and told her how desperate I was for a baby of my own. She scrunched up her face sorrowfully and told me that she prayed to the God of Israel every day, asking him to remember me as he remembered Rachel and give me a baby.

"I'm not barren," I said.

"Then why aren't you pregnant?"

I admitted to her that David refused to give me his seed during my fertile days, and to head off an angry response from her, I explained that it would be impossible to bear children on the road.

"Then why do you continue to wander?"

I replied that David was totally devoted to the people, that nothing was more important to him than fulfilling his duty, but she muttered with obvious scorn that Father needed no messenger to soak up the people's love on his behalf, that he'd managed very well before the son of Jesse had joined our family and could do just as well without him. If her Adriel was able to come home for at least a week every month despite being a senior commander in the army, there was no reason for the son of Jesse to shirk his duties to me, leaving me to live my life as though my husband were lost at sea. All men are inclined to devote most of their energies to all sorts of tasks, some necessary and others utterly frivolous—that is how God cursed them when He banished us from Eden. But to completely squander one's personal life on the altar of work was the province of knaves.

I absorbed her hard words about my beloved with restraint and waited for her to tell me what I wanted to hear. And, indeed, after some hesitation, she held her son close and stated in a decisive tone that when Father came home she'd tell him why I didn't have a child yet and would ask him to order David to return to the palace. I protested weakly, praying in my heart that she would act on her promise, and quickly.

But Father's absence put the matter off. Whenever I asked Merab or Jonathan where he was, they looked down and quickly changed the subject. In normal times, my longing for him would have amplified my assertive nature, helping me get the secret out of them, but my constant yearning for my husband weakened me and turned me into an indifferent daughter whose only interest in her father stemmed from her expectation that he would call her husband back and resuscitate her marriage. I was so preoccupied with the separation from my beloved that when Jonathan summoned me to the palace garden, I immediately told him how grateful I was that he had decided not to wait for Father's return, but rather to take the initiative on his own and bring David back to the palace.

"Your life with your husband is none of my concern," he answered coolly.

I realized that it made him angry to see me operating behind David's back, trying to pull him away from his work against his will. I told Jonathan in a pained whisper that I was willing to pay any price to save my marriage. Jonathan fixed his eyes on me and said in that same detached tone that my married life wasn't the most serious issue in our family these days.

"Father has taken a second wife," he said, hurling the painful news at me without any preparation.

"I cannot believe that he would break his promise to Mother!" I cried in shock.

Jonathan sighed loudly. "That promise was made before he was made king. A king must have many potential successors."

I wanted to give him a hug and tell him that the kingdom had a perfect crown prince and needed no other successors, but his detachment kept me at a distance. It was several moments before I could respond. "I refuse to believe that Father intends to have children with his new wife." That was the best I could come up with.

Jonathan's laugh was short and bitter. "Intends to? He hasn't wasted a moment. She has given him twins."

I was too shocked to speak. Finally, out of my confusion, I asked him the oddest question imaginable: "What are their names?"

He looked at me as if I were insane. "Is that what you care about?"

"I want to know who my new brothers are."

"Armoni and Mephiel." His sad smile broke my heart. "Nice names, right?"

So many things had been going on in my life around that time that I chose to postpone any other questions and take in one thing at a time. I got up and turned toward the bench at the far edge of the fig orchard.

"Don't you want to hear about her?"

I turned to face him. He looked at me expectantly. "Fine." I sighed. "What's her name?"

"Rizpah daughter of Aiah, of Jabesh Gilead."

"And what is her father's name?"

He twisted his face in disgust. "Do you think I used her mother's name for no reason?"

I didn't want to get into the specifics of the questionable family circumstances of this Rizpah daughter of Aiah, but his tense expression made it clear that our conversation was not yet over.

His cheeks twitched nervously. "Do you love David?"

"More than anything in the world."

"Then be careful. The palace is not a place to speak ill of him, even if you mean well."

"You're my family. Who else could help me repair my marriage, if not those closest to me?"

He looked down. "David has enemies."

I leaned toward him and made him look at me. "Merab is not an enemy. She would never hurt my husband."

"I'm not talking about Merab."

I quickly thought back on everything David had done over the past year but could not come up with anything that would have made him enemies.

"I'm talking about Abner son of Ner," Jonathan whispered.

A chill ran through me. "I'm sure Father doesn't take that jealous man's slander seriously."

"Rumors can be destructive. Repeat them often enough, and people eventually start to believe them."

"What does Abner have against David?"

"He claims the people love him too much."

"And that's a bad thing?"

"Abner thinks it's dangerous. He witnessed some of David's visits to the army bases and told Father that the soldiers were like putty in his hands. At first I thought it was a compliment, and I wasn't concerned, but ever since the two of you began appearing before the people, Abner hasn't stopped warning Father that the adulation of the masses is a dangerous force."

My hands shook uncontrollably. I folded my arms to hide the trembling from Jonathan. I wanted to appear calm. "David is doing it for Father," I said, my voice cracking. "He obeys the king's commands as he would obey the commands of God."

"I know," Jonathan mumbled with emotion.

"Then why don't you defend him?" I turned away, trying to hold back my tears. "You love him almost as much as I do."

"Why do you say 'almost'?"

"Because no one can love like I do."

⊰঺⊱

One evening, Mother declared that she no longer cared that Father spent most of his time at the home of his concubine—that's what she insisted on calling Rizpah daughter of Aiah—and that he could stay there forever as far as she was concerned. We didn't believe her, but we were glad she was beginning to accept the situation.

Our happiness was short-lived. A few days later, Father returned to the palace and announced that his second wife and their two sons were going to move in with us. Mother remarked icily that the only available rooms were located in the servants' quarters, but Father, who'd grown accustomed to his old wife's new mean streak, reminded her of the abandoned home of Michal and David, saying that Abner son of Ner, who had been living there for the time being, could go back to live with his family outside the palace grounds.

Only then did Father learn that I had returned. Had these been normal times, he would have summoned me to the throne room right away, descended from his dais, and showered me with kisses. But now I had to wait a long while before being summoned, and even then he remained on his throne, looking down at me from on high. I thought bitterly to myself that he must have been dedicating most of his emotional energy to his new wife and children, and that he had only a few crumbs left for me, if that. I felt my great love for him making way for resentment, but I knew I couldn't afford to fight with him just then, so I stretched my lips into a warm smile, just like I used to do, and told him that I was very willing to give up my house for his new wife and children and that I bore no grudge.

"How long do you plan on staying in the palace?" he asked, ignoring my noble concession.

I could barely contain the rage bubbling up inside me. "Indefinitely."

I thought I detected a hint of excitement in his face, but it quickly regained its rigid expression. "Are you not going back to David?"

"He will come back to me."

I couldn't tell from his reaction whether my confidence made him happy or annoyed. He was straight-faced.

"Surely, you want to know why I left him," I offered, trying to advance the conversation to my ends.

He cleared his throat and looked away. "We have much to talk about, Michal, but not right now."

I knew very well what it meant when he cleared his throat that way: my time was up.

Eleven

Who would have believed that, of all the women in the world, it would be Mother's new rival who would become my soul sister and take the place in my life of the sister I had lost? Why did the sight of her sad eyes make my heart flutter? Why did I take her under my wing rather than make her life miserable, as everyone expected me to? What made me want to protect her from my family's burning resentment?

Perhaps it was the fragrance of the first rainfall rising up from her hair, sweeter than any other smell except, perhaps, for that old scent of lilies. Or perhaps it was something else. To this day, I haven't figured out the mystery of falling in love. I only know one thing: when I woke up early in the morning to the sounds of people arriving, I never imagined that in only a few moments I wouldn't be lonely anymore. I peeked curiously out the window, the way I did whenever something outside caught my attention, and saw two elegant chariots parked next to the house that had been given to me on my wedding day. I got dressed quickly and went out to the palace courtyard. The coachmen had taken shelter beneath the arch of the gate, trying to stay out of the hard rain that had begun to fall without warning, and they were shouting instructions to the servants unloading the chariots.

"The first rainfall came early this year," shouted a large servant carrying a baby crib wrapped in cloth. "You'd better get back inside the palace."

I quickened my stride and slipped in the wet dirt. I tried to grab on to the chariot's ladder, but just at that moment a fragile-looking young woman who looked like a child began coming down. Instead of grabbing the rungs, I accidentally grabbed her dainty ankle. She wiped the rain off her face and burst out laughing. The fragrance of her moist hair filled me with a joy I hadn't felt in a long time.

"Are you my little boys' nursemaid?"

The skinny thighs I could see as I looked up at her made my heart melt. I felt the melancholy that had weighed on me since my return to the palace making way for a liberating sense of lightness, and I was afraid that the spell would be broken if she found out who I was.

"Your nursemaid will be here soon," I said. "I'm your personal servant."

She gave me her hand and climbed down carefully. We stood facing one another in the rain and smiled. Her smile didn't reach her eyes, which remained sad. I couldn't stop looking at her.

"I am Rizpah, of the tribe of Manasseh."

"And I am Rachel, of the tribe of Benjamin."

"Rachel is my favorite name. If I ever have a daughter, I will name her Rachel."

I felt like she could read my innermost thoughts. She paused for a moment, then added sadly, "But it doesn't appear as though that will ever happen for me."

"Why not?" I wondered. "You're a young woman. You'll have many more children."

She blushed, which made my heart race. "I'm not so sure. Besides, the king is the one who chooses the names of his children. I wanted to name one of the twins Gilead, but the king decided to call them Armoni and Mephiel."

It was precisely because she spoke these words with such acceptance that they made me so angry. I wanted to storm into the throne room and demand that Father give their son the name chosen by his new wife. I knew I wouldn't, but my desire to do so perplexed me.

"What is your favorite name?" she asked curiously, as if nothing in the world were more interesting to her than my reply. She was still under the impression that I was her servant but nevertheless spoke to me simply and directly, as if I were a friend or her sister.

"Nebat." I didn't even have to think about it. "The name reminds me of the aroma of moist earth after the first rainfall, just like this smell." I leaned my head closer and took in the fragrance of her hair. "And since my husband is not a king," I added with a smile, "no one can force me to give my son any other name."

She looked around in alarm to make sure no one had overheard me, and only then did she allow herself to laugh. "And what would you call a daughter?"

"Rachel," I said with certainty. "It's my favorite name, too."

She recoiled. "But that's your own name!"

I wanted to throw my arms around her and ask for her forgiveness, but I knew that doing so would frighten her. "I'm Michal," I said, trying to smile. "Your husband's youngest daughter."

Her skinny arms shook and tears of rage filled her eyes. "Why did you do that?" Her voice remained soft in spite of her anger. "I know you all hate me. I would have hated my father's second wife, too, but I was hoping you'd have given me at least a few days of grace."

I held out my arms and took her tiny hands in mine. "Life won't be easy for you in the palace," I whispered. "But I'll protect you. Anyone who wants to abuse you will have to deal with me first."

We said nothing for a while, our intertwined fingers speaking what words could not.

"Princess Michal," she said, barely able to speak through the lump in her throat. "I don't know how I didn't recognize you. The moment I saw you, I knew right away that you were the most beautiful woman in the world."

❦

My family was united in the opinion that my love for Rizpah was instrumental, but each of them had a different explanation for why I would betray my mother. Mother bitterly asserted that I'd always preferred Father over her, Merab conjectured that I was trying to make her jealous to pay her back for resenting my husband, and Jonathan accused me of ingratiating myself to Father as part of my campaign against Abner son of Ner. I didn't try to argue with my mother and sister. I realized that my relationships with them were completely dead and that nothing we could say to one another would bring them back to life. But I wouldn't give up on Jonathan, for the love we shared for David made us allies. I confessed to him that I had initially offered my house to Rizpah in order to gain Father's favor, but, I said, I had truly come to love her, with no ulterior motive.

He didn't believe me. "You're using her in your battle with Abner," he proclaimed.

"I have no interest in hurting Abner. He is not my enemy. His wicked slander has actually been of service to me. It's the reason Father is considering bringing David back to the palace."

Jonathan agreed that nothing would be served by a confrontation with Abner, but his opinion of me didn't change. "David is the only person in the entire world that you truly love. You use everyone else to achieve your own objectives and then cast them aside when you're done with them. You used Merab to reach Paltiel, and you used me to get to David. Now, you have no interest in either one of us. Since your return to the palace, you've been thinking only of yourself. You won't be able to convince me that you care about that frightened, skinny girl who gave our father twins." He paused for a moment before adding, "You even cast Paltiel aside. Do you know that poor man still loves you?"

I realized there was no point in reminding him who it was that encouraged me to abandon Paltiel, and instead I went looking for my soul sister to share my hurt feelings and get her opinion about the strange resentment I seemed to inspire in the members of my family. On my way to see her, I decided to prove to myself that Jonathan was wrong about me, so instead of sharing my troubles with her, I focused my attention on her problems.

"It's time you told me why you're so sad," I said.

She made certain that the doors were closed and fixed her melancholic eyes on me. I could barely hear her weary voice. "Your father doesn't come to me."

"You're still impure from childbirth," I said, trying to find a simple explanation that could put her mind at ease.

Rizpah shook her head. "The twins are three months old. He knows that I've already gone to the wellspring to purify myself."

I wanted to tell her that I could only help her if she finally told me how she had met my father and what circumstances had led him to decide to take her as his wife, but I was paralyzed by what Jonathan had said to me. I didn't know if my motives were pure or if I was merely using this opportunity to satisfy my curiosity.

"Why are you so quiet?" Rizpah asked.

"I'm not sure how to phrase my questions."

"I know what you want to ask. My mother's friends made me swear not to tell the king the truth about our marriage. If they knew I had told his daughter, they'd cross the Jordan River just to kill me."

"Then don't tell me."

A mischievous smile appeared on her face, and for one brief moment even reached her eyes. "I was also given as a gift."

"Why do you say 'also'?"

"Just like you were. You were the prize awarded to David son of Jesse, and I was awarded to Saul son of Kish."

I grimaced in frustration. "The stories about me must not have crossed the Jordan River. One day I'll tell you the truth about my marriage."

I could tell that it took everything she had for her to go on. "My mother, Aiah the Great, was the most famous prostitute on the other side of the river. Men from all over the land would lay aside coin upon coin so that they might enjoy her favors just once in their lives. When I was born, many men were willing to swear they were my father and take me under their wing, but Mother declared that she didn't care who my father was because she intended to raise me only in the company of women. I had a good childhood. I lacked neither money nor love. My mother and her prostitute friends spoiled me and spared me nothing.

"Five years ago, however, everything changed. The rumor was that she'd thrown herself into the river, but I know that she would never have left me alone by choice. The people of Jabesh were certain that I would follow in her footsteps and become the highest-priced prostitute in Gilead. Many men lusted for the young daughter of Aiah the Great, and very large sums were offered for the honor of my first night. But my mother's friends knew that she had intended that I live my life as a respectable married woman, and they swore they would marry me off to the most respected man in the land. I don't remember when the name of the king first came up. At first, it was an absurd suggestion made only in jest, but the idea slowly took hold of them, and they developed a clever plan to trap him.

"At the festival of victory, when the townspeople were all gathered in the temple to reminisce about the war against Nahash the Ammonite, the prostitutes got up and accused us of being an ungrateful people because we had never offered the king a gift to thank him for saving us. The elders rejected

their claim, explaining that Saul son of Kish had received the throne itself
thanks to the victory in that war. But the prostitutes brushed this off, arguing before the large crowd watching the debate that the throne had been given
to Saul by the entire nation of Israel, and that the time had come for the people
of Jabesh Gilead to reward him in the name of our town. In the space of only
a few minutes, the once dignified assembly came to feel like charity collection day in the town's market, with each participant shouting out the gift he
was pledging, trying to make himself heard over all the others. In an effort to
restore calm, the prostitutes generously announced they would be willing to
grant the king the honor of the first night with the virgin daughter of the great
prostitute of Gilead. The people of Jabesh Gilead did not hide their enthusiasm for such an appealing gift, but they expressed concern that the king, who
was famous for his modesty and strict values, would be revolted by the idea
and might even punish whomever had suggested it. Eventually, it was decided
to keep the matter a secret until the king's next visit, and in the meantime
the prostitutes would prepare the girl.

"And my mother's devoted friends did indeed take very seriously their preparations for my royal encounter. But rather than softening my skin with
myrrh and anointing my body with perfumes, they kept telling me the story
of Tamar the Canaanite, who had disguised herself as a prostitute in order
to steal the seed of Judah son of Jacob, and who thus became the venerated
matriarch of the tribe of Judah.

"Two months later, the king crossed the river for a royal visit. But the prostitutes, who knew I was not in my fertile period, told the elders that the gift
would be given to the king some other time. The king's next visit took place
on just the right day, and there was great rejoicing. As expected, the king
turned me down. He declared angrily that the laws of Moses forbade treating
women as objects—not foreign women, and certainly not Hebrew ones—
and he recalled the ancient law of the 'beautiful woman,' which cautioned
soldiers against raping the women of their defeated enemies, the penalty being that when the battle was over the fighters would be forced to marry the
women and take full responsibility for them. But the elders, who'd received
careful instructions from the prostitutes, explained to the king that the people
of Jabesh Gilead would be terribly hurt if their gift was rejected, and they
pleaded with him to take me into his bedchamber, even if he had no intention of touching me.

"I won't tell you exactly what happened that night. A daughter shouldn't hear such things about her father. I must tell you one thing, though: your father is a righteous man, just like Joseph, or maybe even more so. But in spite of my young age, I succeeded where Potiphar's wife had failed. I'll say no more. You can imagine the rest. Three months later, the prostitutes informed the king of the pregnancy of the young girl from Gilead who'd known no other man but him. The king didn't deny it or give a false oath, didn't even call me a whore—as most men do in such cases—but returned to Jabesh Gilead and married me. Initially, he'd planned for me to stay on the other side of the river so as not to cause his wife unnecessary suffering, but after the twins were born, he had a hard time being apart from his little sons and decided that we should move into the palace with him."

The story should have caused me to feel repulsed by the conniving temptress who'd trapped my righteous father and dragged my entire family into her intrigues, but nothing could diminish my love for her, which, in spite of what my family thought, was truly unconditional.

"You got what you wanted," I said, trying to cheer her up. "You're the wife of the king, and your sons are princes. What do you care if he doesn't come to you anymore?"

"Don't you see?" Her eyes were sadder than ever. "I love him. I fell in love with him at first sight. I wouldn't have been able to seduce him otherwise. If you try to see your father through the eyes of a woman, not of a daughter, you'll see that he is irresistible." She stood at the window and looked away from me. The sun cast soft beams of light upon her hair, giving it a truly magnificent appearance. "The prostitutes were right," she whispered, as if to herself. "I really am like Tamar. They forgot one thing, though: Judah acknowledged his paternity, but he refused to touch the woman who'd stolen his seed ever again." She looked back at me and sighed. "Michal, my love, we both know the truth: we can always take their seed, but their hearts and desires remain their own. We can't steal those."

"You're wrong, Rizpah," I said. "We can't always take their seed."

Twelve

David returned to the palace alone. No one came to greet the king's son-in-law. He got down heavily from the dusty chariot, tossed the red curls out of his eyes with the familiar flip of the head, and looked up at my window. I ran outside, my feet bare and my hair wild, but instead of leaping into his arms, I stopped in my tracks and stared at him as if for the first time. It wasn't only that his red beard, which had grown thick, gave him an unfamiliar appearance. The licks of fire in his hair, the steely look in his eyes, the firm jaw, even the boyish roundness of his cheeks—all of these suddenly made him a stranger.

"My love," I said, trying to breathe normally. "There are no words to describe how much I've missed you."

He turned his back on me and began to unload his belongings from the chariot. "I've heard that your father has given our home to his concubine," he muttered in my direction. His voice sounded hard, metallic.

"To his wife," I corrected him. Even at this moment, I couldn't be disloyal to my soul sister. "Rizpah daughter of Aiah is Father's wife, and he is obligated to give her a home in the palace. But we can build ourselves a new house, a larger and more magnificent one."

He turned away and smiled warmly at the guard who came over to take his things. "Hello there, Simeon, my friend."

The guard's cheeks turned bright red. "You remember me?"

"How could I forget? How is your son, the wounded soldier?"

"He lost his arm and cannot make a living, but he's grateful for what he has. He even got married and now has a daughter."

"Blessed be the God of Israel for granting you His graces. Please give your son my best, and tell him I'd be glad to meet with him one day and find him a suitable source of income. That's the least we can do for a heroic fighter who sacrificed his arm for the Kingdom of Israel."

The guard's eyes welled up, and he almost lost his footing. It occurred to me that I saw this guard almost every day and had never asked him his name or taken an interest in his children. I wondered if Father ever had.

"Return to your duties, my good friend," David said, patting him on the shoulder. "I can manage on my own." He hefted a large crate onto his shoulders and went on ignoring me.

I blocked his path. "Have you still not forgiven me?" I yelled.

His eyes were cold, his face motionless. "What is it that I need to forgive you for?"

"Leaving you."

"I forgave you for that long ago. I understand that the rough conditions on the road are unsuitable for a beautiful princess like yourself." He looked me up and down with a faraway look and added, "But I will never forgive you for bringing me back to be the king's musician."

I froze. "You're going back to being Father's player?"

He took the opportunity to squeeze past me with the crate and climbed up the stairs that led to my bedroom.

"David!" I called after him. "My love, it wasn't me. It was Abner. You have to believe me."

He turned around and looked down at me. "Abner started the job, and you finished it. But I have no claim on him. He isn't my loving wife."

Whatever happens, I thought, the important thing is that he is here. We are together again, and that's all that matters. He is tired from the journey, his nerves are on edge from the bitter news. But when he calms down, everything will go back to normal, and he will see that I am not his enemy.

I followed him upstairs and waited in silence for him to finish unpacking. "Go to sleep," I said, trying to use the most tender tone of voice I could muster. "When you wake up, we'll go take a walk in the garden, like we used to. We have some matters to discuss."

He lay on the bed without a word. The sight of his body sent a painful shudder through my stomach. He had the perfect shape and shine of a sculpture. I felt like I might pounce on him at any moment, gripping his waist with my thighs, burying my face in the crook of his neck, and rapaciously tearing out the hairs of his beard with my teeth. When I heard his even breathing, I slipped outside and ran as fast as I could to the only person in the palace who would understand my feelings without judging me.

The baby's cheek rested against her skinny arms, and his little mouth was hungrily sucking at her bare breast. She was totally focused on the sounds of his suckling. Her eyes showed no sign of sadness. When Rizpah nursed her sons, she was happy.

"Is that Mephiel or Armoni?" I asked before she could see me.

She was startled, and her breast fell out of the infant's mouth.

"Sorry for intruding," I apologized.

"You scared me. Is something wrong?"

"David is back."

She tried to put her nipple back into the tiny mouth, but the baby had already fallen asleep, looking content and satiated. The cheek that had been resting against her breast was moist and red. She kissed it and glanced at me.

"I take it the reunion didn't go as you'd imagined it."

Her face maintained an attentive expression throughout my entire story, but the words David had hurled at me from the top of the stairs shocked her, and she couldn't help interrupting me.

"How can he possibly think that about you?"

I looked at the ground, trying to hide my eyes from her.

"Are you crying?"

"He's right," I said against my will.

"He can't be. You love him."

"And that's precisely why I was willing to do whatever it took to get him back. I told Merab that the rutted roads were preventing me from conceiving a child, and I was glad when she understood my meaning and promised to tell Father. David is right. I've collaborated with Abner, his enemy."

She closed her eyes. "Sometimes," she pondered, "it's hard to tell haters and lovers apart. They behave similarly, even if their intentions are completely different."

"And only God, who tests the heart and mind, can tell them apart," I finished her thought.

"Only God," sighed Rizpah.

"In that case, all is lost. David will always see me as his enemy."

She opened her eyes and attempted a smile. "I'm sure he'll come to see that you acted out of love."

"David doesn't need love," I responded without thinking.

Her brow furrowed in confusion. "You told me yourself that love is the breath of life for him and his only reason for existing, that he needs it more than anything else in the world. All people want to be loved, but they make do with a few intimate friends, but David has a need to soak in the love of the crowds."

"Love is nothing but a tool for him," I heard myself say.

"A tool for what?" she wondered.

"For loyalty. He has a need for admiration, he has a need for unconditional acceptance, but what he needs most of all is complete and total loyalty. And those are precisely the things I have not given him."

"When did you realize this?"

"Just now," I said with surprise. "I've never been able to articulate it so clearly before."

"I understand," said Rizpah, and I knew she truly did. She understood everything.

❧

I was a fool to think that David would wake up in a different mood. Instead of acceding to my request to go for a walk in the garden, he ran off to meet Jonathan. I watched them from the side and felt superfluous. The two young men embraced warmly and needed nobody else.

I decided not to wait any longer. This was my only chance. Only if I could repair what I had broken would I be worthy of his forgiveness.

The servants already knew that when I was determined to enter the throne room nothing could stop me.

Father looked at me expectantly, as if he'd been waiting for me, and ordered everybody out. I collapsed onto the rug and asked him to come down from his throne and sit with me like he used to in the past.

"The past is past," he said. "This is the present."

The persuasive arguments I'd prepared fell apart like a sand castle, and the dignified restraint I'd been planning was quickly replaced by a fit of rage. "What's different about me?" I screamed. "I'm the same Michal I always was. What has tarnished your love for me? Why do you all resent me?"

I was so deeply immersed in my pain that I didn't notice him coming down from the throne until I felt his fingers against my cheeks. His smile was sad, but I was glad that at least he was smiling.

"You've inherited my hot temper and my uncontrollable outbursts of rage, but what about my other traits?"

"Do you agree with Jonathan that I'm selfish?"

"Just the opposite. The people think of you not only as the world's most beautiful princess, but also as the princess most deeply in love. That is the only trait of yours they see, and I agree with their assessment. It turns out that the stories people tell about us aren't always unfounded—you are willing to pay any price to fall in love. Actually, 'willing' isn't the right word. You yearn for it. You have contempt for love that isn't wrapped up in sacrifice. In your eyes, the more demanding the sacrifice, the more valuable the love. Jonathan is wrong. You didn't cast aside Paltiel son of Laish out of selfishness, but rather because your love for him demanded no sacrifice."

"You know about Paltiel?" I gasped.

He gave a bitter laugh. "I know much more than that about you. For instance, I know why you've come here and what you want to ask of me. The people of Israel mock my humility. They don't see that it's the most important quality for a king to have, not only because simplicity is a virtue, but also because only a humble person can observe the people around him out of honest interest and learn things about them that they don't always know themselves." He grew quiet for a moment, biting his lower lip anxiously. "But sometimes I'm wrong."

I saw where he was headed and didn't want him to go on. He wrapped his arm around my shoulders and whispered into my ear, "I was wrong about David son of Jesse." He spit out the name with distaste, just like Merab did.

I tried to gather myself so that I could list all the reasoned arguments I had prepared for him in a convincing and orderly fashion, but he beat me to it and listed them himself. "I know that he can be an excellent military commander, not because he was able to kill Goliath the Philistine by himself—

I'm not at all sure that in itself says anything about his abilities on the battlefield—but because of the incredible power of attraction that he has, which can rally soldiers to follow him through fire and flood. I also know that a father shouldn't discriminate between his sons-in-law. I've always promised myself to learn from the mistakes of Jacob the Patriarch and not cultivate jealousy among my children. But your David is not worthy of the same position as Merab's Adriel. What guides Adriel is the desire to serve me and to serve his people, while what guides David is a burning personal ambition, the likes of which I've never seen before in my life."

"You admitted yourself that sometimes your judgments are wrong. It isn't David that you have misjudged, but Abner son of Ner."

Father shook his head with deep conviction. "I've known Abner's short-comings since we were children. He's a vengeful, jealous man, and often mean-spirited, but at the same time he's loyal to those he loves to the death. I can't always turn an enemy into a friend, but in his case I did."

His tone made it clear that it was pointless to argue with him. In despair, I got up and headed for the door. I tried to leave with my head held high, to show him that I still had the power and determination to keep fighting for my husband.

"For now, David will return to serve as my musician. That way I can keep a close watch on him," Father concluded.

"Until when?"

His answer made my blood run cold. "Until the spies following him are convinced that he isn't planning to steal Jonathan's crown."

Horrified, I raced to Jonathan's house and burst inside uninvited. The guards tried to stop me, but I got away from them and entered his bedroom. He was standing by the window looking outside, just as I liked to do. Even in that trying moment, when I was entirely consumed by the terrible revelation, I couldn't help but admire what a handsome man my brother was, almost as handsome as Father. There wasn't a single woman in all the land who would turn him down if and when he decided to fulfill his familial and national obligations and finally start a family. I came over and hugged his waist from behind. I felt love for him just as I had long ago, before something strange and puzzling came between us.

"Father suspects that David is trying to rob you of the throne."

"I know."

My arms dropped to my sides.

He turned to face me, looking hostile. "Father only started paying attention to Abner's slanders after Merab told him that David was seen wearing my tunic, sword, bow, and belt."

I was horrified.

Jonathan's voice cracked. "I gave David my possessions as a sign of friendship. We made an alliance; that's all we were doing in the palace garden."

"Then explain that to Father!" I heard myself weeping. "I'm sure he'll acknowledge his mistake. Father can admit it when he's wrong."

"I tried, but when you look at it from the outside, it can be construed as treason. It looks as if David was taking my right to the throne. Why, Michal? Why did you tell Merab what you saw?"

I didn't answer. What could I possibly have said?

Thirteen

The two years that followed brought mostly good news: David and I were given a new house, more beautiful and more spacious than our last one, which had been built just for us at the edge of the palace grounds, right up against the rear defensive wall. Merab gave birth to Joel, and the proud Adriel announced that, now that he had two children, he intended to sleep at home every night and would no longer stay with his soldiers in the camp. Jonathan finally agreed to start a family and became engaged to Jaarah daughter of Zuri of Ephraim, and the people of Israel enthusiastically began preparing for the royal wedding of the crown prince. Mother came to accept the presence of Father's other wife, sometimes even smiling at Mephiel and Armoni as they played in the palace garden with Elhanan and Joel, her beloved grandchildren. Even Rizpah daughter of Aiah, whose sad eyes had become legendary, couldn't conceal her joy at the sight of the four beautiful boys who looked like brothers, loved one another like brothers, and were not the least bit concerned with the question of which mother was the rival of which grandmother.

Not much had changed between David and me, though. He continued to hate every moment of his job as the king's musician, I continued to stifle my great yearning for a son, and we continued to live our lives in parallel. I had Rizpah, he had Jonathan, and we could spend entire weeks without speaking a word to one another. He didn't accuse me of causing his lowered status in the eyes of the king, except for that one time on the day he returned to the palace, and I preferred not to bring it up. I knew he wouldn't forgive me for what I had done to him, even if I'd done it unintentionally, and I was hoping I would someday get the chance to prove my loyalty and repent my sin. The distance between us manifested itself not only in words, but physically as well. At first I followed Rizpah's example and tried to seduce him on my fertile days, but I failed miserably. His self-control was absolute. His emotions and desires were fully subject to his will.

For months I was able to bite my lip and endure the pain, but when I heard about Merab's third pregnancy I couldn't hold back any longer and screamed out Rachel's ancient cry: **"Give me children, or I'll die!"**

"Am I in the place of God, who has kept you from having children?" David quoted Jacob's cruel response and, in doing so, he tried to treat my lament as if it were nothing but a playful exchange of famous quotes from our ancestors.

I had a special smile that I reserved for these kinds of situations, when I wanted to disguise my suffering and pretend that everything was fine. But I didn't use it that day, and all at once, without planning it, the bitterness I had been stifling erupted out of me.

"The quote from Jacob doesn't apply to our situation. Both of us are childless, not just me."

His face froze. I don't know where I found the courage to go on: "Jacob could wound Rachel by saying that God had withheld a child from her and not from him because he had children from his other wives. But you, David, you only have me. If you don't give me your seed, you won't have any children, either."

He narrowed his eyes, as if unable to fully comprehend. "You think I'm withholding seed from you?"

"I don't think it; I know it. You're punishing me, David."

I assumed that would be the end of our conversation. Past experience had gotten me used to brief exchanges and long silences. His answer, which came several minutes later, shocked me with its directness: "I might not be Jacob, but you *are* Rachel. You told me that's what you wanted before we got married."

Chills ran down my back. I collapsed onto the rug and couldn't control the shaking of my body. "Rachel was a beloved wife."

"Rachel was a barren wife."

"She had a child eventually!" I tried to shout, but the words came out sounding eerily calm. "Give me your seed, David, and I'll ask for nothing more. Not love, not affection, not even friendship. All I want is your seed."

"You'll get it," he said. "I promise."

"When?"

He knelt beside me and fixed his eyes on my wet cheeks. "When your father stops hating me. Sometimes, when I play the harp or the lyre and see the intense hatred in his eyes, I pray for him to hurl his spear at me and pin me to the wall. I'd rather die than rot away in agony like this."

"Nobody hates you. How can you attribute such a terrible feeling to my father?"

"Only hatred can explain my imprisonment. I'm a prisoner in this palace, Michal, a prisoner in my own home."

"A man who goes to Bethlehem the first day of every month is no prisoner."

"I'm allowed to visit my family only thanks to Jonathan. He makes up a different excuse each time so I can go see my old father, but I always have to return within a day, before the king discovers my crime."

"It's true that Father is wary of you, and he might even be afraid, but he doesn't hate you. And if you give him a grandchild he'll go back to loving you like he did at the beginning."

"We mustn't have children, Michal. Not now."

I wanted to say to him that it would be much easier for both of us to handle the loneliness of the palace if we went back to the kind of relationship we had when we were newly married, before our travels spoiled everything. But I knew that it was entirely up to me, and I swore to find a way to prove my loyalty to him and thus repent my sin.

❧

I had my chance at Jonathan's seventh wedding banquet, but the outcome was very different from what I'd expected.

An extraordinary atmosphere took over the palace on the eve of the seventh day following Jonathan's wedding. Unlike the six previous banquets, the last one was an intimate affair attended only by our family and the bride's. I was especially pleased about the absence of Abner son of Ner. The air felt cleaner entering my lungs when that irritant wasn't around. David was loose and relaxed as well. He played and sang songs of love and lust for the young couple, and we all joined him in the chorus: "How beautiful you are, my darling! Oh, how beautiful! Your eyes are doves."

And indeed, the beautiful Jaarah daughter of Zuri of Shechem was endowed with innocent dove eyes that were riveted on her groom throughout the seven days of festivities. But Jonathan's eyes were mostly turned to David. In spite of my joyful mood, I couldn't help but compare the dull expression on his face when he looked at his bride with the fire that blazed from him when he looked at my husband.

"He shouldn't have married her," I whispered to Rizpah sorrowfully.

She shrugged and sighed. "The crown prince must have a family."

"Not with someone he doesn't love."

She chuckled derisively, as if I were being foolish. "Has Jonathan ever loved a woman?"

I stared at her in silence.

"He hasn't and he won't," she continued. "But he must have a family."

At that moment, David leaned over Jonathan, whispered in his ear, and the two of them laughed. I thought I was successfully concealing my emotions, but Rizpah could read me like a book. She said in surprise that it appeared that I had only just now learned the facts of life about my older brother. Her words landed on me like the blow from a sword. She saw my distress and handed me the water jug, looking me over with concern. I heard a great roaring inside me, as if a flood were rushing through my ears. I stood up and gave my chair a hard kick, which made it fall backwards with a bang. The singing stopped at once.

"What's wrong, Sister?" Jonathan asked, looking abashed. The way he blushed proved that he knew the answer.

My stomach heaved. I turned my head away from him, and without a second look I crossed the hall with quick strides, and bounded down the staircase. Before I could reach the gate, I heard the familiar sounds of my husband's footsteps above me.

"What do you want?" I hissed.

"The banquet isn't over yet. Don't humiliate your brother in front of his bride and her family. He's waiting for you."

His strong arms grabbed my waist from behind, pulling me back up the stairs. I started punching him, screaming in rage that the only person Jonathan was waiting for was standing right next to me. He froze in shock, but quickly recovered and continued to drag me up the stairs.

Suddenly an unmistakable thundering voice, full of authority, sounded above us: "Let go of her!"

We looked up at the large figure hovering over us. His expression and tone of voice terrified me. I'd never seen him so angry. He gripped the railing and leaned his enormous body over it to look down at us. "No man will force his will upon my daughter!" he thundered.

The blood ran out of David's face. "She's my wife," he mumbled weakly.

"She is an independent woman," Father roared. "Only an independent woman decides whom she wants to marry and takes any man she wants."

I looked into Father's eyes and saw that David was right. It wasn't suspicion or fear, but hate. "I want to go back to the banquet," I said aloud.

I can't remember the rest of the celebration or anything that happened there. I yearned to fall into my husband's arms and cry with him over the insult that had been seared into his flesh, but I knew I had to demonstrate regal restraint and play down the scene I'd just caused. Only after the bride's family left did I allow myself to give him my hand, but then Father commanded me to join him in the throne room.

"I'm tired," I said. "We'll talk tomorrow."

"Right now!"

I dragged myself after him wordlessly, feeling insulted at the way he was treating me, which was exactly what he had just warned David against. In the course of a single evening I was humiliated and patronized by the two men in my life.

Father paced the throne room like a caged animal. There was something both savage and childish about him at the same time. I feared the outburst that was about to land on me, so I decided to beat him to the punch, declaring dismissively that what he had seen tonight did not reflect the way my life actually was and that my husband adored me.

"You don't realize who you've chosen as your husband," Father cut me off. "Love impairs common sense."

"So does hate," I replied.

He stood before me, his face burning. "David is betraying us." He whispered the awful words with astonishment, as if he himself were hearing them for the first time and was having a hard time believing them.

I couldn't control the shaking of my body. "Don't go on," I whispered. "I don't want to hear it."

"You and Jonathan can shut your eyes and deny reality, but, as king, I cannot allow myself such luxuries. My spies bring me unequivocal proof. There is no longer even the shadow of a doubt: David is a traitor!"

I wanted to grovel at his feet, to beg him to have mercy on the love of my life, but his hard expression made it clear there was no point.

The words flowed out of his mouth as if he'd been rehearsing them. For some time, spies have been tracking David on his family visits to Bethlehem, which had been approved by the naïve Jonathan, who couldn't conceive of the possibility that the friend he loved as a brother was undermining him and preparing to steal his crown. Some of the spies even live in Bethlehem and know Jesse's seven sons and three grandsons, the sons of Zeruiah, personally. The ten heroic warriors, who until recently have been loyal soldiers in Gibeah, are now training a guerrilla army that will have the ability to take the kingdom from the inexperienced crown prince when the time comes. The militia is named for the sons of Zeruiah, known for their cruelty, and is led by Joab, the eldest son, who has a reputation throughout Judah as the most dangerous member of the family of Jesse. At first he recruited mostly the distressed and discontented of Judah, but recently about four hundred debtors and escaped slaves from all over Israel have joined him, ready to give their lives for David.

I decided to make one last effort to try to convince Father that he was wrong, and so I told him what I knew about all the scheming and intrigues that had given rise to this terrible slander. "The sons of Jesse support David?" I laughed derisively. "It's precisely the opposite. They are envious of their young brother for winning the king's daughter and are trying to undermine him in any way possible. I'm sure they themselves leaked the false information to the spies in an effort to bring David down."

"But they'd be bringing themselves down, too," Father said, the loathing in his voice momentarily replaced with a hint of doubt.

"They'd rather die with David. Jealousy is the most destructive emotion in the soul of men. People are willing to hurt themselves as long as the object of their envy is hurt along with them."

Father narrowed his eyes in concentration. His face softened. For a moment I believed he was seriously considering my words, and that they might penetrate his heart and cure him of his hatred. But seconds later the hardness returned to his shoulders and his eyes.

"David will stand trial."

The cry rose up in my throat, but I took a deep breath and stifled it.

He bent his head toward me and laid his hand on the back of my neck. "My messengers are already on their way to Bethlehem, to arrest the sons of Jesse and Zeruiah. I've waited for the end of Jonathan's wedding week. I didn't want to spoil their joy. Tell David he is to appear before me tomorrow at the throne of judgment. I hope my soldiers won't have to drag him there in front of the palace servants."

I pulled my lips into a serene, almost amused smile. "I'm glad you're giving him a chance to stand trial and prove his righteousness. He'll be there tomorrow morning as required, trust me. I can't wait to see Abner's face when the verdict is read. Please tell him I said he shouldn't worry. My husband is a forgiving person. He won't hold it against him."

⌖

The fresh evening air of early spring caresses my face. I skip down the path with little dance steps, loudly singing the tune David composed for Jonathan's marriage celebration, making sure the soldiers can hear me all the way home. They are everywhere, especially around the defensive wall, sneaking quick looks at me and then returning their attention to the gates. There are four of them by our house. I greet them cheerfully, and their eyes follow me up the stairs. Coming from inside the house, I hear the usual sounds of bedtime preparations. I step inside. The servants are fluffing up the pillows and smoothing out the sheets. One maid is bent over the water bowl, washing the feet of the master of the house, as she does every night.

This man, who is currently having his feet washed, is the love of my life. He is sitting on the bed, his back against the wall, his nightgown rolled up above his knees. I walk closer and take in his scent. The moonlight coming in through the window flickers in his pupils, and I see myself in them. His red curls are alight with a mysterious aura, just like the first time I saw him, walking with Merab through the palace garden, when Jonathan called us over to meet Father's new musician.

"It's late," I tell the servants. "Go home."

I get down on my knees, dip my hands in the bowl, and rinse the soles of his feet.

His brow furrows in astonishment. "You're an independent woman," he emphasizes each word with bitterness in his voice. "This is a job for servants."

I dry his feet thoroughly, toe by toe, and then I get up, walk to the dresser, pull out a folded tunic, and hand it to him quickly.

"Take off your nightgown and put this on."

He leans against the bed impatiently and adjusts the pillow under his back. "I'm not going anywhere now. If you have to talk to Rizpah in the middle of the night, call the servants back and have them accompany you."

"Go," I tell him. "Run away. Flee!"

Nothing happens. He sits across from me, his shoulders slumped in exhaustion. A puzzled look passes across his face and instantly disappears.

"If you don't run for your life tonight, tomorrow you'll be killed."

Another moment passes. He still doesn't move.

"You won't be acquitted in this trial."

"What trial?" he asks, confused.

"Abner's spies have exposed the army of Zeruiah's sons. Soldiers are on their way to Bethlehem."

I think I hear his heart beating, but it might be my own. I have no time to find out. I have to take his clothes off myself. His body is completely frozen; the nightgown clings to his skin. I pull it off him savagely. His jaws move up and down, as if he's chewing something. I throw the clean tunic at him sharply. He shudders.

"Get out of bed! I need the sheets."

He begins to rise slowly, then suddenly leaps up, standing beside me and looking helplessly at the tunic, as if he has no idea what to do with it.

"It was Joab's initiative," he mumbles. "I'm not guilty."

I pull the sheets off the bed and tie them together with strong double knots, my fingers turning white from the effort. I purse my lips, blood pulses hard in my neck. My entire body is dedicated to tying the sheets.

He puts on the tunic almost without moving his body. I glance at him quickly. "You look unkempt. Tie the belt and pull down the hem. You mustn't draw attention to yourself."

"I'm not guilty," he says pleadingly. "You have to believe me."

I lower the long rope of sheets out the window, tying the end to the iron doorstop in the wall. "Keep to the sides of the roads. The soldiers will only come looking for you in the morning. I'll stall them as best I can."

"Don't you believe me?"

"I want you to live. That's the only thing I care about."

"Tell me you believe I'm not guilty."

"I am guilty, David. If I'd handled things better at the start we wouldn't be in this situation now."

He climbs onto the windowsill, turns his back toward the outside, and grabs the sheet with both hands. His knees are bent, his shoulders straining, his rounded back tightening with effort.

"This isn't the end," he says. "Soon I'll come back for you, and we'll start again from the beginning. You are my princess. I'll never give you up."

I stand against the window and take his face in my hands. "Promise me you won't take revenge on Father."

He kisses me quickly. "I promise."

⁂

I drag a large statue into the bed and cover it up with the blanket. I scatter goat hairs onto the pillow and wait for Father's emissaries in calm serenity. As the hours pass, I sink deeper and deeper into a daydream that diminishes any sense of time, and in a strange way, almost inconceivably, I start to feel something like profound happiness.

But in the morning, when the soldiers knock on the door, I put on a worried expression and signal them with a nod of my head that they should be quiet. "He's sick," I whisper. "Very sick. Tell the king that the trial has to be postponed."

They watch the motionless figure lying in the bed and nod sympathetically.

And the next day, when Father goes wild with rage and asks why I deceived him and helped his enemy escape, I look up at him, my eyes frozen like a mask, and reply with steady confidence, barely moving my lips, "I love him."

Fourteen

S o, how is it being an abandoned wife at the age of eighteen?

It depends on whom you ask.

Mother never dared voice her own opinions even on less controversial topics, but the tears that welled up in her eyes whenever she looked at me announced her view of my wretched state more clearly than any explicit words could have.

Father forgave me for helping his enemy get away and said that I had escaped a terrible calamity, and that I was still young enough to "take myself"— that's how he put it—to take myself a new man who would give me a real marriage, the kind of marriage that a pretty, independent princess like me deserved. Merab agreed with him enthusiastically, beseeching me to put the past behind me and open my heart to the future.

Rizpah daughter of Aiah changed her mind so many times that I could no longer keep track. Sometimes she consoled me, saying my abandonment wasn't the end of the story, but rather a mere hiatus before David kept his promise and brought me back to him. Other times she would gloomily summarize the details of my three years of marriage and remind me that, aside from the seven days of banquets that followed our wedding, I had not experienced one single day of happiness. Eventually she took the side of Father and Merab and begged me to take another husband.

Jonathan's response was different from all the others. Though he went to bed with a loving wife each night, he felt abandoned himself, and our shared state of abandonment revived the sibling love we had for one another. Once, I was even so bold as to say to him that our competition for David's attentions had turned us into rival wives, just like what had happened to Rachel and Leah. "I've never competed against you, Sister," Jonathan answered expressionlessly and quickly moved on to his favorite topic, describing enthusiastically how his devoted agents had acquired the latest information about David.

And only the abandoned wife herself did not share her views with anyone in her family about what it was like to be an abandoned wife at the age of eighteen. A sober, painful assessment of my few and failed years of marriage led me to the conclusion that I'd been to blame for everything. Had I taken care to hold my tongue like a mature, responsible wife, none of the damage and destruction would have occurred. Merab and Abner had managed to infect Father with their hatred of David only after I'd given them the poisoned arrows with my own hands.

My tortured guilt made me turn inward. I swore never to share my feelings with another person and to deal with the loneliness and longing on my own. My family seemed to take the silence I'd imposed upon myself with equanimity. They must have told themselves that Michal had become withdrawn and introverted, and that it was best to leave her alone rather than risk sending her into one of her out-of-control fits of rage, which made Father's outbursts seem incredibly restrained in comparison. Even Jonathan, my one ally in the palace, didn't demand of me that I share my feelings. Our relationship was limited to the acquisition of credible information about our shared love, to counter the monstrous rumors being spread by Abner's spies.

The only one who objected to my silence was Rizpah. "We are both abandoned wives," she told me. "Who could understand you better than I can?"

"I don't want to be understood," I replied.

"But it would make things easier for you."

"I don't want things to be easier."

"Then what do you want?"

I didn't tell her that what I wanted was for the longing to go on cutting my flesh anew each night.

⟨⟩

I heard of David's marriage from Abner himself, who didn't squander his opportunity and came to take pleasure in watching my outrage with his own
eyes. Though I was used to his horror stories about my husband and thought
I'd become as strong as steel, nothing could have prepared me for such a blow.
At first I tried to tell myself that this rumor was just another lie, but within
a few days Jonathan confirmed it.

"David swore to me he would never take a second wife."

"She isn't a second wife—he's alone," Jonathan sighed as he gave me the
additional details that his agents had gathered about the pretty and clever
Judean bride who was now roaming the countryside with David.

An icy chill ran through my bones, but when I heard her name I gave a
sigh of relief. "Abigail is his sister," I explained. "David has two sisters: Zeruiah is the older one, and Abigail is the younger one. People who saw David in
the company of a young and beautiful Judean woman must have assumed she
was his wife."

"His sister Abigail still lives with her father Jesse in Bethlehem. David's
new wife is a different Abigail, the wife of Nabal the Carmelite, a descendant
of Caleb son of Jephunneh. That odd couple was infamous all across the Carmel region: the husband was mean and stupid, the wife beautiful and clever—
truly, a match made in heaven. David and his men had guarded the couple's
land in exchange for sheep and cattle from their many herds, and when
Nabal died of too much food and wine during one of the sheep-shearing
festivals, Abigail came to David in the desert in the middle of the night and
asked him to take her as his wife."

"She proposed to him?"

"That's what they say."

"And David agreed?"

Jonathan swallowed a gloomy smile. "You know that he's attracted to
strong, independent women."

The image ate away at me and made my nights a living hell. Wherever I
went, I saw the pretty, brave widow heading alone into the dark desert to take
my husband. I might have taken comfort in Abner's spies' version of the story,
which, as always, was completely different from the one told by our agents,
but that alternative version was so shocking that I preferred to imagine my
husband in the arms of a beautiful and independent woman like me than to
believe he'd become a ruthless villain who would murder a rich landowner in

cold blood merely because he refused to give him a tithe at the shearing festival, and who would take his wife by force as a deterrent for others.

When Father summoned me to the throne room, I knew something extraordinarily serious must have happened. Ever since I had extricated David from the palace, Father had avoided almost all contact with me and with Jonathan, focusing all his fatherly feelings on his four other children. Merab had become his favorite daughter and his confidante, but Abinadab and Malkishua received most of his attention and were involved in all matters of state, as if they were to be Father's successors. Even little Ishvi received more time in the throne room than the abandoned crown prince.

"The son of Jesse has taken a third wife."

He flung the news at me without preamble. I had to lean against the wall to stop myself from falling. I had thousands of questions, but I knew I mustn't ask them. Not of Father.

"Are you listening to me?" he asked, coming down from his throne. His eyes were ablaze. "It's one thing to take another wife. We've grown used to that by now. But her name . . ."

I knew he expected me to ask him her name. I bit my lip and looked up at the window. It was pouring rain. The sky was split in two by a zigzag bolt of lightning. I thought about my beloved, wandering in the desert, exposed and at the mercy of the cruel forces of nature, and I felt my heart break with longing.

"Ahinoam," he said, his voice getting through to me despite the crashing of thunder outside.

I continued to stare out the window, my thoughts focused on the rain that was now washing over the desert.

"Don't you understand what this means?"

"It's Mother's name," I said, trying to add a tone of derision to my shattered voice. "David's second wife shares her name with his younger sister, and his third wife has the same name as the queen. Only his first wife was fortunate enough to be given a unique name of her own."

Father stared at me as if I'd gone mad. "And do you think it's merely a coincidence?"

"What?" I spat scornfully. "Do husbands choose their wives based on their names?"

"Husbands don't, but the son of Jesse does! Everything he does is focused on a single objective: to sit upon the royal throne. Do you truly believe he killed Goliath by chance—that he just miraculously happened to run into him?"

For a moment I feared that the tale of Elhanan son of Jair had reached Abner, but then I relaxed. Father ascribed malicious intent to everything David did, but he still believed that he actually killed Goliath.

"The son of Jesse carefully planned the whole thing after all his other plans had failed. First he tried to join my army, assuming that impressive military victories would win him the adoration of the people and give him a chance to gather a group of loyal fighters around him who would stand at his side when the time came. Luckily, my experienced army commander saw right away that the ambitious young man wasn't going to amount to a great fighter and told him to go back to his sheep. At that point, the son of Jesse devised a new plan, invading the palace by way of his skilled fingers with the aim of winning the heart of the elder princess and becoming the king's son-in-law. But that hope, too, was crushed. My wise daughter demonstrated mature judgment and far-sightedness, declaring disgustedly that she wasn't impressed by the royal musician's strained efforts to charm her. But a man like that would never allow such trifles to stop him. The princess doesn't want him? Then we'll take her by force! And so, equipped with my hasty promise of a reward, the son of Jesse roamed the pathways of Judah that he knew so well and managed to track down Goliath and kill him in his sleep. He was certain that the unco-operative princess would be forced to marry him against her will. How disap-pointed he was when he discovered that it had all gone awry and that she'd already been given to another man. Only then, with no other options remain-ing, did the son of Jesse take the younger princess, who gave him her heart and cleaved to him with her love, only to receive goblets of venom and arrows of bitterness in return."

At that point I couldn't hold back any longer and suggested to Father that he forego the rest of his detailed description of the events we all knew and get to the matter of the name Ahinoam already. He shot me a withering look but managed to contain his fury, and he asked me what I thought was the most important thing a man trying to take the throne needed to do. I answered coolly that I'd never considered the question.

"He has to sleep with the king's wife," Father explained patiently, as if he were teaching a class in the laws of usurping the throne. "And it is preferable to do it openly, in the light of day, for all to see. With us—the nation of Israel—that has never happened, perhaps because we've never had a king before me, but it's a common phenomenon elsewhere, practically routine. Almost every king who doesn't inherit the throne sleeps with the previous king's wife. That's the rule: if you've conquered the king's wife, the throne is yours!"

"I don't see what this has to do with David," I hissed. "Just because his third wife has the same name as the queen doesn't mean that . . ." I couldn't finish the sentence.

Father gave me a long look. "You understand," he said at last. "I know you do."

I stumbled toward the door. "I'd better be going."

"We aren't done yet." His voice was harder than ever. I turned to face him.

He fixed a cold stare on a point somewhere above my head, trying not to look at me. "In a week I will give you to another man."

The world heaved beneath my feet, and the room started spinning around me. I put both hands against the wall. I couldn't think.

"You're so young, Michal. I can't allow you to live your life as an abandoned wife. Your sister has already given birth to four boys. What about you? Do you want to remain childless? I see the way you look at the children of Merab and Rizpah, and it breaks my heart."

I felt the anger rising and bubbling up through every part of my body. "Liar," I whispered in a hushed voice, then in a great scream: "Liar!"

His face froze hideously. "What did you say?"

"You don't care that I'm an abandoned wife. You don't think about anything but David. You meditate on him day and night. The distant image of him plagues you by day and haunts your sleep at night. He's your demon, the object of your fears, the source of your nightmares. David is your disease, but instead of seeking a cure, you've banished the only man who could ease your suffering with his music. You say that he used me to fulfill his ambitions? That's exactly what you are doing to me. I'm nothing but an instrument in your war against David—or the son of Jesse, as you call him. I'm the trap meant to bring down your enemy. You don't see me as a daughter, nor do you care about my feelings or my agony. You see me as a snare, nothing more."

He listened to me in silence and didn't interrupt me even once. I expected him to summon his servants and order them to put me on trial for the crime of contempt against the crown. No one, not even a princess, is allowed to speak to the king that way. Deep in my heart, I wanted to stand trial. I preferred to fight openly to stay true to my husband than be led to a wedding like a lamb to the slaughter.

I fell to the floor and looked away from him. "Never," I swore out loud, "Never will I have another husband. David was, is, and always will be my one and only husband. You can give me to anyone you want, but it won't do you any good. I will never be his wife."

I got back to my feet and groped my way back to my house. "Husband, husband, why have you forsaken me?" I whispered to the empty room. "Why don't you come back to take me away, like you promised? I'm no longer the spoiled princess I was at the beginning of our marriage. Today I'm willing to follow you anywhere: to the arid desert, to the isolated border regions, even to the great sea—wherever you desire. I will always be at your side. Take me, my love. I'm not asking for your love, I'm not asking to be your only wife, I'm not even asking for your seed any longer. I only want to be with you."

I sat on my bed and hugged my knees to my chest, laying my cheeks against them. I don't know how long I sat that way. I lifted my head only when I heard the sounds of Jonathan's footsteps. He stood across from me and said nothing. We stared wordlessly at one another.

"Father is giving me to another man."

I heard myself saying the words, and they made me sick. My anger was ignited once again.

"Oh, God," Jonathan whispered.

I took a deep breath. "It won't do him any good. No strange man will touch me."

"Oh, sister of mine." The touch of his fingers against my cheek sent a shiver down my back. "You may be an independent princess, but the rules of society apply to you, too, just like they would to a commoner. A man sleeps with his wife. That's the rule."

"Our family has other rules. Father doesn't sleep with Rizpah, and you don't sleep with Jaarah. Adriel is the only man in our family who sleeps with his wife."

It suddenly occurred to me that David barely ever slept with me, either, so the family principle also applied to me. I was surprised to find that the thought no longer pained me. It only brought up a nagging feeling of curiosity, as if it were an irritating riddle that couldn't be solved.

Jonathan's face was on fire. I knew I'd insulted him, but rather than apologize, I straightened my back and, in a clear and strong voice, repeated the vow I'd made to Father: "Never will I have another husband. David was, is, and always will be my one and only husband."

❦

The night before the ceremony I lay in bed. Being able to fall asleep seemed inconceivable, but sleep was the only thing my body craved. I woke up before dawn and couldn't remember anything at first. Then the dream flooded over me:

I'm fashioning a long ladder out of sheets, tying it to the window, and climbing down quickly, but the ground beneath my feet keeps moving farther away. I suddenly find myself on the desert sands, watching David from afar. He is standing with his back to me, and my heart aches for him. I try to run to him, but my feet are heavy and weak, and they will not respond. I call out his name, but my voice doesn't reach him. Suddenly he turns to face me, and I see that it isn't him. A strange man is reaching his hand out to me.

An unexpected knock at the door cut off my reverie. The maid apologized for interrupting me at such a late hour, telling me excitedly that my fiancé had come to see me before the wedding. I didn't want to know whom Father had chosen for me, but I thought that if he was already there, I might as well take the opportunity to try to persuade him to give up the ridiculous charade that awaited us the next day.

"Let him in," I said.

I wrapped my shawl around my shoulders and sat on the edge of the bed.

❦

He walks in softly, a strange and distant man. I glance at him quickly and turn away. "I already have a husband," I mutter. "No ceremony can change that." I try to quote a few more of the statements I've been rehearsing all week, but I'm not able to recall them.

He comes closer, but I can't see his face in the darkness. I strain my eyes. High cheekbones stand out even through the gloom. Soft velvety eyes glimmer in the dark. I have no need of candlelight to know who he is. I can see that distant image, when the sun blinded me and made me turn toward the chiseled-faced soldier with the long hair riding at the edge of the convoy.

"Michal," he whispers. "My princess."

The familiar words make my stomach turn.

"I'm not your princess. I'm David's princess. I always will be, even if he doesn't come back for me."

"I've been waiting for you for seven years, Michal, just as Jacob waited for Rachel."

Being this close to him makes me shudder. It isn't love, I tell myself. It's something else. A longing for long-gone days, when I was still a young, innocent, happy girl, and when my entire family loved me. Before everything went wrong.

"My love belongs to David, only to him. A woman cannot love two men."

"A man cannot love two women, either. He can marry two, or sometimes even more, but he will always love only one. Jacob loved only Rachel, the mother of our ancestor Benjamin, and Elkanah loved only Hannah, the mother of our prophet Samuel." He pauses for a moment and then comes a step closer. "And some men cannot love at all, not a woman, not their parents, not even their sons—like Abraham, who abandoned his parents, deserted his wives, and was prepared to kill his two sons. Some men cannot make anyone happy, especially not those closest to them, and anyone living with them is condemned to a life of misery."

I understand very well who he means. "Abraham didn't desert Sarah of his own accord. He was forced to leave his home and his people and to wander alone through a foreign land. Two strong kings, each one in turn, took his wife from him."

The soft velvety eyes cloud over. "Let's not discuss the patriarchs. Let's discuss ourselves. I am a man, and I love one woman. Only one. I've always loved and always will."

"I'm not the same girl of fourteen you once knew. I am twenty-two now, having spent three of those years as a married woman, and four as an abandoned wife. Life has worn me down and turned me into someone else."

"I loved you at fourteen, I love you at twenty-two, and I'll love you at eighty."

"I have no love to give you in return."

"I'm not asking for your love."

"I won't give you my body, either."

"I'm not asking for your body."

"Then what are you asking of me, Paltiel?"

"I ask nothing of you, Michal. I only want to be with you."

Fifteen

Immediately after the ceremony, which everyone viewed as my second wedding, Father made Paltiel part of his leadership team, which also included his three sons and his other son-in-law. Father's eldest, the crown prince, was left out. The people of Gibeah gave them the nickname "The Six Days of Work," and spoke proudly of the select group that ran the nation's affairs from the palace and brought the people of Israel security and prosperity as never before. "And who is the seventh day?" someone once joked after hearing the nickname. The seventh day was Abner son of Ner, came the smiling response, for he was resting from any labor and occupied himself only with spying on David son of Jesse. To Father's chagrin, the joke quickly spread throughout the land. Father continued to insist stubbornly that Abner's spies were no less essential to keeping the peace than the soldiers who guarded our borders, for the son of Jesse had become Israel's most dangerous enemy.

When this "Seventh Day" told me the new information his spies had delivered, I put on a casual expression, even managing to choke down a dismissive smile, as if what he said had made no impression on me. Only when he walked out the door did I allow myself to cry. I tried to stifle the sounds, for I didn't want the servants to call Paltiel out of the throne room, as he'd ordered them to do anytime they thought my mood was deteriorating. I buried my face in the blanket and bit down hard on it, my teeth nearly breaking from the effort, but after only a moment, my sobs erupted out of me with all their might.

Paltiel arrived immediately. He knocked on the door, and when I didn't answer he opened it and came inside. Until that moment he'd kept his promise not to come to my room.

"Ahinoam and David have a child," I wailed over my shoulder.

"I know. His name is Amnon."

My crying ceased at once, replaced by a terrible fury that momentarily dulled the stabbing pain in my ribs. "Why didn't you tell me? Why did you let me hear it from Abner?"

"Your father and I decided to spare you the pain. We never imagined Abner would be so bold as to go behind our backs. He must be disciplined. That man really takes pleasure in upsetting you."

He sat beside me on the bed and leaned his head toward me. His long hair fluttered against my cheeks. I felt the heat of his body against my thigh. My hand reached for his arm, and I pulled it back with great effort, which made my muscles ache as if I'd been lifting a heavy load.

"You aren't barren, Michal. You could have a child, too."

I turned to lie on my back and looked up at him. My lips fell open slightly and came near to his on their own accord. At the last moment, I pulled my head back.

He reached his hand to my face. My body shuddered. "No!" I cried out louder and more harshly than I'd intended. "I am a married woman. You are forbidden to touch me."

His hand hung in midair. He let it fall and said distantly, without looking at me, "Did Abner also tell you about Abigail's pregnancy?"

I felt like I was choking.

"Amnon will soon have a little brother. It appears that the happy father is a very fertile man."

"Stop it!" I cried.

Tears welled up in his eyes. "Let me give you a child, Michal, and then I'll stay away from you. I swear."

I got up and dragged my body to the edge of the room. "There is only one man who can give me a child, and he isn't you." I held on to those cruel words with all my strength. Without them, I didn't think I'd be able to stand my ground.

He looked at the ground with a wounded, helpless expression. "You won't ever have a child from him. Surely you now realize what everyone else realized long ago: the son of Jesse doesn't want a son from you. He wants to form his own dynasty, one that carries his own name, not Saul's." He looked up at me slowly. "I must tell you something else. Do you know where he is right now?"

What difference does it make, I wondered, where my beloved is roaming? Does it matter if he is in the desert of Maon or in the desert of En Gedi, at the strongholds of Horesh or at the Hill of Hakilah, in the wilderness of the Arabah or of Jeshimon, in the region of Carmel or of Ziph? What matters is that he is alive. I suddenly saw a terrible image that gave me pleasure. I saw little Amnon dying of thirst in the arid desert, just like the son of Hagar, except that no angel came to Ahinoam to raise up a well for the child. I was appalled by the possibility that jealousy had turned me into a monster, just like it did to Hannah, the mother of the prophet Samuel, who had wished for the deaths of the sons of Peninnah, her rival wife.

"He is in the palace of Achish, King of Gath," Paltiel went on.

At first I thought he was joking, but his handsome face was serious. I must have burst out laughing anyway. I couldn't tell that I was doing it, but the offended Paltiel commented that the ridicule Jonathan and I expressed couldn't counter the solid intelligence that was delivered by Abner's spies.

In spite of the wave of rage that flooded over me, I remained outwardly serene and broke into a disparaging description of David's travels in the city of Gath, hoping that Paltiel would see how baseless the rumor really was. "Achish must have been very excited to receive the famous guest who'd killed his strongest fighter. He must have opened the palace gates wide for him and ordered his servants to give a warm welcome to the young Judean who killed Goliath. At the same time, he must have also taken the opportunity to remind them of the famous song the women of Israel had composed for the occasion: 'Saul has slain his thousands, and David his tens of thousands.' He only forgot to mention that those thousands and tens of thousands were his own dead soldiers."

"The report we've received from the spies is even more amusing than your version, and if we weren't talking about a real threat to the security of Israel, we might have all had a good laugh. The son of Jesse was forced to flee to Gath after Abner's soldiers spread out across the land, and he had no place left to hide. He was hoping that no one would recognize him in the kingdom of the Philistines, but he underestimated his notoriety. When he was captured and brought to trial before the king, he made incomprehensible grunting noises and drooled all over his beard. People said Achish almost threw up in disgust and ordered his embarrassed soldiers to stop bringing him lunatics. Or, to quote his juicier phrasing: **'Am I so short of madmen that you have to bring this fellow here to carry on like this in front of me? Must this man come into my house?'"**

"Well then, you need not fear him any longer," I said, trying to use a teasing tone of voice to disguise the pangs of doubt that had begun to gnaw at me. "Madmen are no threat to the security of Israel. Tell Father that, now that David has been officially pronounced insane, you can disband Abner's army of spies and let the soldiers return home."

"I might have agreed with you if that were the end of the story, but David didn't make do with the role of the madman of Gath for very long. Eventually, he revealed his true identity to Achish and asked for refuge for his family and the criminal militia of the sons of Zeruiah. In return, David agreed to serve as the king's senior advisor on affairs relating to Israel. In other words: he agreed to reveal our most confidential security secrets."

I opened my mouth, but the scream lodged in my throat.

⚫

When I noticed Jaarah's round belly, I thought to myself with pride that the hard things I'd said to Jonathan about the celibacy of the men in our family had helped bring about his wife's quick impregnation. I felt like the prophet Miriam, who reproached her father for abstaining from her mother and thus brought about the birth of her brother Moses. When she grew older, she also reproached Moses for abstaining from Zipporah and, in doing so, reunited them as well.

"I wish you could reproach your father, too," Rizpah said painfully when I shared my feelings with her.

I looked at her in surprise, for Father's opinion of me had become so low that any attempt by me to intervene in his personal life would be worse than unhelpful; it might even make things worse. I suddenly recalled how, when I'd burst into the throne room years ago to demand that he not offer Merab as a prize, he didn't castigate me, but instead declared before his stunned servants that he was proud to have a daughter like the prophet Miriam, who dared to lecture her father. The memory was so painful that I was only barely able to keep my expression under control beneath the watchful gaze of Rizpah. I'd already made my peace with being the rejected daughter, along with my brother Jonathan, but every once in a while the pain came back and plagued me, as it had at the beginning, when I'd returned home after my year of traveling with David, only to find that I'd lost the family I once had.

The pride I felt over Jaarah's pregnancy renewed my lust for life somewhat, but these shreds of happiness ended when she died in childbirth. When I saw that the stricken Jonathan was unable to give his son love, I made up my mind to raise him in my home with Paltiel. Around the same time, I heard the rumors of Kileab, Abigail's first son, who was born in the town of Ziklag, which had been given to David by Achish as a reward for his dedicated service to the Philistine people. I felt like Rachel, who watched all the women around her constantly giving birth, not to mention the cattle and sheep being fruitful and multiplying, while her womb remained empty. To my disappointment, Father decided that the orphaned Micah would be given to Rizpah to be raised in her home with Armoni and Mephiel. It was never said explicitly, but it was clear to everyone that I was not considered suitable as a foster mother precisely because I was childless. I couldn't be trusted to give up the child and return him to his father when the time came.

The sorrow over the death of Jaarah was heavy, but life has its own force, and the sounds of the merriment of the seven beautiful children scampering all through the palace on their little feet brought happiness back to our family. Only Jonathan would not be comforted. He walked among us, grief stricken, and even the sight of his delightful baby boy couldn't put a smile on his face. He was haunted by the knowledge that he hadn't brought his wife joy in her short life, and this made him turn morose. Needless to say, the continuing erosion of his status in the family only exacerbated his bitterness. My heart ached to see him suddenly become old before his time, and I asked myself painfully if people also saw me as a downtrodden, bitter woman, who had only ten years before been considered the most beautiful woman alive. Paltiel kept swearing that my beauty only increased with the passing of the years, but I knew I would be beautiful forever in his eyes, even when my hair turned white and my face grew wrinkled.

❧

When rumors reached the palace of a slaughter carried out in the desert of southern Judah by the army of the sons of Zeruiah, I felt my body turn to stone. That night I cried out in my sleep. Paltiel came into my room and hesitantly ran his hand over my damp hair.

"Tell me that this time you also know that Abner is lying," I begged.

"He claims to have witnesses from the desert of southern Judah."

"They are false witnesses! If the army of the sons of Zeruiah killed everyone—man, woman, and child—then there were no witnesses left alive."

"Perhaps there were a few survivors. These things happen."

I steadied my rigid body and sat up in bed. My face twisted with pain, and my breathing grew heavy, as if I'd exhausted my body with hard work. Paltiel watched me with concern.

"I know you hate David. Unlike Father and Merab, you at least have good reason. But do you truly believe an Israelite is capable of killing an entire village of his own people only to prove his loyalty to a foreign king? Does it make sense to you that a man would kill children and babies from his own tribe only to make the king in whose land he has taken refuge believe that he has betrayed his people?"

"No." Paltiel cast down his eyes. "It does not make sense to me."

I slipped back into bed and turned to face the wall. "I want you to stay the night with me," I whispered to him.

"I'll always stay with you, my love," I heard his voice saying behind me.

❧

The Philistine attack was like a lightning strike on a sunny day. In the weeks that preceded it, there had indeed been reports of a suspicious deployment of Philistine forces, but Father's ministers and advisors, including his three sons and two sons-in-law, all declared confidently that we had never been in a better situation and that no enemy would dare attack us in the near future. Our soldiers sat complacently all along the western border and did not even have time to pick up their weapons when the Philistines invaded their camps in a surprise attack. Their accurate intelligence helped them gain control swiftly. They knew which gates to enter, how many guards were stationed at each gate, where the other soldiers would be, where the horses were stabled, and which structures served as weapon stores.

The tribes of Israel received the king's emergency decree with utter shock, refusing to believe that all the military camps along the western border, from Aphek in the south to Shunam in the north, had fallen to the Philistines. But the call-up took place without a hitch. Husbands left their wives, fathers said good-bye to their children, and boys kissed their old mothers, vowing to stop the uncircumcised ones and save the people of Israel.

My three brothers also took their leave from Mother, and Jonathan even managed to snap out of his detachment from his baby boy before he left. "Micah, my son" we heard him mumble. "When I return from the war, I will take you back."

Mother's body shook with the force of her weeping. Merab and I held her shoulders and tried to hold back our own tears, while Rizpah, who stood to the side, gave herself permission to wipe her eyes.

"I can't be worried about all my sons," Mother wailed. "My heart cannot take so much worry."

Merab reminded her that her youngest son, Ishvi, and her two sons-in-law were not going out to battle, but this only made her cry harder.

Adriel and Paltiel did not easily accept their fates. First, they declared firmly that the crown prince was the one who should stay in the palace, but after Father reminded them that Jonathan had been out of touch with the affairs of state for years, they suggested leaving behind Abinadab and Malki-shua, who were well versed in leadership and could take over if the situation required it. But a stone-faced Father declared that the sons of the king had to participate in the battle for the sake of the fighters' morale, and he ordered his sons-in-law to remain at young Ishvi's side.

⁘

No news came from the front at Mount Gilboa. Though my nerves were nearly shot, I managed to put on a calm face and tell Mother that I was certain we would soon be welcoming the king and the three princes home with music and dancing as they returned victorious from the battlefield. But when I learned that Abner son of Ner was not joining the battle, I lost control of myself and burst into his room of secrets in a fit of rage.

"You coward!" The roar that came out of my throat frightened even me.

"Go and defend Father instead of lying around the palace. It's your job! It's what you were appointed to do!"

He looked up contemptuously from the scrolls laid out before him. "And who will expose the critical intelligence about the son of Jesse?"

"There's nothing more to expose. The Philistines have already overrun our military camps."

He got up and walked over to me. His body cast a menacing shadow over my face. "There's still much left to expose. Your first husband will not rest until he sees the Kingdom of Israel fall."

I stared at him wordlessly.

"You don't believe me? I understand you. Even the Philistine commanders had a hard time believing that a man could betray his people to such an extent. You should have seen how shocked they were when the son of Jesse begged Achish to let him join them in their war against Israel."

I continued to gape at him until servants came in to announce that a messenger had arrived from Mount Gilboa with important information. I ran to the throne room as fast as I could. Father's empty throne made my throat catch, but the news gave me hope. Our fighters had managed to block the Philistine invasion. The Israelite towns in the valley and beyond the Jordan River were saved. But Mount Gilboa was lost. There were many casualties, but the precise number was unknown. The fighters were being counted to see who was missing.

"Are my father and my three brothers safe?" I asked boldly.

"Have no fear, Princess," replied the messenger. "If something terrible had befallen the king or one of his sons, God forbid, the entire land would already be in an uproar."

⟨⟨⟩⟩

But at midnight another messenger arrived, and the horror on his face spoke what words could never say.

The whole land cried with us.

Even the heavens wept.

The Israelites fled before the Philistines,
And many fell dead on Mount Gilboa.
The Philistines killed Saul and Jonathan and Abinadab and Malkishua,

So Saul and his three sons and his armor-bearer and all his men died
    together that same day.
The next day, when the Philistines came to strip the dead,
They found Saul and his three sons fallen on Mount Gilboa.
They cut off their heads,
And stripped off their armor,
And fastened their bodies to the wall of Beth Shan.

Sixteen

Paltiel forcefully grabbed me and shouted that we shouldn't go inside. Merab surrendered. She didn't have the power to resist. But I wouldn't give in. I hadn't kissed Mother in many years, and I felt I had to kiss her now. I wanted her to have a last kiss from the younger daughter with whom she'd never been close. I struggled wildly, trying to free myself from the strong arms that were gripping me. Paltiel wouldn't let go. He wanted me to remember Mother the way she used to be.

The pierced body was buried surreptitiously, wrapped in a thick shroud. We told the servants there was no way we could have a large public funeral for our mother while the bodies of our father and three brothers were hanging on a wall. But that wasn't the whole truth. We were trying to hide the circumstances of the queen's death from the people. We hoped they would believe that her heart couldn't bear the news that the messenger had delivered.

But the rumor spread throughout the land. "Queen Ahinoam fell on her sword," people whispered in horror, trying to imagine what a woman who has lost her husband and three sons in a single day feels the moment before throwing herself upon the sword. They didn't know that her faithful maid, who couldn't bear the extended death throes of her mistress, had pulled the sword out of her belly and pierced her heart in order to put an end to her misery.

Ishvi's coronation was recorded in the chronicles of Israel as a heartbreaking affair. Not one of the tens of thousands of people that crammed into Gibeah could remain dry-eyed at the sight of the two grieving sisters accompanying their only remaining brother to the royal throne. When Abner son of Ner, commander of the army of Israel, anointed the young prince, great moans rose up out of the crowd, rather than cheers of joy. Only when the new king managed to steady his feet and stand up straight, supported on both sides by his older brothers-in-law, and the people could see that he was no less tall and handsome than his dead father and brothers, did the cries of fealty begin to sound. At first they were quiet, almost hesitant, and then gradually louder, until they filled the streets of Gibeah: "Long live Ishvi son of Saul, King of Israel!"

Over the course of my brother's sad coronation ceremony, I recalled the moving stories of the ceremony that had been held for my father so many years before, while I was still in my mother's womb. "We should never have agreed to let Abner fill the role of the prophet Samuel," I whispered to Rizpah.

She shrugged her skinny shoulders in a gesture of despair. "What choice did we have? Since the death of Samuel, no prophet has been able to command all the tribes of Israel."

"Any prophet, no matter how small, is better than this man. A man of God should conduct the holy anointment ceremony, not a man of war."

"If we had made do with a prophet who lacked authority, the people might have gotten the impression that the previous king's men did not stand behind his young son. Abner's public support grants Ishvi the authority he needs so badly these days. Many of our people have been disparaging his youth and inexperience, and an entire tribe has failed to appear at his coronation ceremony." She grew quiet for a moment, then whispered with revulsion, "I loathe Abner even more than you do. He's been visiting my house every day since the tragedy. I've had enough of his condolence visits."

I reached out a compassionate hand to her face, and I was relieved to feel her anguish at becoming a widow and at her sons becoming orphans. But my own calamity was inconceivable. I still couldn't feel the gaping hole inside me left by Jonathan's absence. I still couldn't feel my desperate yearning for Father. I still hadn't tried to sketch the features of Abinadab and Malkishua in my mind's eye. The pangs of longing only began gnawing at my heart some time later.

Abner's soldiers had no need for sophisticated spying methods to expose the coronation ceremony that the sons of Jesse held for their younger brother in Hebron. People across the land were talking about it. The people of Israel were pinning their hopes upon their new king, Ishvi son of Saul, and prayed aloud that despite his youth he would have the determination to take the army of Israel into the rebellious town of Hebron and use force to put a stop to the attempt to divide the young kingdom his father had established. The disparate tribes of Israel had dreamed for so many years of becoming a single nation. How could the dream be cast aside only a single generation after it had been achieved? While it's true that only the tribe of Judah seceded from the rest of Israel and crowned David son of Jesse as its king, and the rest of the tribes swore fealty to Ishvi son of Saul, we are all the children of Jacob, and we mustn't give up on any tribe.

Adriel and Paltiel were attuned to the will of the nation and decided to launch a fraternal war to prevent the division of the kingdom, but Abner son of Ner objected, arguing that the army of Israel was still licking its wounds after the difficult battle at Mount Gilboa, while the army of the sons of Zeruiah was growing stronger. While it was no longer part of the army of Gath and received no more support from the Philistines, many young people from Judah were joining every day, prepared to kill and be killed for the sake of the kingship of the son of Jesse.

Young Ishvi was torn between the various opinions that were presented to him. After weighing the possibilities, he finally decided to take Abner's advice and not go to war against Judah.

"Merab is furious with Ishvi and has nothing but contempt for him, but I actually understand him," Paltiel told me. "The decision to launch a war of brother against brother is one of the hardest decisions for a king to make. Ishvi sees the secession of Judah as a fait accompli and prefers to focus on the post-war reconstruction."

I tried to change the subject and began talking about Abner's increasingly frequent visits to Rizpah, which were making her life miserable. My emotions were complex and confused, as they were whenever I thought of David. In the first days after the tragedy, Paltiel waited for me to come seek comfort in his bed. When he saw that I wasn't coming, he asked me brazenly if I were still waiting for the son of Jesse to take me back and give me his seed. I told Paltiel that I wasn't waiting for any seed, not from him, and not from David. The calamity had worn me down nearly to death, and the only thing keeping me alive was my duty to protect the kingdom Father had established by assisting young Ishvi in his first steps as ruler.

"And after that?" Paltiel asked.

"I don't know, Paltiel," I replied.

When we sat down to have dinner, I noticed that Merab was impatient for the meal to end and for the servants to put the children to bed. Ever since the calamity, we made sure to have a family dinner every night, trying to give the children a sense of security, a sense that the world hadn't completely shattered, that life goes on. Since we no longer felt we could dine in the large hall we had used for family gatherings in the past, we moved to a smaller room that made the tragic contraction of our family less glaring. Out of the same desperate desire to provide the children with a semblance of stability, we kept to assigned seats on the four sides of the table. Each adult sat with at least one child: Merab and Adriel sat with Asahel and Benjamin, their two younger children; Paltiel and I sat with Elhanan and Joel, their two older children; Rizpah sat with Armoni and Mephiel, the twins born to her and to Father; and Ishvi sat with Micah, the son of Jonathan and Jaarah.

Abner son of Ner asked to join our family dinners and even raised the issue with Ishvi, but my family knew I wouldn't sit at the table with him and turned down his request. Merab also had no desire for friendly conversation with the army commander who had failed to stand at Father's side in the battle at Mount Gilboa. The great esteem in which she had once held Abner became further diminished following his firm objection to war with the rebellious Judah.

"What did you want to tell us?" Paltiel asked Merab after the children left the table.

Instead of speaking normally, her voice came out sounding strangled. I knew it had to be something especially bad, for Merab was always able to express her opinions fluently even in the most stressful situations.

"The sons of Jesse are manufacturing a powerful weapon."

Ishvi's lips trembled. "Are they preparing to go to war against us?"

Ishvi's frightened question raised Merab's ire and brought back her ability to speak. "What reason could they possibly have to fight us?" she mocked.

"The Judeans would have to be complete fools to make sacrifices for something that's been given to them on a silver platter."

"Then what kind of weapon are you talking about?" Paltiel interrupted her. He wouldn't stand for anyone belittling Ishvi, demanding that we treat him with the same respect we'd given Father.

"The weapon I'm talking about is stories. The son of Jesse has recruited many scribes to his cause. Their leader is Seraiah, the most talented scribe in Judah. This group is disseminating awful stories about Father. Today I heard one from a palace maid who is engaged to a Judean man, and I felt as if Father was being murdered a second time."

Silence prevailed at the table. None of us urged her to go on. We just looked at one another in horror, waiting.

"The story is so terrible that I can't bear to repeat it. The Judeans are trying to convince the nation of Israel that Father did not die a hero defending our nation, but rather that he was punished by God for his sins."

"What sins?" whispered Ishvi.

"All kinds. It seems to me that they themselves haven't yet decided exactly which sins to ascribe to him. But what's so terrible about this story is the way they use the ghost of the prophet Samuel."

"*The what?*" Ishvi's eyes threatened to pop out of their sockets.

"The story describes how an old witch from Endor conjured up the ghost of the prophet Samuel the night before the battle on Mount Gilboa, and heard from him that Saul and his sons would die the next day as punishment for their sins, and that the man chosen by the God of Israel as the next king was none other than his former son-in-law, David son of Jesse of Bethlehem."

I could barely restrain the urge to scream. The shock I felt at what she had told us was like nothing I'd ever felt before when hearing stories of David. I tried to imagine Samuel's ghost rising up from the underworld, but I couldn't.

"No Israelite would believe such a story," I finally whispered.

"Why are you trying to diminish the seriousness of this?" She looked at me with suspicion, or at least that's how it seemed to me.

"Michal is right," Paltiel said. He always came to my aid when he felt I was being attacked. "The word of God is not given to the nation of Israel by mediums and spiritists, but by priests and prophets."

"No story can ever distort Father's image," I added. "The people of Israel will always be grateful to him and will never forget what he did for them."

"The Israelites have always been ungrateful toward their leaders," Merab replied bitterly. "Remember what they did to Moses. The nation has a short memory, especially with regard to a king such as Father, who didn't bother to record his deeds and spread tales of his greatness."

"The nation of Israel will condemn false stories about Father," I said confidently.

"It's Father, Jonathan, Abinadab, and Malkishua who have been condemned!" Merab shouted. "Their bodies are condemned to hang on the walls of Beth Shan, and the people of Israel, who owe so much to their first king, are listening to the monstrous stories of Judah instead of risking their lives for him and bringing him and his sons back for a proper burial in Israel."

"That is the king's duty," Adriel intervened, giving Ishvi an angry stare. "People will only risk their lives if their leaders lead the way."

Ishvi paled. "I ordered Abner to plan a military operation to recover their bodies, but he claimed that if our soldiers entered the occupied territory, the war with the Philistines might be reignited, and our army, which has not yet recuperated, might suffer an even worse defeat than it did in the last war."

"So what do you want from the people?" Adriel asked, turning to Merab. "Instead of taking action, their king sits idly and takes the bad advice of his cowardly army commander. Do you then expect the common people to risk their lives and try to recover the bodies on their own?"

Paltiel tried to catch Ishvi's eye to see if he needed help responding to the combined onslaught of his sister and brother-in-law, but Ishvi was looking at Rizpah, who generally tended to assume a low profile at our family meals and almost never got involved in our conversations.

"Tell them," he said.

"But you've ordered me not to . . . ," she stammered.

"It's all right," said Ishvi. "It's time."

Rizpah fidgeted uncomfortably and turned to face me, trying to draw encouragement from my loving eyes.

"The people of Jabesh Gilead will take the bodies down from the wall of Beth Shan and bring them back for burial in Israel."

We all stared at her wide-eyed.

"How do you know?" asked Merab.

"My late mother's friends heard it from . . ." Her delicate face turned red.

"Their clients," Ishvi completed her sentence.

I admired his matter-of-fact tone. No embarrassment, no contempt. Strangely, he seemed almost to take pride in the ancient profession of the good friends of his father's wife.

"Are you sure they'll actually do it?"

"My townspeople are prepared to give their lives for King Saul. They feel they've finally been granted the opportunity to repay him for the benevolence he showed them twenty-five years ago when he saved them from the hands of Nahash the Ammonite."

"Why didn't you tell us?" Merab asked, tears flowing from her eyes.

"The Philistines mustn't find out. The king ordered me to tell no one, not even the commander of the army."

"Especially not the commander of the army," said Merab. She turned to face our little brother and cast down her eyes. "Forgive me, Your Majesty," she whispered.

⊸✦⊶

Ishvi's self-confidence continued to grow. He needed the respect of his older sisters to believe that he was worthy of taking the place of his great father as ruler, and when we gave it to him wholeheartedly, he revealed his hidden talents and became a true king. When he gave his first speech, his voice was still too soft, and the heralds standing beside him on the stage were forced to repeat what he said word for word. But his next speeches were made in a voice almost as loud as Father's, and his eloquent words easily reached the ears of the most distant heralds, who passed them on further.

But my little brother wasn't only talented with words. His inclusion as part of our father's leadership team had taught him to rely on the efforts of others. Adriel took over the finances and managed to improve the tax collection process, Paltiel was in charge of relations with neighboring nations, and Abner son of Ner remained the commander of the army. Ishvi also gave roles to Merab and me, but we carried them out in secret so that it wouldn't be publicly known that the king was including women in his leadership team. And what was left for the king to do? To sit on the throne of judgment, to make speeches, to meet with envoys of other nations, and to make important decisions. And the people of Israel, what did they do? Well, the people of Israel—who had once looked dubiously at the young man who'd assumed the throne, asking one another with contempt, "How can this fellow save us?"

just as their parents had asked about the king's father in the early days of his reign—now asked God to guard their king from all evil and grant him a long life, so that he might continue to nurture the Kingdom of Israel.

But their prayers weren't answered.

⟨❧⟩

Rizpah arrived at the hour of the morning watch with ashes in her hair and wearing a torn nightgown. She was scratching at her forehead, pacing and wailing.

I didn't need to ask her what had happened, nor who did it to her.

I held her trembling body and laid her head in the crook of my neck. "Hush, Sister," I whispered. "Don't take this thing to heart."

I tried to take the advice I'd given her and attempted to get the terrible picture out of my head, but the image of the gigantic man abusing my soul sister wouldn't let go of me. I wiped the ashes from her hair with gentle strokes, hearing a distant voice, almost like an echo, repeating the words Father had said to me when the rumor of David's marriage to Ahinoam had reached his ears: "If you've conquered the king's wife, the throne is yours!"

Paltiel decided to wait until morning. We assumed that Ishvi would take the news much harder than Merab and Adriel, as their trust in Abner had already been shaken, while Ishvi still believed in him without qualification.

"The king will execute that traitor," Paltiel promised Rizpah.

"Abner will tell him that I seduced him!" she cried. "And who will the king believe? The commander of his army or the daughter of a whore?"

"He will believe his father's wife," Paltiel told her.

I looked at him in wonder and thought that a woman as flawed as I was, who dragged a bundle of mistakes and sins behind her, was undeserving of this pure man's seed. Perhaps that was the real reason I kept my body away from him, not my fading fidelity to my first husband.

But Paltiel's assessment was mistaken. Ishvi actually did believe Rizpah, and her claims were also supported by the testimonies of servants who had heard her screams, but the king decided not to execute Abner for treason, and instead banished him from his palace like a dog. "Father also forgave the rebels who tried to undermine his rule in the early days," said our good brother.

Merab reminded him that the people Father had forgiven were not rebels, but mere slanderers and naysayers, while a man who sleeps with the former king's wife is declaring that he sees himself as the next king. But Ishvi wasn't capable of killing any member of his nation, and certainly not his father's cousin.

"Your intuition about Abner was correct," Merab said to me.

It was the first time in many years that I'd heard a kind word from her. I felt a flutter of pride, but it disappeared in an instant. I knew that there'd been another time, long ago, when it had actually been her intuition that turned out to be correct. I couldn't speak about it out loud. The pain was still too great.

"I'm afraid of him," I whispered, uncertain as to whom I was referring.

"So am I," said Merab. "Abner is a dangerous man. How can our brother not see it?"

Ishvi was convinced that the situation with Abner had ended with his banishment from the palace. He appointed Adriel commander of the army and gave the responsibility for collecting taxes to two brothers, Baanah and Rekab, the sons of Rimmon the Beerothite, who had been the wheat assessors of Benjamin. His brief life experience had taught him that it was possible to recover from any kind of disaster, and that if we had managed to restore the kingdom after the great calamity, we would certainly be able to deal with Abner. No one, not even Merab or I, could conceive of the disaster that could be wrought by a vengeful man who had lost all his inhibitions.

The rumor spread quickly, and it terrified the nation more than any rumor that had come before.

"Abner son of Ner has defected and joined the son of Jesse."

"It can't be!" I cried. "There is no greater hatred in the world than that of David and Abner. Father first became suspicious of David only because of Abner. Had it not been for Abner, this all might have been avoided. I refuse to believe that they are now collaborating."

"Abner is helping David plan the war," Paltiel said, his voice breaking.

"What war?" Merab asked, appalled. "Judah received its independence from us on a silver platter. What more do they want?"

"They want it all," said Adriel. "Abner promised the son of Jesse that he had the power to turn all of Israel to him."

Ishvi collapsed onto his throne, looking around glassy-eyed. "I'm all alone," he mumbled to himself. "Everyone is defecting to the son of Jesse."

I hurried over to him, hugged his broad shoulders, and rested my cheek against his chest. "Ishvi, my brother," I whispered. "You are not alone. You have Adriel, Paltiel, Merab, and me, as well as Rizpah. Together we can defeat Abner son of Ner."

I was quiet for a moment, then I steeled myself and added, "And the son of Jesse."

⁂

But Ishvi died alone. In his sleep. His head was cut off by his two tax collectors while he took his afternoon nap. He was twenty years old when he died. All of Israel lamented the death of their young king, taken from them after only two years on the throne. David son of Jesse lamented for him as well, or so said his messengers when they came to Gibeah.

"David son of Jesse, King of Judah, sends his condolences to the Kingdom of Israel," they said. "The two contemptible murderers, Baanah and Rekab, the sons of Rimmon the Beerothite, brought him the king's severed head, but they performed the wicked deed on their own accord, without his instruction or prior knowledge. The king commanded that their hands and feet be cut off and that they be hung over the pool in Hebron. He despises traitors."

I didn't move a muscle. I felt nothing.

"We demand that our brother's severed head be returned to us," said Merab.

"That isn't possible," the messengers explained. "King David has already buried the head in Hebron. He made sure to perform a proper burial, as befits a righteous man."

"A king," I corrected them. "Ishvi son of Saul was a king."

Merab added, "Tell the son of Jesse that the people of Israel want to bury their king themselves."

⁂

The House of Saul had two grown daughters, two young sons, and two sons-in-law left. Five grandchildren. One wife.

We all swore to carry on for the sake of the nation of Israel. For the God of Israel. For Father.

"Saul, King of Israel, lives and breathes."

Word of our vow spread far and wide and imbued the people with the hope that, in spite of it all, there was still a king in Israel, or rather, two kings, Adriel the Meholathite and Paltiel son of Laish, and that in six years, when Armoni turned sixteen, they would give him the throne and crown him the next King of Israel, the third of the line of Saul.

We held on for three years against Abner son of Ner, our father's cousin, Israel's former army commander, who waged a bloody war against us at the head of the army of the sons of Zeruiah, which had become the army of Judah.

Everything collapsed around us. People were murdered, families were slaughtered, cities were destroyed, tribes surrendered. But we didn't break. We continued to rule in Gibeah and to defend what was left.

Every day a little less was left. Each day, more soldiers were killed, another city was lost, another tribe surrendered.

We had almost no soldiers left, nor cities, nor people.

We were left all alone.

The war between the house of Saul and the house of David lasted a long time
David grew stronger and stronger
While the house of Saul grew weaker and weaker.

And after three years, when the army of Judah conquered Gibeah, it was met with almost no resistance. We didn't have to wait for the messengers to bring us news to know what was going on. The sounds of horses galloping into the city and the cries of Benjaminites surrendering had reached us. We knew that the emissaries of David son of Jesse would soon arrive at the palace, demanding that we announce the surrender of the House of Saul. Deep in my heart, I had been waiting for it all to be over. I didn't know what would happen next, but at least we would be spared the uncertainty.

We decided that each family would remain in its own house. We were afraid that the enemy might still decide to use military force to break into the palace, and we thought it best for the invading soldiers to see three normal families with small children, not royalty that needed to be subjugated. Paltiel decided to take Micah, Jonathan's five-year-old son, into our home, so that we would also look like a normal family with a small child. His nursemaid came with him. He was unwilling to be separated from her.

Then we heard the screaming. For a moment I thought it was the maids surrendering, but it sounded much worse. Paltiel decided to step outside and look to see what was going on. I wanted to join him, but he wouldn't let me.

"Lock the door," he ordered. "Don't let anyone in."

The screams grew louder. Micah cried in terror. The nursemaid took him in her arms and tried to calm him, but he fought her and threw his little body in all directions.

After a short time, there was a loud knocking at the door. I hissed at the nursemaid to get under the bed with Micah, but the door was broken down before we had a chance to move.

It was Paltiel. "Quickly," he shouted, "we have to flee!"

His appearance petrified me. I couldn't move. He grabbed my arm and dragged me behind him. I felt no pain. The nursemaid ran after us with Micah. He continued to kick and scream, and she had to hold him tightly so he didn't slip out of her hands. We ran across the garden. The servants were running in every direction like madmen. Their voices sounded strangely hoarse to me. One wing of the palace was on fire. The servants trapped inside were screaming. Some of them jumped out the windows. They looked unreal, like ghosts. One maid threw herself off the roof and lay motionless on the ground below.

I yelled at Paltiel that we had to stop at the houses of Rizpah and Merab, but he dragged me on without speaking or stopping.

"I won't leave without my family!" I screamed.

He dug his nails into me. "Merab and Adriel are dead. I saw their bodies. Elhanan and Joel managed to take their little brothers and escape to Rizpah's house. I told them to run to the back gate. We must get there. It's our only chance."

It was as if he were speaking a foreign language. I understood nothing.

Suddenly I heard a bang behind me. Paltiel looked toward the sound and froze. I looked back, too. Micah was lying on the stones, blood trickling from his head. His nursemaid tried to get him up, but he didn't move.

Paltiel continued to drag me along, but I managed to release myself from his grip and reach Micah.

"He's dead!" Paltiel yelled. "We have to get to the back gate."

I leaned over the small body and heard a soft gurgling. I took him in my arms and continued running after Paltiel. I saw the back gate from a distance. There was no one there. The chariot hadn't waited for us. I stopped running and held Micah close.

"They're gone," I said to Paltiel. "We have no way to escape."

"Keep running!" he shouted. "Don't stop for a moment."

I suddenly realized that this was the day I would die. Twenty-eight years old, eight years older than Ishvi was when he died. I whispered a silent prayer to the God of Israel, asking that He allow me to do just one more thing before He took my soul: to save Micah, my brother Jonathan's son.

I kept running, through the gate and outside. The chariot was waiting on the other side of the wall, and standing beside it were Rizpah and the boys. They hadn't left without us.

Paltiel took the reins and we all crowded into the back. The chariot slowly made its way toward Gallim, the town where Laish, the father of my husband Paltiel, lived.

On the way, in flashes of clarity that broke through the dark fog I was in, I realized that I was the only remaining daughter of Saul and that the seven trembling children sitting around me in the chariot—the eldest was thirteen years old, and the youngest, who might never see the light of another day, was five—were the last of Saul's line. I also realized that, from that moment on, Rizpah and I had become the children's mothers, and Paltiel had become their father, and that we bore the responsibility for the survival of the House of Saul.

⟡

At night, after we reached the home of Laish, after we dressed Micah's wounds and fed the boys, I came to Paltiel's bed.

"My husband," I whispered.

He didn't move.

"I want to bear your child," I continued.

His limbs remained cold and rigid.

"Give me seed," I begged. "I want a son of your seed."

In the moonlight, I could see the wrinkles fade away from his forehead. He took me in his arms, and for one single, brief moment he was once again that long-haired, chiseled soldier I'd seen at the edge of the convoy.

He'd waited for me for fourteen years, twice as long as Jacob had waited for Rachel.

Seventeen

Micah remained paralyzed from the waist down, but he did not remain trapped in the house. The six other boys made sure to include him in their games and took him everywhere. They brought him down to the stream in a special wheelbarrow designed by the elderly Laish, Paltiel's father, and they took turns pushing him on the swing that Rizpah put up for them in the yard. They even managed to carry him up to the house that Paltiel built for them high up in the carob tree.

And when evening came, as I sat in the garden with Paltiel and Rizpah watching the boys at play, their good looks and great height announcing even from far away that they were sons of Saul, I marveled at the power of the flow of life, which is able to break through loss.

Even my will returned. For many years I had wanted nothing, but the day I lost my sister and we became refugees in Gallim was actually the day that I felt that distant craving knocking on the locked doors of my heart, demanding that I make room for it again. It began with the desire for a child and continued with other desires, which grew more frequent and imbued me with a lust for life the likes of which I hadn't known since I was a girl of fifteen. I wanted to play with the seven boys and to make Micah laugh, to chat with Rizpah, to be pretty, to eat, to drink, and to live. Most of all, I wanted to lie with Paltiel. Not only for his seed, but also to feel his arms around my neck, to take in the scent of his body, to hear his breath in my ears, to sense his love.

The image of my first husband grew hazier and hazier, and if it hadn't been for the many stories about him that reached Gallim, I might have been able to wipe him away entirely. I asked Paltiel to pass along no information about David son of Jesse. I don't care about his incredible military successes, or the palace he's built in Hebron, or how many more wives he has taken, or the names he's given his many children.

But rumors of his coronation ceremony reached me against my will. I couldn't avoid them. All across the land, people were talking about the celebrations for the restoration of the kingdom that were to be held in Hebron, at which representatives from all the tribes would swear their allegiance to David son of Jesse, who would no longer be the king of Judah alone, but the king of a united Israel.

And then Abner arrived.

More than five years had passed since Ishvi had banished him from the palace, and I never imagined that I would ever again see his thick figure with the cruel smile. He stood in the doorway and gave me a deep bow.

"Queen Michal, I'm glad to see that you are still the most beautiful woman in the world."

The paralyzing waves of terror returned all at once. I tried to control the trembling of my legs, but I knew that he could tell I was afraid. If he could terrorize me when I was a safe and protected princess in my father's palace, he would certainly be able to do so now.

My eyes hurt from the effort, but I didn't lower my gaze. "I am not a queen. I was once a princess, but now I am a farmer's wife."

He tried to enter, but I blocked the door with my body. "My husband is working out in the fields," I told him. "Come back in the evening."

His broad shoulder cleared a path between my body and the doorframe. He apologized for his lack of manners and stood across from Rizpah, who had come into the room at that very moment, carrying Micah and breathing hard from the effort. It wasn't easy for such a small woman to carry a crippled boy of seven on her own. The smile disappeared from Abner's face. He was unable to look at her directly. But she actually did manage to look at him.

"Abner son of Ner," she said, and I admired the restraint in her quiet voice. "To what do we owe the pleasure of receiving such an honored guest in our humble abode?"

"The home of two queens is no humble abode."

"Two queens?" She raised her eyebrows and set Micah down on the rug, his back against the wall. "I am the king's widow, and Michal is a princess. There are no queens here."

Micah examined Abner with his intelligent eyes and asked us who the guest was.

"He was once your grandfather's army commander," Rizpah said contemptuously in a teasing tone of voice. "And now he is the commander of the army of Judah."

"Joab son of Zeruiah is the commander of the army," Abner said, the sourness in his voice sending a rush of pleasure through my body and momentarily distracting me from the unceasing shaking of my legs. "And in three days, after our king's second coronation ceremony, he will be the commander of the army of the united Kingdom of Israel."

Then Abner looked back at me. "I've come to take you back to your husband."

Painful flashes of light flickered in my eyes. "My husband is here with me," I whispered.

"You've waited many years for your husband to fulfill his promise and take you back."

"My husband is Paltiel son of Laish."

Abner looked over at Rizpah and then at the ground. "Our king will marry you as well. It's as I said, there are two queens in this house."

I collapsed onto the rug. My teeth were chattering. I couldn't see a thing. My trembling hands groped in the darkness and found Micah. I hugged his shoulders, trying to draw strength from the heat of his body.

But Rizpah did not lose her wits. Her clear voice rang out through the room, increasing my adoration of this gentle woman, who could transform herself into a lioness when she needed to. "If you try to drag us out to your carriage against our will, we'll scream as loud as we can, and the residents of Gallim will come and see for themselves how David son of Jesse takes his women by force."

"My carriage? What are you thinking, my queen? A golden chariot awaits you outside the house. You're welcome to look and see it for yourself. Beautiful queens cannot travel in a simple carriage. And as for the residents of Gallim, they are already gathering around the chariot, eagerly awaiting your arrival. This town has never had such an honor before."

"Abner son of Ner," I said, able to speak, though my teeth were still chattering, "do you not fear our God?"

He rolled his eyes. "My entire life is dedicated to His people, Israel. When God chose your father, I served him with devotion and was prepared to give my life for him. He didn't have a more loyal servant than me. But when God rejected Saul and chose David, I followed God's will. The man chosen by God is my king."

The words "God rejected Saul" revolted me. I couldn't believe that people were saying that about Father. But Rizpah, who was more well versed in the Judean tales than I was, took the opportunity to run outside and call for help. Abner showed no concern about her flight and continued to calmly describe David's astounding successes, how he was going from strength to strength, and his plans to conquer all the lands in the region and turn the Kingdom of Israel into a power without rival.

Suddenly, the sounds of screaming pierced the air. I raced for the door, but guards appeared to block my way. From where I stood, I could see Rizpah being dragged to the chariot by soldiers. Mephiel and Armoni screamed at the tops of their lungs while the soldiers held them back at a distance from their mother. Then I saw Paltiel. Two armed soldiers were standing on either side of him, holding his arms and not letting him move. He stood opposite me and wept. I'd never seen him cry before. Even at the worst moments, when everyone around him had broken down and collapsed, he always kept his cool, never shedding a tear, like on the day Gibeah was conquered.

And now there he was, my strong husband, weeping.

The two guards bowed deeply and asked me to accompany them to the chariot. Paltiel's sobbing grew louder. The people of Gallim watched in horror. Many of them were wiping tears from their eyes. I looked back at Abner. "Let me take my leave from my husband," I said, "and I promise to get into the chariot without resisting."

Abner spat scornfully that my husband was King David son of Jesse, but that he had no problem with my exchanging a few words with the whimpering farmer who'd once been an officer in the king's army and was now a blubbering female. The soldiers let go of me and let me approach him. Silence fell all around us. Everyone watched me with bated breath.

I came near to my husband and buried my head in his chest and put my arms around his waist. His hands were shaking, but he was able to hug me back. "I'll return to you," I told him. "David son of Jesse owes me his life. He'll release me. Rizpah will return to her boys. It will be his reward for the benevolence I showed him. I'm sure of it. Besides—" I ran my lips over his chiseled cheek and put them to his ear. "Besides," I whispered quietly, so that no one else could hear, "your child is sprouting in my womb."

As I got in and sat beside Rizpah in the chariot, he was still frozen, but as the chariot began moving, he gave a great shudder and began to walk after us.

Weeping as he went, my husband followed me, **weeping as he went.**

All along the road people gaped at the strange sight of a golden chariot riding along in regal splendor, accompanied by the king's horsemen, and behind them a tall, long-haired man walking alone and wailing.

Abner son of Ner, who was riding on his horse alongside us, called for the coachman to speed up, but it did no good. My husband ran after us and managed to catch up.

When we reached the village of Bahurim at the outskirts of Judah, Abner lost his temper. He stopped his horse, jumped off, and attacked Paltiel with his large body.

"Go back home!" he yelled.

My husband did not fall. I stuck my head out the window and looked at him. He looked back at me. The chariot drove on.

That was the last time I ever saw him.

Eighteen

Fifteen years ago, I met a ruddy boy with beautiful eyes. An aura of light surrounded his curly hair. Everyone who saw him was enchanted. Some were afraid. I loved him.

Now that boy is a man in his prime. Life has turned us into enemies. He is the reason my father is dead, my mother is dead, my five siblings are dead, my brother's little boy is crippled, and our kingdom is destroyed.

Do I still love him?

His red curls have faded, the wrinkles around his eyes have deepened, his jawline has hardened, but his charm is ever present, perhaps even stronger. I can see the enchantment in the faces of his ministers and advisors. I can feel it inside of me.

Did the man I once loved plan his betrayal of my father, or did things just become complicated and get out of hand? That question has plagued me ever since the battle of Mount Gilboa. At times, I believed it had been merely bad luck that sent David down a slippery slope from which he could not return, dragging him into the army of the enemy. At other times, I was certain it had all been carefully planned, step by step: playing music in the palace, marrying the princess, appearing before the people, defecting to the Philistine army, the war, the occupation, the coronation.

And now, as I stand before him, the question still nags at me, but I know that whatever the answer, he still makes my heart flutter.

"My queen." His voice is the same, but it's firmer now. "I've brought you back to me, just as I promised."

He rises from his seat and holds out his hands. I recoil instinctively. He puts his arm around my shoulders and says in a festive tone to his ministers and advisors, "Bow to Queen Michal, daughter of King Saul, anointed of God."

They bow before me as one, their foreheads touching the ground. No one has ever bowed to me this way. David notices my embarrassment and tightens his grip. "My queen," he whispers, "I'll come to you tonight."

⚜

There are so many questions I want to ask him, but the wall I've built around myself might crumble if I do. I must stay close to the window and harden my body. I mustn't look at him. "Return me to my husband!"

He is quiet, but a moment later I hear his firm voice behind me. "I am your husband. I betrothed you with a hundred Philistine foreskins."

I turn to face him. His expression is serious, devoid of any smile.

"My husband is Paltiel son of Laish. Return me to him! Return Rizpah to her sons! That will be my reward for saving your life. I will ask you for nothing more. I swear it."

"Jonathan is the one who saved my life. His messengers brought me regular reports on your father's movements. If it hadn't been for his warnings, the soldiers would have trapped me. I will never forget what he did for me."

His words make my skin crawl. I examine his face in astonishment, looking for a hint that he is joking. His expression remains serious, though, and he says in a tone of appeasement that he feels no ill will toward me. True, it was my fault that he lost my father's affection, but he forgave me for that long ago, and now that he has fulfilled his promise to bring me back to him, we can put the past behind us and revive our marriage.

The tears burst out of me all at once, along with all those questions I swore I wouldn't ask: Why didn't you give me your seed? Why did you marry other women? Why did you give them your seed? Why did you wait so many years to bring me back?

He comes closer, wrapping his arms around my waist, looking into my eyes, and he answers my questions one by one. For a long time, he had been looking forward to the moment when he could bring me back, but by fleeing from him when we were making appearances before the people, I showed him that I couldn't handle the difficult conditions of the road. Only now, as a king, could he finally grant me a life of luxury befitting a refined princess like myself. He remembers the promise he made before our marriage—he always has—but our lives didn't go according to plan, and the terrible loneliness forced on him during his long years as a fugitive led him into the arms of other women. And as to the hardest question of them all, he wishes he'd had a son with me. He would have made him the crown prince. But God prevented me from becoming pregnant. In spite of my barrenness, however, I would always be the wife of his youth, his favorite.

Just as suddenly as my tears had burst forth, laughter erupts out of me. At first it is a quiet laughter of sharp broken breaths, but by the end it has become a roiling wave that washes over my body and makes my shoulders shake. My entire body takes part in this laughter. "Barren? Me? What are you thinking? My womb is bearing fruit even now. The son of my husband Paltiel is sprouting within me."

He looks down and gives my belly a glassy-eyed look. "I mustn't come to you. I will make Rizpah my wife. You will remain a celibate widow till the day you die. That is the law."

"Return me to my husband!"

"If you go back to him, you would be sealing his fate. Anyone who lies with the king's wife is punished by death. That is the law."

He turns his back on me and strides to the door. "I remember the devotion of your youth, how as a bride you loved me, and I will allow you to raise the bastard child in my palace. But you will have to hide him. If it becomes known that the king's wife has given birth to another man's child, I will be forced to banish him, or perhaps worse. That is the law."

⌁

That very night, the king's servants came to take Rizpah. She followed them without resistance. She left in the evening and returned in the morning. "He won't come to me again," she said upon her return. "I promised to sit beside him on the stage tomorrow during the coronation ceremony, and in return he will permit me to visit my children once a month."

I looked at her imploringly.

"I tried," she said, her eyes welling up. "I told him that if he would permit you to visit Paltiel, you would also sit beside him tomorrow for all to see, but it didn't work. He forbids you to leave the palace."

I watched the coronation ceremony through the window. The crowds filled the square in front of the palace and the streets all around it, watching in silence as the representatives of the tribes swore allegiance to the king. I focused on the delegates from Ephraim and Manasseh, and even more so on the representative of Benjamin, trying to detect signs of pain or rage on their faces, but their expressions remained calm and serene. The prophet Gad anointed the new king's forehead, and the entire nation cried in a single voice, "Long live David son of Jesse, King of Israel!"

There was no apparent difference between the tribes of Rachel and the tribes of Leah. All were merry on this day of celebration. I recalled the things Merab had said about the nation's short memory, and I wanted to jump out of the window and reproach the nation for its forgetfulness and ingratitude, but I bit my lip and continued to look out in silence. Only when Abner son of Ner handed the crown to the prophet Gad was I no longer able to hold back, and I cursed Abner that he should die by the sword, like Father, but not in a glorious war and not at the hands of an enemy, but rather out in the fields, alone, like a dog, at the hands of someone he trusted.

That wish was granted in full.

Only after Abner's death did the existence of the vicious games in which soldiers from Judah fought soldiers from Benjamin become publicly known. The people of Israel were shocked to hear how the victims of these contests, euphemistically called "Let the Young Men Play Before Us," were buried surreptitiously so that no one would find out how they had died. The terrible secret might have remained hidden for much longer, but unfortunately, or perhaps fortunately, no fewer than twenty-four soldiers were killed in one of the tournaments, half from Benjamin and half from Judah. Asahel son of Zeruiah decided to call off the games and eliminate their creator, Abner son of Ner. But Abner, who was more experienced, struck first and put his sword through him. When Joab and Abishai found out, they avenged the death of their younger brother by killing Abner in the fields. David tore his clothes and ordered the people to wear sackcloth and ashes in mourning for the hero Abner son of Ner, who had died at the hands of villains, but the people of Israel knew that the king was secretly happy to be rid of a scoundrel like him, whose betrayal of the previous king had proved that he couldn't be trusted.

I thanked God for His benevolence and asked that He continue to show me grace by turning David's heart to my favor, so that I might give birth to my son in Gallim and raise him with Paltiel, my husband. But this prayer was not answered.

My only son, Nebat, was born in Hebron, far away from his father.

⤛❦⤜

Paltiel was working in the fields when he received the news of the birth of his son. He got on his wagon and began to ride for Hebron, but the king's soldiers stopped him as he was about to leave Gallim.

"I have a son!" Paltiel shouted. "I must get to my wife, Michal daughter of Saul."

"Michal daughter of Saul is the king's wife," the soldiers replied. "And she has not given birth to any son."

"Let me go to the palace," Paltiel begged.

The soldiers brought him back to Gallim, and his son remained in Hebron. Paltiel never got to see Nebat's face, hear his cries, take pleasure in his laughter and his first steps. He never got to hear Nebat call him "Father."

But that word was often on my son's tongue. I spoke it to him from the moment of his birth, as if he were growing up with his father and seeing him every day. I believed that David would eventually acquiesce to my pleas and permit me to go home. But the days went by, and Paltiel only got to know his son through the letters I sent him with Rizpah once a month. I told him everything: when Nebat got his first tooth, how many words he knew, which songs he liked, and whether he had gotten used to the city of Jebus, now called Jerusalem, to which we had moved from Hebron after the king declared it the new capital of his kingdom. I tried to tell Paltiel different things in each letter, but I always ended with the same words: "Stay strong, my husband. Soon we will meet again." Paltiel always ended his letters in the same manner as well—a heartbreaking vow of love that made my stomach clench and brought tears to my eyes. But he grew more and more desperate with each letter. "I'm prepared to give my life for your release," he wrote in one of his last letters. "But I cannot die before I see you one last time. Have you done everything you can, my beloved? Is there nothing more to do?"

This letter upset me more than any of the previous ones had and caused me to burst into the throne room without any forethought or planning.

"Do you still have need for the daughter of the previous king to affirm your status through her presence in the palace?" I screamed at David in front of his slaves and advisors. "When will you feel secure enough on your throne to release me from my prison?"

David nodded at his servants, who exchanged looks with one another and hurried to seize hold of me.

"You are not a prisoner," I heard the clear voice of the king call after me as they dragged me out. "You are a queen."

Desperation led me to conceive of a bold plan. I was certain that Rizpah would join me, but when I told her what I was planning she beseeched me not to go through with it.

"When David smells a threat he becomes dangerous," she said.

"What choice do we have? Nebat is four years old already, and his father has never seen him. We must take advantage of this opportunity. All the tribes of Israel will be in Jerusalem tomorrow. David won't be able to ignore my distress if he knows that the nation supports me. It's time to act. It's now or never."

"The nation is fickle," warned Rizpah. "It cannot be relied upon."

"Then go sit on the stage tomorrow with Ahinoam, Abigail, Haggith, and Abital." The names of David's four other wives rushed out of my mouth in a single breath. "I can carry out the plan myself."

"You've forgotten our king's newest asset," Rizpah answered coldly. "Maakah, the daughter of the King of Geshur."

⤞⤝

The masses began arriving in Jerusalem that same day, and by the next there was no empty space in the city, not even in its most remote streets. All the tribes of Israel wanted to watch with their own eyes as the Ark of the Covenant was carried by the priests into the new city. In the months that preceded this event, the king's scribes had been spreading a new lie, claiming that the ark had been in the hands of the Philistines ever since the defeat at Ebenezer in the days of Eli the Priest and that it had been taken to Edom a few years ago, after the Philistines decided that it cursed whoever held it. Only now, so they said, after dozens of years in captivity, had David managed to conquer Edom and free the ark from its captors. I told Rizpah confidently that no one would believe the story, that the nation of Israel would never forget that it was Father who liberated the ark from the Philistines in the early days of his reign. But deep inside I was afraid the nation's short memory would disappoint me yet again.

I watched out the window, waiting impatiently for David to get to the stage and begin his speech, but he was dancing wildly before the wagon carrying the ark, showing no sign that he would stop anytime soon. The dancing girls waved cypress branches over his head and shook their cymbals, and the crowds skipped and danced to the music of the lyres, harps, and drums. I had to admit that this celebration surpassed the ones that were held in Father's day.

"Why are you wearing a new dress?" Nebat asked me. He wasn't used to seeing me in new clothes.

I picked him up and carried him to the window so that we could look outside together. "Do you like the dress?"

He shrugged. "It's too sparkly."

I was moved by the thought that the first king's modesty had been transmitted to his little grandson. "I'll only wear it one more time," I whispered. "Do you know when?"

He looked at me curiously.

"When we meet Father."

I waited a few moments longer, and when I saw that David had no intention of climbing onto the stage I set Nebat down on the bed and went out to the stairs.

"Mother!" he called after me. "Where are you going?"

"To persuade the king to let us go home."

My limbs felt oddly heavy. I nearly retreated, but I managed to catch my breath and walk outside. Suddenly I felt a heavy hand on my shoulder, followed by a second one. The guards were holding me and wouldn't let me go. David was dancing right in front of me, but his back was to me.

"David!" I called. "David!"

He stopped dancing and looked backward, a self-satisfied expression filling his sweaty face. *Release her*, he mouthed to the guards, and spread his arms out. "Queen Michal, I'm so glad you have come to celebrate with us."

He turned to the herald. "All hail my wife, Queen Michal, daughter of King Saul, anointed of God."

The herald turned to the crowd and called out, "Long live Queen Michal, the wife of the King, daughter of King Saul, anointed of God!"

The people replied as one: "Long live Queen Michal, the wife of the King, daughter of King Saul, anointed of God!"

I turned to face the cheering crowd. My heart almost leapt out through the open neck of my dress, but I succeeded in focusing my mind on the words I'd spent the past day memorizing.

"I am not the king's wife!" I called out to the crowd. "I am the wife of Paltiel son of Laish."

The people closest to me heard my cry. I could see it in their eyes.

"I have given birth to his son," I said, straining my voice as much as I could, hoping what I was saying would be heard far away. "My son and I are captives in this palace. Help me persuade the king to let us go."

I turned back to David. He was watching me with cold, piercing eyes. I recognized that look. I was overcome with terror, but I didn't stop yelling: "Help me persuade the king to free my son and me!"

David walked over to the herald and whispered something in his ear. The herald nodded and turned to the crowd. I was paralyzed by shock. Did David want what I had said to be heard?

The herald gave a signal to the heralds positioned farther away and yelled out, "Queen Michal mocks the King of Israel for his dancing!"

All the other heralds repeated after him, "Queen Michal mocks the King of Israel for his dancing!"

"That isn't true!" I screamed. "All I want is my freedom!"

The herald listened intently and then called to the others, "Michal daughter of Saul says that a king who skips and dances with slaves reveals himself to the nation as an undignified and vulgar fellow!"

The other heralds repeated, word for word, "Michal daughter of Saul says that a king who skips and dances with slaves reveals himself to the nation as an undignified and vulgar fellow!"

The people standing in front of me, who had heard what I'd said, stared at me in silence, while those farther away began shouting angrily. I couldn't see the expressions on their faces, but their cries did reach my ears. They hated me.

David held his hand up. "Hear the king's response!" called the herald, and the crowd hushed at once.

"I am dancing before my God," David declared with a smile, "the one who has chosen me and appointed me ruler over Israel. I am most certainly willing to degrade myself for the God of Israel, but dancing with slaves is actually a great honor for me."

The heralds cried out the king's response as loud as they could, and the crowd brayed with laughter.

"A greater honor than dancing with the daughter of Saul!" someone shouted.

I hadn't heard him, but the heralds loudly repeated the joke, and the growing laughter of the crowd pierced my ears.

In the days that followed, the entire land spoke of Michal daughter of Saul, who had tried to humiliate the humble king by mocking his delightful simple ways. "She will not have a son until the day she dies," people gloated. "That will be her punishment."

And in all of Israel, there was not one person to be found who would be so bold as to remind the nation that this princess, whose haughtiness all were now denouncing, was the daughter of King Saul, the most humble man who ever lived, who had been so harshly criticized during his reign for his excessive humility.

Rizpah tried to console me with the hope that out of the strong something sweet might come. "The people hate you so much that they might demand that David banish you from the palace. You'll be able to go back to Paltiel, I'm certain of it. In the meantime, keep writing to him. Your letters are the only way he can get through each month."

I asked myself despairingly how many more letters I'd have to write him. Two weeks later, when Rizpah returned from Gallim with her clothing torn and her hair unkempt, I knew that letter had been my last.

⬥⬥⬥

My husband Paltiel died alone in the fields. No one saw who stabbed the sword through his heart. No one heard his cries. He was forty years old when he died. The days of his life had been few and difficult.

"Father is dead," I told Nebat.

"Are you going to die, too?"

I was standing at the window. For a moment, I had the urge to throw myself out and join the ones I had loved and lost. "No," I said, clutching Nebat to my breast. "I won't die. I have something to live for."

"How did Father die?"

"They murdered him."

"Who murdered him?"

I let go of Nebat and ran outside, my legs galloping of their own accord, as if I were being blown forward by a storm. It was raining. Lightning flashed, and thunder exploded all around me. I burst into the throne room, wet and leaving muddy footprints on the gleaming rug. The servants tried to stop me, but I reached the platform before any of them even had a chance to move.

"The blood of my husband, Paltiel, cries out to you from the ground!"

David fixed his eyes on me. There was neither contempt nor hatred in them, only compassion.

"You are just like your father. He blamed me for every tragedy that befell him also."

He got up from his throne and came down to where I was standing. I wanted to pounce on him and wring his neck with my fingers, but my feet would not obey me.

"Man of blood," I managed to whisper.

"I did not kill your husband, God forbid."

"You ordered your agents to kill him, just as you ordered your two servants to murder my brother Ishvi in his sleep years ago. I know you will send your emissaries to Gallim again to murder the seven boys as well, and that you are also scheming to murder my only son, Nebat."

He stared at me in shock, paralyzed by the enormity of what I was saying. "Have you gone mad with grief?"

"Order your scribes to spread the rumor," I said with scorn. "The people of Israel will surely believe that I have become a mad princess, just as they believed I was mocking your dancing at the celebration of the Ark of the Covenant."

He walked over to me and ran the back of his hand down my cheek. I hated myself for the way his touch made me shiver.

"I apologize for what happened, but I had no choice. I trusted you. I thought you'd come to express your support, but you tried to incite the people against me." He paused and then added softly, "I am willing to have the seven sons of Saul join me in the palace. You'll be able to watch over them and raise them together with your son. We'll tell people he is one of Merab's so that he isn't harmed. The boys will be under my protection. No one will touch a hair on their heads, I promise you."

"Your promises are worthless to me. You promised not to take another wife. You promised to give me your seed. You promised to come back for me right away. You promised not to take revenge on Father. You break your promises as if they were nothing but foolish prattle."

"What can I do to make you believe me?"

"Swear to the God of Israel that you will not kill off the descendants of Saul."

Before I could even finish, David got down on his knees and placed his hands on his heart. "I swear to the God of Israel that I will not kill off the descendants of Saul."

"That isn't enough. I want you to swear before Seraiah, your scribe, and command him to write down your vow in a scroll."

A few moments later, Seraiah entered the throne room and sat at the desk. He spread open a scroll in front of him, dipped a feather in ink, and nodded to signal that he was ready. David repeated his vow slowly, and Seraiah took down every word: "I, David son of Jesse, swear to the God of Israel that I will not kill off the descendants of Saul."

I thought that the ceremony was over, but then David glanced at me for a moment, closed his eyes in concentration, and added, "And also that I will not wipe out his name from his father's family."

Before leaving the throne room I audaciously asked David why he had added the last part of the vow. His reply astounded me. "That was the vow composed by your father."

I couldn't believe my ears. "Father asked you to swear not to kill off his descendants? When was this?"

"After I fled the palace, Jonathan still believed that the rift between your father and me could be mended. He persuaded him to meet me in a cave in En Gedi and made him promise not to harm me. The meeting was kept completely secret. Even those who had accompanied him thought he'd gone into the cave because even kings have to answer the call of nature. I tried to convince him that I had no intention of robbing Jonathan of the throne, but he forbade me from returning to the palace. Then, before we parted ways, he told me that he knew I would be the next king of Israel and that he wanted me to swear to him not to kill off his descendants. I repeated the vow to him exactly as he had phrased it, and that was the last time I ever saw him. Jonathan tried to arrange other meetings from time to time, but we both knew it was pointless."

David's story managed to arouse within my frozen heart a warmth that I didn't think I could ever feel for him again. "I believe you," I whispered. "Have your slaves bring the seven sons of Saul here. I know you won't harm them."

⇌

Armoni and Mephiel were the first to climb out of the chariot, and they bent down to hug their mother. The last time I'd seen them, they had been boys of fifteen, and now, at age twenty, they towered at least a head taller than everyone around them. Elhanan and Joel had also become tall, powerful men, and even Asahel and Benjamin, who hadn't yet finished growing, were impressive. Only Micah remained short. His legs, which had barely grown since he was five years old, dangled over the edge of the three-wheeled wheelbarrow like two thin sticks.

"That's the last wheelbarrow Father built for Micah," I told little Nebat, who was staring at his new large family with a gleam in his eyes. "Remember I told you about the wheelbarrows Father built him every year?"

Before I had a chance to show the boys to their rooms, the servants summoned us to appear before the king. We walked to the throne room, and I was glad to see that Micah was able to propel the wheelbarrow by himself. His strong arms turned the wheels effortlessly, and he steered it using the muscles of his shoulders and upper back.

I stood before David and introduced the seven boys in order of age. They all bowed and thanked him for his grace. For a moment, I recalled a distant image of a young musician who was invited to dinner at the palace being introduced to the royal family, but I managed to push it away. My life experience had taught me to subdue memories rather than allow them to drag me into pain that I could not bear.

I saw that David was also surprised by the height of the boys, some of whom he'd known as small children, but he did not share his feelings, instead giving each of them a restrained smile. His face softened only when I introduced Micah.

"Forgive me, I cannot bow to you, Your Majesty," said Micah.

Rather than replying, David got up from his throne, came down from the platform, and leaned over him.

Micah stared at him in surprise. "Thank you, Your Majesty, for bringing us to your palace to eat at your table."

The king reached out a hand to the twelve-year-old boy's soft face and ran it over his cheeks and hair.

"Your father was a good friend of mine," said David, "the best friend I ever had."

Nineteen

Two servants and one cook were the only people who ever set foot in our home, which became known as the "House of Saul" and was located in its own wing of the palace. We lived in utter solitude, never taking part in the lively social life that surrounded us. When I ran into David's wives, which happened only rarely, I would exchange a few words of greeting with them, glance at their children, and hurry back to my family. Abigail was the only one of the wives who made me curious. During our brief conversations, I got the impression that she was a strong and interesting woman. The other wives seemed like a boring herd of women with no personality, and I could barely tell them apart. Every so often a new girl would join the band, looking lost and scared for a few weeks, but in a matter of months she would be carrying her pregnant belly with pride and holding her head up high, and she would be staring down the next girl with a mixture of contempt and loathing. The princes were quite dull as well. At first, when I could still tell them apart, I noted to myself that Amnon, Ahinoam's son, the eldest, seemed pathetic, while it was actually Absalom, the third son, the grandson of the King of Geshur, who looked like a king. But after the birth of Shephatiah, the sixth son, I lost interest and told Rizpah with great satisfaction that none of them, not even Absalom, had inherited even a smidgeon of their father's exalted charm.

Our isolation, which was so well suited to two tired women who'd had enough of life and only wanted rest, was agony for the eight effervescent boys blossoming into young men. They especially missed the sweet encounters with girls their own age that had been such a part of their previous lives. They understood that the two of us, as the wives of the king, were required to remain inside the palace, and since they were noble and kind, it had never occurred to them to leave us alone in Jerusalem and return home without us, but they asked, at the very least, to come and go as they pleased, to wander the streets and markets, to meet friends in Gallim, and to dance with the girls out in the fields and vineyards on holidays and festivals.

But David firmly refused. "I am responsible for their safety," he declared, describing for me at great length the many terrible dangers to Saul's descendants that lurked outside the palace gates. At first I accepted his view, but as the days went by, I was increasingly tortured by feelings of guilt. I wasn't certain that I had done the right thing by bringing the boys here. The palace was the safest place for them, but is danger not preferable to life in prison?

Many months went by before David found time for an audience with me.

"You are responsible for the boys' safety only inside the palace," I told him. "I release you of any responsibility for their safety outside."

"You cannot release me from my vow. I swore to protect them."

"You swore not to exterminate them."

"They are under my protection. If even a hair falls from their heads, I won't be able to face your father's memory."

"But you allow your sons and daughters to go outside."

"Only on rare occasions, and only under heavy guard."

"Our boys will also leave only occasionally and only accompanied by guards. They are asking to go to Gallim for the upcoming Festival of Harvest so they can dance with the girls in the fields. Micah will join them. The Festival of Harvest is enjoyable even for those who cannot dance."

David fidgeted uncomfortably and ordered his slaves and advisors out. "I don't want to upset you," he said, "but you must know the reason for my absolute refusal."

His tone frightened me. I realized there was a threat involved.

"The descendants of Saul face graver dangers than my own sons. Your father's enemies have been popping up everywhere, not only in Judah, waiting for a chance to take revenge on his descendants."

"Who would want to take revenge against the descendants of Saul?" I asked in shock.

"Refugees from Nob, the city of priests your father destroyed."

Waves of fury flooded over me. "The army of Edom, led by Doeg, destroyed Nob!" I cried. "Everybody knows that."

"There are other stories."

"My father wouldn't even destroy his enemies. His critics railed against him for letting the Amalekites live. Who would believe that he destroyed a city in Israel?"

"It's what people have been saying about him," he said, sounding puzzled, as if he were astonished by the stories as much as anyone.

"You are the one who has destroyed a city in Israel, not my father."

"Me?!"

"When you fled the palace, you wanted to prove to Achish, King of Gath, that you had cut off all ties to your nation and your tribe so he would trust you and grant you refuge in his land, so you destroyed the towns of the southern desert of Judah on his behalf."

"Do you believe that?"

"It's what people have been saying about you." I said it in the same tone of voice that he had used.

"I destroyed the Amalekites that your father let live, and since I'd left no remnant of them, I was able to use the opportunity to tell Achish that the dead were members of my own tribe. But the people of Israel know the truth."

"They know the truth about my father as well. The false tales his enemies are spreading about him will be scattered by the winds. They will never stand the test of time."

"Those eight boys may not leave the palace," David said, ending the discussion.

When I recounted the details of the argument and its sad outcome to Rizpah, she turned white with fury. I had never seen her so angry before. "David plays innocent, but the ones spreading the monstrous tales about your father are his own scribes. They just haven't made up their minds yet whether to portray Saul as a weak and cowardly king or as a cruel and bloodthirsty one. On the one hand, they say that he failed to destroy his enemies and that he didn't die a hero's death on the battlefield but rather fell on his own sword like a coward. And on the other hand, they spread rumors that he was constantly throwing his spear at anyone he didn't like, including, of course, his innocent musician, David son of Jesse. The first time I heard that one I thought it was laughable, for everyone knows that King Saul was the greatest warrior in Israel. If he'd thrown his spear at his musician even once, David son of Jesse would have been skewered to the wall, and all the calamities that have befallen us would have been prevented. But Merab was right. The nation does have a short memory. Repeat a story enough times, and, better yet, write it down in the book of chronicles, and it becomes reality. So, now David is trying to convince you that refugees from Nob wish to take revenge on our sons!? He himself has countless bitter enemies who would love nothing more than to hang his children from the pillories. Because, unlike King Saul, who only fought those who attacked us and never killed women or children, David conquers peaceful nations and orders his army commander not to leave alive even a single dog pissing on the wall. He tortures his enemies with saws and iron picks and draws lots to decide who will live and who will die. After he conquered Moab, he ordered all its people to lie down on the ground, and he measured them off with a cord. Every two lengths he put to death, and he spared the third so he would have slaves to pay him tribute. And that's nothing compared to what he did to the people of Aram-Damascus. David's sons are the ones in real danger of blood vengeance, not ours."

I knew where she had gotten all her detailed information about David's vicious conquests. Micah liked to ride his wheelbarrow all around the palace and eavesdrop on the conversations of servants and members of the royal family. He heard everything and forgot nothing. I had no interest in this gossip—I wanted to hear nothing of David's deeds, good or bad—but Rizpah and the boys were captivated by it, and they encouraged Micah to continue to carry out his spy missions.

"Then what could the real reason for David's decision possibly be?" I asked.

"He is afraid of our boys," Rizpah said confidently.

"Why would David be afraid of gentle boys who are only allowed to study languages, read books, play music, ride horses, and listen to the latest gossip their crippled brother brings them?"

"David knows that if the people of Israel got to know Saul's descendants up close and compared them to his own sons, the future of his dynasty would be in danger." She glanced at me hesitantly and cast down her eyes. "And I can think of another reason for him to keep our boys locked up. He doesn't want them to marry and give birth to sons and daughters. He cannot destroy us by the sword, but no one would be able to lay the blame on him if we just naturally disappeared."

Her words filled me with dread. "What is your basis for saying this?"

"No one in the world plans his moves in advance as cleverly as David does."

That's what Rizpah thought, but eight years later she would come to realize that there were two people who planned their moves in advance even more cleverly than David.

Twenty

Bathsheba was the first to arrive at the palace, and Ahithophel followed her. They seemed equally dangerous at the beginning. Only after the rebellion was over, when Ahithophel had strangled himself to death while Bathsheba returned to the palace in full force, did we come to understand that the granddaughter surpassed her grandfather.

Bathsheba entered the palace with the usual feminine ploys, and while we found them interesting, we didn't perceive them as anything out of the ordinary, and we had no idea that they were about to shake up our lives and change the balance of power in the king's court.

"David's new wife is no girl," Rizpah said, trying to draw me into the discussion of Micah's latest gossip. He was already twenty years old at that time, but his handicap made it possible for him to go on eavesdropping around the palace uninterrupted; he took advantage of the fact that people tend to regard the disabled as mindless creatures and allow themselves to talk about anything they want in their presence, as if they were nothing but air. His great intelligence and terrific memory helped him find out everything. Nothing remained hidden from him. The isolation that had been forced upon us made us all the more dependent upon his discoveries, and his spying methods became increasingly sophisticated.

I reminded Rizpah that I had no interest in hearing the stories of David's new wives or of his old ones, and I remained indifferent as I continued embroidering the coat of many colors I was making for my son, Nebat.

"This isn't just routine gossip." Rizpah laughed. "This woman has done to David exactly what I did to your father."

Needless to say, I couldn't remain indifferent to a teasing comment like that. I put down my embroidery and looked at her intently.

"Eliam, the father of Bathsheba, and Uriah the Hittite, her husband, are two of David's heroes, and they live just opposite the palace. When they were called up to fight in the ongoing war against Ammon, she began walking around naked on the roof of her house at the precise time that the king liked to step out to the palace roof for some fresh Jerusalem air following his afternoon nap. Her persistence paid off, and eventually she received the coveted invitation for a onetime visit to the royal bedroom. But Bathsheba had come to the palace to stay, and less than a month later, the king was told that she was carrying his son."

"You think she planned the pregnancy?"

"That's how I snared your father, and that's how Tamar, the matriarch of David's line, snared Judah. Since the dawn of time, it's been the way women have snared husbands they had a hard time getting by conventional means."

"But your mother's prostitute friends made sure you encountered Father when you were in your fertile time, while Bathsheba was trying to seduce David over a long period. She couldn't have known when he would invite her to his bed."

"You're right, but don't forget that Micah is no expert on women's matters. Perhaps Bathsheba only walked around the roof naked on her fertile days."

"And what did David do when he found out she was pregnant?"

"He brought Uriah home from the battlefield right away."

"That's not the move I would have expected."

"Uriah hadn't been home for three months, ever since the war broke out. David wanted him to sleep with Bathsheba so that when he found out she was pregnant he would believe the child was his."

"But you told me that David eventually married her."

"Because Uriah wouldn't sleep with Bathsheba when he came home. Or so she says."

"So what did David do?"

Rizpah looked at me intently. "You know the answer."

"He killed Uriah?"

"David never kills with his own hands. He sends people to do the unpleasant task for him, while he tears his clothes in grief and composes heartbreaking lamentations in memory of the dead."

We were sure that the death of Uriah the Hittite would be the end of the story of David and Bathsheba, that the ambitious woman who had fulfilled her dream of marrying the king would give birth to her prince and live happily ever after in the palace. But before long we came to see that the story was more tangled than we'd thought. When Micah first told us, we couldn't believe our ears.

"Bathsheba isn't pregnant?" we asked in astonishment. "Are you sure?"

"The king's wives hate her, but they also revere her as the only person in the world who has ever outwitted David."

Past experience had taught us that Micah was never wrong, but a few weeks later he appeared with an embarrassed look on his face and reported that Bathsheba indeed was pregnant.

"Are you sure?" we asked in chorus.

"Her belly precedes her."

And then, just as we had all become convinced once again that it really was just another case of the old story of a woman becoming pregnant in order to bag a desirable husband, Micah brought us new information that turned everything upside down and left us baffled.

"Bathsheba has been tying a feather pillow to her belly," he told us excitedly. "One of the maids saw it peeking out from under her dress."

We couldn't conceive of an explanation for such odd behavior that made any sense. Only after the death, as it were, of the unborn child did Micah manage to put together the fragments of information he'd collected and form one clear picture to explain it all: Unlike the previous times that David's rivals suddenly found themselves dead, the death of Uriah the Hittite had aroused an outcry in the kingdom. The people of Israel refused to believe the stories being spread by the king's scribes, which claimed that Uriah had been killed in the normal course of things in the war against Ammon. "Joab son of Zeruiah killed him on the battlefield," they told one another angrily, "so that the king and Bathsheba could marry unchecked."

Bathsheba realized that she had become the most hated woman in the kingdom and hurriedly introduced the king to a venerable old man visiting the palace from the neighboring town of Giloh.

"Meet Ahithophel," she said proudly, "the father of my father, Eliam. He is the only person who can get us out of the dire straits we're in. His advice is like the word of God."

"My advisors are no less clever than your grandfather," replied the king in despair.

But the plan that Ahithophel laid out left David agape. He knew it would restore the people's love for him.

Bathsheba stuffed a feather pillow under her dress and walked around the palace appearing quite pregnant. Half a year later, the king's heralds spread word of the new son born to the king and Bathsheba, his wife. This news delighted the nation not one bit, but rather only intensified the outrage. "She is not the king's wife!" the people cried. "She is the wife of Uriah the Hittite."

Ahithophel reassured David that everything was going according to plan and let his good friend Nathan the Prophet in on the secret. Nathan was overjoyed at the opportunity that had fallen into his lap to take the place of Gad as court prophet. One day, as the king was sitting as usual upon the throne of judgment, Nathan appeared before him, demanding that David listen to what he had to say about a matter and pronounce his judgment.

Everyone who was there followed the prophet's sad story with bated breath as he described the two neighbors, one a wealthy man and the other a pauper, and they wiped the tears from their eyes as they heard about the ugly fate of the pauper's lamb.

"Well," the prophet asked the king when he had finished his story, "what should be done to the rich man who slaughtered the beloved lamb of his impoverished neighbor?"

"As surely as the God of Israel lives," the outraged king cried, "the man who did this deserves to die!"

"*You* are the man," Nathan thundered.

The people gasped and regarded with admiration the brave prophet who would dare to reproach the king without fear or prejudice.

"This is what God says," the prophet went on. "'I anointed you king over Israel in place of Saul. I gave his house to you, and his wives, and his kingdom. And I gave you even more. Why did you despise the word of God? Why did you strike down Uriah the Hittite with the sword? Why have you taken the pauper's lamb?"

"I deserve to die," David mumbled the words that Ahithophel had put in his mouth, while at the same time bursting into rather convincing tears. "I have sinned against my God."

The furious eyes of the prophet softened abruptly. "God forgives those who confess their sins." He was silent a moment, looking around at the people standing before him. "What punishment befits the king who has taken the pauper's lamb?"

They stared at him, perplexed. "You just said God forgives those who confess their sins," they mumbled.

"There is no forgiveness without punishment," the prophet declared firmly, and turned back to face David. "The God of Israel will take away your sin, but the son born to you will die."

The people moaned in sorrow. "Ask our God to let the child live!" voices cried from all directions.

But the prophet insisted, "The man who stole the pauper's lamb must be punished. The child will die!"

Seven days later, news of the baby's premature death spread through the land, and the nation was moved by the king's impressive ability to accept the judgment that had been imposed upon him.

"He ended his mourning two days later?" they marveled.

"That very same day," came the reply. "The king washed, put on lotions, changed his clothes, and went to the Tabernacle to pray that God might send consolation to his miserable wife, Bathsheba, who had lost a husband and a son in a single year."

The people of Israel joined in his prayers, asking God to give the pauper's innocent lamb another son in place of the son who had been taken from her.

Rage bubbled up through my body and made my blood boil. How dare Nathan say that God gave David Saul's house and kingdom? Who does this prophet mean when he speaks of Father's wives that were given to David? Rizpah is one wife, so who is the other? Who do the people think of when they hear this nonsense?

"Nathan's parable is completely backwards," Nebat said, breaking the silence. "The one who died was the pauper, not his lamb."

"Eventually, the people will realize they've been deceived," said Mephiel hopefully. "The entire nation can't be deceived for long."

Rizpah chuckled. "The parable of the pauper's lamb will yet become the very symbol of fearless and profound prophecy. This Ahithophel is a genius."

"It's too bad Father never had such an advisor," Armoni sighed.

The word "Father" on the tongues of Mephiel and Armoni stirred my emotions anew every time. It was only when they spoke it that I remembered they were my brothers. The rest of the time I felt as if they were my sons.

Armoni glanced at his mother, expecting her to agree, but Rizpah furrowed her brow and said nothing. "Bathsheba didn't come to the palace to stay," she said at last.

We looked at her in confusion, trying to decipher her meaning.

"She came to the palace to bear the crown prince."

"That's impossible," said Micah. "If and when Bathsheba gives birth, her son would be the youngest of the king's sons."

Rizpah did not argue, but a year later, after Solomon was born, she reminded me of her conjecture and even reiterated it with greater confidence. "Bathsheba came to the palace to bear the crown prince."

"Solomon is the king's youngest son," I said dismissively.

"People assume the firstborn son will inherit the crown, but the prostitutes who raised me heard stories of the palace intrigues of neighboring peoples, and they told me that most of the kings who have ultimately risen to the throne were not firstborn sons. Do you know what has enabled them to inherit the crown?"

"They must be the most ambitious sons, the craftiest, the most devious, and possibly the cruelest," I replied.

"Those are important qualities indeed, but you are ascribing them to the wrong person. Most kings rise to the throne thanks to their mothers. A king has many wives, and each of them dreams of giving birth to the crown prince and becoming the queen mother. The competition is fierce, and the winner is the most ambitious, craftiest, most devious, and cruelest *woman* of them all. I know David's wives, at least the most prominent ones, and I have no doubt that Bathsheba will be able to defeat them all. On top of everything else, she has at her side the wisest advisor there ever was. Solomon will be the crown prince, unless she bears another son and decides to push for him."

"Amnon, the firstborn, will never surrender his position. He isn't especially impressive, but he has no shortage of aggression and ambition. That's what Micah says about him."

"But his mother, Ahinoam of Jezreel, is a weak woman, and it's the mother that counts."

"Not always. The nation of Israel crowned my father when his mother was no longer alive, and David lost his own mother when he was three. Israel's first two kings took the throne by themselves; no mother pushed them along."

"You're right about your father and wrong about the son of Jesse. It's true that David did lose his mother at a young age, but he was raised by his eldest sister Zeruiah, who was like a mother to him, and she decided that he would be a king."

"How can you say that? You don't know her."

Rizpah laughed scornfully. "I know Joab and Abishai, and I knew Asahel before he was murdered by Abner, and I know that David would have never captured the throne without them. And what do the three of them have in common? Zeruiah, of course. It is no coincidence that they decided to take her name rather than their father's."

She grew quiet and lowered her head. She blushed. "For many years I accused myself of possibly being a member of that breed of women who push their way into the king's bed in order to try to bear the crown prince. You must remember that after Ishvi was murdered, Adriel and Paltiel declared that they would serve as mere temporary rulers, and then after six years my son Armoni would assume the throne. I couldn't understand how I was capable of rejoicing at the thought of my son's future coronation after the terrible tragedies that had crushed our family. I feared that maybe deep inside I'd wanted it to happen."

"The tragedies were not your fault."

"I suddenly wasn't so sure."

Rizpah's odd confession brought back the memories I'd been working hard to forget. My life experience had taught me never to look back. The longing for my dead loved ones could be the end of me. I must look forward and hold on to what I still have, and I still do have so much: Nebat, the seven boys, Rizpah.

I got up and hugged her. "You are not a member of that breed of women. While you're no less intelligent than Bathsheba, you lack her kind's most important trait: cruelty. You don't have a cruel bone in your body."

We both laughed with relief and went on gossiping about the schemes of Ahithophel and Bathsheba. We regarded the court intrigue of David's palace as amusing theater that had nothing to do with us. Could we have foreseen the calamity hovering over our heads? And even if so, could we have prevented it? These questions have been eating away at me for twenty years, and they drive me mad.

⚉

As if to confirm Rizpah's suspicions, Nathan the Prophet appeared before David and informed him that God loved Bathsheba's son very much and, thus, the boy would be named Jedediah—"friend to God." The king was very glad to hear that God could fall in love with babies the moment they were born but reminded the prophet that the parents were the ones to name their children.

"The God of Israel has decided that the child's name will be Jedediah," the prophet insisted.

"His name is Solomon," declared David.

"Fine," the prophet growled in submission. "I will call him Jedediah for God's sake, and you can go on calling him whatever you want."

Micah described this public event in such an entertaining manner that we were nearly choking with laughter. Our days in the palace were nothing but dull routine, and in the absence of anything new in our own lives, we took a great deal of interest in the scheming of Ahithophel and Bathsheba, and we thirstily drank up the stories that Micah brought us. The one who was most keen for them was Rizpah, who began to devote the majority of her time and thought to them. The seven boys had other things to do, like riding horses, reading, playing music, and studying. Micah's stories amused them and brought some color into their lives, but the stories never became their main interest.

"Ahithophel has killed two birds with one stone," Rizpah marveled. "He has turned Solomon into the favorite son, the beloved of God, and also put him on a par with Abraham and Jacob, the fathers of our nation, whose names were changed by God himself."

"Perhaps it was Bathsheba's idea," I said. "I'm curious to see that woman in the flesh."

I only got the chance to do so five years later, at the proclamation ceremony of the crown prince. David was fifty-six years old, and judging by his robust health and sharp mind he still had many years ahead of him on the throne, but Ahithophel had convinced him to officially proclaim Amnon his crown prince so as to spare the younger princes, who might otherwise have aspirations for the position and allow themselves to be dragged into dangerous scheming. When Micah brought us this news, I teasingly told Rizpah that she might have been wrong about Bathsheba and Ahithophel, for here they were submissively accepting the appointment of the firstborn son as crown prince. But Rizpah remained confident in her assertion that all of Ahithophel's counsel was aimed at nothing other than making Solomon king, and that even if the details of his plot were not yet clear, they would become so in time.

I had no interest in taking part in the proclamation ceremony, but the king's messengers delivered the invitations to our doorway and ordered us all to appear.

"What's changed?" I wondered. "Why has David suddenly remembered that we exist?"

"He wants the crowds to see that even the descendants of Saul are swearing allegiance to the crown prince," explained Micah. "Ahithophel told him it was important."

"Of course," Rizpah added proudly. "Everyone in the land loves our boys. Whenever they see them, they long for King Saul."

Indeed, even though we were imprisoned in the palace and forbidden from leaving the grounds, our boys' reputations were known everywhere. I don't know who spread the tales, but it must have been that the visitors who ran into them in the palace courtyard from time to time brought back admiring stories of their beauty and height, and perhaps even about their wisdom and kindness, so reminiscent of their father and grandfather that hearts ached with longing for him.

"Don't delude yourself," I said bitterly. "The people have quite forgotten their first king."

We attended the ceremony as required, watching indifferently as Amnon struggled to squeeze his broad face into the expression of a crown prince. He looked so pathetic in his elegant royal gown that we could barely contain our laughter. I noticed that almost everyone's eyes were pinned on Absalom, who stood beside his father with Kileab, the son of Abigail. I tried to look away from David. Whenever I saw him, or even merely thought of him, an involuntary shiver still sliced down my body and filled me with feelings of guilt.

"Absalom is gorgeous," I whispered to Rizpah. "We have to admit that he is even better looking than our boys."

"Too good looking," Rizpah declared scornfully, and she put her arms around her twin sons, standing on either side of her. "Our sons are men. Absalom looks like a statue."

Nathan the Prophet announced importantly that, by the king's decree, his firstborn son, Amnon, would inherit the throne when the time came, and the crowd replied with a recitation of the oath of allegiance. Out of boredom, I looked to my side, at the seating area of the wives and princes, and ran my eyes over them, trying to figure out which ones I was able to recognize. They all appeared focused on the ceremony, so I could stare at them as much as I liked. I suddenly noticed that one of the wives standing across from me had turned her head in my direction. Standing at her side was a chubby boy of about five, chewing on a mouthful of figs.

I immediately knew who they were.

Bathsheba's eyes ran over my ankles, up to my waist, past my neck, and locked in on my face. I tried to smile at her, but her gaze paralyzed me. I couldn't move.

After the ceremony I told Rizpah about the petrifying way Bathsheba had glared at me. "That woman scares me," I admitted.

"Amnon is the one who should be afraid. He's the first one she'll take out to make way for her fat son. I still don't know how she'll do it, but it's only a question of time."

That time arrived sooner than expected. Rizpah had assumed that Bathsheba and Ahithophel would wait for Solomon to come of age, but the fate of the crown prince was sealed within only seven years, when desperate screams sliced through the air in the middle of the night, and everyone in the palace awoke with a start. We, too, were awakened, and before we could figure out what was going on, Micah got into his wheelbarrow and rode quickly to the center of the action. But this time we had no need for his spying. The information quickly made its way to us in the form of Tamar daughter of Maakah, Absalom's sister, who was running amok all through the palace, ashes in her hair, her gown torn, scratching at her forehead with her fingernails, pacing and screaming.

Rizpah watched her in horror. I knew she was recalling what Abner had done to her, and I tried to get her to come back home, but she wouldn't move and kept her piercing gaze fixed on Tamar.

"Amnon!" Tamar screamed. "Amnon has defiled me!"

By the time Micah returned with the rumors he'd been working so hard to collect all morning, Rizpah had already recovered. She had recovered so much, in fact, that she grilled Micah about the relationship between Absalom and Ahithophel.

"They're friends," Micah admitted. "But what has that got to do with the rape of Tamar?"

"How friendly are they?" Rizpah demanded to know.

"Ahithophel is Absalom's advisor."

"And what does David have to say about that?"

"David only rarely needs Ahithophel's counsel, and he doesn't mind if the man spends his many hours of leisure time with Absalom."

Rizpah nodded her head slowly. "That's what I thought," she muttered.

We knew she wouldn't share her thoughts with us before she formed a full and clear picture in her mind. In the meantime, Micah satisfied our curiosity, reporting daily on any new developments. David's reaction surprised us. Rather than putting his rapist son on trial and punishing him, or at the very least removing him from his position as crown prince, the king demanded that his daughter keep quiet, and he returned to his usual business as if nothing had happened.

"David knows that Tamar wasn't really raped," Rizpah said, not hiding her pleasure at the astonished looks on our faces. "The moment I saw her screaming I knew it was an act."

"How did you know?" Nebat interrupted.

Rizpah and I exchanged quick looks. The five older sons remembered Abner's rape and understood that Rizpah was speaking from experience, but Nebat, and perhaps Micah and Benjamin as well, were probably too young to remember and most likely had heard nothing about it.

"Why would she do such a thing?" Elhanan asked in wonder, and Joel seconded him, adding that a girl lying about rape caused much more harm to herself than to her alleged rapist. No one would want to marry her, and she would remain alone and desolate her whole life. He said the word "desolate" with such empathy that my heart ached. Rizpah and I had decided long ago that our survival hinged on remaining focused on what we had left and not what had been taken away, but every once in a while we gave in and cried in each other's arms over the isolation our beloved boys had to suffer. We yearned to see them marry and have children, but we knew the chances were slim. They did visit the whorehouse of the king's soldiers, which David had given them special permission to do, and sometimes we allowed ourselves to dream of a girl, even a prostitute, who would win one of their hearts and become his wife. But the years wore on, and none of our sons started a family.

"You're right," said Rizpah. "I knew right away that Absalom was behind the rape story, but I couldn't figure out how he could have convinced his sister Tamar to do that for him. That's how I arrived at Ahithophel. Only a mind like his could have conceived of such a brilliant plan, in which everyone involved is certain that he or she will be its biggest beneficiary, but it is actually the one standing behind the scenes who takes home the entire pot—Solomon, of course."

"How?" Micah shouted. He felt frustrated that he was always the one who collected all the facts, but it was his grandfather's clever widow who was able to spin them together into riveting tales of intrigue.

Rizpah's eyes sparkled. Nothing could be more exciting for her than getting inside the heads of Ahithophel and Bathsheba. "Let's start at the beginning. Solomon is the youngest son. Who is his main rival?"

"Amnon," we replied all together.

"Bathsheba and Ahithophel have to get rid of Amnon. They can wait patiently for Solomon to grow up and do it himself, with their help, of course. But when you have a rival, it's preferable to send someone else to take care of him, and it would be even better if the person you send has a motive to harm your rival, because then no one would suspect you. That's precisely what Bathsheba and Ahithophel did. They looked for another prince who would want Amnon out of the way. Kileab, the second son, isn't right for the job. He doesn't aspire to inherit the throne, and even if he did, his mother, Abigail, would have put a stop to it. That's how Absalom, the third son, was chosen. He is ambitious, selfish, and, most importantly, good looking. His beauty draws the nation to him, which makes him believe that he should be the crown prince. Now, all that is left is to convince Absalom that Ahithophel has his best interest at heart and wants to help him clear Amnon out of his way. The rape story is a very good way to do that because the king would surely disinherit a rapist, and even if not, what could be more justified than a brother killing his sister's rapist? No one would accuse him of murder. On the contrary, the nation would only think more highly of him. I can already imagine the songs his adoring maidens would sing for him."

"And what does Tamar have to gain?" asked Micah.

"If Amnon takes the throne, she will be nothing but a distant princess, whereas the coronation of Absalom would ensure her status as sister to the king. Never fear, the sister of the crown prince isn't likely to remain alone and desolate."

"Do you think Absalom is going to murder Amnon?" I asked in a high-pitched voice.

Rizpah looked at me with surprise. "I see that you care."

"I don't like murder," I mumbled in embarrassment.

She smiled affectionately. "I'm sorry to say it, Michal, but the answer is yes. Unless David declares that his eldest son will not inherit the throne, Absalom will murder him. Again, it's only a question of time."

"But Absalom would be murdering Amnon to become king himself, so what do Ahithophel and Bathsheba gain? Instead of having to get rid of Amnon, now they will have to get rid of Absalom."

I can't remember who asked that question, but we all nodded in agreement. It was clear to all of us that if Rizpah didn't have a satisfactory response, her fascinating analysis would go down the drain.

But her explanation came easily and quickly. "It's much easier to get rid of a prince who isn't the firstborn, and it's even easier to get rid of a prince who has murdered his brother, even if he was justified in doing it and was adored by the nation after he did. Ultimately, the nation would rather see a peace-loving king on the throne whose hands are clean of blood."

"And how do you think Ahithophel and Bathsheba plan to get rid of Absalom?" Micah asked curiously.

"We'll see," Rizpah answered cheerfully. "It won't be dull around here."

⇽⟐⇾

This time, Rizpah's forecast was proven right somewhat later than expected. By then, we were all certain she'd been mistaken and that Absalom was either unable or unwilling to kill his brother. But two years later, in the midst of the shearing festival, Absalom's agents slit Amnon's thick neck, leaving him to wallow in his own blood. It took place in the land of Ephraim, far from the king's watchful eyes.

"Absalom is patient," Rizpah said admiringly when Micah brought us the news of the murder. "An outstanding quality for someone who wants to be a king."

"How did David react?" I asked Micah.

Everyone stared at me. I tried to pretend that I didn't actually care, but I knew they didn't believe me.

"He was glad," Micah replied, not hiding his pleasure at our surprise. "At first a messenger came to the palace and told David that Absalom had murdered all the princes. The king almost died of sorrow. He fell off his throne like a dry tree trunk, and he jerked and coughed and drooled on his beard. It was not a pleasant sight."

I shut my eyes at this description. I couldn't imagine David in such a state.

"But shortly thereafter a second messenger arrived," Micah continued, "and told the king that only Amnon had been murdered. Instead of crying over his dead son, the king rejoiced over the living ones."

We looked to Rizpah for an explanation. "Ahithophel thinks of every detail," she said, impressed. "He found a way to portray Amnon's death as a trivial matter so as to ensure that David would not execute Absalom."

"But Ahithophel wants Absalom out of the way," Nebat said, puzzled.

"Not so quickly, though," Rizpah explained. "If Absalom is taken out at this stage in the game, an accomplished and worthy son might take his place and serve as a much more challenging rival."

"It's even more sophisticated than that," Micah began to say, then he lost confidence and grew quiet.

I encouraged him to keep going and hoped that Rizpah would listen to what he had to say. I knew her opinion mattered to him more than mine did. He considered us both to be his mothers, but Rizpah was his favorite one. Sometimes I would try to recall how young men usually related to their mothers. I loved the strong bond we had with the boys, but it also concerned me. I knew they were overly dependent on us, and I would ask myself whether their dependence was still within the realm of reason, or if their imprisonment in the palace was preventing them from becoming men. The only examples I had ever seen up close were my brothers, but Mother was a quiet, introverted woman who always remained in Father's great shadow. Rizpah and I were so different from her that it was impossible to make a comparison. All the time we had lived in Father's palace, Rizpah had also been quiet and introverted, but ever since we escaped Gibeah she'd become a formidable woman. I had changed, too. I was once a blazing bonfire, but all the tragedies that landed on me extinguished it, leaving me only a few embers to sustain my love for my only son, Nebat, for my soul sister, Rizpah, and for the seven boys.

"Ahithophel wanted Absalom to be compared to Simeon and Levi," Micah said, looking intently at Rizpah. "Such a comparison puts him in a positive light. When the first messenger informed the king that Absalom had murdered his sons, everyone would have naturally thought of Simeon and Levi, who avenged themselves not only upon the man who had raped their sister, but also upon his entire family and city. When the second messenger arrived and said that Absalom had only killed his sister's rapist, the ministers told the king that Absalom was a righteous man and deserved no punishment. David decided to banish him to the home of his grandfather, Talmai, King of Geshur, and there were some voices of protest against even that light punishment."

"The righteous murderer," Rizpah laughed, and she praised Micah for his fine distinctions.

"Now all that's left is to see how and when Ahithophel and Bathsheba are going to drive this righteous man away from the throne," Nebat said with a smile.

"I'll warn you in due time," Rizpah declared. "I've gotten into the heads of Ahithophel and Bathsheba; they can no longer surprise me."

<hr>

Rizpah was wrong. None of us foresaw Absalom's rebellion. We all watched him with great interest after his return from Geshur following three years of exile, and we were impressed by the techniques he used to gain the love of the nation. But we never imagined that Ahithophel and Bathsheba would try to speed everything up and overthrow David instead of patiently awaiting his death. Only after the rebellion started did Micah bring us the one piece of information we had been missing, without which Rizpah hadn't been able to put together all the pieces of the puzzle.

The missing piece was named Adonijah.

Now that his firstborn son was dead, David had decided he was free to choose a crown prince based on merit, rather than birth order. The choice was easy: Adonijah son of Haggith. David knew that no one was worthier.

Indeed, Adonijah was a very worthy son. He'd inherited his mother's kindness and gentleness, and from his father he'd received not only red hair and pretty eyes, but also wisdom and a sharp mind. He was even ambitious and very charming. He lacked only one thing: cunning. Adonijah was an honest man.

"Too honest," Rizpah sighed after the rebellion was put down and David had proclaimed Adonijah crown prince. "He won't be able to handle Bathsheba's deviousness."

I recalled what she'd said back then two years later, as Adonijah's body, full of stab wounds, was taken from the altar, and the queen mother's scribes hurried to spread the rumor that he had asked to have the king's widow for himself, thus declaring himself a rebel against the crown. But all this happened after the calamity, and by that time there was no one left to be impressed by the fulfillment of my soul sister's prophecy.

⊰♋⊱

Ahithophel tried to persuade David to choose Absalom. He knew it would be much easier to get rid of a crown prince who had been convicted of his brother's murder than one who was entirely unsullied. David's choice remained firm, but he agreed temporarily to postpone Adonijah's proclamation ceremony. Ahithophel wasted no time and quickly taught Absalom how to win the love of the nation. When I first heard about his methods, I thought they resembled those of David, which I'd seen up close when I had accompanied him on his journeys among the people. But it quickly became clear to me that the son had surpassed his father. Absalom didn't have David's charm, but his spectacular beauty made up for it. While the other princes traveled outside the palace in two-horse chariots, Absalom would appear in all his glory in an eight-horse chariot of gold, with some fifty people running ahead of him. It was a sight to behold. His long hair fluttered in the wind, and he knew how to move his perfect body to the beat of the horses' hooves. When he would wave his arms, the crowds would catch their breaths. When he smiled at them, their hearts melted with love. It was impossible to look away. But he was not content with the wonders of his body on the chariot. He also knew how to charm people inside the palace. When litigants left the king's courthouse, they

would meet a handsome prince at the gate who took an interest in them, asking to hear what city and tribe they were from and what judgment the king
had given them. The flattered litigants would describe how their trials had
gone, and the prince would express his displeasure at the way they had been
wronged and would tell them sadly that, had he been the judge, their demands
would have been met. But the technique that won the adulation of the nation
more than any other was his refusal to allow them to bow to him, or in other
words, kisses instead of curtsies. When people would walk through the palace gate and try to bow to him, he would grab them with his muscular hands,
pull them in, and exuberantly give them a kiss on their foreheads.

"The nation wants Absalom," Ahithophel told the king.

David waved his hand dismissively. "I don't care what the nation wants.
I know what it needs. The nation of Israel needs a king like Adonijah. Soon I
will officially proclaim him crown prince."

David couldn't imagine the intensity of the nation's love for Absalom, and
even worse, he couldn't imagine how intensely the nation had come to hate
him.

We couldn't imagine it either. We'd been imprisoned in the palace for so
many years that we had little idea of what was going on outside. Micah managed to gather stories from within the palace, but it never occurred to him
that on the outside the nation hated David. When we received the first bits
of information about the scale of the rebellion, we were certain they must be
wrong. We were willing to believe that the people of Benjamin resented
David, and maybe the people of Jabesh Gilead as well, but the entire nation?
Even Judeans? It couldn't be. Why would the people of Israel hate their successful king, one who had conquered all the neighboring lands on their behalf and expanded the territory of their kingdom to a size that not even
Joshua had dreamed of?

"They call him 'Man of Blood,'" Micah reported with pleasure. "The
people of Israel have had enough of the Sons of Zeruiah's reign of terror."

"They long for King Saul," Rizpah added hopefully. "They want a king
more like him."

"Is Absalom anything like Grandfather?" cried Nebat.

"In the way he looks," said Rizpah. "Absalom is tall and handsome. He
reminds the people of the king they long for."

Her words angered me. "Absalom is the complete opposite of Father. Everyone remembers King Saul's humility. Even David's scribes can't dispute it. In contrast, Absalom has fifty people running ahead of him and weighs his hair on a scale. The people of Israel might hate David, but don't delude yourselves into thinking they miss our father and grandfather."

⁓

When news of the rebellion reached David, he believed his army would be able to easily defeat the rebels, but the messenger who came to the palace left him no hope.

"The hearts of the men of Israel are with Absalom!" cried the messenger. "The rebel army has managed to invade Jerusalem."

The frightened king ordered his slaves to prepare the chariot, but the shouting of the rebels was so close that he knew there was no time to spare, and he fled on foot. All his men fled with him. He ordered that ten of his wives be left behind to tend to his palace.

"Only a coward of a husband flees for his life and leaves his wives behind as guards," Rizpah spat with disgust when it became clear to us that we were not alone in the palace.

When the rebels burst in, we were startled at the sight of Micah's terrified expression. We realized he must have been remembering the invasion of the palace in Gibeah, which had left him crippled, and we tried to reassure him, telling him that Absalom had no reason to harm us. We honestly believed this. Even Rizpah didn't foresee Ahithophel's satanic plan.

Absalom's soldiers entered our home and ordered Rizpah and me to accompany them to the roof of the palace. The boys tried to inquire about the reason for this strange order, but in response the soldiers drew their swords and dragged us out by force. Nebat fell upon the soldier who had grabbed me and began to punch him, but the other soldiers pushed him to the ground and kicked him all over. I grabbed onto their legs and cried that we would go with them peacefully. They led us up the stairs to the roof. David's ten wives were standing there. They were naked. The palace courtyard and all the surrounding streets were filled with crowds of people, looking up. Some of them were rhythmically cheering, "Long live Absalom, King of Israel!" but most of them were standing silently.

The soldiers ordered us to undress. My hands were frozen. I couldn't feel my body. I closed my eyes and tried to convince myself I was in a nightmare and that soon I would wake up at home with the eight boys. One soldier grabbed the hem of my dress and raised his sword. Rizpah's voice stopped him before he had a chance to tear it off of me.

"We are not the king's wives," she said.

As always, she was the first one to regain her composure.

Just then, Absalom walked out onto the roof, Ahithophel at his side. The crowds down below cheered even louder, and Absalom smiled at them, waving his perfect arms.

"Your Majesty," Rizpah said calmly.

Absalom turned to face her. His face took on a puzzled look. It appeared to me that Ahithophel was also surprised to see us.

"We are not David's wives," Rizpah went on. "I am Rizpah daughter of Aiah, widow of King Saul, and this is Michal, Saul's daughter, the wife of Paltiel son of Laish."

Absalom and Ahithophel exchanged looks.

"Release them," Ahithophel ordered the soldiers.

On our way downstairs we heard from above us the screaming of the women being raped on the roof. Only then did I allow myself to cry. Rizpah cried, too.

⋘⋙

"David continued up the Mount of Olives, **weeping as he went, weeping as he went;** his head was covered and he was barefoot."

Micah heard this quote, word for word, from Absalom's men, who roamed the palace with the pride of victors.

"Measure for measure," I interrupted him. Rizpah looked up. She knew it wasn't my usual practice to speak ill of David. "Just like Paltiel," I choked. "He was also weeping as he went, the whole way from Gallim to Bahurim."

After Absalom was defeated, the king's scribes admitted that during his flight David had run into a distant relative of Saul's by the name of Shimei, who had thrown stones at him, yelling, **"Get out, get out, you man of blood, you scoundrel! God has repaid you for all the blood you shed in the household of Saul, in whose place you have reigned. Because you are a man of blood!"**

But the truth was much worse. Shimei was the supreme judge of the council of tribal courts and a descendant of Ehud son of Gera, who had long ago saved Israel from the Moabites. And he wasn't the only one brazen enough to openly express his glee. Throughout the king's journey, crowds of people gathered along his path, celebrating his downfall. Had it not been for Joab son of Zeruiah and his men, who protected David at great risk to themselves, he would have met his death at the hands of the masses. Joab's reign of terror had suppressed any hint of protest, which had led David to believe that his people loved him and were grateful for his conquests; he was stunned by their animosity toward him.

But what frightened David most of all was Ahithophel's betrayal. He knew that whoever had the good fortune of that man's counsel would be assured of victory. "The advice of Ahithophel is like the word of God," the king told his people. "That man is cleverer than any other. If we can't find a way to thwart his ability to advise Absalom, we're doomed."

David's terrified men were beside themselves. The only one who was able to get himself under control was Hushai the Arkite, one of the court advisors, who was not about to miss the opportunity that had befallen him to inherit Ahithophel's lofty position as the king's master of secrets.

"I'm willing to go frustrate the advice of Ahithophel," Hushai told David. "Absalom will believe I've joined him, too, and he will listen to my advice."

Joab and Abishai, the sons of Zeruiah, were afraid that Hushai wasn't clever enough to formulate his own plan, but the king assured them that cleverness was not necessary to frustrate Ahithophel's advice. "It's very simple," David explained to Hushai. "You need to listen very carefully to Ahithophel's advice and then say the opposite. Absalom likes convoluted advice, so try to prove to him that your advice is more complicated than Ahithophel's."

Absalom received Hushai with suspicion but eventually took him into his confidence and revealed that he planned to follow Ahithophel's advice and pursue David and his men that very night.

"That is not good advice," Hushai declared.

"David's soldiers are panicked and confused," Absalom explained. "This is a golden opportunity that we can't afford to miss."

"Panicked soldiers are dangerous soldiers," Hushai said confidently, and he launched into a long lecture, seasoned with proverbs and analogies to the world of nature, explaining to his perplexed audience that Ahithophel's plan should not be carried out precisely because it was so simple and logical. "David's soldiers are certain we will track them down tonight. When they see that we aren't attacking them, they'll assume that a plague has swept through our army, and they'll complacently disarm, which is when we'll attack them and kill David."

Hushai described his convoluted plan to Absalom and his men for a long time, and when he was finished they called out excitedly, "The advice of Hushai the Arkite is better than that of Ahithophel!"

Ahithophel realized that the fate of the rebellion had been sealed and didn't need to use much imagination to know what David would do to him upon his return to the palace. He didn't wait for Absalom to meet his own spectacular death upon the oak tree and for Absalom's defeated soldiers to declare their surrender. Instead, he saddled his donkey and set out for his hometown of Giloh, and he hanged himself.

And Bathsheba?

Bathsheba waited at the home of her father, Eliam, until the rumors of Absalom's death were confirmed. Then she hurried back to the palace, along with her son Solomon, to welcome home her husband the king, who had returned to the throne.

⚜

But the events of the rebellion sapped David of his strength and turned him old before his time. His wives had nothing but contempt for the young girl from Shunam, who had been brought to his bed to warm his wizened body. Only one of the wives treated her kindly: Bathsheba. Abishag the Shunamite would have done anything for her, but Bathsheba asked for only one thing: to be the first to find out of the king's death. Abishag wanted very badly to fulfill Bathsheba's wishes, but unfortunately the king's soul returned to his God while Joab son of Zeruiah and Abiathar the Priest were at his bedside, and by the time Bathsheba heard about it, the heralds had already spread the word throughout the kingdom that the coronation ceremony of the crown prince would be held that very day, even before David's funeral, in order to prevent anyone from taking advantage of the vacancy and trying to take over by force.

The masses gathered in Jerusalem, crying, "Long live Adonijah son of David, King of Israel!" as they excitedly looked at the red-haired man with the beautiful eyes who so resembled his dead father.

Abiathar the Priest anointed Adonijah's forehead, and the commander of the army, Joab son of Zeruiah, placed the crown atop his head.

At that very moment, Nathan the Prophet and Zadok the Priest leapt onto the stage, accompanied by dozens of armed soldiers. "Adonijah is a rebel!" they cried. "David, King of Israel, lives and breathes!"

The people still remembered how David had taken revenge against anyone who had joined Absalom, and they began running for their lives. Joab and Abiathar tried to stop them, swearing that they had seen the king die with their own eyes and that his final words had been to reiterate his long-standing decision that the throne would pass to Adonijah son of Haggith. But no one listened. The people were convinced that David was still alive.

Three days later, the heralds spread the bitter news of the king's death and called the people to return to Jerusalem for the true coronation ceremony. Most people chose to remain at home this time and await updates there, but the few who did arrive stared in astonishment at the young boy sitting confidently upon the throne. Nathan the Prophet and Zadok the Priest stood before them, reading the king's will aloud:

"As surely as God lives, who has delivered me out of every trouble, I will surely carry out this very day what I swore to you by the God of Israel: Solomon your son shall be king after me, and he will sit on my throne in my place."

Those present didn't know to which woman this vow had been directed, but they got their answer momentarily when Bathsheba climbed up to the stage and tearfully described the last moments of her husband's life and the will he'd dictated to her with the last of his strength.

Nathan the Prophet anointed Solomon's forehead, and Zadok the Priest placed the crown atop his head.

"Long live Solomon son of David, King of Israel!" cried the heralds.

The crowd repeated their cry in obvious confusion, then rushed home to tell their families that a child was now sitting on the throne in Jerusalem.

"A child?" their families asked in shock.

"A child!" they confirmed. "But they say he is the wisest of all men."

⁂

Joab son of Zeruiah fled to the Tabernacle immediately after Solomon's coronation and grabbed hold of one of the altar's horns. He thought that no Israelite would dare slaughter a man in a holy place, but Benaiah son of Jehoiada, the new commander of the army, who had chased him there, explained at length that the order to kill him had been given directly by David, who had even made the effort to put it into writing in his will, and that even the altar could not frustrate the will of the king.

Adonijah son of David realized he was next, and he tearfully took his leave from his beloved wife and from Ithiel, his baby boy. But Bathsheba placed him under her protection, and her writers quickly spread the uplifting news that instead of hanging the rebel by his hair and shooting him with three arrows, as had been done to Absalom, the king had decided to spare him.

Shortly thereafter, the queen mother told her son that Adonijah had asked for her permission to marry Abishag the Shunamite. Bathsheba innocently believed that there was nothing at all wrong with this request, but Solomon, the wisest of all men, gave her a short lesson in palace intrigue and explained that anyone asking to marry the previous king's widow is incriminating himself by revealing his desire to undermine the king.

"Is that so?" Bathsheba asked, appalled. "Now we must kill Adonijah. What a pity."

Adonijah also fled to the Tabernacle and held on to the altar's horns, and he was also killed by Benaiah son of Jehoiada. Thus, right there on the holy altar, the two people most dear to David met their deaths: the one, his nephew and army commander, who had devoted his life to him; and the other, his son and inheritor, who was the most worthy of sitting on his throne.

So, Solomon sat on the throne of his father David, and his rule was firmly established.

Twenty-One

Rizpah had foreseen all of Bathsheba's moves. There was only one thing she hadn't seen, hadn't known, hadn't expected.

Our seven boys were taken to Gibeah at the start of the barley harvest, less than a year before Solomon took the throne. There was a gloomy atmosphere in the palace at the time. The king of Israel, David son of Jesse, was preparing for death. Nathan the Prophet and Zadok the Priest were spending long hours with him behind closed doors, all the servants and advisors having been ordered out. Even Hushai the Arkite, his master of secrets, wasn't allowed inside. Everyone understood that the king was concerned about the hateful things being said about him among the tribes of Rachel, and that he wanted to ensure that the throne would pass to his son without turmoil, but no one knew what kind of advice they were giving him behind the closed doors.

The servants didn't know.

The ministers didn't know.

The advisors didn't know.

Micah didn't know.

Rizpah didn't know.

And I didn't know either.

Had I known, I would have fallen at his feet, and I would have cried and begged and repeated the vow he'd made to Father and to me, and I would have told him that he owed his life to me, and I would have reminded him of my love.

⊷❧⊶

Early that morning, the commander of the palace guard arrived at our home and announced that the king had decided before his death to allow our boys to leave the palace and visit Gibeah. I was moved by David's gesture. I missed the city of my birth so much, having not seen it for thirty years. But the commander apologized and explained that it was a long journey that only the seven healthy boys could undertake, not the crippled son or the old mothers.

We walked them to the chariot and kissed them good-bye.

> **The king took the two sons of Rizpah daughter of Aiah, whom she had**
> **borne to Saul,**
> **Armoni and Mephiel,**
> **Together with the five sons of Michal daughter of Saul,**
> **Whom Merab had borne to Adriel son of Barzillai the Meholathite.**

When we returned home, Micah told me with a mischievous grin that Rizpah had managed to sneak into the chariot. I was jealous. Only a tiny body like hers could squeeze itself under the seat.

> David took
> Armoni,
> Mephiel,
> Elhanan,
> Joel,
> Asahel
> Benjamin
> And my son, my only son, whom I love,
> Nebat,
> And handed them over to his emissaries, who took them to the land of
> Benjamin and led them up a mountain.
> Together.
> All seven of them.

And the people didn't know it, didn't guess it, didn't see it.

But Rizpah saw it.

Did she hear them scream? Did she try to protect them with her tiny body? Did she swear to avenge them?

Rizpah saw how they hanged our sons at the top of the mountain, and she saw how they tacked their bodies to the pillories, and she saw the birds and the wild animals approaching, and she stayed with our sons' bodies and protected them. She guarded them day and night, on that day and on the next. She didn't leave them after a week, nor after a month. Day and night, night and day, Rizpah protected our dead boys, driving away the birds and the wild animals.

Rizpah daughter of Aiah took sackcloth
And spread it out for herself on a rock.
From the beginning of the harvest till the rain poured down from the
     heavens on the bodies,
She did not let the birds touch them by day
Or the wild animals by night.

The people of Gibeah heard about the bereaved mother standing alone on the mountaintop day and night—another day, another week, another month—driving away the birds and the wild animals from the bodies of her sons, and they climbed up the mountain and asked her to go home, promising to guard the bodies in her place. But she continued to drive away the birds and the wild animals from the bodies of her sons, not seeing, not hearing, not stopping.

The news spread across the land, and the people of Israel flocked to Gibeah from all the tribal lands to climb the mountain and look at the mother guarding the bodies of her sons.

And David sat in his palace in Jerusalem, hearing about the people gathering in Gibeah, thinking they would disperse on their own. Summer was about to start, and the sun would beat down upon their heads and drive them away, back to their shaded homes.

But another day went by. and another week, and another month, and Rizpah continued to drive away the birds and the wild animals from the bodies of her sons, and people continued to gather around her and watch.

And the cry rose up from Gibeah, rolled into Jerusalem, burst through the palace walls, and made its way to the king:

Why?

Why did you kill them?

Why did you kill the sons of Saul?

⤙✥⤚

David ordered his scribes to immediately compose stories to justify the deed, but even his talented scribes, who could resolve any problem with the help of an appropriate story, failed to compose a tale that could explain the murder of the sons of Saul. Even Seraiah couldn't do it. The alarmed king summoned his advisors, prophets, and priests, but none of them could advise him. The spirit of rebellion was in the air, and the protests became ever more direct and aggressive:

> *You killed the seven boys because you know that we long for our first king.*
> *You killed them because you realize that as long as we still have hope that one*
>   *of Saul's descendants might become king, your son's reign would not be firmly*
>   *established.*
> *You've taken away our last chance for a king from among the sons of Saul.*
> *That's why you didn't kill Micah. A cripple cannot become king.*

⤙✥⤚

David demanded that Nathan the Prophet and Zadok the Priest find a way to extricate him from the bind he was in. The two of them knew that the protest would die down only if the nation could be convinced that the boys had been murdered for its own good. They ordered the palace scribes to remind the people of Israel that the land had been plagued by a terrible drought every year for the past three years, and that all their pleading and praying and begging had done them no good. Left with no other choice, the prophets and the priests had decided to make a sacrifice—and not just any sacrifice, but the sacrifice of seven princes—so that God might be appeased and inundate the land with rain.

The story drove the entire nation mad. *The God of Israel despises human sacrifice!* the people cried. *And if David son of Jesse is so devoted to us, why doesn't he sacrifice his own princes?*

Nathan and Zadok consulted with the granddaughter of the wisest advisor there ever was and managed to adjust the problematic explanation that had been rejected with such outrage. They sent the king's scribes to tell the people that God does indeed despise human sacrifice, but that He also punishes sons for the sins of their fathers. King Saul had committed terrible sins that had brought the drought down upon us, and only the deaths of his sons could appease God's wrath.

What sins? the people cried. *What did King Saul do to deserve such a punishment?*

The scribes reminded them that Saul had failed to wipe out the Amalekites and that he hadn't waited for Samuel, as ordered, but instead had made the war sacrifice himself. But when the scribes saw that the people actually respected Saul for doing those things, they brought up the gravest sin of all: the massacre of the town of Nob. But almost every person in Israel personally knew refugees that had fled Nob and had heard from them more than once that the man who had destroyed that city of priests was Doeg the Edomite.

Only then did the scribes inform the people of Saul's massacre of the Gibeonites, the woodcutters and water carriers of Israel. *How is it that we have not heard of this massacre before?* the people asked, mocking the new tale, and the scribes explained that the cunning Saul had managed to conceal his act and that only now had God decided to publicly reveal it.

But the people didn't believe it, and the crowds went on flocking to Gibeah.

⌁

The king realized that there was only one thing left that he could do to calm the nation. His advisors warned him that it was a risky move that might well heighten the people's longing for Saul, but David knew that their longing would make no difference anymore, for Saul had no descendants left. David sent out his heralds to call the people of Israel to a magnificent state funeral that would be conducted for the heroic King Saul son of Kish and his ten loved and admired sons.

The bones of Saul and his three sons who had been killed in the battle of Mount Gilboa were dug out of their grave in Jabesh Gilead and brought to Gibeah, and the bodies of the seven boys were taken down from the pillories on the mountaintop.

On the day of the funeral, furious rainstorms pounded the entire land without respite, but the people of Israel did not stop flocking to Gibeah. And when the bones and the bodies of the dead were lowered into the grave, and the king began to play a melody and sing a lament he'd composed for them himself, the cry rose up from the people, "We will not forgive! We will not forget!"

⋘⋙

But they did forget. The nation has a short memory.

⋘⋙

When the seven boys were lowered into their grave, the mother who had guarded them for half a year was not there. No one knew where she had gone. Some said she had fallen on her sword, just like Saul's first widow. Others said she'd thrown herself into the Jordan River. And still others said she had returned to Jabesh Gilead.

⋘⋙

The first mother had disappeared, but the second mother remained in the palace and lit seven candles, yelling and screaming and making strange noises all night long. She did the same thing the next day, and all that week, and the week after that, month after month, year after year. Night after night she lights her candles and screams from dusk until dawn. Her house is no longer called the House of Saul, but the Palace of Candles, and her name is no longer Michal, but the Mad Princess, and the nation has long forgotten who she is and how she came to be mad.

That's how it is. The nation has a short memory.

⋘⋙

Only King Solomon and the queen mother did not forget who it was that dwelled in the Palace of Candles. But they didn't fear her. The mad are as good as dead. If she wants to go on living, let her live. She must be too mad to understand that she has nothing left, and that she has nothing to live for.

⋘⋙

But Michal daughter of Saul does have something to live for.

Twenty-Two

I have finished my story, my beloved boy. I have nothing more to tell you. I only want to hug you, to hold you close, to feel what I've been waiting twenty years to feel.

You are looking at me intently. The effort has etched two tiny lines in your high forehead. Your beautiful eyes have darkened, and they hang on me in supplication. You're biting your lip. Fear grips your throat.

"Did any of the boys have a family?"

"Not a single one of them was able to marry. They were prisoners in the palace."

The tension in your face eases in relief. I need to turn my heart to stone and find the strength to say the words that will bring the dark shadow back over your eyes. "But my only son, Nebat, had a lover."

Your brow furrows again.

"Her father was the leader of the tribe of Ephraim. She once came with him to the palace and met Nebat. Their love was kept secret."

Your thoughts have paralyzed you. You stare at me and say nothing.

"Ask me her name."

Traces of anxiety slip into your voice. "What was her name?"

My voice betrays me. I want to give it all up and say nothing. To say nothing so that you can be free to live a simple life. To say nothing and not to cast upon your young shoulders a burden too heavy to bear.

I catch my breath and, with effort, pull out the word that will change your life. "Zeruiah."

The walls of the room collapse.

"The beautiful, brave Zeruiah, the prettiest girl in Ephraim."

A current slices through your body. You smile a twisted smile, and your mouth gapes open in a wail that threatens to tear your lips apart. The scream is silent, piercing directly into my heart.

"Zeruiah bore Nebat a son, but he never got to meet him. My grandson was born after the death of my son."

Your eyes are squeezed shut. You've dropped your head and are gasping for breath. You're unable to straighten your neck to look at me.

I stand up, my feet dragging as I make my way to you, and I collapse onto the mat in front of you. "Ask me the name of my grandson."

Your face twists in pain. The horror cleaves it in two.

"Ask me the name of my grandson!" I cry. "Ask me the name of my grandson!"

Tears flood your eyes. You try to make a sound, and then immediately go quiet, as if the sound of your own voice makes you afraid.

Ever so slowly, I lean toward you and bring my lips to your ears, and I whisper the words that have been bubbling inside me for twenty years. "Shelomoam, my grandson, my only grandson, whom I love."

The King

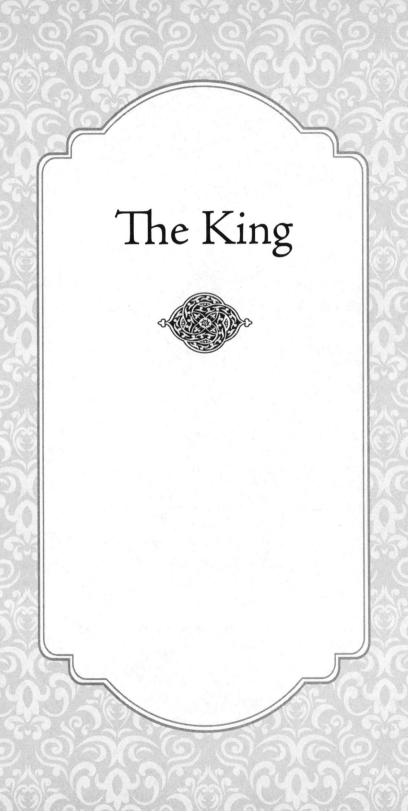

One

When I was a child I liked to embellish. I felt trapped within a life of gray, and I wanted to add some color to it. I wanted a more interesting life.

I know now that my life is beyond what any embellishment could possibly have made up.

It's hard to believe, but that was the first thought I had when the Mad Princess finished telling me the story of her life and I realized it was my life story, too. At that moment I had only thoughts, no feelings. I didn't need to freeze myself to dull the pain, for I felt nothing.

The lips of the Mad Princess were nearly up against my cheek. Hadad sat across from us, watching. I could see that he expected me to fall into her arms in a tearful embrace, and to be honest, that's what I'd expected of myself as well. But I had no feelings, not love, and not joy or sorrow. Not even compassion.

Hadad continued to watch me expectantly, waiting for me to at least say something.

"I want my Aner back."

A deep silence fell over us, the kind you only hear when you're holding your breath alone in the middle of the desert. The silence weighed heavily on me, and I tried to come up with something better to say, but suddenly the Mad

Princess burst out laughing. A moment later Hadad joined her. He laughed wholeheartedly, the way only he does, his fat body jiggling, his face turning red, and the veins in his neck swelling up. At a certain point I, too, joined in the laughter.

The servants who rushed in stared at us in shock. Even the Benjaminite thugs were astonished when Hadad called them in and ordered them to return Aner to me.

"Did she finish telling the story?"

Hadad nodded.

"And?" They gestured toward me with their heads. "What does he say?"

"He says he wants his horse back." Hadad was actually choking with laughter. "That's what he says."

Hadad then led me to a side room at the end of the hallway, as the Mad Princess followed me out with her eyes. I didn't turn to face her. The room was small, but it had everything I needed: a large lamp, a nicely made bed, and a warm meal on the table, richer and more delicious than anything that I'd been served over the full day I'd spent listening to the story.

"Sleep tight," Hadad said softly. "Don't let anything disturb your sleep. You know how to block out unwanted thoughts."

I stayed inside that room for almost a week. That's what Hadad told me, anyway, when I finally came out. I remember very little of those days. Most of the time I was in a haze that did not abate even while I was eating the meals the servants brought me. I wasn't able to think about the Mad Princess's story. Every time I tried, I was quickly enveloped by a darkness from which I would later awake with a sudden start, breathless. I stayed awake for entire days, but I have no idea what I was doing; it all faded into oblivion. I remember only one moment, which I think took place on the fifth day: I was standing in the center of the room, waving my fists in the air and screaming, "I have a father!" Then I collapsed onto the bed and whispered over and over to myself, "I am the son of Nebat. I am the grandson of Paltiel. I am the great-grandson of King Saul."

Another day, maybe two, passed before I felt ready to come out. I was sure the room was locked, as I had grown so used to being imprisoned, but the door opened easily and I found myself back in that dark hallway. The servants rushed to summon Hadad.

"Take me to my grandmother," I told him. The words "my grandmother" slipped out of my mouth as naturally as if I'd been speaking them my entire life.

Tears flooded his eyes. I could see them twinkling in the dim light of the torches.

"First come see your horse," he said.

I accompanied him down the stairs, and we made our way to a large barn. Aner was standing at the trough, drinking peacefully. His brown coat aroused an irresistible feeling of yearning from within me, but I waited a few minutes before I fell upon him. I didn't want him to get spooked. I took in his scent and stroked his whole body. I knew that he was the last remnant of my old life, and I needed to make sure that at least one thing had remained the same.

"Now we'll go see Grandmother," I said to Hadad.

"It's nighttime. She's working."

I stared at him uncomprehendingly.

"Why are you so surprised? Your grandmother works very hard. Have you ever tried to scream and light candles all night long?"

I wanted to cry, but instead I began asking him questions. They helped me sort out my feelings, which had started returning to me. I bombarded him with the questions one after another, not even waiting for his answers. Hadad seemed pleased, telling me that he'd been concerned that it might be many more days before I'd recovered from what I had heard and was ready to face new revelations. He said he was glad to see that I already had the strength to hear the truth about his life.

"Tell me about your life some other time. Now I want to get the full picture of mine."

"Your life and mine are connected. Do you think that I just happened upon your grandmother?"

We climbed the stairs and entered a large, well-lit hall. Hadad began telling me his story while we were walking, but when I laid my hand on his shoulder for a moment, he stopped talking and embraced me. His embrace is what released my pent-up tears. Hadad cried, too. It was a long time before he was able to pull himself together and go on with what he was saying.

"When I told you I was married to an Egyptian princess, you didn't ask me what had led me to be living in Egypt. You must have assumed I left my homeland in order to marry Lady Eno, sister of Tahpenes, wife of the Pharaoh. But the truth is that I came to Egypt at the age of eight, a bit too young to

marry, and far too young to be alone in the world. My father, the King of
Edom, had been murdered, along with my mother and the rest of my family.
All the males in the large cities of Edom had been murdered with them, including children and the elderly. The slaughter lasted almost six months, and
by the time it was over, very few males remained in Edom."

Hadad paused for a moment to see if his words were making any impression on me. I wanted to confess that I'd heard too many tales of slaughter of
late and that I'd become immune to them, but I chose instead to keep my eyes
focused on him, attentive and silent.

"I was saved thanks to my father's slaves, who'd managed to hide me. They
brought me to Egypt, where the Pharaoh Siamun agreed to grant me refuge. I
grew up in the palace with his sons and was given the education of a prince.
I learned all the languages of the area—Moabite, Ammonite, Aramaic, Hebrew, and, of course, Egyptian—and I was trained in all the fighting methods
of Edom and Egypt. When I grew up, the Pharaoh appointed me as the commander of the training program for his army's elite units and gave me his
wife's sister as my wife."

Hadad paused again and waited for me to ask him something, but I had
trouble uttering the one question that had occurred to me.

"Who slaughtered the Edomites?" I finally asked.

Hadad gave a huff of contempt. "Have you forgotten that I can read you?
Ask the question the way you have it formulated in your mind."

I took a deep breath. "Was David son of Jesse behind this slaughter as
well?"

"It was carried out by Joab son of Zeruiah and his soldiers. David, as usual,
declared sadly that it had been done without his consent or knowledge, but
my father's slaves told me the truth, imbuing me with the aspiration to liberate my vanquished land and take revenge against the man who murdered my
parents and my people. But an aspiration is not enough. You need power to
realize an aspiration, and Pharaoh Siamun declined to assist me in going to
war against Israel. I tried to find other partners in my quest for revenge. There
were plenty. Almost all of the neighboring kings, with the exception of
Hiram, King of Zur, and Siamun, King of Egypt, wished to be released of
David's yoke and avenge his cruel conquests, but none was prepared to take
the risk of rebellion. The only man that had the necessary courage and will
was not a king: Rezon son of Eliada, commander of the army of Aram Zobah,

which had been destroyed by David. Rezon was able to take refuge in Aram-Damascus, or what was left of it after David's conquests, and planned his revenge from there. But in my estimation, his small army wasn't going to be able to overpower the army of Israel, so I searched for another partner.

"At that time, word of David's slaughter of the descendants of Saul was spreading throughout the area, and I had a brilliant idea: instead of searching for an army that could stand up against the invincible army of Israel, I would be better off joining forces with the House of Saul and assisting them in rebelling against David son of Jesse in return for the liberation of Edom. That way, I could kill two birds with one stone: I would both take revenge on my parents' murderer and also take back my homeland.

"The gates of the Kingdom of Israel opened wide to welcome a relative of Pharaoh, even if he was an Edomite, but I quickly came to see that my plan would not work. Saul had only one descendant left, a cripple, unsuitable to take the crown. At first I thought of consulting with Rizpah daughter of Aiah, Saul's widow, who stood atop the mountain in Gibeah, guarding the bodies, to find out if she wished to be queen; but when I saw her I realized that she no longer wished for anything other than a proper burial for her sons. That's how I got to Michal. The people who were gathered in Gibeah told me that Rizpah was the mother of two of the hanged boys, while the five others were the adopted sons of Michal daughter of Saul, born to her sister, Merab. My heart pounding, I asked them where I could find this adoptive mother, afraid she might be dead like the rest of Saul's descendants, and I was shocked to hear that she lived in Jerusalem with her husband, David son of Jesse. My initial thought was that I should return to Egypt and search for other allies, but before I did so I decided to pay a quick visit to the palace.

"The king was happy to play host to the Pharaoh's brother-in-law and instructed his slaves to fulfill my every wish. Crafty man that I am, I took advantage of his generous hospitality in order to meet with his first wife and try to determine whether she was willing and able to replace him on the throne. One meeting was enough. I knew that the miserable woman was not capable of ruling her people. But then, just as I was about to give up, I heard that there were rumors of a girl from Ephraim who had been the lover of one of Saul's descendants and was carrying his child. I decided to take my chances and tell Michal why I had come to Israel. I suspected that she wouldn't inform on me to the man who had killed her two brothers and five adopted children. It wasn't easy gaining her trust, but ultimately she couldn't resist my charms, or perhaps she saw me as her last lifeline. Either way, the important thing is that she confirmed the rumor. I must admit that, until that very moment, I hadn't allowed any emotion other than revenge into my plan, but when she told me that one of the dead boys was actually her own son, and that the last scion of the House of Saul was in the womb of his lover, I couldn't hold back and cried like a little child. Now do you understand what you are to us? We've been waiting for you for twenty years. Twenty years!"

"What do you want from me?"

Hadad looked at me as if he were seeing me for the first time.

"Don't you understand?"

"I don't want to understand. The fact that I'm the last scion of the House of Saul doesn't mean I need to sacrifice my life for your plans."

"You need to become king. That's what you need to do. 'Need' actually isn't the right word. It's your destiny."

"No one can decide my destiny for me. I know that you and Grandmother have been hanging your many hopes on me, perhaps all the hopes you have left, but you'll have to find someone else to fulfill them. I've suffered enough. Now that I've finally uncovered the secrets that have tormented me all my life, I intend to start living."

"You are speaking out of fear, and I can certainly understand you. I would also be afraid if someone suddenly ordered me to lead a rebellion against the king. But when you hear our plan, I'm confident that you'll be convinced it's a winning one."

I didn't want to tell Hadad that I wasn't only speaking out of fear, but out of disappointment, too. I was disappointed to hear that my grandmother hadn't brought me to her in order to get to know the only descendant she had remaining, but merely in order to use me as an instrument to achieve her goals. I recalled what she told me about David, who had used her as a stepping stone to reach the palace, and bitterly thought to myself that she was doing exactly the same thing. I was afraid that Hadad would read my mind and begin poking around at my emotions, but he was entirely focused on the success of the plan. That wondrous ability I'd thought he possessed must not have existed after all; it was just that his spies had collected detailed information about me, and that was what had given me the impression that he could decipher the secrets of my heart.

"We've waited twenty years for you to grow up, but we haven't been idle. Your grandmother's madness has afforded us the privacy we needed. That was my idea. I explained to her that if she learned how to freeze herself, the queen mother would become convinced that it was no longer necessary to watch us so closely. No threat can possibly be posed by an empty and hollow shell under which nothing is hiding."

"So you tortured her, too? Did you bury her alive? Did you starve her to death? Did you force her to slaughter an animal she loved and eat its flesh?"

Hadad blushed. "Your grandmother has a natural talent for disengaging. I've never seen anything like it. I only gave her a few exercises, and we were ready to get started. We didn't have much time, either. Don't forget that we only had three months between the time I arrived and when she turned into a frozen block that awakens only at night."

"Wouldn't it have been better for her to remain frozen all hours of the day and night?"

"That's what I thought, too, but she decided she wanted to create a loud ruckus that wouldn't allow the nation to forget the slaughter of the House of Saul. She hoped that everyone would remember that her screaming and candle lighting had begun at the precise hour of the royal funeral David held for Saul and his descendants in Gibeah. But the nation has a short memory and a great ability to adapt. No one gets too excited about her madness anymore. If you go out on the street and ask the older residents of Jerusalem when the Mad Princess lost her mind, most of them will tell you she's always been mad, and the few who remember will tell you it had something to do with the first rain that came down after many years of drought."

"So, when did you create the army of the Palace of Candles?"

"Only after Solomon took the throne. When David died, I returned to Egypt and tried to persuade Pharaoh Siamun to invade Israel and liberate Edom for me, but he preferred to form an alliance with Solomon and give him his daughter Hatshepsut as a wife. His wedding gift to the young couple was the town of Gezer in the land of Ephraim, which he'd conquered from the Canaanites. I understood that he would not be any help to me and suggested that Eno and I go with Hatshepsut to Jerusalem to help her settle in and not be lonely. After we brought the Pharaoh's daughter to Solomon and gave him the town of Gezer, it was quite easy to convince the queen mother to appoint me captain of the guard of the Palace of Candles and to give me soldiers and money so that the Mad Princess could have enough playthings to keep her busy. Bathsheba was surprised that I would request such a worthless position, but I explained that I'd worked hard enough in Egypt and now wanted to rest. Ever since, I've dedicated my entire life to one thing and one thing only: making you king. Everything is ready for the rebellion. I've got trained soldiers, mostly from the tribes of Rachel—you've met four of them in person, and the memories of that encounter will remain etched into your leg forever; I have spies throughout the land; and, most importantly, I'm about to be joined by the most powerful country in the world."

"You've managed to convince Pharaoh Siamun to help you bring Solomon down?"

"I haven't and I won't, but the military will soon seize the throne of Egypt, and Pharaoh Siamun will be replaced by a Libyan warlord named Shishak, the leader of the Libyan mercenaries in Egypt, who will become the new Pharaoh. Genubath, my son, has returned to Egypt to help Shishak bring down Siamun. In return, he's been promised that the great Egypt will support the rebels against the House of David and will help the new king of Israel establish himself on the throne."

I had a hard time believing what I was hearing. "But Pharaoh Siamun is like a father to you!" I cried. "He gave you refuge in his land, and your wife is his wife's sister. How can you betray him?"

Hadad's face grew hard. "I'm willing to betray everything that's dear to me, even my wife and son, as long as it helps me liberate Edom and take revenge on the House of David."

I was stunned by the cruelty in his voice. It was more than I had the strength to bear.

"You are exactly like David," I finally said.

"True," he said. "To defeat your enemy, you must become like him."

Two

Hadad was confident that my grandmother would do anything in her power to pressure me into becoming the next King of Israel. For twenty years, it had been all she had to live for. How could she give up on the only dream she had left? He trusted her powers of persuasion, as well as the natural compassion a young grandson feels when facing his old grandmother, whose entire life was incomparable agony.

His error became clear to him the very next time we all met together, when he saw how she accepted everything I said with a proud smile and a look of adoration, as if I were speaking rare words of wisdom.

"Yes, Shelomoam."

"Correct, Shelomoam."

"You're right, Shelomoam."

"He doesn't want to be king!" Hadad shouted. "Do you understand what that means?"

"It means he'll do what he wants," Grandmother said with a smile, never taking her velvety eyes off me.

Hadad's perfect self-control fell apart all at once. He was wild with disappointment. His pain made me feel sad, and I tried to cheer him up as best I could. Later, it occurred to me with surprise that I hadn't ever paid attention to other people's emotions before. I had been concerned only with myself.

"You'll find someone else to rebel against Solomon and be King of Israel," I tried to console him.

"There is no one else. Don't you see? You are the last scion of the House of Saul."

"Not all kings come from royal families. Shishak is not a descendant of the Pharaohs. You need to seek out a young and attractive man of the tribes of Rachel with a lust for leadership. Even Ithiel admitted that leadership qualities are more important than a royal lineage."

"That viper! That accursed redheaded fox!" Grandmother's lips twisted in loathing. The mention of Ithiel's name turned her all of a sudden from a loving grandmother into an angry lioness.

"He's my best friend. I miss him."

The roar that burst from her mouth petrified me, but, oddly enough, her fit of rage also aroused in me a hint of longing for her father, my great-grandfather, whom I never got to meet.

"Promise me you won't put your trust in him."

"The fact that he's David's grandson doesn't make him a viper. You told me yourself that his father, crown prince Adonijah, was an honest man."

"Don't be naïve, Shelomoam," she said, her voice softening. "Ithiel is Solomon's spy. Do you think he just happened to find the tunnels we dug for you?"

"If we tell him who really murdered his father at the altar he will become Solomon's greatest enemy."

Hadad almost fainted at these words, and he made me swear not to reveal my identity to anyone, and certainly not to one of Solomon's spies. "The king's soldiers have been searching for you since before you were born. Do you think your poor mother decided to imprison herself in a cave and cover her face with a mask for no reason? Have you ever heard of Sheba son of Bikri?"

"They told me my mother was the commander of his rebels in Ephraim and that was the reason she needed to hide in the cave, but I know it isn't true."

"You'd be surprised, it actually is somewhat true, but it's more interesting than what they told you. David had hoped that the royal funeral of the House of Saul would quiet the voices of protest over the murders of the seven boys. He was only partially right. The protest did weaken, but it didn't die down entirely. Sheba waved the flag of rebellion and swept up tens of thousands of young people from the tribes of Rachel."

"Bilhah told me about that rebellion."

"Do you know who Sheba son of Bikri was?"

"Some man from Benjamin."

Hadad swallowed a little smile. "Your grandfather."

I look at him in confusion. "Which grandfather?"

"The father of Zeruiah."

"That can't be. Mother's father was the leader of the tribe of Ephraim, but Sheba son of Bikri was from Benjamin."

"That's what he wanted people to think. A man who initiates an attempt to overthrow the king doesn't want his identity revealed, at least not in the early stages."

"Bilhah told me that Zeruiah ran away from home and joined the rebellion against her father's wishes."

"That's a very nice story, but the truth is her father, Sheba son of Bikri, was the one who instigated the rebellion. After the seven boys were murdered, he realized that his daughter was carrying the last scion of the House of Saul in her womb, so he decided to rebel against David and sit on the throne himself until his grandson came of age and was able to inherit the crown. But, as you know, the rebellion failed. Your grandfather died in Beth Maakah, and his body was thrown to the soldiers who were surrounding the city."

"I know," I whispered. "Bilhah told me about the failed rebellion, but I didn't know he was my grandfather. So, when did my mother go to the cave?"

"David's spies searched for her everywhere. David was determined to put an end to the hopes for a king of the line of Saul. The lepers' cave is the only place where a person can erase her identity and keep her face concealed. It's been twenty years, but the danger has not yet passed. That's why we brought you to the Palace of Candles in such a violent manner. I always thought that when you reached adulthood we'd reveal your identity to you, and then, when you were ready, we'd initiate the power play that would put you on the throne. But to our great distress, we learned that your anger and rebellious nature were leading you right into the lion's den in Jerusalem. You can imagine how frightened we were. A reckless word here, a slip of the tongue there, and someone in the king's court might have put the pieces together and discovered who you were. We had to stop you before you reached Jerusalem and bring you to my excellent training cells. Your training wasn't only meant to provide you with fighting skills, but also, or mostly, to teach you to keep yourself under control even while being tortured. No one can know that you are the last scion of the House of Saul."

"For how much longer? I want to get out of the thicket of secrets of my childhood. I want to proudly carry the name of my ancestors. I want my mother to be able to feel the light of the sun on her face."

"Until you are king. Only then will we be able to reveal your true identity to the nation. You'll have a big, strong army to protect you and to get rid of your enemies."

"This isn't going to do you any good, Hadad. I will not be king."

"Doesn't the lust to avenge your ancestors burn inside you?"

"The people who murdered my ancestors are long dead. The only lust burning inside of me right now is the lust for life. I want a simple, peaceful life, without wars or struggles. If I could turn back time, I'd return to Benaiah's vineyards and never join the army. But what's done is done, and now I have to report to the examinations you've arranged for me and become a commander. And I intend to carry out my military duties in the quietest way possible."

"When I met you two years ago you were a ruthless and bitter savage even though you had no reason to be that way. Your adoptive parents raised you with love and gave you a life of comfort that other children in Zeredah or any-place else could only dream of. So what if they had a few secrets? Was that any reason to become so vile? And now that you've heard your grandmother's story, instead of becoming vicious and vengeful, you suddenly turn into an innocent and placid little lamb without a hint of anger at anyone. What's happened to you?"

"I know who I am and who my ancestors were. That's all I ever wanted."

"And your ancestors are calling out for you to avenge their blood."

"I want to live, Hadad. I don't want to waste my life in schemes for revenge, like you have."

"Live, Shelomoam," Grandmother said, putting an end to the argument between Hadad and me. "That is the greatest revenge you can have against the House of David."

⚭

Hadad had it all wrong. Grandmother's story hadn't made me calm and serene. My nights were plagued by horrifying nightmares that left me with dark shadows under my eyes. But he was right about one thing: I didn't feel any

desire for vengeance whatsoever. I don't know if it was because David and
Bathsheba were long dead, or because I didn't perceive Solomon as someone
worthy of hatred. It's true that when I was a child, I abhorred his tyranny and
couldn't forgive his destruction of the temples and his imposition of such a
heavy tax burden, but the stories I had heard about him made me see him
now as a ridiculous character, unworthy of hatred. More than anything, I
despised the stories his scribes had made up. Of all of Grandmother's and
Hadad's secret assets—spies, soldiers, arms, and allies—I was most excited
about their undercover scribes. I wholeheartedly believed what Bilhah had
taught me in my childhood about stories being more decisive weapons than
any other. My belief in the great power of stories lived on into my adulthood,
even as I exchanged literary embellishments for fists and spears, and so I
asked Hadad to introduce me to grandmother's undercover scribes in the
hopes that I could hear more details about the stories they were planting in
the king's book of chronicles.

"Our scribes are out of work," Hadad said, yawning. "They have nothing
to fight against."

"Does Solomon have no scribes?" I wondered.

"He has many, but he's such a boring king that stories about him aren't
worth fighting against. They'll put future generations to sleep anyway."

"That bad?"

"Far worse. Most of the stories are basically endless lists of the materials
used to construct the great buildings that have been built for him, especially
the Temple and his private palace, which was only just recently completed
after thirteen years of hard labor. Sometimes, for variety's sake, of course, the
stories also detail the precise weight of said materials, the types of sacrifices
that were made on special occasions, the dimensions of the ten copper sinks
in the Temple, and, most fascinatingly, the number of steps leading to the
king's throne and the exact shape of the animals carved into them. I'd rather
listen to his father's horror stories, believe me."

"But they say he's the wisest of all men."

"That's another one of the queen mother's brilliant ideas. Bathsheba knew
who she was dealing with and used that to elevate her own status. She was
the one who ruled the kingdom, while her genius son devoted all his time to
solving riddles, building palaces, buying horses, and what he loved more than
anything else: collecting women. As we speak, his collection has reached seven

hundred and fifty items, and he's still going strong. In order that his subjects wouldn't ask too many questions about the king's odd pastimes, his mother declared him the 'wisest of all men' and spread a sweet little story about how he judged a dispute between two prostitutes over a baby, at the end of which the people were left in awe of his great wisdom. It's the only interesting story that has been written about him to this day, perhaps because ever since deciding that case he's been mostly concerned with the shovels and fountains his good friend Hiram, King of Zur, has been making for him, with the three thousand fables of beasts and fishes that he has been busy writing, and with the fifteen thousand songs he is working so hard to compose in celebration of the cedars of Lebanon and the hyssop on the walls. Poor Ahithophel—if he ever met the great-grandson who inherited his nickname, he would want to go right back to the underworld."

"And who's been ruling the kingdom since Bathsheba died?"

"His wives."

"All of them?"

"A select team of foreign women, mostly Moabites, Sidonians, and Hittites. Their leader is Naamah the Ammonite, mother of Rehoboam, the crown prince. She married Solomon when he was sixteen, even before he became king, and is considered the most powerful woman in the kingdom. And do you know who her second-in-command is?"

"I can guess: Hatshepsut the Egyptian, your wife's niece."

"Solomon admires her more than all his other wives. After you finish your examinations in the new palace, don't forget to stop by the house he built for her. He hasn't built a house like that for any of his other wives. Which means I've got a mole in the most intimate circle of the king's court. Now do you see how easy it would be to take down the king? Just say yes, and the crown is yours."

"No," I said. "No. No. No!"

Three

Grandmother's story turned me old before my time as well. It was as though the sixty-five years that were unfurled before me over the course of a day and a night had been added to my own life. I had no energy. I also considered the upcoming examinations at the palace an irritating burden, but I knew that I had no choice. Hadad had set the date, and I couldn't disappoint him again. He'd invested so much in me and wasn't getting the return he'd expected. This was the least I could do for him.

"Show them what you've got," he said, unable to disguise the trembling in his voice.

"It's nothing for me," I said, trying to appear fresh and energized. "After everything you've put me through, these examinations will seem like a party."

After about an hour, two servants came to take me to the new palace. Rumor had it that the palace was even more magnificent than the Temple, which was considered the most beautiful building in the world. Up to that point, I had only been able to get a sense of the size of the palace because a high wall surrounded it on all sides, concealing it from outsiders. I was glad for the opportunity to see it from the inside. When I passed through the first gate, I didn't notice anything out of the ordinary and was prepared to dismiss the rumors as exaggerations, but after we passed through the fifth gate, a castle of gigantic proportions came into view, unimaginably beautiful and glamorous.

We entered the outer courtyard, and my breath caught at the sight of the garden. The carpets of multicolored flowers resembled spectacular mosaic floors, and small animals I'd never seen before were playing among the rare trees. There were birds of every feather, tiny monkeys, and bizarre fish swimming in a lovely pond with waterfalls. The walls of the castle were made of giant cedar beams interrupted by at least thirty arches lined with gold that gleamed blindingly in the sunlight. We walked into a large hall whose walls were adorned with precious gems embedded in enormous bricks. I couldn't figure out how they had transported bricks of that size, how they had made the steps gleam like polished sapphire, how they could have woven thread of gold and silver into the rugs, and how they had sculpted the lions to look so real.

But this palace filled me with an unpleasant feeling that increased the longer I observed it. I thought about the high taxes that had been required to build it, of the children who had been forced to leave behind their childhood games and go to work to help feed their families, of the women getting callouses on their tender hands clearing stones from the fields, of the men breaking their backs plowing and threshing, and I couldn't help but ask myself what my great-grandfather King Saul, who had gotten so angry when his pretty daughters wore elegant dresses to victory parades, would have said of such splendor.

⤜⧽⤛

The examinations began right away, without any warning. I walked into a closed room, and before I could tell what was going on, an armed fighter attacked me, engaging me in prolonged and persistent combat. I fought ceaselessly for hours without so much as a water break. Each fighter they put in against me was stronger and more skilled than the one before. One of them even managed to hurt me, but it was a tiny cut, and I didn't need to freeze myself to keep fighting. I was allowed to sleep at night, but only for a few hours before they woke me up to solve arithmetic problems. I solved them instantly. They were easier than the ones I had been given by my teacher in Zeredah. Then I was instructed to write on three different kinds of parchment. They asked if I knew any languages other than Hebrew, and when I said I was fluent in Egyptian and knew a little bit of Aramaic, an awed silence filled the room. At the end, I was once again subjected to hand-to-hand combat, this time against two fighters at once. That fight wasn't easy, but after the simple examinations I had just completed, I couldn't really complain.

After the two fighters ended up lying motionless on the ground, a tall, skinny man walked into the room and consulted with my examiners in hushed tones. I could see that he was important by the way they bowed and huffed with excitement. I was glad to see the satisfied smile bending up the corners of his mouth.

"Do you know who I am?" he asked.

I shook my head no.

"I am Adoram, in charge of the taxes."

"The tax minister?"

He smiled, but the smile didn't reach his eyes. "I have plans for you, but first I need to speak to Hadad."

The next morning, I woke up to a heavy hand shaking me impatiently. I opened my eyes to find Hadad standing before me.

"Not good," he muttered. "Not good."

"Did I fail the examinations?"

"You succeeded too well."

"And that's a bad thing?"

"It's very bad. Adoram has decided to appoint you head of the tax collection corps in Ephraim."

I couldn't speak.

"You're going to be the most hated man in Ephraim. Maybe in all of Israel. When you finally decide you want to be king, you won't be able to launch a revolt. The people will hate you to death."

"I'm not going to launch any revolt, but I also have no desire to collect taxes for the king's insane construction projects. Tell Adoram you've trained me to be a fighter and that I don't know how to deal with miserable peasants who have nothing left to eat."

"There's no point. Adoram told me he's been looking for someone like you for years and that he needs you now more than ever. Ben Hur of the tribe of Judah, Ephraim's current tax commissioner, is unable to meet the new demands for supplying the king with the required quota of construction workers. The personal tax rate and the tax rate on crops are both about to rise, yet Ben Hur can still somehow manage his tax collection duties—you expropriate some land, put a few people in prison, and sometimes, when you have no

choice, you do some less pleasant things. But now Solomon is about to build
the Millo."

"What does that mean?"

"You leave that to his architects. What Adoram needs from you is another three thousand strong young laborers from the tribe of Ephraim, in
addition to the five thousand who are already in Jerusalem and have just finished building his palace."

"Solomon needs eight thousand builders in Jerusalem?" I asked, incredu-
lous.

Hadad chuckled. "So few? Eight thousand is only the number he's getting
from Ephraim. Until now there have been ten thousand forced laborers in
Jerusalem and another ten thousand in his store cities and his cities of
horsemen, and now the number will go up to thirty thousand. Do you understand what this means?"

I preferred not to understand too much. I had no time to think about it,
either. Things happened at a dizzying pace. An hour later, I found myself
facing Adoram again, as he repeated Hadad's frightening words in a slightly
different way. He summarily explained what my duties would include and
promised that the seasoned tax collectors of Shechem would give me all their
lists and help me start up my work. In conclusion, he stretched his thin lips
in an amused smile and said, "You won't be very popular in the eyes of your
tribe."

I wanted to punch him in the face, but instead I politely replied with what
Hadad had taught me to say: "I didn't come here to be popular. I came here
to do whatever job you gave me."

He looked satisfied. "I told the king you were quite a man. He's looking
forward to meeting you."

I felt like I was about to suffocate. "When?"

"Now."

⟨≫⟩

Later, when I recounted the meeting to Hadad, he didn't believe me. The event
had been so strange and different from what I could have expected that I wasn't
even able to explain to myself what had happened. I stood before the king.
He signaled for me to come closer. I bowed. He asked, I answered, and that
was it. I only realized that had been the end of the matter after I left.

"Didn't you want to tear his head off his fat neck?" Hadad asked with disappointment.

"I barely saw him. I was much more interested in his throne, especially the fish swimming so happily inside the glass steps. Where does he get these ideas?"

Hadad's eyes welled up. "So, Shelomoam, is this good-bye?"

"Adoram has given me half a day to take my leave from my friends in the Palace of Candles. In the meantime, he's putting together everything I'll need. Guess how many soldiers are going to accompany me."

"Even a thousand soldiers won't be able to protect you from the torrent of stones the people of Ephraim will rain down on you when you enter their land. And the worst part is, each and every stone will be justified. And as for your redheaded friend, fine, go take your leave of him; perhaps it's better this way, so that it won't occur to him to try and find out why you ran off without a word. But don't tell your grandmother that you got my approval."

"I don't need your approval anymore. Soon enough, you'll need mine."

I entered the Palace of Candles through the main gate. My friends were waiting along the path, cheering loudly for me. Uzziah was the most enthusiastic. "I told you!" he yelled. "Our Shelomoam is going to be the next commander of the army of Israel!"

I hugged each one of them. Some of them asked me if they could join the tax collection corps of Ephraim when they completed their service in the Palace of Candles. I made no promises but left them all feeling good.

Ithiel stood at the end of the line. We looked at each other and laughed, but suddenly our laughter turned directly into a powerful burst of tears.

"Our youth has ended," he said.

I couldn't tell him that mine had been taken away ten days earlier.

We walked over to the edge of the garden. As we walked, I reminded myself that he was the grandson of the man who killed my father, but I wasn't able to hate him.

"I want us to swear allegiance to one another," he said.

I swallowed and said nothing. When I spoke again, my voice was trembling. "All right," I said. "Let's swear it."

We knelt and extended our hands to one another.

"My brother, Shelomoam," said Ithiel, "I am prepared to give my life for you."

I shut my eyes. I didn't know what to say.

"You don't have to repeat the same thing I said," he whispered. "Just say what's in your heart."

"My brother, Ithiel," I said in a loud voice. "I love you. Always remember that I mean it, no matter what you hear about me."

⋯

Then I went to Grandmother. I sat down across from her on the mat, rested my head in her lap, and took in the smell of old age. She leaned over me, her warm breath caressing my face.

"We'll meet again," I whispered.

"I think I'm old enough not to be so sure of that."

"I'll come visit you."

"You mustn't, Shelomoam. It might raise suspicions."

"People will think I've come to visit Hadad and my friends."

She thought this over for a few long minutes. "All right," she said at last. "Come see me one more time."

"When?"

"When you have a child. I want to see my great-grandchild before I die."

"I promise."

"And one more thing." She stroked my cheek and put her lips to my ear. "Follow your heart, Shelomoam. You have a good heart. You can trust it."

Four

The whole way to Ephraim I kept the curtains closed and didn't peek out the window even once. I knew the familiar views might make me overly emotional, so I preferred not to look outside. The soldiers who accompanied me rode their horses on all sides of the chariot and closely guarded Aner, who galloped freely beside them. They understood how dear he was to me.

So many things had happened in such a short time. I tried to concentrate and organize my thoughts. I hadn't come to a decision about whether I wanted to help the elders of Ephraim divide the tax burden or whether, as Hadad had suggested, I would be better off presenting the requirements to them and letting them work things out themselves. Adoram had decided to augment the tax army in Ephraim with two thousand more armed soldiers, but I have no intention of using them. I am going to meet with people directly, without bodyguards, and speak to them face-to-face with my whistling *sh* sound, so that they will know I am flesh of their flesh, not some sealed-off despot dropped on them from above.

I ordered the coachman to pass through Zeredah on the way to Shechem and instructed the soldiers accompanying me to stop at one of the stalls and buy raisins and almonds for the children. They asked with puzzlement what children I was expecting, and I told them that when I was a boy my friends and I used to gather up the sweets that the king's horsemen would throw in our direction, and that one time the commander gave me a ride on his horse and asked me my name. I didn't share the part about the pleasurable feeling that had taken hold of me when I saw the other children looking up at me and I felt like a king.

The soldiers exchanged looks and asked me how long it had been since I'd last visited Zeredah. When they heard my reply, they said things were different now and that there wasn't a chance the children of Zeredah would be running after us. I didn't argue, but in my heart I was thinking that they would soon come to see that children are children and that when you throw candy to them, there isn't a chance that they won't gleefully run after you, even if their parents have warned them about you and told them you're a bad man. I climbed onto Aner's back and rode at the front of the convoy. I decided to freeze myself a bit in preparation for the familiar sights so that my soldiers wouldn't see that I am an emotional man.

The main street was empty, though there were still at least two hours until sunset. I suddenly realized the sights weren't really familiar at all. I stopped for a moment in an effort to recover from the anxiety that had seized me and from the shaking that had come over me, and then I continued riding past neglected fields and abandoned houses as the tears ran freely down my cheeks. They'd come so suddenly that I hadn't had time to wipe them away. Had it not been for the soldiers riding alongside me and watching my every move, I would have allowed myself to fall off my horse in a fit of sobbing.

"What happened to Zeredah?" I cried. "It's like a ghost town."

"Why do you say 'like,'" the soldiers said. "Are you sure your family still lives here?"

I began galloping in the direction of my house like a madman. I noticed a few houses that were still inhabited, but they were in such a sorry state that my anxiety only intensified. From a distance, I could see that the wall surrounding our thicket had been torn down, apparently because the secrets had left the house along with me. I ordered the soldiers to ride on to the house of administration, and I directed Aner to keep going. I breathed a sigh of relief at the sight of the familiar vineyards, which were just as I'd remembered them. I assumed that Benaiah was at work there, but I didn't want to take the time to look for him. I rode into the thicket, jumped off Aner's back, and tied him to one of the fruitless trees.

I knocked on the door and held my breath. My face burned when I saw

Bilhah. I wanted to fall upon her shoulders but held back, afraid that her heart couldn't take the excitement.

"There you are," my adoptive mother said in a restrained tone of voice. "We thought you'd be here much sooner."

I felt dizzy. I couldn't tell if it came from excitement or disappointment. Her tone was so normal, as if she'd seen me only an hour ago.

"You knew I was coming?"

"Your grandmother's messengers are speedier than you are. They told us last night."

"Quiet!" I heard Benaiah's frightened call coming from behind me.

I turned to face him. He was standing by the window and didn't come any closer. I opened my mouth to say something but couldn't find the right words. What is one supposed to say in such a situation? I love you? Thank you for raising me? I know I've been ungrateful? Forgive me for what I've done to you? Let's start over?

None of these statements expressed what was in my heart. I suddenly felt that old yearning spreading through my body. I leaned down to hug Bilhah.

"I'm sorry," I whispered.

"I know," she said. "So am I."

Her arms were still hanging at her sides. I didn't know how to get her to hug me.

When I straightened back up I saw Benaiah standing in front of me. He hesitated for a moment and then came closer. I wrapped my arms around him and he leaned against my chest. I let out a small sigh, and a moment later his arms folded around me.

"I'm sorry," I said again. It was all I could say.

Then Elisheba entered the room. I pretended not to notice her. I didn't mean to do that, but I wasn't able to look her in the eyes.

"Shelomoam," she said.

I looked up at her. Her black curls flowed freely past her shoulders. I was glad to see that they weren't confined in a headscarf. She'd become a woman but had remained so small and thin that I could have wrapped one arm around her waist and lifted her up over my head.

"Greetings, Elisheba." Her name scorched my tongue and paralyzed my body. I didn't dare go near her.

Bilhah watched us intently and suggested that we sit down to eat right away because the lentil stew was already warm in the oven, and the bread was ready to eat. The familiar flavors flooded my stomach with a warmth that climbed up my neck and relaxed the muscles of my face. I made an effort not to look in Elisheba's direction, but when I asked Bilhah and Benaiah what had happened to Zeredah she burst in and interrupted them, saying in a choked voice that the high taxes were destroying the land. The farmers weren't being left with sufficient crops to sustain their families and had to become laborers or even slaves on foreign soil. The estate owners were still somehow able to bear the weight of the tax burden, but the villages and small towns barely had any peasants left, and many of them were deserted.

"We wouldn't have been able to make it either, if not for the money your grandmother sends us," Bilhah said in a whisper.

Benaiah glanced outside anxiously. The memories flooded over me. I wanted to cry, but I managed to smile at him.

Five

The thought that Mother was imprisoned in a cave because of me filled me with guilt. I knew it wasn't my fault, but how can I enjoy the feeling of sunlight on my face when I know that my mother has been buried alive since the age of twenty for the sole purpose of saving my life? How can I find the right words to say to her if I haven't even been able to say what I feel to my adoptive parents? I was afraid I might never be able to develop the feelings I should have had for her. I'd known her since the age of eight. She wanted to know everything about my life and was attentive and sensitive, but seeing a person once a month cannot replace having a mother who prepares meals for you and sits beside you when you're sick. I actually was able to form a warm relationship with Grandmother in spite of the short time we had together, but a grandmother and a mother are entirely different things. I didn't have to love Grandmother, and when I realized that I did feel love for her, it was an unexpected gift that filled me with happiness and pride. But I *have* to love Mother, especially after all she has sacrificed for me.

And then, of course, there was the last time we'd met, when I had shoved her onto the bed. Even to myself, I couldn't repeat the terrible thing I'd said to her.

Instead of dealing bravely with my guilt and trepidation like an adult who takes responsibility for his actions, I put off my visit to the lepers' cave time and again, telling myself that I had to get everything organized at the house of administration in Shechem before I would have the mental energy to go see her and mend the tears. I knew it was just an excuse, but I couldn't stop myself from shivering every time I thought about those sad eyes that would be looking out at me from behind the mask.

Bilhah told me that Elisheba visited Zeruiah every week and that they'd become close friends. She and Benaiah didn't lecture me, but the looks on their faces were testament to their disappointment in me. How could it possibly be so unimportant to me to see my mother? How selfish could I be?

That wasn't the only thing putting a damper on my relationship with my adoptive parents. Bilhah did begin to hug me again after that first visit, but the atmosphere remained tense, and the conversation didn't flow. I had so many questions to ask them, but I couldn't muster up the courage to open old wounds and reveal my feelings. We barely even spoke of my job as head of the tax collectors. They were afraid to bring the topic up, treating it as a sore subject that it would be best to ignore. I sometimes got the feeling they were afraid of me.

But what troubled me most was my aversion to Elisheba. I visited Benaiah and Bilhah only on days when I knew she was off dancing with her friends in Shiloh. I yearned to confess my feelings for her, but whenever I tried to imagine such an encounter, I was paralyzed with fear.

◆❧◆

In contrast to the stinging failure of my efforts with the members of my family, which made me feel like an insecure child, the soldiers actually treated me with awed respect. It was flattering to have tough, rugged men, older and more experienced than I was, accepting my authority. I had the sense that their attitude toward me wasn't merely a product of the title Adoram had given me, but also of that slippery, inexplicable quality that my friend Ithiel had described with the lovely phrase, "the personality of a king." I preferred not to think of myself as having such a personality so that I wouldn't be tempted to give serious thought, God forbid, to Hadad's plans for me to seize the throne.

As if to help me convince myself that I really was meant for a simpler life, my meetings with the elders of Ephraim failed miserably. They nearly lost their minds when I told them about the new tax ordinances I had brought with

me from Jerusalem. A few of them burst into tears, while others bellowed that
the barrel was empty and that there was nothing left to scrape from the bottom.
A few days passed before I dared tell them that Adoram was also demanding
another three thousand of our young men for the forced labor tax.

"Don't say 'our,'" the town elder of Bethel shouted at me with loathing. "You
aren't one of us. Your whistling *sh* sounds and the sighs of sorrow that come
out of your mouth don't change the fact that you're collaborating with the
devil."

"Would you rather that the commander of the tax army in this region be a
tyrant from another tribe who treats you harshly?"

"The burden is becoming harsher anyway." The elders scoffed bitterly.
"We'd rather have a Judean commissioner standing against us, like Ben Hur,
than someone from Ephraim. At least we could stone Ben Hur without feeling
guilty."

At one of our meetings, I was unable to conceal my tears when I heard
the story of a young mother who had lost her husband and was forced to sell
her children in order to pay her taxes. I wept right in front of the astonished
elders. I didn't care anymore if they saw that I was an emotional man.

I didn't dare make public the plan that was ripening inside me to alter the
way that the tax burden was being divided, but I was eager to share it with
someone close who would understand me. Without another thought, I set
out on the road. My soldiers wanted to accompany me, but I informed them
that I traveled to Zeredah alone.

I reached the thicket at midnight, and less than a minute later I was standing at Elisheba's bedside.

Her frightened eyes shone at me through the dark. "What are you doing
here?"

"When we were children, I couldn't fall asleep before telling you all about
my day."

She said nothing.

"I want you to hear me now as well."

I sat on the edge of her bed, pressing my hands tightly against the sheet so
that they wouldn't even think of slipping toward her body. She sat up and
leaned her back against the wall, pulling the blanket up over her bent knees.

I told her about the additional taxes Adoram was imposing on Ephraim and
about the three thousand young men he was demanding for the construction

work in Jerusalem. "Don't be like the elders and ask me why I accepted this position," I requested. "Right now, I'm only trying to figure out how to collect the taxes in the most just manner."

"That other question is more burning for me than it is for the elders. How can the great-grandson of King Saul possibly collaborate with the son of David? Why are you helping Solomon lay his yoke even more heavily upon the nation of Israel?"

"One day I'll tell you about the chain of events that brought me to the palace, and you'll understand that I didn't have a choice. In any event, what's done is done."

"You need to become Solomon's adversary."

"And then what will happen? He'll replace me with a different commissioner who will tyrannize Ephraim. Ever since I came back here, all I've been thinking about is how to more justly divide the tax burden. The things you said to me described the situation perfectly: the poor peasants are forced to sell their ancestral lands, and only the large landowners are able to bear the burden. The idea I've developed would make things harder for the rich, but I believe that they will eventually come to see that we have no other choice. If we don't make the change, there will barely be any farmers left in this region, and we'll all starve to death."

"I belong to a rich family." I could hear her smiling through the darkness. "Try to convince me why it's in my interest to pay more taxes."

"Let's start with the labor tax. Who are the ones sent to do forced labor in Jerusalem?"

"The poor, of course," she said with a sigh.

"Those miserable people have to waste their strength on excruciating construction work far from home while their own families are desperate for an extra pair of hands. Is it too much to ask that families whose sons are sent as forced laborers for the king receive complete exemptions from taxes?"

"Go on."

"The head tax isn't just, either."

"But that's the most common tax there is. All the kings in the world impose it on their people. Even Moses imposed a head tax during the time in the wilderness, and no leader ever had more compassion for the poor than he did."

"Moses imposed a tax of a half shekel, which was a symbolic amount that anyone could afford. The tax rate imposed by Adoram causes people to lose their lands. I'm not saying that the head tax should be eliminated, but it must be significantly lowered and made affordable for everyone."

"I don't understand your plan. If you lower the personal tax and exempt the families of forced laborers from all taxes, you will be forced to increase the rate of tax on crops by a large margin."

"I want to change that, too."

"That's the most just tax there is. Unlike the head tax, which is the same amount for every person, the tax on crops is set according to the yield actually produced by each person's fields. Moses imposed a high rate for that tax as well."

"A tenth, Elisheba. Moses imposed a tax rate for crops of one tenth of the yield. Do you know what Solomon's rate is?"

"Four tenths," she whispered.

"And now Adoram has ordered me to raise it to five tenths."

"Half the yield?" Elisheba cried. "We really won't have any farmers left."

"I need to set variable tax rates. The poor will pay a little, and the rich will pay much more."

"How much more?"

"Seven tenths of their yield."

In spite of the scant light coming through the window, I could see her eyes widen with astonishment. "That's almost three-quarters. Who could possibly bear a tax like that?"

"In spite of the difficult situation, there are still wealthy landowners. We just have to convince them that it's within their power to save Ephraim."

"I don't believe they'll be convinced. You'll have to send your armed soldiers and collect the tax from them by force."

"I'm sure that Bilhah and Benaiah will be willing to give up three-quarters of their grapevines to the king in order to save their land."

"Our situation is different. I'm not familiar with any other family in Ephraim that receives regular monthly payments from Jerusalem. Besides"— her voice broke—"why do you call them by their names? Adoptive parents are still parents."

I felt my hand letting go of the sheet and sliding in her direction. "Only if I call them by their names can I have any hope that you'll be mine."

She drew back from me. The vehemence of her response was discouraging, but I knew that whatever wasn't said now might never be said.

"I love you, Elisheba."

She paused for a moment. "I love you, too," she said. "You're my brother."

Her distant tone of voice tormented me more than the last part of what she'd said.

"I'm not your brother, Elisheba. When you became a young woman, I tried to push you out of my thoughts and fantasies. I tried not to see the image of you at night. I banished you, Elisheba. I know you remember that. The vestiges of that banishment are still etched into your heart. You can't forgive me for what I did to you. You begged me to be your brother the way I used to be, but I couldn't be your brother, and I sent you away in tears."

I knew that revealing my feelings would turn me into a different person in her eyes, and I waited for her to say something to me, but she said nothing.

"I'm not your brother, Elisheba," I whispered. "I'm a man in love who is begging you to love him back."

She brought her lips close to me, her breath making my head spin, but before I could wrap my arms around her, she shoved me with a sudden sharp movement.

"You're my brother." Her voice was metallic and cold. "I can offer you the love of a sister. That's the only love I have for you."

Six

After that night, I didn't know what to believe. The words Elisheba had hurled at me were clear, but her tone and body had told me something else. I was faced with two irreconcilable realities.

Only my professional accomplishments gave me air in the swamp of sorrow and confusion I'd sunken into. The elders fully supported the new tax plan I'd presented to them, but they used almost the exact same words Elisheba had and they advised me not to attend the meeting with the wealthy men of Ephraim without armed escorts. I told them that I was determined to make the plan work by appealing to the hearts of the people of Ephraim, and not with the help of my soldiers' weapons.

I had never spoken before a large audience before. The thought that I was standing before the most powerful people in Ephraim made me anxious, but strangely, that anxiety didn't paralyze me. It actually loosened my tongue.

When the wealthy men of Ephraim realized that I was talking about a comprehensive tax rate increase, they interrupted me with angry cries of "Who needs this Millo? Why should our best young men waste their strength filling the breaches in the walls of Jerusalem while our own cities lie in ruins? Why are we forbidden to build our temples, while more and more temples to other peoples' gods are built in Jerusalem? Are Chemosh the abomination of Moab and Molek the abomination of Ammon better than the God of Israel?

If Solomon wants to collect foreign women, let him build temples for them using Judean taxes. We aren't willing to finance his whims any longer."

Instead of summoning my soldiers and ordering them to lock up the protestors, as Ben Hur used to do, I waited for the shouting to die down and declared in a loud voice that I agreed with every word they said.

The effect on them was immediate. At first, there were still a few whispers of protest, but these soon died down. I told them that we were in the midst of a difficult period, that Israel had never before had a king who made his construction projects the supreme goal of the kingdom, that the small farmers were unable to meet the frightfully high tax rates of this builder king and were being forced to abandon their lands, that entire families—men, women, and children—were losing their homes. It was clear to me, I told them, that the wealthy were having a hard time, too, but they were the only ones who could save Ephraim, if only they would agree to shoulder higher tax rates and take the burden off the destitute. And then, when a new king takes the throne one day and declares a different set of priorities, they will be able to look their children and grandchildren in the eyes and tell them that it was thanks to them that Ephraim was not destroyed.

When I finished my speech, no one got up. I tried to interpret their expressions, which fluctuated between solemnity and shock. The surprise came a moment later, and it was so great, so sensational, so earthshaking, that I had no choice but to agree with what Ithiel had said about the unique quality of my personality.

The wealthy men of Ephraim got up on their feet and cheered.

But there were a few witnesses to this festive occasion who were not as impressed by me. Though I'd arrived at the meeting without an armed escort, four soldiers came in during my speech and stood listening with stony expressions on their faces. After the wealthy of Ephraim had dispersed, one of the soldiers commented that I was walking a tightrope and that it was safe to assume that the king would not reward me for the names I was calling him. I realized I was dealing with Adoram's spies and that I would have to convince them of my loyalty. Too much interest from Jerusalem could cost me dearly.

"The king doesn't care what I say," I declared confidently. "He cares only about how much money I deliver. Why should he care what names I call him? The important thing is that the taxes be paid properly. What's better, a Judean commissioner like Ben Hur, who turned the people of Ephraim against him and couldn't meet the required quota for construction workers, or someone like me who is one of them, who understands their distress and is able to deliver the goods?"

I was glad to find that my powers of persuasion worked on spies as well.

The problems actually came from the place I'd least expected. The tax exemption for the families of forced laborers presented me with a difficult challenge. Rather than having to order my soldiers to drag three thousand men out of bed in the middle of the night, as all the other tax commissioners in the kingdom had to do, I was flooded with some ten thousand volunteers from all corners of Ephraim. Almost no poor family failed to send me one of its boys. The strong young men filled the streets of Shechem and refused to return to their homes. "Take us," they begged whenever I stepped out of the house of administration. "We want to build the Millo in Jerusalem."

I had no choice but to make another speech, this time to the masses. There were so many people that my strong voice wasn't enough, and I had to use heralds. I stood on the steps of the house of administration and gave them my word of honor that my soldiers would inspect each volunteer individually and choose the strongest among them, the ones who could best withstand the exhausting work of construction.

"And what if there are more than three thousand strong men?" came their cries.

"Then we will take the poorest ones among them," I said. "They need the tax exemption more than the others."

The heralds repeated my words throughout the streets of Shechem, but I only heard the gasps of the people standing right in front of me. I took advantage of the silence and explained my new tax plan in simple terms. I wanted to make sure that even the uneducated people who didn't know arithmetic could understand it.

I didn't need to wait long for their response.

"Shelomoam son of Benaiah!" cried the crowd. "You are our brother!"

When I went back into the house of administration, I saw a few young men waiting for me by the gate. I recognized them at first sight. They fell upon me and crushed me in their muscled arms.

"These are my friends from Shiloh," I explained to my baffled soldiers. "The best friends I ever had in Ephraim."

A moment later we were sitting around the table together, eating and reminiscing.

"We always knew you'd become a great man," they said. "But you promised to take us to Jerusalem with you, and then you disappeared without saying goodbye."

I cast my eyes down and apologized for being so despicable, and I told them that they hadn't been the only ones I'd hurt during those very bad years.

"They weren't so bad," they said. "We made quite a gang, and we enjoyed every moment."

I asked each one of them what he was up to, and I was glad to hear that most of them had put wild living in the past and started families. But, like almost everyone else I'd met in Ephraim, even they were suffering great financial distress and were having a hard time finding work. A few even admitted that they still committed acts of thievery every once in a while when opportunities presented themselves. I immediately offered to renew our friendship and let them join my army of tax collectors. They hesitated, but I convinced them that the training we'd been through together was more than sufficient. "Besides," I added, "I promise to keep training you."

"You are our king," they said. "We'll go through fire and flood for you. Just point us in the right direction."

"I already have your first orders." I laughed. "Bring me Tirzah the midwife. I want to apologize to her, too."

Their expressions made my heart skip a beat.

"You haven't heard?"

I tried to tell myself it was just something trivial. A simple illness, a small accident. Perhaps she had moved to a different city.

"She died."

The room spun all around me. I grabbed the arms of my chair and shut my eyes.

"After you left, she took a new lover, and her husband caught her in the act. The neighbors heard her screaming all night long. In the morning, he hung the pieces of her body on the wall of his house. Israel hadn't seen anything like it since the concubine in Gibeah."

It was a long time before I was able to utter a sound, but instead of the scream that had been strangling me, something strange came out of my mouth: "The story of the concubine in Gibeah is nothing but a fiction. The scribes of Judah made it up to besmirch the tribe of Benjamin."

"Fact or fiction, how can we possibly know?" They had trouble concealing their bafflement at my response. "We didn't see the body of the concubine in Gibeah, but the body of Tirzah was seen by everyone in Shiloh. Her husband left her there as a warning for all to see until she started to rot."

I had to run to the washroom to throw up. When I returned, they apologized for their graphic descriptions, adding that they must have forgotten that I was excessively sensitive to bloodshed.

"What was done to that villain?" I interrupted. "Was he hanged on a tree or burned at the stake in the town square?"

"A husband can do as he pleases to his whore of a wife."

The word "whore" raked my skin with iron combs. I felt the air running out of my lungs and nearly passed out. My friends' embarrassed looks attested to the hard time they were having digesting the turmoil I was in. One of them even tried to give expression to their confusion.

"Listen," he said. "You used to be so tough. What happened?"

They wanted to stay with me until I calmed down, but I ordered my servants to bridle Aner. I felt an unbearable yearning for the soft caress of a woman, someone who could pull the iron combs from my body and massage my wounds with warm oil. I had no idea where I was riding. The crowds that still filled the streets of Shechem cheered and cleared a path for me. I was surrounded by love, but I felt as lonely as a dog. Elisheba didn't want me, Bilhah was pulling away from me, and I couldn't allow myself to go see Grandmother.

Riding on the open roads did me good. I felt the rain drops on my face. I took in the fragrance of the wet grass. I fingered the sticky trunks of pine trees, and I hopped off Aner's back so I could knead moist clumps of earth in my hands. I felt my strength returning, and then, in a sudden flash of understanding, I knew I could no longer resist my yearning for the woman who'd been waiting twenty-one years for me.

⁂

Here is the cave I first saw thirteen years ago. Just like then, it is wet from the first rains of winter. It hasn't changed at all—the same wide threshold, the same spacious hall, the same incense torches, the same colorful rugs on the floor and walls, the same long corridor leading to the small cell.

Here is the woman with the cloak, sitting in the torchlight. Her body is wrapped, her face covered. Her two eyes blaze at me from behind the mask.

I stand opposite her at the other end of the cell and utter the word that burns inside of me, quietly at first, then louder, eventually in a shout: "Mother."

Her entire body shakes, as it did back then. Her arms, her legs, even her face.

"Shelomoam."

Her voice cracks as she whispers my name, exactly as it did back then.

I come closer, kneel before her, and gently lift her mask off her head. The sight of her face makes my eyes sting, but I open them wide, feeling as though I want to look at her until the day I die. I will never get enough of the tiny wrinkles in the corners of her eyes, the black hair streaked with white, and the slightly loose skin of her neck.

"'Sorry' is an unworthy word, but I have no other."

"Then say the word again that you said before. I've been yearning to hear it for twenty-one years."

"Mother."

She pulls me in and grasps me around the waist. She explores my hair and my face with her fingers, buries her lips in the crook of my neck, runs her trembling hands down the length of my back.

I don't know how my large body manages to curl up in her small lap. I rest my head on her shoulder, close my eyes, and feel swaddled like a baby.

"Why don't you take off your mask?"

"They mustn't see my face."

"The people who wanted to kill me are long dead."

"The danger has not yet passed, my beloved child."

"Come out of the cave, Mother. Let me see the sunlight on your skin."

"I might be recognized."

"I want you to come live in my home with me."

Her warm hand wipes at my tears and presses into my cheek.

"The cave is my home, Shelomoam. At my age, it's hard to get used to new homes."

Seven

The next day, I sent two armed soldiers to Shiloh and ordered them to bring me Ramiah son of Perez, the sycamore fig gatherer. He arrived at the house of administration in chains. His pleas for mercy disgusted me. I told the guards to drag him off to the jail and informed him that he would be tried for the crime of murder.

He gave me a blank stare. "She was my wife," he said. "You have no right to intervene in what goes on inside people's homes."

At my next meeting with the council of elders, I informed them of the murder and implied that, contrary to the firm views I had expressed in the past, this time I wouldn't object to freshening up the abandoned noose in the town square. Instead of a reply, I got a murmur of displeasure, but they didn't protest openly, and the matter remained unsettled. In light of their chilly reaction, I set the issue aside and only raised it again at my next meeting with the elders, two months later. I took comfort in the knowledge that in the meantime the murderer was rotting away in a cold and moldy cell. I quoted the law of Moses regarding the unfaithful wife, which forbade a jealous husband from taking the law into his own hands and killing his wife, even if he was absolutely certain that she had been with another man. Instead, he was required to bring her to a priest and make her swear her innocence.

"It's a different situation now," the elders said. "We no longer have any temples or priests in Ephraim, and we cannot demand that a jealous husband take his wife to Jerusalem anytime he becomes suspicious."

"But he *can* murder her?"

"A wife is her husband's property. He paid a bride price for her. That is the law."

Before our next meeting, I prepared a moving speech about the fates of miserable women who were unlucky enough to be given to cruel men, and about Moses the lawgiver, who had given extensive authority to the elders of the nation. While I was making my speech, I wasn't thinking of Tirzah, as one might have expected, but about Elisheba. I imagined her sitting across from me on one of the benches, her long curly hair flowing over her delicate shoulders and her black almond-shaped eyes sparkling at me with an encouraging twinkle.

"The helpless ones are holding out their feeble hands to you in desperation," I raised my voice in an emotional conclusion. "You are the only rays of light in the darkness of their lives. God hears the cries of the oppressed and hopes that the elders of Israel will gather their strength and courage to judge His people with righteousness and compassion. Do not stand idly by. This is your moment."

An hour later, the elders gave me their word that Ramiah son of Perez would not live another year. I immediately ordered my soldiers to disperse throughout Ephraim and invite the people to the trial that would begin in Shechem the following month. I wanted as many men as possible to be there, and I wanted the verdict to reverberate throughout the land. A few soldiers twisted their faces in anger, but most of them expressed gladness and set out willingly.

At the end of the day I rode to the lepers' cave to tell Mother about the trial. Ever since our reunion, I would visit her at least once a week, and I was glad to discover that, in contrast to the uncomfortable tension that continued to prevail between my adoptive family and me, with my real mother I was actually able to build a warm bond that only grew stronger as we spent more time together.

"I'm so proud of you, Shelomoam," she said.

Her response was predictable, but it made me happy anyway. I'd had a hard day, beginning with the long speech and the excruciating longing for Elisheba, and ending with open disdain from some of my soldiers. I needed a mother's stroking. We sat down to eat, and I told her again about the success of my tax plan. I wanted her to compliment me, but she barely had any reaction to what I was saying. Her mind seemed elsewhere. When I stood up and was about to clear the table, she looked at me and said, "Why are you giving up on your love?"

It took me a long time to reply. "If I act on my love, people will know she isn't my sister, and my identity will be revealed."

"We'll find a solution, Shelomoam, just as we found solutions for all the other problems that sprung up at every turn throughout your childhood and youth. Your grandmother has fine advisors, and she's managed to come up with a cover story for every problem. Who do you think composed all those stories we told you?"

I didn't know what to say, and I sat back down. "Elisheba doesn't want me," I finally whispered. "I'm like a brother to her."

"Every woman dreams of a brother's love," Mother said. She was silent for a moment, then she stood up and sang in a clear, pleasant voice:

"If only you were to me like a brother,
"Who was nursed at my mother's breasts!
"Then, if I found you outside, I would kiss you,
"And no one would despise me.
"I would lead you and bring you to my mother's house.
"I would give you spiced wine to drink,
"The nectar of my pomegranates."

⁂

The next few months were intense, and I had no time to think about the trial. I trusted the elders to be properly prepared and didn't ask them too many questions. I devoted most of my time to individual meetings with the three thousand young men who were about to leave for Jerusalem as forced laborers, and I promised them that my soldiers would visit their families regularly and make sure that all their needs were taken care of. Many young men tried to bow to me, but I wouldn't let them. Had it not been for the revulsion I felt for Absalom son of David, I would have grabbed them with both my hands and kissed them on their heads and perhaps even on their faces. I felt as if they were my children, even though most of them were older than I was. The old age that had come over me in the wake of Grandmother's story no longer consumed all my strength. Most of the time I felt fresh and active, but the sixty-five years that had unfurled before me had been added to my own, and they had turned me into a man with life experience.

On the day of the trial, crowds of people flocked to Shechem from all over Ephraim. They gathered outside the house of administration and listened intently to the heralds, who repeated every word that was spoken inside. The elders' verdict was accepted with cheers of joy, and many girls even began dancing and singing songs of praise for me, their faces bursting with adoration. They were pretty and sweet, and they made me feel great yearning. I knew I could have any girl I wanted, that I could cling to her soft skin, taste her breasts, push my loins against her thighs, and feel I wasn't alone.

To my disappointment, the elders acceded to the murderer's pleas and postponed the date of his execution by four months in order to allow him to celebrate the last Festival of Freedom of his life. When I told Mother about this turn of events, she consoled me by saying that the postponement didn't make any difference. It was thanks to me, she said, that all men had learned the lesson that there was a higher law and that the blood of women is not forfeit.

⌘

A week before the Festival of Freedom, I was awakened in the morning by a thundering male voice coming from the back gate of the house of administration, which was just beneath my bedroom. It took a few seconds before I was able to shake off the cobwebs of sleep long enough to realize that it was the voice of Hadad. I raced outside in my nightgown, intending to attack him unceremoniously, but at the last minute I noticed a tall, skinny figure at his side, which put a damper on my joy. Adoram and Hadad stood side by side, instructing the stablemen as to how to handle the horses. Hadad spoke louder than usual. I knew him well enough to understand that he was trying to warn me.

"Hello, Your Excellencies," I said tentatively.

They turned to face me. I could tell that Hadad was proud of the speed with which I managed to freeze my emotions, just as he had taught me. I tried to catch his eye to get a sense of what was in store for me, but he ignored me and instructed the servants to unpack their things. I invited them to breakfast, and Adoram ordered me to have the meal served in a side room so that we could have privacy.

The moment we sat down, Hadad declared gravely that troubling news had reached Jerusalem of unusual authority I had taken upon myself.

"What authority?" I asked, trying to give my voice an apathetic tone.

"Legal authority," Hadad answered gravely.

"Have you come to look into the trial of the fig gatherer from Shiloh?"

Adoram loudly chewed a piece of moist honey cake, looking me over with his narrow eyes.

"And at the same time," Hadad continued, "we intend to clarify the nature of the extreme changes you've made in matters of taxation."

The news was certainly not encouraging, but having Hadad at my side in my time of need made me confident that I'd get out of this bind. I maintained a calm demeanor even as Adoram met with the elders and asked to hear them describe the chain of events that had led to the strange trial and the surprising verdict. The elders didn't mention my involvement and completely left out the speech that had led them to change their views and put a husband who had killed his wife on trial. When Adoram commented angrily that word of my speech had reached his ears, they answered dismissively that I had been giving a great many speeches, and they weren't able to remember every word I said. The leader of the elders went even further, emotionally telling Adoram that what had led them to deviate from the law and put the man on trial was the extremely cruel manner of the murder, the likes of which Israel hadn't seen since the concubine in Gibeah. "A cruel murder deserves a cruel punishment," the elder concluded. "That was the lesson that the Judeans taught us when they punished the people of Benjamin to the full extent of the law."

When Adoram finally retired to rest, I waited to hear the door lock before I hugged Hadad. He patted my shoulder, hard.

"So?" I said. "Am I in trouble?"

"It's nothing."

"Do you think I'll get out of it in one piece?"

"In one piece? Every other commissioner in the country wants to study your method and set varying tax rates. The wealthy are trembling in fear. They're afraid their fate will be the same as that of the wealthy of Ephraim, but they have no one to make compelling speeches to them, to convince them that higher taxes will turn them into saviors of the people and ensure the admiration of future generations. Where do you get these ideas?"

"Just read our Torah and look at the reasoning Moses used to convince the people to set aside a weekly day of rest for every person, to free their slaves after seven years of service, and to let their fields lie fallow every seventh year, and you'll see that I've come up with nothing new."

"You truly are as great as Moses. Your grandmother says so, too. She asked me to remind you of his birth story and said you would figure out the rest for yourself."

I pondered the story of Moses's adoption and reached the conclusion that we were actually opposites. He was raised as a prince and discovered as an adult that he was the son of slaves, while I was raised a son of slaves and discovered as an adult that I was a prince.

"Did Moses also teach you how to recruit forced laborers?" Hadad said, interrupting my thoughts. "The exemption you gave their families has turned them into the most diligent builders in Jerusalem."

"Do you think Adoram would agree to raise the quota of forced laborers in exchange for lowering the tax rate? The wealthy of Ephraim are having great difficulty bearing the heavy tax burden, and every so often signs of protest pop up. I've been meeting with each one of them personally to calm them down, but we won't be able to hold on much longer with such high tax rates. Eventually, even the wealthy will collapse under the weight and abandon their lands. On the other hand, forced laborers are easy for me to recruit. I have five thousand additional young men waiting in line and prepared to go to Jerusalem even today."

"I think Adoram would gladly approve that deal. The three thousand new laborers you've sent him build more in a month than the ten thousand workers from the rest of the tribes do in a year."

"Then why did you come to Shechem to threaten me with your inspections?"

"What's the matter? Don't you want to see your old trainer anymore?" He burst out laughing, but then his face turned serious. "Why did you decide to put the husband who murdered his wife on trial? You know that I've got nothing personal against executions, but it's best not to put any ideas in Adoram's head. He needs to believe that you're a tax collector who only cares about money, not some kind of judge or a man with leadership ambitions. We don't need him to start fearing you too soon. I'd also advise you to go easy on the names you've called Solomon. They fit too well, and Adoram knows that."

"So what's going to happen?"

"I trust your powers of persuasion. Explain to him that you got carried away trying to persuade the elders to accept your tax plan."

"And will he accept my explanation?"

"That's the beautiful thing about Adoram. He loves money and doesn't really care how you get it. Do you think he'll give up a gold mine like you?"

"And what about the trial?"

"The murderer will return to Shiloh alive and well, and you won't even be able to send your gang over to make him disappear. If you had just killed him quietly, no one would have said a word, but you decided to teach the people a lesson and turned his trial into a spectacle, so now you'll have to sit quietly and let Adoram set him free."

"It will undermine my position in the eyes of the people of Ephraim."

"Nothing can undermine your position in the eyes of the people of Ephraim, Shelomoam. I saw how the elders went out of their way to protect you. They love you."

"I don't understand you, Hadad. If everything is so good, why did you take the trouble to make the trip?"

Instead of answering, he wrapped his arm around my head, crushing the back of my neck. I felt like my bones were about to break, but it was a pleasant kind of pain. "To tell you I was wrong," he said.

"About what?"

"About your becoming king."

"You don't want me to be king anymore?"

"I'm not worried about it anymore. It doesn't make a difference whether you want it or not. In the end, you will become king despite your objections. Your grandmother and I thought that we'd have to reveal your identity to put you on the throne, but it has become clear to us that you're doing well enough without the people knowing about your royal ancestry. You took on the most hated position in the land, and within a year and a half you've become the most beloved and admired man in Ephraim. I have no idea how you did it. As far as I can remember, I didn't include developing that skill in your training program."

"Thank you for the compliments, but I already have a plan for myself, and becoming king isn't part of it."

He looked at me intently. "Would you like to hang the villain who murdered your lover?"

I could tell I was blushing.

"Would you like to make new laws for your people?"

I remained silent.

"Those are all things," said Hadad, "that only a king can do."

We continued staring at each other for a long moment. "I miss Grandmother so much," I finally whispered, totally beside the point.

He smiled. "You'll see her again. She won't leave this world before you bring her the great-grandchild you promised her."

Eight

Adoram returned to Jerusalem reassured and satisfied, while Hadad stayed in Ephraim another two weeks to help me make improvements to the training program for my soldiers. Before he left, he reminded me again of the great-grandchild I'd promised Grandmother. He advised me not to sink too deeply into work and to leave time and energy available for other pursuits. I thanked him with all my heart for his helpful advice and commented, as if as an aside, that it was too bad he didn't live by it himself, as his wife, Eno, lived in Hatshepsut's grand palace and only saw her dear husband once a month despite the fact that the Palace of Candles was so close to Solomon's palace compound.

Hadad's expression told me that I'd touched a sore spot, and I regretted having brought up the subject.

"She went back to Egypt."

"With her niece?"

"Have you gone mad? If Hatshepsut left Solomon, a war would be liable to break out between Israel and Egypt. She's the wife he most adores."

"You've been yearning for such a war."

"Not yet. First we need to put Shishak on the throne, then we can plan the liberation of Edom."

"Then why did Eno return to Egypt now?"

"She wants to help our son, Genubath, put Shishak's takeover into action."

"And she doesn't care that her sister is the wife of Pharaoh Siamun?"

"Eno is a smart woman. She'd rather help our son become the king of Edom than remain the sister-in-law of the king of Egypt."

"And you? I thought you wanted to be the king of Edom."

"I'm old already, and it'll be many more years before we free Edom."

I gathered that his plan to become king of Edom would have remained unchanged had I agreed to work in concert with Shishak and seize the throne in Israel. Happily, he said nothing more on the subject, preferring to focus on my private life and showing great interest in the nature of my relationship with Elisheba. He was disappointed that I was a man only at work, while I remained a frightened, insecure child in my family relationships. For a moment, I thought about trying to subtly change the subject, but I knew that cheap ploys like that could succeed with ordinary people, but not with the man who pretended he could read the secrets of my heart, and who often succeeded in doing so.

"She's my sister," I said, trying to dismiss him with my usual response.

"Sisters are wonderful. Almost all the great kings of Egypt have taken their sisters as wives."

"I'm not a king, and I'm not an Egyptian. It isn't really the practice among us Hebrews."

"You're half an Egyptian and three-quarters of a king," he laughed. "The mother of Ephraim, your ancient patriarch, was Egyptian, and your great-grandfather was a king."

"I could understand if you said I was half a king, but how did you get to three-quarters?"

"Your great-grandfather counts as a quarter, and the other half is an advance on what you'll become in the future."

"You're very good at arithmetic," I said, ending the debate. "As to prognostication, however, you leave something to be desired."

"Everything I predict for you will come true, you'll see. In the meantime, you'd best stop working so hard and get to work on that great-grandchild you promised your grandmother."

⋘⋙

Indeed, work was my entire world. In addition to never-ending tax calculations and the weekly meetings with the elders of Ephraim, I also devoted time to regular tours of every city and village and to getting to know the simple people, who would tell me about their woes and inundate me with their love. But at the end of the day, I was alone. Sometimes I passed the nights chatting and laughing with the members of the Shiloh gang, but even such pleasant pastimes couldn't take my mind off how lonely I was.

Throughout the long period of time that had passed since my late-night visit with Elisheba, I had been trying to see her as little as possible. I made sure to visit Bilhah and Benaiah when I knew she wouldn't be home, making up a different excuse every time to avoid celebrating Sabbaths and holidays with them. The tension between us remained as it was, and I'd grown used to it. My love for Mother was the best thing that had happened to me since my return to Ephraim, other than work, of course, and I was beginning to make my peace with the likelihood that she would always remain the one person I was close to in my life.

On one of my regular visits to Zeredah, I was surprised to find Elisheba standing at the door. I asked with eyes downcast where Bilhah and Benaiah were, and she answered sadly that they had gone to the funeral of a fig gatherer's baby boy, who had died in his sleep. Needless to say, the mere mention of that profession made me shudder. Elisheba saw the trembling in my hand and said with emotion that she knew what I'd gone through after Adoram freed the Shiloh murderer, and she added that she'd been wanting for some time to tell me that she admired my brave attempt to change the law and to protect women in their homes. I thanked her for what she had said, and I was about to return to Shechem, but she begged me to stay, saying with a shy smile that Mother had prepared my favorite lentil stew before she left, and it was waiting for me in the oven.

We sat across from one another at opposite ends of the table, and so as not to allow my embarrassment to paralyze me, I chattered nonstop, not letting myself be silent for even a moment. Elisheba tried to focus, but I could tell that her thoughts were drifting elsewhere. For a few moments I concentrated on the stew I loved so much, warm and fresh as always. When I had finished eating, before I even had a chance to get up, Elisheba asked me if it was true what people were saying, that the unfortunate woman from Shiloh had been my lover.

I wanted to confess it all, but my tears were strangling me. "I'm building a city to commemorate her name," I said at last.

She reached out from the other end of the table and laid her small fingers in my palm. "You don't have to say anything more. I understand."

I couldn't breathe.

"Where are you building this city?"

My knees were shaking under the table. "North of Shechem."

She removed her hand from mine and got up to boil water. "Adoram allows you to build new cities?"

I told myself that she had only stroked me the way that any sister strokes her brother. "Tirzah is being built on the ruins of an abandoned Hittite town," I said, managing to restore my normal breathing and speak clearly. "If anyone complains, I can claim that it's part of the restoration project of towns and villages that I've been conducting all over Ephraim."

Elisheba brought over a hot infusion of herbs and poured it into two clay mugs. "Your new tax plan is saving our land." She returned to her seat at the other end of the table and carefully sipped her hot drink. "I'm so glad you accepted the position, and I regret the things I said to you that night."

I could see the little girl who used to listen to my stories every night: her fine eyebrows that had hardly thickened, her luminous pale skin, her perfect white teeth, the childish swell of her cheeks, her slanted almond eyes, the innocent but determined expression on her face, even that little spot on her nose, the one she hated so much, which made me want to cry with love.

"Which things do you regret saying that night?"

She got up from her chair and walked over to me. Without a word she was on top of me, taking my face in her hands. A moment later, her tongue was in my mouth.

She kissed me with tenderness and with hunger. I heard her breath catch in her throat. I held her close with one arm and touched her body with my free hand. My fingers found their way under her dress and caressed the warm, soft skin of her back and her waist. I breathed in the scent of her hair, the taste of her lips, the whisper of her breath. I'd never been so happy in my life.

Suddenly she jumped to her feet, weeping, and fled to the edge of the room. I looked at her in shock.

"You love me, Elisheba."

"I mustn't love you."

"You may love me. You aren't my sister."

She was sobbing loudly. Her hair clung to her wet cheeks, and her shoulders were shaking. The way she was gasping for breath was so painful for me that I stopped breathing myself.

"Don't you see, Shelomoam? Do you really not know why I mustn't love you?"

I furrowed my brow in confusion, not knowing what I was supposed to say.

"I cannot be married to a king."

I blew out a long breath and tried to smile. "I won't be king."

She shook her head and kept crying.

I knelt down and placed my hand on my heart. "I'm willing to swear it."

"Don't swear, Shelomoam."

I'd never seen her so determined in my life.

"I want to swear, Elisheba."

"We mustn't swear to things that aren't in our control."

"Then what can I do to make you believe me?"

She came closer and looked into my eyes. "Ask me why I can't be married to a king."

Her clenched jaw gave her face a forceful look that I didn't recognize.

"Why can't you be married to a king?"

"I cannot share my husband with other women. Such a life would turn me into an embittered woman. I'm sure of it."

I got up and stood before her. "I will never take another wife."

She looked up at me. "If you become king, you will have no choice. Solomon has eight hundred already, David had dozens, even your grandfather had two."

I took both her hands and wrapped my fingers around them. "My grandfather had one wife his entire life."

"Ahinoam was his first wife, but then he took Rizpah daughter of Aiah as a second wife."

"I'm not talking about King Saul. He was my great-grandfather. My grandfather, Paltiel son of Laish, loved one woman his whole life. Only one. He waited for my grandmother for fourteen years, twice as long as Jacob waited for Rachel."

Her cheeks twitched. I leaned toward her and gathered her into my arms.

"Most men have two wives and one mother," I whispered. "I have two mothers, but only one wife."

Nine

Our firstborn, Nadab, was born on a scorching hot summer day that kept the people in their homes and the midwives at their birthing stones. It was a good thing, because the birth was so quick that, had we needed to bring the midwife all the way from her home, our baby would have had to come into the world on his own. My memories of Bilhah's difficult labor terrified me throughout the months of pregnancy, mostly because I worried that Elisheba would have trouble giving birth to a child of my seed, who might have inherited the great height and broad shoulders of the line of Saul. Indeed, when I held him in my arms I couldn't understand how her narrow, delicate body had been able to give birth to such a large baby.

We decided to name our children after members of the family of Moses, Aaron, and Miriam, who were still the leaders both of us admired most. Elisheba liked the name Gershom, who was Moses's firstborn, but I convinced her that Aaron's eldest had a nicer name, and we even agreed that if we were blessed with more boys, we would call them Abijah, Eleazar, or Ithamar, after Aaron's other three sons. Deep in my heart I knew that the beauty of the name Nadab wasn't the true reason I preferred it to Gershom. Ever since we had made public the revised story of my birth, people had started comparing me to Moses, and I didn't want to amplify the similarities between us by giving my son the same name he gave his.

The story itself hadn't been made up in order to aggrandize me, but because there was no other choice. I couldn't marry Elisheba without some kind of explanation, so Grandmother's scribes hurried to make up a new birth story for me that would put the minds of the people of Ephraim at ease and make it clear to them that she wasn't my sister. Many aspects of the new story were true, but my connection to the lepers' cave was completely left out and replaced with the story of a little basket floating along on the waters of the Jarkon river. According to the story, Bilhah was walking alone on the banks of the river one day when she was astonished to find a basket floating on the water, inside of which was a newborn baby, stained with blood. She fell in love at first sight with the baby and decided to adopt him, but since she was only fourteen and her husband only sixteen, she worried that her neighbors might decide to give the abandoned baby to some childless family, and so she pretended to have given birth to him on her own, in a carriage by the side of the road. The people of Zeredah were shocked to discover that this young woman from their town had suddenly given birth without anyone having known of her pregnancy, but the fact that she liked to wear loose-fitting dresses that blurred the outlines of her body gave them a satisfactory answer. They also told themselves that a young woman's strong, firm belly sometimes remained quite flat all the way through the end of a pregnancy.

My birth story spread quickly all through Ephraim, and it aroused wonder and veneration. "Our commissioner is the second Moses," people said. Some of them winked at one another and whispered with delight that now all that was left was to wait and see who Pharaoh was.

⁕

After the marriage ceremony, I went back to live in my childhood home. I only came to the house of administration in Shechem once a week for my regular meeting with the elders of Ephraim. The rest of the week, I worked out of the small house of administration in Zeredah. The painful rift in my relationship with my adoptive parents had healed almost entirely, and the tension between us had dissipated. I knew I couldn't ask Mother to live with us, but after Nadab was born I couldn't help myself and begged her to leave the cave at least once to stand at my side during his circumcision ceremony.

"The danger has not yet ended," said Mother, "and now it has also passed to your son."

"Will he also have to wait eight-and-a-half years to see you?" I spat bitterly.

She lowered her eyes. "Now we must be even more careful."

"It's been more than twenty-five years. David son of Jesse is long dead, and no soldiers are looking for me."

"The new story they're telling about you only makes the danger greater. The people of Ephraim are comparing you to Moses."

"That comparison is embarrassing, but how is it dangerous?"

"Moses was hidden in the basket because the king found out that the savior of Israel was about to be born, and he wanted to kill him. I'm sure the scribes of the Palace of Candles didn't consider this, but their story actually reveals the truth about the circumstances of your birth. The danger is now greater than ever. You must promise me that you will do everything possible to protect Nadab."

I realized that she had a point, but I wasn't willing to raise my son the way I was raised. "My son won't grow up surrounded by a thicket of secrets," I declared.

After the circumcision, I brought Nadab to her and placed him in her arms. She hugged him to her with steady hands and raised her head heavenward. "Thank you, God," she whispered. "Now I will forgive all that You have done to me."

"For now, God only deserves partial forgiveness," I said, trying not to reveal my emotions. "You should forgive Him in full only after you remove that mask from your face and breathe the outside air."

Mother's ongoing imprisonment in the lepers' cave was now the only dark cloud over my life. In spite of the terrible circumstances of my birth, which had robbed me of the chance to know my father and caused immeasurable suffering for my entire family, I felt like a lucky man. I was living with the love of my life, cultivating a warm and close relationship with my mother and with my adoptive parents, and I was a father to a healthy and handsome baby boy. There were hardships, of course, especially in my work—I wasn't always able to find a solution to the poverty and suffering I encountered, but I dealt successfully with most problems and took pleasure in the love and admiration of the people of Ephraim, whom I considered to be my tribe-mates. "I'm even stranger than I thought," I told Elisheba when I found out that the Benjaminites had sent a delegation to Adoram asking him to appoint me their commissioner in place of the hated Shimei son of Ela. "I have two mothers and two tribes as well."

When Nadab was six months old, I set out for the Palace of Candles to fulfill my promise. Elisheba was very excited at the prospect of meeting Grandmother, whom she thought of as a practically superhuman character. "Imagine if you suddenly had the chance to meet our matriarch Rachel," she tried to explain. "That's precisely how I feel."

On our way, we stopped in the land of Benjamin to receive final instructions from the spies of the Palace of Candles. I was so used to their being everywhere that I didn't give the encounter any thought. When I'd returned to Ephraim six years earlier, I was astounded to find that Hadad's secret loyalists had infiltrated the most sensitive positions in the house of administration. Bilhah also reminded me that as a child I once saw her smiling at one of the soldiers, and she explained that he had been the one who had delivered the money Grandmother sent us every month.

We arrived at the meeting place, and I warmly embraced the four men who were there waiting for us. "Meet the Benjaminite thugs who almost cost me my leg," I said to Elisheba.

They laughed and patted little Nadab's head. "Why didn't you bring the horse with you? We miss him."

"Aner is old now. I only take him out on short rides."

I had expected our meeting to include having a meal together. I wanted to catch up with them and ask about Grandmother, but to my great sorrow it became clear to me that we would have to quickly disperse.

"We mustn't be seen together," they said. "Adoram's spies have been tracking you ever since you left Ephraim, and they'll be here shortly."

Elisheba froze in horror. "Why is Adoram tracking us?"

"The story of the basket reached Jerusalem and caused a commotion in the palace. The similarity to Moses was a mistake."

"My mother saw it right away." I sighed.

"What's done is done, but now we need to plan the visit more carefully. Do not go to the Palace of Candles before you meet with Adoram. Tell him you've brought your family with you because your wife yearned to see the most glorious temple in the world with her own eyes."

Elisheba clenched her teeth in the expression of restrained anger that I knew so well. I squeezed her shoulders to let her know I felt the same way. Neither of us wanted to visit the temple of Judah when the temples of Israel's other cities were in ruins. "You think Adoram will talk to me about that story?"

"Let's hope so. Because if he doesn't, it would be a sign that he suspects you made it up to appear more like Moses."

"So, what should I tell him?"

"You must convince him that you made the story up out of despair and insecurity, with no ill intent, because your true origins are so lowly. Tell him your mother was a whore."

My hand pressed into Elisheba's. "I won't do it!"

"Your grandmother's scribes have determined that it's the only way to fix their mistake. Tell Adoram you were born at the whorehouse of Shechem and that Benaiah, who was a regular visitor, took pity on you and took you into his home. After Elisheba was born, your adoptive parents decided that you would marry her, so they told you that you weren't their son. To make you feel better, they told you that you were like Moses, an orphan found in a basket. But after you ran away from home, they became angry and revealed the bitter truth to you about your dubious origins."

"Adoram will ask me why I spread the story if I knew it wasn't true."

"Tell him that after you married Elisheba you had to convince the people of Ephraim that she wasn't your sister, and you decided to use the old lie you were raised with so as not to humiliate yourself."

"There are too many stories about my birth floating around now. Adoram won't believe me."

"He's used to these kinds of complications. Anyone who lives in the court of the king knows that every episode has several versions. Do what we're telling you, and everything will be alright. You have to trust us. Your visit won't go as planned, that much is true, but the important thing is for it to go peacefully."

"Hadad won't allow me to visit the Palace of Candles in the end."

"He really did wonder if it was worth the risk, but he doesn't have a choice. This is the only thing keeping your grandmother alive. Tell Adoram nonchalantly that you're planning on visiting Hadad and your old friends. Most of them have left the Palace of Candles, including your good friend Prince Ithiel, who is married and living with his wife's parents in Hebron, but you still have a few friends left there."

"Why isn't Ithiel living with his wife in the king's palace?"

"That's a long story. We'll tell you some other time."

❦

We arrived in Jerusalem near evening and were given the largest room in the palace's guest wing. The conversation with Adoram went exactly according to plan and ended with his solemn promise not to make my lowly origins known. The next day, I gave him a detailed report on the tax collection in Ephraim, reading him endless columns of numbers. I was hoping he'd grow weary of it and let me be on my way. My longing for Grandmother and Hadad was excruciating, and I felt like I couldn't wait any longer, but he was riveted and showed no signs of impatience. At a certain point, I couldn't take it anymore and told him that before I returned to Ephraim I had to take my wife to see the Temple and visit my friends at the Palace of Candles, but he just muttered coolly that our work was not yet finished and that I would have to prolong my visit so that we could go over all the calculations and make important decisions that would help us successfully execute the changes.

"What changes?"

"The king is going to fill the gap in the wall of the city of David."

"What does that mean?"

"It means we need five thousand more forced laborers from Ephraim."

"How soon?"

"In six months."

"I can do it. Many young men will be willing to work in Jerusalem to free their families from their tax burden."

"We cannot give you any further tax reductions. The king's treasury is empty."

I was so flabbergasted that I was speechless. "Without tax exemptions, we won't be able to recruit anyone," I finally said.

"I have faith in you," Adoram said with an amused smile. "When the people of your tribe hear about this important building project, they will accept the burden with love."

"The people of Ephraim enthusiastically built the fortifications of Hazor, Megiddo, and Gezer. The Judeans should build Jerusalem themselves."

Adoram furrowed his brow. "Am I hearing criticism of the king's judgment?"

"I'd be happy to meet with him in person and explain my views."

"The king has more important matters to deal with. That's what you have me for."

I only managed to get away from him two days later, and I was so upset and shocked that I waited a few hours before taking Elisheba and Nadab to the Palace of Candles. I didn't want Grandmother to see me in such a state. Hadad deciphered my mood immediately and asked me what new edicts I'd received from the great taskmaster, as he called Adoram. When I told him what the situation was, his red face grew suddenly pale.

"What are you going to do?"

"I don't know. These edicts will bring about a famine in Ephraim. All my accomplishments are liable to go down the drain."

"We'll discuss it later. Your grandmother can't wait any longer."

"How is she?"

"Not well. At night, she lights her candles without screaming. That's how weak she is. But she became twenty years younger when I told her you were coming."

There was nothing I wanted more than to bound over and hand her my son, but I knew I had to take care to introduce her to my family gradually. Elisheba remained in the doorway watching her from afar, her eyes wide with wonder. I walked in slowly, cradling Nadab, trying not to let the excitement cause my knees to buckle. Grandmother saw us and burst into tears. Her crying stunned me. Six years ago I sat across from her on the mat, and she told me how her father died in the battle of Mount Gilboa, how her mother fell on her sword, how her brother was murdered in his sleep, how they slaughtered her sister, how her loving husband died alone in the fields, and how they hanged her only son on the top of a mountain. She told me all this with dry eyes; not a single tear ran down her cheek over the course of the entire story. And now this strong woman was sobbing at the sight of my little boy. I bent down and placed him in her lap. I hoped he wouldn't cry at the sight of the old, unfamiliar woman now suddenly hugging him and staining his face with her tears. To my relief, he was looking at her with curiosity, then he reached out his little hands and yanked the golden tiara off her head.

Grandmother was laughing and crying at the same time. "He wants the crown. It's obvious that the blood of kings runs in his veins."

I put the crown back on her head and took Nadab from her.

"'I never expected to see your face again, and now God has allowed me to see your children too. Now I am ready to die.'" Grandmother mumbled the familiar words Jacob had spoken when his son Joseph had presented him with his grandsons.

"You will not die," I whispered. "You'll have the chance to see more great-grandchildren."

I turned and signaled for Elisheba to approach. She walked over to Grandmother with quick strides and bowed before her.

"Princess Michal." Her voice trembled with excitement. "I don't know what you looked like when you were younger, but you are still the most beautiful woman in the world."

Grandmother took her in her arms. "My sweet child," she said. "You remind me so much of my sister."

"Of Merab?" I marveled.

"Of Rizpah daughter of Aiah," whispered Grandmother.

Now even Hadad couldn't hold back his tears.

We talked for a few minutes, and then Grandmother asked to speak to Elisheba in private. I wanted to stay with her a little longer, but Hadad gave me a pat on the shoulder and pushed me out.

"Come," he said. "We'll leave the girls alone."

Ten

Elisheba wouldn't tell me what Grandmother had said to her. On any other day, I would have interrogated her and managed to get her to tell me the secret, but now all my strength was focused on the new forced labor tax that had been imposed upon us. I convened the elders of Ephraim for an emergency meeting and gave them a report on the harsh edict. I was so angry that I let them yell and curse to their hearts' content, and I didn't stop them in time, as I had been doing ever since Hadad had come to Ephraim and warned me not to call King Solomon names, especially if they actually fit him.

"The new Pharaoh is afraid of us because we're the most populous tribe in Israel!" cried the chief elder of Bethel. "He is making our lives bitter with harsh labor and weighing us down with bricks and mortar so that we'll be unable to reproduce!"

By the time I realized what was going on, it was too late, and I couldn't stop the flow. The nickname "new Pharaoh" made its way not only through Ephraim, but also throughout the rest of the kingdom, and it reached Jerusalem, too, of course. A commission of inquiry headed by Adoram appeared at the house of administration in Shechem and questioned me about the nickname's origins. The investigation went on for many long hours and included explicit threats to my servants and veiled, but rather obvious, remarks about the poverty my wife and son could anticipate if the head of their family was sent to prison and their land was expropriated by the king. It was the first time I felt that the torture I had experienced in the tunnels hadn't been in vain. Thanks to the ability to freeze myself that I had learned from Hadad, I managed to get through three days without sleep and still not give away the name of the elder from Bethel.

With relaxed confidence, I reported on the recent chain of events and told Adoram that the elders had indeed compared the new tax edicts to Pharaoh's hard labor, but that no one ever imagined comparing King Solomon to Pharaoh, and that I had no idea how any such expression might have come about. After a week, Adoram's patience wore out, and he decided to return to Jerusalem, but not before I was warned that the next royal slander to come out of Ephraim would result in my going to prison, along with all the elders.

"If you forego the additional forced labor tax, I promise you that the people of Ephraim will compose songs of praise for the king and spread them throughout the kingdom," I told Adoram.

To my surprise, he replied that my request would be seriously considered. I didn't get my hopes up, but within only a few days a special messenger arrived to inform me that the most gracious king had decided to make do with the forced laborers who were already in Jerusalem. I immediately convened the scribes of Ephraim and ordered them to sit in the house of administration and compose songs of gratitude for Solomon.

"How long do we have?" asked the scribes.

"As long as you need," I replied.

When the songs were finished, I summoned players of harps, drums, flutes, and lyres so that the songs could be turned into a musical performance that would draw crowds. I planned to send companies of musicians to the market squares of the cities of Ephraim, in the hope that doing so would spread the songs throughout the land. The first performance was scheduled to take place at the large house of administration in Shechem, in the presence of the elders and their families. The scribes asked me to bring my family as well. Elisheba stated with revulsion that she wanted no part of such a disgrace, but she finally gave in and attended with Benaiah and Bilhah.

When I heard the first song, I froze in fear and ordered them to stop the show, but the crowd had already memorized the words and sang them again enthusiastically:

Moses freed our ancestors
From Egyptian slavery,
Shelomoam will free our sons
From Jerusalem's slavery.
Shelomoam will say to Solomon:
Let Ephraim go,
Let my people go.
Shelomoam will make Ephraim grow.
Make my people grow.
Let Ephraim go,
Let my people go.

I had to act quickly. I knew that Adoram's spies might be in the crowd, and even if they weren't, the song would reach their ears shortly. I silenced the audience and delivered a speech. I appeared calm on the outside, but I'd never been so scared in my life. I'd faced my share of dangers in the past, but back then I'd been a reckless, adventurous youth. Now I was a husband and father to a little son.

When I finished my speech, the people didn't stand up and cheer, as they usually did, but rather they remained in their seats with reserved expressions on their faces, their lips quivering with disappointment. My declaration of absolute loyalty to the king had convinced them that I wasn't the redeemer who would save them from his hands. And, though I didn't say so explicitly, they understood that if the song were to become public, I would no longer be able to serve as commissioner.

I don't know whether it was that Adoram didn't hear about the performance, or whether he decided to forgive me because the songs written for Solomon by the scribes of Ephraim met his expectations. Either way, the matter ended peacefully, and no delegation led by him came to see me in Shechem. But from my perspective, the event had long-lasting repercussions, for it led me to meet Ahijah the Shilonite.

That day, I was sitting in the small house of administration of Zeredah making complicated calculations in order to figure out how many peasant families I could return to their lands in return for the excess taxes I had in my treasury. I was trying to concentrate, but constant shouting from outside kept interrupting my thoughts, which forced me to step outside. The servants apologized for the disturbance and said they were trying to get rid of a young musician from Shiloh who had been part of that performance in Shechem and had been waiting for me since the early hours of the morning. I asked them to tell him I'd gladly meet with him the next time I visited Shiloh, but the fellow was persistent, and I could see that I had best let him in and try to get this unwelcome meeting over with as quickly as possible.

He fell to his knees and bowed deeply before I could stop him.

"A quick bow of the head would have done just fine," I said coolly.

He looked around quickly and brought his head closer. "I know who you are," he whispered.

I chuckled loudly and told him I was the commissioner of Ephraim.

"You're a prince."

"Very funny."

"My grandfather and your grandfather were friends."

"Which grandfather?"

"King Saul."

Now it was my turn to look around. Just in case, I decided to freeze myself and weigh my next moves carefully. It was the first time I had ever felt deep in my bones the danger that Mother and Hadad, and Grandmother for that matter, were so afraid of. Until now, for me it had been merely an event from the distant past that had caused my mother's imprisonment, but now, in a single instant, it had become a real and tangible danger that threatened not only me, but my little son, too.

"Do you know that he was a prophet?" the man asked.

"Who?"

"Your great-grandfather."

I blew out a sigh of relief. I realized there was nothing to worry about. No sane person would take seriously the words of a madman claiming that King Saul had been a prophet.

"You think I'm mad."

I spoke in my commanding tone and ordered him to leave willingly, so that my servants wouldn't have to drag him out by force. I don't like it when people read my mind. Hadad was one thing; I'd grown used to him. But not some odd character who had somehow managed to discover the most hidden secret of my life.

He smiled. "Let me tell you a short story, and after that I promise not to bother you anymore. You've heard many stories in your lifetime, so what's one more to you?"

That statement also made me anxious. How did he know which stories I'd heard?

At first, I listened to him impatiently, but I soon realized that I did find him interesting, and not only because I like stories. I was smiling from the very beginning, as he vividly described the way my expression had changed all of a sudden the moment I'd absorbed the words of the song at the performance in Shechem.

"The final lines were mine," he said proudly. "You will make the nation of Israel grow. That isn't a hope or a prayer; it's a prophecy. I'm a member of the company of prophets of Shiloh."

I was familiar with the various companies of prophets that operated throughout the kingdom, and of course I admired them. Many of them did not experience revelations even after long years of study, but the ones who did reach that exalted level had the honor of delivering the word of God to the nation. There were, of course, also prophets like Nathan, whom Grandmother had told me about, who was mostly concerned with the palace intrigues of Ahithophel and Bathsheba, but most prophets were dedicated to spreading morality and knowledge, as well as to helping us cope with hardship and draw faith and strength.

"How long have you been studying?"

"Five years."

"And have you had a revelation yet?"

He laughed. "Listen to my story, and you will see how my revelation is connected to you."

And this is what Ahijah the Shilonite, the young novice prophet, told me:

"My grandfather is an unknown prophet who was once a member of the company of prophets of Samuel. My father did not follow in his footsteps, becoming a fig grower instead, but I have known that I would become a prophet ever since I can remember. I have friends who've studied for fewer years than I have and who have already experienced several revelations, but my grandfather consoled me, telling me that sometimes a great deal of time passes before someone's first revelation comes. In the meantime, until I become a prophet, I make my living playing music. In the context of my studies of prophecy, I've learned to play six different instruments. The harp is the instrument that brings me closest to God, but when I found out about your scribes' performance and arrived in Shechem, the only instrument they offered me was a drum. Oh well, what won't one do to make a living?

"In the middle of one of the rehearsals, as I was drumming energetically along with the other musicians, I suddenly felt myself levitating above my body. I don't remember anything else, but the people who were there told me I tore off my clothes and fell naked onto the stage. It lasted a few minutes, and when I woke up and heard what had happened, I realized that I'd had my first revelation. It was very important to me to know exactly what I had said, but everyone around me had been so startled that they could only reconstruct a single sentence, which I had repeated several times: 'Shelomoam will make the nation of Israel grow.' The scribes liked the line and decided to include it in the chorus of the first song.

"When I returned to Shiloh after the performance and told my grandfather about the revelation I'd experienced in the middle of the rehearsal and about the strange statement I'd made about you, the blood ran out of his face, and he revealed to me that you were the great-grandson of King Saul. At first I was afraid that he'd lost his mind, for everyone knows that David son of Jesse destroyed Saul's descendants. But when I heard his story, I became convinced that he knew what he was talking about.

"Saul son of Kish and my grandfather met as young men in the prophet Samuel's company of prophets. Saul had already experienced several revelations, and everyone expected a bright future for him as a prophet. Samuel, however, told him that he would be the first king of Israel and demanded that he leave the company. The humble Saul ignored Samuel's prophecy and returned to plow the fields of his father, Kish. But when Nahash the Ammonite threatened to enslave the people of Jabesh Gilead and put out their eyes, Saul could no longer deny the duty that Samuel had given him and the spirit of God that came upon him, so he cut up the oxen into twelve pieces before the astonished eyes of the elders and recruited all the tribes to the great battle on the other side of the Jordan River. The rest of the story is familiar. After the glorious victory that the unknown young man from Benjamin delivered to the nation of Israel, Samuel pulled him out from among the supplies and anointed him the first King of Israel. Only he didn't tell anyone that this tall, handsome king had once been his student. Sometimes, however, when Saul wasn't being careful, he would suddenly experience a revelation, and his stunned ministers and advisors would ask in astonishment: 'Is Saul also among the prophets?' A rumor also spread that he'd once had a revelation in the midst of a mass meeting, and the question 'Is Saul also among the prophets?' became a famous saying that expressed the adoration of the nation for him.

"After the calamity at Mount Gilboa, my grandfather offered Merab, your grandmother's older sister, that he or another one of the members of the company of prophets could anoint Ishvi, but Merab decided it was best to have someone famous like Abner do it, rather than an unknown minor prophet. That was the end of my grandfather's relationship with Saul's family. Years later, he lamented the death of Saul's descendants along with the rest of Israel and was certain that the dynasty had been annihilated, but then an old prophet, who had been with him in the company of prophets of Samuel, revealed to him that the daughter of Sheba son of Bikri had borne a son to Nebat son of Michal, and that the child, the last remnant of the House of Saul, was living in an isolated house in Zeredah. Ever since you returned to Ephraim as tax commissioner, he has been following you from afar, and he is very glad to see that you've inherited your great-grandfather's exceptional leadership abilities. I don't need to tell you how excited he was when I told him that my first revelation was about you.

"Now do you understand why I've come to see you? You're the one who will save us from those who torture and oppress us. Thanks to you, the people of Israel will be fruitful and multiply and grow exceedingly numerous. And I will be your prophet, just as Samuel was your great-grandfather's prophet. I will give you the word of God and spread the word that you are our God's anointed one. I will anoint your forehead with anointing oil and declare your reign in the sight of all the people. You will be our next king—not only the king of Ephraim, but the entire nation of Israel."

Sweat poured down my forehead, and my hands were shaking. "I will not be king," I said.

"But it's the will of God," said Ahijah the Shilonite.

"I have my own will. God has given us the freedom to choose our own path."

"Not always. Moses didn't want to redeem Israel, but God forced it upon him. Your great-grandfather didn't want to be king, but—"

"Samuel forced it upon him," I finished his sentence. "Do you know what my life would have been like had Saul son of Kish not given in, had he stayed back to herd his oxen and plow his fields? I'll tell you: I would have been raised by my father, Nebat, and my mother, Zeruiah, in a small house in Benjamin. Grandmother Michal would have come by to play with me every day, and Grandfather Paltiel would have taught me to ride a horse and would have built me a swing in the yard. And Grandfather Sheba would have visited from Ephraim from time to time, telling me all about his ancestor Joshua son of Nun. And I would have had many aunts and uncles, and cousins, and nephews, and we would all be . . ."

I wasn't able to continue.

"I know," whispered Ahijah the Shilonite. "Your family paid the highest price a royal family has ever paid, but—"

"No!" I said. "There will be no 'but' for me."

Eleven

Grandmother died two months after the birth of Abijah. I didn't place him in her lap; I didn't give her a farewell kiss; I didn't hold her hands as she took her final breaths; I didn't close her eyes when she'd returned her soul to God; and I didn't bury her body in the ground. My grandmother died alone, far away from her only grandchild and from her two little great-grandchildren. Only Hadad was by her side when she died.

Grandmother's death pained me greatly. Even Elisheba, who had gotten to meet her only once, wept over her for many days. Her profound sorrow gave rise to disturbing wisps of envy in me over the mysterious bond that had formed between them, and in which I hadn't been included. I asked her at least to tell me now what they had discussed in private, but I was met with a fortified wall.

"In due time," she said.

"When will the time come already?" I asked angrily.

A stubborn silence was the only response I got. I felt as though my grandmother was casting a shadow between my wife and me, and the odd sensation grew even stronger five years later, when our little daughter was born. I wanted to name her Michal, but Elisheba vehemently refused and demanded that we call her Jochebed, Miriam, or Zipporah, as we'd agreed when we got married.

"Don't you want to perpetuate my grandmother's name?"

"It was her will."

"You discussed our children's names in that conversation?" I asked in astonishment.

She was silent. "Choose any name you please," she said at last.

I named her Miriam.

⸎

Before this happened, just after Grandmother's death, Hadad had returned to Egypt, and three years later the military overthrew Pharaoh Siamun and installed Pharaoh Shishak, leader of the Libyan mercenaries, in his place. Hadad sent me letters through his messengers and reported that everything was going according to plan. The Egyptian army would invade Israel and receive minor—but crucial—help from Rezon son of Eliada, who had been appointed army commander of Aram-Damascus. The coordinated invasion from the north and the south would leave the army of Israel with no possibility of victory, and Edom and Aram Zobah would finally be released from the yoke of occupation and gain their independence.

I was careful not to upset Elisheba and pretended everything was fine. Slowly but surely, however, my nervousness was beginning to show. I felt pain in my chest and a burning sensation in my stomach. One day I couldn't get out of bed. My limbs were paralyzed, and there was a huge lump blocking my throat. Elisheba begged me to tell her what was bothering me, saying all the things women say when they want their husbands to open up to them. After several attempts, I was finally able to speak and replied with pent-up anger that a wife who won't share with her husband his grandmother's will should not expect him to share his secret misgivings with her. My reply made her almond eyes fill with tears, and I regretted it immediately. I asked her to forgive me for speaking such nonsense, the words of a desperate and confused man who could not find any peace.

"Is this about your grandmother's death?"

"It's about Hadad."

"Do you miss him?"

"I'm afraid of him. He's persuaded Shishak to go to war against Israel in order to liberate Edom and Aram Zobah. I love him and want his son Genubath to take the throne, but I love my own people more."

"Is it impossible to liberate Edom and Aram without a war?"

"Only if Solomon agrees to give them up."

"And what is the chance that will happen?"

"The same as the chance that he will give up his lavish construction projects in Jerusalem and release the forced laborers to their homes. He's given Hiram, King of Zur, twenty Israelite cities in the Galilee region in exchange for one hundred and twenty talents of gold, but he will never give up foreign soil conquered by his father."

"Not even in exchange for gold?"

"Hiram, King of Zur, is his friend. He calls him 'my brother.' He would never turn over the lands his father conquered to those who aren't his friends, not for all the treasure in the world."

Elisheba sighed. She didn't say so explicitly, but I knew she understood what was driving me mad. Only if a king arose who would agree to free Edom and Aram Zobah could a war with Egypt be prevented.

❧

I wrote to Hadad in vague terms that I was willing to reconsider the position he had offered me years ago. Afterward, I went to the lepers' cave and revealed my misgivings to Mother, hoping she would persuade me not to risk my life and the lives of my children. Her bare face remained expressionless, and only at the end, as I got up to give her a farewell kiss, did she whisper in my ear that she loved me and was sure that my good heart would lead me down the right path. I recalled that Grandmother had also said similar things.

My misgivings grew deeper each day. I would return home from work in the evening, kiss Elisheba, play with Miriam, help Nadab and Abijah solve arithmetic exercises and memorize new Egyptian words, and ask myself in terror whether I had the right to burden them with a weight that might turn their lives into a nightmare, like Grandmother's had been.

One morning I arrived at the house of administration of Zeredah as usual and found an official chariot waiting for me by the gate. Adoram's messengers politely requested that I accompany them, and before I knew what was happening, I was on my way to Jerusalem. I had many long hours to formulate a plan, and I reassured myself that even if my letter to Hadad had been discovered, it would have been completely indecipherable. When we passed the Palace of Candles, I wanted to jump out of the chariot and run to Grandmother's grave, but instead I fixed my gaze on Solomon's palace and told my escorts in a tone full of wonder that the new garden, whose construction had just recently been completed, was even more magnificent than its predecessors and that I'd never seen such colorful birds before.

Adoram apologized for the unexpected journey he had suddenly imposed on me with no advance notice and informed me that Solomon's construction advisors had finished planning the new project that would be built in Jerusalem, which was the reason I was needed so urgently. I felt the muscles of my face relax with relief and asked what the project would be—the Temple, the king's palace, the Millo, and the City of David had all been completed, so what else was left to build? Adoram pursed his lips and whistled, though it wasn't clear whether he meant it admiringly or contemptuously. He spoke with accentuated deliberateness as he said that anyone with eyes could see that the walls of the king's city could not remain breached, especially not now, when there was a new ruler in Egypt, and the new Pharaoh was hinting at war.

"We are building up the walls of Jerusalem," Adoram declared cheerfully. "You must recruit five thousand new forced laborers within a week. This time we cannot give you any reduction in the tax rate on crops, but I'm absolutely certain that the people of your tribe will be glad to take part in this formidable challenge and will volunteer in large numbers."

"Of course," I whispered. "They'll be delighted."

He narrowed his eyes disapprovingly. "Do I detect mockery in your voice?"

"God forbid. The people of Ephraim are always happy to contribute to their countrymen. But in order to contribute, they need to be alive, and in order to live, they need to eat. I don't know how we'll feed our children after five thousand working pairs of hands are taken from us in the course of a day."

Nothing I said made any difference. If I were strong as I once had been, I might have been able to get at least some relief in the tax burden, but of late I'd become weak and despairing.

The chariot took me back to Ephraim. As we were leaving Jerusalem we suddenly stopped, and I heard the coachman arguing angrily with someone. I pulled the curtain aside and saw a young man standing on the seat of a wagon and blocking our way. His new cloak stood out against the background of the tattered wagon and drew my gaze.

"He says you ordered him to wait for you on the road!" the coachman called to me.

I looked up at his face and saw that it was Ahijah the Shilonite. I recognized him instantly. I would sometimes run into him in Shiloh, and we would exchange a few neutral words about nothing much.

"Go back to Jerusalem!" I told the coachman and got onto Ahijah's old wagon.

He directed the horses in silence, never turning to face me. When we crossed out of the land of Benjamin, he stopped the wagon and ordered me off. The light in his eyes and the radiance of his face gave him the look of a holy man, and I couldn't refuse him. I followed him along side roads until we arrived at a large empty field.

"Do you know the story that David's scribes made up about your great-grandfather and the prophet Samuel?" asked Ahijah.

"They made up lots of stories about them."

"The one about the tearing of the coat."

"That's one of the most loathsome stories I've ever heard. I don't want to think about it."

"Tell it to me!"

In any other situation, I would never even have considered telling that story, but my great willpower was now entirely at the mercy of Ahijah. "The prophet Samuel informed King Saul that God had rejected him and his kingship, then he turned his back on him and started to walk away. King Saul ran after him, grabbed the hem of his robe, and tore it, and the prophet Samuel said to him, **God has torn the Kingdom of Israel from you today and has given it to one of your neighbors—to one better than you.**"

Ahijah pulled a knife from his belt and handed it to me. I looked at it, confused, and I had no idea what I was supposed to do next.

"Tear my cloak!"

"It's a new cloak," I mumbled. "It would be a shame to tear it."

"Tear it!" Ahijah repeated his order. "We are about to correct the story that David's scribes made up about your great-grandfather."

I wanted to ask him how stories could be corrected, but instead my hands grabbed the knife of their own volition and reached for Ahijah's cloak. Oddly—I don't understand how—I knew that if I tore it, my power to choose would be taken from me, and I would never again be a free man. I had fought against Ahijah's order with all my might. I knew I mustn't surrender.

Ahijah stared at me intently. I could see that he understood my struggle. "So be it," he said, taking the knife from my hand.

The great tension inside me eased at once. He cut off a large piece of fabric from his new cloak and commanded me to spread out my hands. This time I didn't put up a fight. I felt I was doing it of my own free will.

Ahijah cut off a small scrap of the piece of fabric he was holding, placed it in my hand, and called out, "Joseph!"

Then he added another scrap and called out, "Benjamin."

Then, scrap after scrap:

"Dan.

"Naphtali.

"Reuben.

"Simeon.

"Issachar.

"Zebulun.

"Gad.

"Asher."

❦

I cupped the ten scraps of the cloak in my two hands, and suddenly something strange happened to me, something hard to explain: I felt love for them. My love was so strong that I held the scraps to my heart and ran my lips over them. Had anyone ever told me I would fall in love with scraps of fabric, I'd have been certain that person was mad.

Ahijah threw the scrap that remained in his hand to the ground and looked away from it. I wanted to pick it up and brush off the mud that had stuck to it and hold it to my heart along with the ten other scraps, but he stopped me.

"This is what the God of Israel says," Ahijah thundered. **"See, I am going to tear the kingdom out of Solomon's hand and give you ten tribes."**

I looked longingly at the scrap that lay on the ground, feeling unwilling to give it up. "Give it to me," I begged.

"That scrap is the tribe of Judah."

"The Judeans are our brothers."

"They rebelled against Saul and divided the nation."

"I want to add them to the ten other tribes."

"No," said Ahijah. "The Judeans will not be part of the Kingdom of Israel."

❦

When I arrived home, Elisheba ran into my arms, buried her head in my chest, and told me in a strangled voice that she'd nearly gone mad worrying about me. She asked me to tell her how Jerusalem had been and whether, God forbid, my letter to Hadad had been discovered. When she realized I wasn't answering her questions, she looked up at me with concern. "You look so different," she whispered.

I fell to my knees and begged for her forgiveness. I always wanted to live a simple life. I have no lust for power, and I know it's wrong to put our children and her at risk. But there is a power stronger than me, and I can no longer resist it.

She looked at me for many long minutes and then started to bring her lips toward me, but she paused midway.

"I want you to say it explicitly," she said.

"I will become king."

The frozen expression on her face melted all at once, as if she'd received a piece of comforting news that gave her peace and joy. She asked that we sit at the table, and she brought us warm beverages and a sweet, fragrant pastry.

"What are you going to do?"

"I don't know."

"I do. Your grandmother told me."

"Is that what you discussed when you were alone?"

"Yes."

"She knew I would become king?"

"Of course she did. She was a prophet."

I couldn't help but think that if Grandmother had truly been a prophet, she would not have married David.

"So, what do I have to do?"

"Change your name."

"Why?"

"Our two greatest patriarchs changed their names after they accepted their roles as fathers of the nation. Abram became Abraham, and Jacob became Israel."

I swallowed hard and felt my entire body stiffen. "The fact that I'm willing to take on the burden of the kingship doesn't mean that I'm going to become someone else. I struggled with Ahijah the Shilonite in the field today and wouldn't give up my freedom of choice. Besides, I like my name."

"Your grandmother liked it, too," Elisheba said softly.

"Then why do I have to change it? Moses didn't change his name after God revealed Himself in the bush and commanded him to redeem the nation of Israel."

"Moses's name suited his mission: he drew—*mashah*—the people of Israel out of Egyptian slavery. Your grandmother was glad that we chose to name our children after members of his family. She knew you were the second Moses even before the people of Ephraim called you that."

"That's true. Hadad hinted as much." My eyes grew moist. I wanted to fulfill Grandmother's request and change my name without delay, but I didn't think I could.

"My name fits my mission. There's no need to change it."

Elisheba smiled sadly. "That's what your grandmother thought when you were born. The days of David's reign were filled with war and bloodshed. She asked your mother to name you Shelomoam in the hopes that you would become king one day and bring peace—*shalom*—to the nation of Israel."

"But the name Solomon also comes from the word *shalom*."

"And he's lived up to it. Thirty-six years ago, the nation was desperate for peace, but now it's desperate for something else."

"What is the nation desperate for?"

She got up and stood in back of me. "You know the answer. The prophet Ahijah the Shilonite foresaw it for you in his first revelation."

"My grandmother never heard his revelation."

"She didn't need to hear the revelations of other prophets. She was a prophet in her own right."

I stood up and walked to the door. Elisheba followed me and grabbed my hand. "That was her will."

I turned to face her. "What is my new name?"

"You can guess it yourself."

"I want to hear you say it."

She stood on her tiptoes and stretched her neck up to me. "Jeroboam," she said, pressing her fingers into the palm of my hand. "From the word *jerob*—to multiply—because you will cause the nation of Israel to multiply and grow exceedingly numerous, just like Moses did."

⋘⋙

That night, I tossed and turned in bed, but I could not fall asleep. It wasn't because of the fateful decision that was about to turn my life and my family's life completely upside down, and it wasn't because of the imposition of the forced labor tax that would bring disaster upon Ephraim. It was actually the name change that stabbed at my heart and made my chest feel tight. I rolled the strange name around on my tongue and knew I would never be able to love it. The name Shelomoam flowed out with a pleasant gentleness, beginning at the roof of the mouth, moving to the tip of the tongue, and then sliding out the lips with a warm kiss. Jeroboam, on the other hand, was a hard name that twisted the jaw, got stuck in the mouth, and ended up biting the lower lip.

Fortunately for me, I couldn't spare much time to worry about my name. The new tax edict required me to gather up all my strength. I had to convene the elders right away, and I knew the meeting would be stormier than ever. For that reason, I decided we should meet in my own home, inside the dense thicket of trees that had concealed the secrets of my childhood and youth, and I invited only seven elders I knew with certainty weren't spies for Adoram.

I reported on the project to build up the walls of Jerusalem in a quiet, matter-of-fact tone, but they could tell that something awful had happened. When I arrived at the number of forced laborers that Adoram was demanding from us, a shocked silence fell over the room. It took all that I had to leave them with a bit of hope. "We'll find a way out," I said with false confidence, "just like we have in the past."

Their shoulders slumped as if I'd dropped a heavy weight on them. "The only way out is rebellion," the chief elder said.

"No!" I shut him down. "We mustn't put our children's lives at risk."

"Don't you understand the situation?" cried a different elder. "It's better to die by the sword in a war for our freedom than to starve to death."

"It wouldn't be a war. It would be a slaughter. Solomon will put down the rebellion before we can even gather weapons. You remember the rebellion of Sheba son of Bikri." I paused and took a deep breath so that I could get over the feeling of suffocation that had come over me when I'd mentioned my grandfather's name.

"David was the one who put down the rebellion of Sheba son of Bikri."

"And what about the Rebellion of the Temples? Have you already forgotten about that?"

"This time we'll succeed. All the people of Israel will join us, not just the tribes of Rachel."

"All the tribes joined the Rebellion of the Temples, too."

"This time, it's a war for our survival, not for proximity to God."

I was trying to think of more counterarguments when I suddenly realized that it wasn't the rebellion that scared me, but rather what would follow it. All night, I had managed to push to the side the decision I'd made the day before and keep it locked in a box in the back of my mind. But now the moment of truth had arrived, and I could no longer ignore it and go on with life as usual.

"We're not yet ready for a rebellion," I said softly. "We need someone to get us ready."

The chief elder was about to interrupt me, but he was so shocked that his words got stuck on the tip of his tongue. Long minutes passed before the question that was floating in the air of the room was spoken aloud. "Who is that someone?"

The answer shot out of my mouth by itself. "I will redeem the nation of Israel."

Twelve

The elders eagerly awaited the preparations for the rebellion. How disappointed they were when it became clear to them that I wouldn't be training any fighters or caching any weapons.

"Our rebellion is going to be a clean one," I informed them. "Not a drop of blood will be spilled."

"How is that possible?" the elders asked in astonishment. "Even Moses killed Egyptians when he redeemed the people of Israel from Pharaoh's house of bondage."

"My mission is to multiply the nation of Israel, not to diminish it," I said. It was a major hint at my new name, but they had no way to see that. A name change symbolizes a most significant transformation, and I knew that I mustn't raise unnecessary suspicions. Members of my family called me Jeroboam only inside the four walls of our house and in the cave, but never in the presence of my children. Nadab, my eldest, was already twelve years old, but Mother was able to convince me that knowing a secret can be an even greater burden than not knowing it, and that I'd be better off not sharing my family's convoluted history with my children prematurely. It made me angry that I was raising them in a world of secrets, but what choice did I have?

Elisheba and Bilhah supported the clean rebellion I was planning and encouraged me not to give the idea up, while Mother and Benaiah were full of anxiety and implored me to gather weapons in case they were needed, should worse come to worst and Solomon decide to send armed soldiers into Ephraim. I replied by saying that weapons were the kinds of things that ended up being used if they were available. "In every previous rebellion, the rebels were armed with weapons," I reminded them, "and they all failed. The time has come for us to try a different kind of uprising."

"And if it fails?" Mother asked anxiously.

"Then at least no one will die."

A week later I told Adoram that I'd managed, with great effort, to draft fifteen hundred forced laborers who were prepared to leave for Jerusalem immediately to build up the walls, and that in order for their families not to starve I had to lower the head tax and the tax on crops in Ephraim. I had made a calculation that he wouldn't remove me from my position or order his soldiers to seize laborers from their homes by force. For now, it was in his best interest to make do with fewer workers, rather than risk a violent confrontation with the strongest tribe in Israel at the height of the largest construction project Jerusalem had ever seen. I knew that his restraint wouldn't last forever, but I now had a relatively quiet period in which to plan my next steps. I asked the elders of Ephraim not to push me to escalate the rebellion prematurely so that we didn't end up in a war of brother against brother, God forbid. They eventually accepted my stance, but they urged me not to delay too much. "We want to see the new king take the throne in our lifetimes," they said.

Hadad also agreed to be patient and continued to send me secret letters hidden in opaque jars of perfume. "It's best that the Libyan mercenaries of Shishak not hear about your strange rebellion," he wrote in his characteristic style. "The expression 'clean rebellion' would get them so riled up that they would be forced to invade Israel just to dirty it up."

I didn't know how long it would take before more tribes joined our tax rebellion, but I knew which tribes would be the first. And indeed, the tribe of Benjamin sent only a third of its quota of forced laborers to Jerusalem, and six months later the people of Manasseh on both sides of the Jordan announced that they were absolutely certain that the building of the wall would be unaffected by the absence of the two thousand new workers they were supposed to recruit. In response, Adoram called an emergency meeting and summoned representatives of all the tribes. Mother trembled in fear, but I explained that the rebellion was going exactly as I'd planned.

"Maybe Solomon is plotting to kill all of you when you arrive in Jerusalem?"

"Solomon does nothing on his own other than plan construction projects, compose riddles, and collect women, and Adoram wouldn't dare kill the tribal representatives and risk a war with the entire nation of Israel. He knows how to collect taxes, not wage wars."

"And what about Solomon's foreign wives who run the affairs at the palace court?"

"They are too busy doing what they're doing and have no time to deal with peripheral issues like some strange tax rebellion, something they've never even heard of in their home countries. Naamah the Ammonite must make sure that her dear son Rehoboam maintains his position as crown prince despite his meager abilities, and the others are investing all their strength in intense competition over the grandeur of the temples that Solomon has built for their gods. Each is trying to obtain more gold, more gems, and more rare treasures for her god. It is being said that the god Chemosh is currently in the lead, that his temple in Jerusalem is even more magnificent than the ones built for him in his own land of Moab."

My description managed to amuse Mother, and she commented jokingly that Hadad's spies were certainly doing their job well, adding that as long as the most current information they provided me revolved solely around the misdeeds of Solomon's wives in their battles over their temples, she could rest easy.

When I returned home, I remembered that it was market day in Zeredah and decided to stop and buy a Philistine shell necklace for Elisheba from her favorite jeweler. I would often roam the markets of Ephraim alone, like an ordinary person, and I tried to do so at least once a week. It was important to me to get to see from up close how the simple people lived and to hear from them directly as they talked about their troubles and concerns. Zeredah's market had always been and still was my favorite, as it aroused bittersweet memories of the distant days of my childhood.

I tied up my horse at the entrance to the market, near the food stalls, and I turned in the direction of the performance tent. I stopped every few steps to answer the greetings and expressions of love that were heaped upon me from every direction, and I noticed that while I was chatting, I was also glancing around nervously. I had the feeling that I was being followed, but I saw nothing out of the ordinary and figured that it was just my imagination. In addition to the necklace, I also bought a swing for Miriam and two cedar boxes for Nadab and Abijah. I returned to my horse and began strapping the gifts onto him when I heard a familiar voice coming from behind me.

"Is that Aner?"

"Aner is dead," I answered, turning toward the voice. A man of average height was standing opposite me. I examined his face with interest. I didn't recognize him at first, but a moment later the gifts fell from my hands, and I found myself falling on his neck.

"Ithiel," I whispered in a strangled voice. "I've missed you."

He hugged me with all his might. "I was starting to doubt we'd ever meet again."

"Every time I traveled to Jerusalem, I hoped to see you, but you were always at the home of your wife's family in Hebron. Why don't you live in the palace anymore?"

"Long story. I'll tell you some other time."

I recalled that this was the same response, even in the same words, that my friends, the Benjaminite thugs, had given when I asked them about him years ago.

"Come home with me," I pleaded. "Meet my wife and three children, and we'll talk until morning. We have seventeen years to catch up on."

He licked his lips, which had grown dry from the excitement. I felt like I was melting with love, and I tried again to hug him, but he let out a groan and grabbed my arms.

"I've come to warn you."

For a moment, the troubling thought occurred to me that he'd become one of Adoram's emissaries and had come to persuade me to put an end to the tax rebellion.

"They are going to kill you on your way to Jerusalem tomorrow. To make it look like just another robbery on the roads, your coachman will also be killed, and they'll steal your money."

My legs were shaking so badly that I couldn't even sit down. I leaned against my horse, gasping for breath. "Thank you, Ithiel, for warning me," I managed to whisper. "I won't go to Jerusalem tomorrow."

His ginger eyelashes fluttered and closed for a moment in pain. "Don't you understand? They are determined to get rid of you. If you don't come to

Jerusalem, they'll kill you here in Ephraim, and perhaps they'll take the opportunity to attack your family as well. Adoram is calling you 'Solomon's Bane' and saying that your tax rebellion is really a euphemism for a rebellion against the king."

"It isn't a euphemism. It's a clean rebellion."

"Adoram says you want to overthrow the king."

I fixed my eyes on him. "And what do you think?"

"I don't think. I only want you to live."

Those words also sounded familiar, but I couldn't recall where I'd heard them.

"Aren't you afraid of warning me?"

"Of course I am, but I'm more afraid of losing you."

I was overwhelmed by his love for me and made no move to leave. He shook me savagely. "You need to take your family and get outside the borders of Israel. Do you have someplace to go?"

"I'm not going anywhere. All the tribes of Rachel have joined my rebellion. They've put their trust in me. I cannot abandon them. The tax rebellion must go on and—"

Ithiel pushed me toward my horse with both his hands before I could finish my sentence. "Flee, Shelomoam!" he screamed. "If you don't run for your life tonight, tomorrow you'll be killed!"

The memory hit me all at once. My grandmother had said those exact same words to his grandfather. More than eighty years ago she saved David's life, and now his grandson was saving her grandson.

"Go!" Ithiel shouted. "What are you waiting for?"

I got on my horse without thinking. The feelings, the sensations, the terror—everything in me was frozen. There was only one thing I didn't freeze in that moment: my powerful love for him. I leaned down from the horse and fixed my eyes on his. "Ithiel," I said, my voice now much softer. "Do you know who your father was?"

He looked up at me with a puzzled look in his eyes.

"Adonijah son of David was the crown prince."

His face went blank. I had a feeling that he was hiding something from me.

"He was the favorite son," I continued in the same soft voice, like a quiet melody. "There was no one in the palace like him—blameless and upright, a man who feared God and shunned evil."

He didn't look surprised.

"Did you know that?"

"One of the elderly wives of my grandfather once ran into me at the Temple and asked if I was the son of Adonijah. When I replied that I was, she muttered some strange things about how I should have been the crown prince. I didn't take her seriously. I thought she was confused by my resemblance to my grandfather, which everyone always talks about."

He bent his head down and wiped his forehead with the back of his hand. "I don't understand why no one ever told me."

"So that you would go on thinking that he was murdered by a mad priest."

His face froze in shock.

"He escaped to the altar after learning of false charges being concocted against him by the queen mother, Bathsheba, who claimed that he was scheming to take Abishag the Shunamite, the last woman your grandfather had married before he died."

His mouth dropped open a bit, and his eyes widened in horror. "Who killed my father?"

"Benaiah son of Jehoiada, the commander of Solomon's army."

"Oh my God," Ithiel mumbled with the last of his strength.

"I don't know if you believe me, and there isn't anyone still alive to confirm what I'm saying, but I had to tell you what I knew about you."

I pulled sharply on my horse's reins and began galloping forward when I heard Ithiel call from behind me, "Wait a moment!"

I stopped and turned my horse to face him.

"I do have someone I can ask. The old lady I mentioned earlier . . ."

I held my breath.

"Her name is Abishag."

I felt the distant characters from Grandmother's story coming to life and standing before me. No matter where I went or what I did, no matter how far I ran, they would always pursue me. I tried to steady my hands so that I could ride on, but Ithiel stood in front of me and blocked my path.

"How do you know all this?"

I said nothing.

He didn't take his eyes off me. "Who are you, Shelomoam?"

At that moment I did the thing I'd been warned about and cautioned against, the thing they made me fear and that caused my torture in the tunnels. All my senses fought against me, but no power in the world could stop me.

I got off the horse, stood before him, and looked into his eyes. "The Mad Princess was my grandmother."

His eyes widened. "You're . . . you're . . ."

"Yes," I said. "I am the great-grandson of King Saul."

Thirteen

My great-grandfather and his three sons were killed by the Philistines, but I breathed a sigh of relief when I got to their land. As we rode swiftly along the Jarkon River, I sat on high alert in the carriage. Each soldier who passed us made my heart beat faster, but when we entered Ashdod, I could finally slow down and glance back at my family, sitting crowded in the back, signs of terror still upon their faces. A distant image suddenly flashed before me: my grandmother fleeing Gibeah with my grandfather Paltiel and her soul sister Rizpah, looking at the seven boys sitting around her in the carriage, knowing that if she couldn't get them safely to Gallim there would be nothing left of the House of Saul.

"I'm hungry," whined little Miriam.

Had I not insisted on stopping at the lepers' cave, we would have had time to bake a few loaves of bread for the road, but I couldn't flee without taking my leave of Mother. I had begged her to come with us, but she'd refused absolutely. "If I flee with you, they might begin to make inquiries about me and discover my identity," she said firmly. I tried to explain that the king wanted me killed anyway. What difference did it make if he knew who I was?

Mother sighed and shook her head. "What is a tax commissioner, insubordinate and rebellious as he may be, compared to the last scion of the House of Saul?"

"Our exile is liable to last a long time," I said. "Who knows when we'll meet again."

My words pierced her heart like a dagger. I didn't think I had ever seen her so sad. "Sometimes a mother's love is tested most powerfully in parting, like Jochebed, who let go of her son and abandoned him on the waters of the Nile in order to save his life. I parted with you the moment you were born; I have the strength to part with you again."

She covered her face with the mask, and I went outside to call my children to come into the cave to say farewell to Zeruah, the leper who was Mother's and Father's friend. Elisheba hugged her, wiping the tears from her own eyes as she did. Miriam kissed her covered-up hands, and the boys promised to send her letters.

I bent over and rested my head on her shoulder. "We'll come back to you," I whispered.

"I know," she said.

"Come back from where?" Miriam asked.

"Where are we going?" Nadab and Abijah joined in.

I didn't reply. I was afraid someone might stop us during our journey and ask our destination. I didn't want to burden them with keeping the secret.

Only four days later, after we had left the city of Gaza, did I dare speak aloud the name of the land we were about to enter.

"I knew it!" declared Abijah proudly. "I could tell we were riding south along the coast."

"I'm afraid of the Egyptians," Miriam said.

"Our matriarch Asenath was an Egyptian," Nadab reminded her.

"The Egyptians are bad," insisted the girl. "That's why Moses struck them with terrible plagues."

Bilhah seized the opportunity, of course, and began excitedly describing the powerful friendship of Joseph and Pharaoh, King of Egypt. I listened to her with mixed feelings. I was glad she was imbuing my children with love for our patriarchs, just as she'd done for me in my childhood, but I was sorry that I still couldn't tell them that the patriarch of their tribe was not Joseph, but rather his younger brother Benjamin. I wanted so badly to raise my children without secrets.

When we finally arrived at Shishak's palace, I got down from the carriage alone and approached the guards to introduce myself and ask them to call for Hadad the Edomite. To my surprise, they took me right inside and pointed toward the large silhouette standing in the garden in front of the intimidating statues of Pharaoh. Two minutes later, I found myself being crushed between his arms.

"How did you know I was coming?" I asked.

"You wanted to surprise *me*? I nearly passed out when I heard of your escape. What luck that you were able to get out in time. And a job well done by your spies. They're even better than mine."

"I don't have spies."

"Then who told you that Adoram was plotting to kill you?"

"My good and beloved friend, the one you and Grandmother liked to call the 'red fox.'"

Hadad grimaced in disgust. "I'm certain that he planned it together with Adoram so that you would trust him and reveal your secrets to him. Be careful that he doesn't become your Ahithophel."

What he said startled me, but I felt that I could trust my heart, as Mother and Grandmother had told me.

"What's wrong with you? Your face has turned as green as the Nile."

I knew how to deal with cross-examinations and quickly find the excuse that made the most sense. "I just remembered that the Benjaminite thugs once hinted to me that Ithiel had left the palace under mysterious circumstances, and I'm curious to know what they were referring to."

"Rehoboam's mother is stirring things up just like Bathsheba before her, though she wasn't endowed with her predecessor's cunning or cruelty. She notices that there are a few impressive princes walking around the king's court, overshadowing her sorry little treasure. Bathsheba would have made sure to exterminate them, but Naamah, merciful Ammonite that she is, just throws them out of the palace."

"Ithiel is no threat to Rehoboam. He isn't the son of a king."

"But Solomon adopted him as a son, and he glows far more brightly than the hundreds of princes swarming around in that palace. Besides, don't forget that he's the spitting image of his grandfather."

"Only when it comes to outward appearances."

"That's precisely where we disagree, kid. Listen to me, don't trust him."

"So now you're calling me 'kid' again?" I tried to change the subject. "I thought we were over that a long time ago."

"I can't call you Jeroboam. I told your grandmother—that name makes my mouth hurt. But she insisted. Has your family gotten used to it?"

"My children don't know about it yet. I think that here of all places, far away from Jerusalem, I'll be able to tell them everything I've been hiding from them all these years."

"Not everything. You mustn't tell them the dangerous secrets quite yet. I have to train them first."

"My children will never go through your torture. You'll have to kill me first."

"That's a very good idea. Your clean tax rebellion is going nowhere anyway."

His hard slap on my back almost knocked me to the ground. I grabbed his head in a hug, and we went out to the carriage. Hadad bowed deeply to Elisheba and gave Nadab a sidelong glance.

"Tall and handsome like a real descendant of Saul," he whispered to me with satisfaction. "He'll make an excellent crown prince. The only problem is that his father is playing childish games of rebellion instead of taking the throne by force."

"I'm not a traitor like you are," I replied. I could tell he was hurt by my undisguised criticism of his rebellion against Pharaoh Siamun, but it was important to me to make it clear to him that I would never agree to go to war against my own people.

I was invited to come alone to dinner with his family. Hadad's excuse was that it would be better to let Elisheba and the children get settled in their new home in peace, but I understood that he wanted to have a difficult conversation with me. Indeed, the unpleasant topic came up even during the introductions. I bowed to his Egyptian wife, the princess Eno, and before I had a chance to approach his son, whom I had liked instantly, Hadad jumped in between us, pointed to each of us with a flourish, and announced ceremoniously:

"Genubath son of Hadad, the next king of Edom."

"Jeroboam son of Benaiah, the next king of Israel."

"You know I'm not the son of Benaiah," I said with annoyance.

"We mustn't speak your father's name out loud. It's dangerous."

"For how much longer? I'm in Egypt. Solomon's spies are very far away."

"Until you take the throne," Hadad decreed, and he immediately started up his campaign. He confidently argued that Shishak's army could quickly defeat Solomon's soldiers, and that the casualty count would be extremely low. I answered that even if he promised me that not one of my people would be killed, I would still object to an Egyptian invasion of my homeland. I wasn't about to let a foreign army intervene in our internal affairs.

"Then what are we going to do?" Hadad sighed. "Wait for Solomon to die? He's not even sixty yet. His father waged difficult wars and bitter struggles and still lived seventy years, so someone who lies around the palace all day making up proverbs and riddles can certainly live to be a hundred. And what about me? I'm not willing to die before seeing with my own eyes that my son Genubath has taken the throne in the liberated land of Edom."

Genubath nodded in agreement, and Eno looked at me suspiciously. I decided to lay out my plan for them and try to convince them that a tax rebellion might not be as fast as a war, but that it could eventually produce a much better outcome. I don't know what helped more, my speaking skills or my fluent Egyptian, but by the end of the meal Genubath told Hadad that he was willing to wait for the tax rebellion to be taken up by the majority of the tribes of Israel so that the overthrow could be carried out without bloodshed.

"How long will it take?" asked Eno.

"I believe that within five years it will all be behind us."

"And what if it isn't?" Hadad asked.

"Then we'll wait a little longer," I said.

"How much longer?"

"I don't know, Hadad, but this is the only way I'm willing to take the throne. If you take a foreign army into Israel, you'll have to find yourself a different king to liberate Edom."

"Or we can liberate Edom by force of arms and make Israel the slaves of Egypt," Eno said coldly.

※

Even after everything had been made clear and Genubath and I had become allies, I continued to be concerned about the possibility that the Egyptian army would invade my homeland. My meeting with Shishak only exacerbated my fears. Hadad was surprised that I wasn't more overwhelmed by the great occasion, for it isn't every day that a mere mortal comes face-to-face with the Pharaoh. He ascribed my equanimity to the wondrous ability to freeze myself that he had taught me. I explained to him that I'd never gotten too excited about powerful men, even when I was a little boy facing an intimidating commander all alone, and it was all the more the case today, knowing that the blood flowing in my veins was far superior to the blood of the rebel Libyan mercenary warlord.

"So I gather you're not enthusiastic about Shishak," said Hadad.

"I'm grateful for the refuge he's providing in his land for me and for my family, of course, but he isn't going to become my friend."

"No matter. What's important is that you like Genubath."

"I've got good taste."

"I'm not so sure. A man of good taste doesn't fall in love with the grandson of his father's killer." He fixed me with his penetrating gaze and added, "Why do I feel like you're trying to hide something from me? Whenever I bring him up, your face turns green."

I wanted to change the subject, but as had happened with him so often in the past, I found myself a few minutes later giving him a detailed report of the last things I had told Ithiel before we parted.

He listened to me in shock. His face went pale, and all at once his gaze became vacant of all expression. "You're insane," he mumbled. "Completely insane. How did I not see this earlier?"

"Spare me your fine distinctions," I replied scornfully.

I knew I shouldn't have told Hadad that I'd revealed my secret to Ithiel, and that once I had told him, I needed to understand his concerns and not intensify them with my bitter mockery. Looking back, when I try to reconstruct the harsh quarrel I had with him, the only excuse I can come up with is that the flight from my homeland had brought back some of the poorer qualities of my youth, ones that I had been certain I had gotten rid of permanently. Although I had given my family encouraging examples of our ancestors— Abraham, Jacob, and Moses—who, like us, had been forced to flee their homes, I hadn't been able to draw comfort from them myself. In Israel, I'd been the venerated commissioner of Ephraim who'd had a mass following and who'd been able to hold his own even against a prophet of God, but here, in Egyptian exile, far from my mother and my people, I had once again become the wounded, intimidated boy Hadad had met twenty years before in Gibeah.

"I am under an obligation to save your life. I promised your grandmother to protect you at all costs." There was no anger in his voice, nor censure, but only exhaustion.

"The person who saved my life was Ithiel. If I'd relied on your spies, I would be a corpse today."

"You cannot take any chances. You must become the king of Israel."

"And what if I refuse? What if I tell you to forget all about it?"

"What's wrong with you, Jeroboam? Has the new name changed you?"

"Leave me alone, Hadad. I'm thirty-eight years old already. It's time you stopped meddling in my life."

His voice rose gradually, becoming almost a shout. "I can't not meddle after you told the grandson of the son of Jesse who you are! Why did you do it?"

"Because I love him."

"How can you love the grandson of your father's murderer?"

"So what if he's David's grandson? Parents eat sour grapes, and the children's teeth are set on edge?"

His lips trembled. "You've sentenced him to death. I can't let him live now that you've revealed the secret to him."

Hadad turned away heavily and made to go. I felt like my hands and feet were bound in iron chains, but I still managed to spring upon him. Though he was already an older man, his senses were still as sharp as those of someone much younger, and a moment later the two of us were rolling around on the floor. I had no control over what I was screaming at him; the words just came out: "If a single hair of Ithiel's head falls out, I'll become your worst enemy. I'll hunt you down for all time, and I'll hunt down your wife and son, too. And when I become king, the destruction that David and Joab brought down upon Edom will be nothing compared to what I'll do. I'll leave it in ruins and put not only the men to the sword, but the women and children, too."

Hadad sank into a sad silence. "Then why don't you just kill me right here, right now?" he finally murmured.

I sat down on him and clamped my thighs around his wide waist, and I began to squeeze my fingers around his throat. Then I burst into tears.

He gave me a broken smile that made my heart ache. "I never wanted to hurt you, kid."

I hugged him as tight as I could. Only then did I realize how much I loved him.

He gave a long sigh. "My hands aren't as clean as yours. When killing is necessary, one kills; when betrayal is necessary, one betrays. That's life. But I would never hurt you, and do you know why? Because of your grandmother.

She's the only person in the world to whom I've been faithful to the end, unconditionally. I'd give everything up for her, even the liberation of Edom. Don't ask me why because I've got no answer."

I felt a lump in my throat, and in the absence of words, I was silent.

Fourteen

Solomon died two and a half years later, at the age of fifty-nine. He reigned in Jerusalem for forty years, just like his father. And unlike his father, the days of his life were few and good.

"His end was gloriously awful, though," Hadad stated with satisfaction. "Your tax rebellion made his life miserable. When even the tribes of Leah joined the protest and unilaterally reduced the number of forced laborers, he was completely helpless, and he truly lost his mind with rage. That's what killed him. Had it not been for this clean rebellion, he would have gone on collecting Egyptian horses and foreign women until the age of one hundred and twenty, and they would have had to build many more palaces and stables to house them all."

"And many more temples for his wives' gods," Elisheba added in disgust.

"The only god he didn't build a temple for was our Qos," Hadad said, his face turning glum. "I didn't feel comfortable saying it to him, but the truth is that his collection was worthless because it had no Edomite women in it."

"He barely had any Hebrew women, either," Elisheba said, trying to console him.

"A collection is a collection," Hadad concluded. "You don't get excited about the objects that are right under your nose."

◦◦◦

Hadad's messengers left Egypt urgently to spread the word about my return throughout Israel, also using the opportunity to introduce the nation to my new name.

"Your annoying name has actually been received rather well," Hadad reported to me with surprise. "It's used in most of the songs they're writing in honor of your return."

"My people care about the meanings of names, not about the way they sound," I explained.

"You're telling me! Only a nation like the Hebrews is capable of calling its god Jehovah. Or is it Yahweh? How *do* you pronounce that word?"

"What are you talking about? Don't you know we never say it out loud?"

"Of course I know. Moses taught you that your god is the One Who Must Not Be Named. And you're still trying to tell me your people are in their right minds?"

Despite his great joy, Hadad was also troubled by concern for my well-being, and he instructed the Egyptian soldiers escorting us home not to take their eyes off me. I tried to convince him that the protection was only necessary when we were passing near Judah, but I understood that it was pointless to argue, and I made my peace with the situation. In contrast to the small carriage in which we'd arrived in Egypt two-and-a-half years earlier, trying to appear like just another simple family traveling the roads, this time we were riding in a large and spacious four-horse chariot surrounded by twenty armed horsemen. Pharaoh Shishak had actually commanded his people to prepare an eight-horse chariot of gold for us, but Hadad explained to him that my great-grandfather Saul had been the most humble king in the world and that, unfortunately, I seemed to be taking after him.

The most exciting part of the journey took place before we even reached Israel. During the two days we spent traveling from the Pharaoh's palace to the city of Gaza, we told our children the truth about their family. I chose to spare them a detailed description of the murders of the seven boys, and I didn't see the need to discuss at length the palace intrigues of Ahithophel and Bathsheba that had put Solomon on the throne, but even the little I did tell them shook their tender souls and caused a few bursts of tears. What stunned them the most, even more than the fact that their father was about to seize the throne, was the moment they realized that there was a healthy woman hiding under the mask and that woman was their grandmother.

"She has no sores at all?" Miriam asked again and again. "Not even one?"

"Your grandmother is beautiful, and her skin is smooth," Elisheba said as she stroked Miriam's hair. "And soon you will see her with your own eyes."

Bilhah and Benaiah wiped the tears from their eyes and added admiringly that Zeruiah, the only daughter of Sheba son of Bikri, had been the most beautiful girl in Ephraim forty years before, which was why Prince Nebat had chosen her. I didn't want to tell my children that their grandfather had spent his life imprisoned in the palace and only got to meet their grandmother by sheer luck. The family story they had just heard was shocking enough as it was, and I thought it best for the time being, at least with regard to the subject at hand, to allow them to remain in the world of legends where a prince gets to choose the prettiest girl in the land.

The Pharaoh's chariot was faster than the carriage we'd arrived in, and by the middle of the fourth day we were already at the gates of Jaffa. The curtains were closed against the sunlight, so we couldn't see what was happening outside, but suddenly we heard the sounds of music and singing. We peeked out through the window and what we saw left us speechless. Crowds of people were lining the side of the road, going wild with joy at the sight of our convoy. They were drumming, trumpeting, dancing, and singing at the tops of their lungs. We couldn't catch the words of their songs, but we heard their calls loud and clear.

"Jeroboam!" the crowd screamed. "We've missed you!"

Hadad was agape at the sight. "Unbelievable," he mumbled. "I never imagined that they loved you to this extent. We don't even need to tell them you're Saul's great-grandson. They want you for your own sake."

I came out of the chariot and got on one of the horses. Many in the crowd were waving tribal flags, and I was excited to see that it was not only members of the tribe of Ephraim who had come to welcome me, but also members of the tribes of Benjamin and Manasseh. The tears ran freely down my face. I no longer cared if my people knew that I was an emotional man. "I love you, children of Rachel!" I cried in a choked-up voice.

"We love you, Jeroboam," they answered as one.

I wanted to get off my horse and approach them, but Hadad was standing behind me, shouting at the soldiers not to let anyone come near me. The ride turned into a crawl, and we only reached Zeredah at night. An especially large gathering awaited us at the entrance to the town and wouldn't let us ride on. I proposed walking to our home on foot, but Hadad ordered his soldiers to clear a path for us through the crowd and to keep me surrounded on all sides. He also rejected out of hand the suggestion that we stop at the lepers' cave on the way. "You'll visit your mother tomorrow morning," he determined in a tone that brooked no argument. "Not now when the eyes of the entire nation are upon you."

"I no longer have secrets," I complained.

"You've waited forty years—you can wait a little longer," came the reply.

⚜

The closer we got to our home, the more excited we felt, though we knew we would find it neglected and abandoned and terribly shabby in comparison to the splendid palace Shishak had given us in Egypt. How surprised we were when we discovered that the people of Ephraim had been taking care of both the house and the thicket during all the years we had been away.

"They believed we would come back to them," Elisheba whispered, her voice cracking.

"They knew we would come back to them," I said.

Miriam was so overwhelmed that quite a few minutes passed before she noticed the figure sitting on her bed. Her cries of alarm echoed through the entire house. The first to respond was Hadad, of course, whose sharp senses surprised me anew every time. He burst into the room, sword in hand, and managed to subdue the figure, pinning it against the wall. I raced into the room behind him, took a look at the intruder, and felt my heart fluttering wildly inside me.

"Greetings, Commander," the uninvited guest said to Hadad. "I see that the years have weakened you not at all."

"Ithiel," Hadad said, dumbfounded. "What are you doing here in the middle of the night?"

Nadab and Abijah came in at a run, and following close behind were Elisheba, Benaiah, and Bilhah. They stared wide-eyed at the sight.

Ithiel looked them over with curiosity and then focused his gaze on me. "You told the truth."

I approached him and hugged him with all my might.

"Why do you love this man?" Miriam objected. "He really scared me!"

Ithiel stood before her, got down on one knee, and asked for her forgiveness.

"Aside from my family, there are two people I love more than anyone else in the world," I explained to her, "and both of them are here."

I could tell that Hadad was touched by what I'd said, but he steeled his face and turned to give Ithiel a suspicious look. Elisheba told the children to go unpack their things and suggested to the three of us that we go out to the thicket so that we could speak without being disturbed.

On the way outside, Ithiel put his arm around my shoulders and told me that he'd been waiting two-and-a-half years for the chance to thank me for what I'd revealed to him. In the light of the full moon I could see his eyes sparkling with love.

"Abishag the Shunamite was willing to tell you the truth?"

"Why are you so surprised?"

"She was Bathsheba's ally."

"A young, innocent girl is taken by force from her home and brought to the bed of an elderly king who is about to die, and you're surprised that she falls head over heels for the only woman in the entire palace to give her a smile? After my father was murdered, she was plagued by terrible feelings of guilt, which have lasted to this day. She wanted to tell me the secret years ago, but she was worried that the revelation might make me want to take revenge. You know what? She was right. Solomon was like a father to me, but ever since I learned the truth about him, I have wanted only one thing: vengeance—and if not upon him, then at least upon his son."

"Forget about vengeance, Ithiel. It will lead you nowhere. If I'd had any interest in vengeance, I would have killed you the moment I found out who you were."

"I won't kill Rehoboam. I have no desire to see him dead. But I won't let him be king. The son of Solomon will not inherit his throne."

It was hard to believe that Ithiel could become my enemy, but I saw no other possibility. "We're both planning to fight for the crown," I said in pain, "because we both believe with all our hearts that becoming king would right the wrongs that were done to our ancestors."

"I don't want to be king," Ithiel said with such serenity that it made me distrust him.

"You said you wanted to dispossess Rehoboam of his crown," I mumbled.

"Not in favor of me."

"Then in favor of whom?"

"In favor of you, Jeroboam." He spoke my new name so naturally.

Hadad had been watching us throughout the conversation, his eyebrows squeezed together with suspicion, but now he gulped in astonishment.

"You will be the next king of Israel," Ithiel went on, "and I will stand at your side and help you manage the affairs of the kingdom. And do you know what gift you'll receive from me?"

I looked at him and waited for him to continue.

"The tribe of Judah."

I shook my head sadly, staring at the ground. "The prophet Ahijah has foretold that the Judeans will not be part of the Kingdom of Israel."

"Is that some kind of punishment?" asked Ithiel.

I didn't answer him.

"For the fact that my grandfather rebelled against your great-grandfather and severed Judah from Israel?"

I stayed silent.

Ithiel bit his lip. "Even prophets can be wrong sometimes." I could see that he was trying to reassure himself. "I'm sure the Kingdom of Israel will be united, just the way your great-grandfather founded it."

We sat down on the bench, my arm around his shoulders. Hadad went on standing across from us, watching him intently. His face had softened. I asked myself if he trusted him now, or if nothing would be able to change his attitude toward him. In spite of the darkness, it seemed to me that I could see a spark of affection in his eyes. "In that case," said Hadad, "all that's left is to prevent Rehoboam's coronation. The tribes of Rachel hate him already; now we need to get the tribes of Leah to love to hate him, too."

Even though I was used to Hadad's style of speaking, I joined in Ithiel's laughter. I wanted to lift his spirits after the prophet's bitter revelation that I'd shared with him. "Why didn't you ever make us laugh at the Palace of Candles?" he asked Hadad.

"That's all I needed," groaned Hadad. "As it was, my soldiers thought too much of themselves—snooping around, being so bold as to find the tunnels I'd worked so hard to dig."

All at once, Ithiel's face darkened again. "I really was Solomon's mole," he said extremely quietly. "But—"

"Don't apologize," I said, cutting him off. "You pulled me out of Hadad's tunnels at the very last moment. His torture had nearly killed me."

Hadad sat down on the other side of Ithiel and gave him a hard pat on the shoulder. "The worst is behind us. Let's put in one last effort, and all our aspirations will be realized." He turned to face me. "What are you up to, kid? How do you plan to disrupt Rehoboam's coronation ceremony without having to dirty up your dainty hands by separating his head from his body?"

The words flowed out confidently. All throughout our journey from Egypt I could see the images in my mind's eye, and I had not a shadow of a doubt that my plan would succeed. "I plan to leave for Jerusalem right away at the head of a large delegation that will include distinguished representatives from the tribes of Rachel, and I will inform Rehoboam that we are demanding significant reductions in the tax burden. As the date of the coronation approaches, I'll return to Jerusalem, and when the ceremony begins I'll burst onto the stage and demand an immediate answer from him. Rehoboam will, of course, reject my demands out of hand and ignite the fury of those present. Our boys will cause havoc and prevent the prophet from anointing him with the oil. I'm sure most of the audience will join in."

"What if Rehoboam accedes to the demands and agrees to reduce the tax burden?" Hadad wondered.

"My demand will be so audacious and irritating that he won't be able to accede to it."

"You're wrong," said Ithiel with concern. "We can depend on Rehoboam to make every possible mistake, but he has a wise mother who has appointed old and experienced advisors for him. They'll see right away that your demand is a trap, and they'll teach him a basic principle of how to be a king: if you want the people to worship you forever, be their servant at the start. I'm afraid that Rehoboam will follow the elders' advice and reduce the tax burden, not only for the tribes of Rachel, but also for the rest of the tribes, and the grateful Israelites will accept him as king."

"In that case, we'll be forced to invite the Egyptian army here," Hadad interrupted.

"Absolutely not," I said firmly. "If Rehoboam lowers the tax burden, I'll let him to reign in peace."

"And give up the throne?" Hadad cried.

"I want to be king, but it isn't a sacred cause. The important thing is for the people of Israel to be released from the hard labor imposed upon them by Solomon and to be a free people once again, as Moses wanted."

Hadad was nearly suffocating. I'd never seen him so upset before. "You're demonstrating your absolute loyalty to your people," he said, his voice suddenly sounding old. "But what about me? I dedicated my entire life to your grandmother and to you, and now you're throwing me to the dogs?"

My heart ached for him. I wanted to swear that I wouldn't rest until Edom was free, but Ithiel beat me to it, giving him a smile of reassurance. "It'll be alright, Hadad. I'll make sure that Rehoboam doesn't heed the elders' advice."

"How are you going to do that?" Hadad asked doubtfully.

"I'll tell him that his aged advisors understand nothing, and that if he wants to rule, he needs to make a show of strength because the people of Israel only understand power, and the only viable response to their audacious demand is to increase the tax burden. That's what Pharaoh did when Moses dared to demand that he give the people of Israel three days off." Ithiel stopped and gave a mischievous wink. "Don't worry, I won't say that last part to him."

A burst of relieved laughter erupted from Hadad's chest. He lifted up his hand and grabbed Ithiel's arm. "Have you heard of Hushai the Arkite? He frustrated Ahithophel's good counsel and caused Absalom to act like a fool and be defeated by David. You, Ithiel, are going to be our Hushai. You will frustrate the elders' good counsel and persuade Rehoboam to raise taxes instead of lowering them."

"I'll make an excellent Hushai," Ithiel said, his eyes twinkling.

"Rehoboam's answer has to be completely unacceptable," Hadad continued enthusiastically. "I want the crowds to leave in the middle of the ceremony so that he's left alone on the stage. That's exactly what his grandmother did to your father."

Ithiel looked at him thoughtfully, and a veil of sadness covered his eyes. "Measure for measure," he whispered.

Hadad got up onto his feet. "I'm going out to give the soldiers a few orders. In the meantime, the two of you should prepare Rehoboam's response. It has to be obnoxious and insulting. That is a lethal combination."

The children were already asleep, so we were able to go back inside and consult with Elisheba, but we couldn't come up with anything that all three of us agreed on. When Hadad returned, he was disappointed to find us still debating. "I can't count on you," he grumbled. "How long does it take to think? What's so hard about what I asked you to do?"

We answered despairingly that we had put together a few lines, but we weren't sure they were good.

"Let's hear them," Hadad said curiously.

I stood across from him, placed a hand on my hip, and said in a self-important tone:

"My father made your yoke heavy,

"And I will add to your yoke.

"My father also chastised you with whips,

"But I will chastise you with scorpions."

"Not bad," Hadad said, furrowing his brow. "But something is still missing. We need to come up with one more sentence, something really disgusting."

He stood up and paced back and forth, then stopped, spread his legs, and placed his hand on his loins. "Do you see this little thing of mine?" his voice thundered. "It's thicker than my father's fat hips."

A stunned silence fell on the room, but a moment later we exploded into laughter. Ithiel was holding his belly, Elisheba was wiping tears from her eyes, and I collapsed onto the table, gasping for breath.

"Where did you get that idea?" Ithiel groaned in admiration.

Hadad laughed with delight. "Why should Jeroboam have the only name with a meaning? Doesn't Rehoboam deserve the same? Now he can explain proudly that he's the widest—*rahab*—of them all, and everyone will finally understand his strange name."

"You're a genius."

"My delivery wasn't good enough," Hadad said modestly. "We need something short and rhythmic, like a song. The people of Israel will have to spread it all over the country, and quote it with great anger."

"This song will be quoted till the end of time," Ithiel promised. "Trust me."

I noted to myself with amazement how, only a few hours ago, Hadad had been prepared to kill Ithiel with his own hands, but now there was friendship, perhaps even love, between them. I didn't want to put a damper on their joy, but I knew that I had to.

"I don't believe Rehoboam would agree to repeat those lines," I said. "He can't be that stupid."

Ithiel smiled. "Oh, but he is."

"That bad?"

"Much worse."

Fifteen

Mother felt my head, my shoulders, and my face, as if checking me to see if anything was broken. I looked at her, and I couldn't stop the waves of joy coursing through me at the thought of the rays of sun that would soon be caressing her face.

"Don't go to Jerusalem!" she begged. "Stay in Ephraim, my child, please!"

"I have to stop Rehoboam's coronation ceremony! It's my only chance to overthrow him without bloodshed."

"And what if his soldiers attack you with swords?"

"Rehoboam wouldn't dare hurt me while the nation that loves me so much is right there watching."

"The *nation?*" She spat out the word with scorn and rage. "The nation has a short memory, Jeroboam. They love you today, and tomorrow they'll love some other leader. This is the same nation that forgot everything King Saul did for it. It's the same nation that accepted the son of Jesse as its king. It's the same nation that made your father's murder possible."

"The people will protect me, Mother," I said.

When I returned home, I was happy to find the prophet Ahijah the Shilonite waiting there for me. His face shone so brightly that I knelt before him.

"Forgive me for remaining standing," Ahijah said, smiling and giving me his hands, "but you don't allow people to bow to you, or so you said the first time we met."

I briefly told him about my experiences in Egypt and gave him a longer description of my meeting with Ithiel and his absolute confidence that the tribe of Judah would accept me as its king. Ahijah listened carefully, then closed his eyes and wrinkled his forehead. I watched him, my heart pounding. I was excited at the possibly that I would see him experiencing a revelation, but to my disappointment nothing about him looked any different. A few minutes later he gave me a sober look and said flatly that no power in the world would be able to attach the tribe of Judah to the Kingdom of Israel. I believed he was wrong, but I didn't argue with him. Instead, I asked for his blessing as I prepared to go to Jerusalem for my meeting with Rehoboam. Ahijah raised his hands, laid them upon my shoulders, and began saying the words of his blessing, when suddenly Hadad burst in and fell upon both of us with kisses. I told him sternly that Ahijah was a holy man, but Hadad ignored my rebuke, shouting loudly, "All the tribes of Israel are joining your delegation, even the tribes of Leah!"

Ahijah reacted to the news with equanimity. "Of course," he said. "All of Israel will follow you, Jeroboam, except for the tribe of Judah alone. You remember the scraps of fabric that I placed in your hand."

"I want to tear your cloak, too," Hadad said pleadingly. "And you will look at the tear and say, 'This is what God says: "See, I am going to tear Edom out of Solomon's hand and give it to Genubath son of Hadad of the royal seed."'"

Even a serious man like Ahijah wasn't able to keep a straight face around Hadad. "Great idea," he laughed. "There's only one problem: I'm a prophet of the God of Israel. Why don't you ask your Qos to send you a prophet so that you can tear his cloak?"

"Our prophets don't like having their cloaks torn," Hadad said sorrowfully, and looked over at me. "I envy you. The bumpy road to the throne is much easier when you have a private prophet putting together favorable prophecies for you."

Ahijah laughed for the second time in a minute. "I have faith that the scribes of Judah will spoil my favorable prophecies, just as they did Samuel's. They'll write in their books that I rejected Jeroboam and prophesied a terrible future for him and his family."

"For all I care, they can also write that the Benjaminites joined up with

Judah because of their great admiration for Rehoboam, the grandson of their beloved son of Jesse," Hadad said.

"That's something even the scribes of Judah wouldn't be able to make up," I chuckled.

"Oh, but they would," replied Hadad. "Why not? They've got excellent imaginations. I heard they summed up the years of Solomon's reign in one sentence: **The people of Judah and Israel were as numerous as the sand on the seashore; they ate, they drank, and they were happy.** But who cares about these lies? We have a lethal weapon fighting against them most effectively."

"What weapon?" Ahijah asked curiously.

"Michal daughter of Saul recruited scribes to work as moles. They disguise themselves as Judean scribes, and they scatter short, cunning sentences throughout Judah's books, which will reveal the truth to future generations."

"We no longer have any need for such a weapon," proclaimed Ahijah.

"But you said the scribes of Judah would write terrible lies about Jeroboam," Hadad said in puzzlement.

"Let them write whatever they want," said Ahijah the Shilonite, as he fixed his pure eyes upon me. "Only Judeans will read the books written by the scribes of Judah, while the chronicles that our scribes write will be read by all of Israel."

I didn't argue with him, but deep in my heart I prayed that the Judeans wouldn't have their own books and that they would eventually join the united Kingdom of Israel, as Ithiel had promised me.

───※───

A short while later, I was already on my way to Shiloh to meet the tribal elders so we could travel to Jerusalem together. Cheering people lined the entire route, and when I got to Shiloh the cheering grew much louder. Armed young men from Ephraim surrounded the elders, not letting them mix in with the crowd. In any other circumstances, I would have reprimanded the young guards for their intransigence, but right now the only thing I really cared about was for the journey to go peacefully without anyone getting hurt. The elders gave me an emotional welcome, and the chief elder of Benjamin even burst into tears, telling me that he'd been waiting his entire life for this moment, believing with all his heart that, even though it tarried, it would most certainly come. I wanted to tell him who I really was and amplify his happiness even more, but I was held back by Hadad's directive not to reveal the secret prematurely. Instead, I said to him and to the other elders that, for now, I was not declaring a rebellion against Rehoboam, but rather only demanding that he lower the tax burden; only after we received his reply would I consider my next steps.

"We don't care what Rehoboam does," the choked-up elder answered. "He can accede to your demands or reject them—it makes no difference at all. Either way, you will be the next king of Israel."

Before we set out, I ordered the young men to lay down their weapons and accompany us unarmed. The frightened elders tried to convince me that Rehoboam's soldiers were liable to attack us before we even entered Jerusalem. Instead of replying, I looked to the crowds that had gathered around us.

"My brothers, my people!" I called. "I command the young people of Ephraim to join me on the journey to Jerusalem. The tribal elders will ride their horses, and every man under thirty will walk with me on foot."

The young men raced over to me before I could even complete the order, competing against one another to see who could reach me first. A few of them reminded me that I was already forty years old and that I should be riding on horseback with the elders, but I replied with a smile that I still had strength in my loins. By the time we left Shechem, there were already hundreds of escorts surrounding us, and many more joined us in the land of Benjamin. The great parade attracted women and children, too, who brought us water and bread and cheered with great enthusiasm.

We reached Jerusalem toward evening and traveled through the streets of the city of David. The Judeans watched us with concern, but I didn't think I detected any signs of hate in their faces. A few of them even smiled at us encouragingly. Shortly afterwards, I presented myself at the palace gates, heading the delegation of elders, as my thousands of young escorts stood quietly behind me, filling the square and all the surrounding streets. I ordered the astonished guards to inform Rehoboam that a delegation of the elders of all the tribes was waiting for him outside. They went in immediately and returned a few minutes later with Adoram, who looked just as I'd remembered him.

"Shelomoam, Commissioner of Ephraim," he said. Even his narrow gaze remained as it had been. "You're a bit late. I summoned you here three years ago."

"I ran into a few delays," I told him. "And by the way, my name is Jeroboam."

"Jeroboam son of . . . ?"

My heart skipped a beat, but my face remained calm. "We will discuss my ancestry another time. Now, we demand to see Rehoboam."

"You demand? What a rude word. Why don't you say 'ask'? Or, better yet, 'beg'?"

"We demand," I repeated.

A lengthy silence hung over us. "We'll leave it at that," he finally said, trying to sound measured and calm. "Come inside the palace, and I'll try to arrange a meeting for you with the crown prince."

"The meeting will take place outside, before the eyes of the entire nation."

Adoram's tranquil mask fell away all at once. "The crown prince will not be coming out here to you!" he bellowed. "The coronation ceremony will take place in one week, and that will be your opportunity to see him up close in all his glory!"

I moved to stand beside Adoram and looked to the crowd gathered before me. "Listen carefully to what I tell you, and deliver the message to Rehoboam word for word—do not neglect anything: **Rehoboam son of Solomon, your father put a heavy yoke on us, but now lighten the harsh labor and the heavy yoke he put on us, and we will serve you.**"

Adoram's eyes almost popped out of their sockets. "What is the meaning of **and we will serve you?** Are you dictating terms to the crown prince?"

"Most certainly," I replied. "If he refuses our demand, we will not crown him king."

"In another week you will all stand here and bow before him, and you will also be punished for these words that you have spoken. **Put a heavy yoke on us?!** The **harsh labor** of your father?! His **heavy yoke?!** Is this how you speak of the father of the crown prince? Was King Solomon your Pharaoh?"

"You said it," I replied, and the crowd laughed uproariously and repeated my words, "You said it!"

⊰⊱

Among the crowd that had joined me on my journey by foot to Jerusalem were the four Benjaminite thugs and the members of the gang from Shiloh, my good and dear friends who'd sworn their allegiance to me years ago and were willing to lay down their lives for me now. They advised me not to lead the convoy back through the night because walking for an entire day and night was difficult even for strong and powerful men, and the people would need a good night's sleep to recover their strength. Since we didn't feel safe among the Judeans, we kept walking for another hour until we got to the land of Benjamin. I wanted to reach the town of Ramah to pray at the grave of our matriarch Rachel, but my friends suggested stopping somewhere closer, rather than dragging the exhausted people all the way to Ramah. To convince them of why it was so important to me to reach Rachel's grave, I told them that the Judean scribes had recently begun to spread a new lie claiming that Rachel was actually buried in Bethlehem, the birthplace of the son of Jesse. The Benjaminite thugs were familiar with the story, but the members of the Shiloh gang, who were hearing it for the first time, reacted with utter shock. "The scribes of Judah have long asserted that the patriarchs and matriarchs of Israel are buried in Hebron and not Shechem," one of them said angrily, "and now they are trying to claim that our very own matriarch is also buried in their land?"

I eventually took my friends' advice, and we stopped in the nearby city of Gibeah. The tribal elders stayed in the homes of the city's wealthy, while the rest of us scattered through the fields and vineyards and lay on the ground to sleep under the open sky. I very much yearned to visit the graves of my father and great-grandfather, but I knew that I mustn't do so. "You've waited for so many years," I heard Hadad's words reverberating within me. "So, you can wait a little longer. The worst is behind us." I thought of the mask that would soon be removed from Mother's face, and from mine as well, and of the cave of secrets we would be leaving behind, and knew I wouldn't be able to fall asleep.

It quickly became clear that I wouldn't have been able to sleep anyway. Rumor of our arrival had spread all through the land of Benjamin, and the people flocked to be with us and hear from up close what had happened in Jerusalem. The women brought out trays of food, heaped with everything good to eat, and the tall girls of Benjamin danced and danced until the morning light as the excited crowd accompanied them with wild applause and sang along with them. I knew their favorite song well, but the new lyrics filled my eyes with tears:

Moses freed our ancestors
From Egyptian slavery,
Jeroboam will free our sons

From Jerusalem's slavery.
Jeroboam will say to Rehoboam:
Let Israel go,
Let my people go.
Jeroboam will make Israel grow.
Make my people grow.
Let Israel go,
Let my people go.

In the morning, as we prepared to go on with our journey, I said to my friends with a smile that stopping for the night not only failed to restore our energy, but also made things even worse because, after a full night of dancing and singing, the people were now even more tired than they had been.

"You don't need to sleep to restore your energy," one of the Benjaminite thugs replied. "Anyone who experienced this night will remember it for as long as he lives and will recount it to future generations, almost like the night our ancestors left the house of bondage in Egypt."

"Our night of redemption will be celebrated in a week," I told him, "when we return to Jerusalem to attend the coronation that will not take place."

"And what if Rehoboam accedes to our demands?" he asked with concern.

I couldn't tell them about my beloved Hushai, who was in the palace at that very moment frustrating the counsel of the elders who were advising Rehoboam.

⌇

Elisheba greeted me in tears, saying she couldn't bear my going to Jerusalem again, especially now that I had become Rehoboam's declared enemy. I told her about the massive numbers of young men from Ephraim and from Benjamin who had protected me all along the way, and I promised her that this time we would be joined by young men from other tribes as well, maybe even from the tribes of Leah. My answer actually made her anxiety worse.

"Do you trust them?"

"Who?"

"The people of Reuben, Simeon, Issachar, and Zebulun?"

"You forgot Levi," I corrected her with a smile.

"The Levites are our flesh and blood. I trust them completely."

"I trust the other sons of Leah, too. I spoke with their tribal elders along the way, and it became clear to me that they loathe the dynasty of the son of Jesse no less than we do. Do you want to hear the song that members of the tribe of Reuben composed for Rehoboam's coronation ceremony?"

She nodded.

I picked up our daughter Miriam's drum, tapping it with my other hand, and singing:

"We have no share in David,
No part in Jesse's son!
Every man to his tent, Israel!"

"Who taught you that song?" Elisheba asked excitedly.

"I told you," I said, puzzled. "The elders of Reuben. They said that it's so popular in their land that it has no fewer than four different tunes."

She came over, buried her head in my chest, and wrapped her arms around my waist. I could feel her shaking and wrapped my arms around her. "My love," I whispered. "Remember what Hadad said: the worst is behind us. Only good things will happen to us from now on."

"Your grandfather wrote that song," she whispered.

I pulled back my head and looked down at her in shock. "Which grandfather?"

"Sheba son of Bikri."

"How do you know?"

"Mother sang it to me after you found out the truth about Zeruiah and ran away to Jerusalem to become a soldier in the king's army. It was the rallying cry of Sheba son of Bikri's rebellion, which spread all through the tribes of Rachel, and then all through the land."

"Why didn't they tell me?"

"There's a lot more they didn't tell you," I heard Hadad's powerful voice say from behind me. He'd burst into our room without knocking and looked even happier than he had two days earlier, when he'd informed us that the tribes of Leah were joining our delegation.

"Forgive the interruption, my dear lovebirds, but you can't expect me to hold back when I hear about what our Hushai is doing in the palace."

"How can your spies already be here with new information? We just got back from Jerusalem."

"They are much speedier than your cumbersome convoy."

"Do you mean to tell me that Ithiel has already frustrated the elders' counsel?"

"Even a talented man like him cannot frustrate advice that has not yet been given."

"Then what has he done?"

"A short time ago, an official announcement left the palace, carrying the initial response to the audacious request of the former commissioner of Ephraim. Guess what city will be playing host to the coronation ceremony of the widest man alive?"

Our obvious impatience gave Hadad much pleasure and made him draw out his words with intentional slowness. "Not Jerusalem, not Hebron, not Bethlehem, not even the lovely city of priests Beth Shemesh."

"Please, Hadad," I begged. "Take pity on us!"

"The coronation ceremony will be held in the city of . . ."

He was enjoying every minute.

"Shechem!"

We stared at him wordlessly.

"I admit that I was still somewhat suspicious of Ithiel," Hadad continued. "You know what it's like—it isn't easy to get rid of old habits. But now I'm sure he's on our side. Only a dirty mind like his could come up with a crazy idea like this."

I shook my head doubtfully. "I suspect your information is erroneous. Even Rehoboam is not so stupid and drunk with power as to dare hold his coronation ceremony in the central city of Ephraim."

"What does Ithiel like to say?" Hadad laughed. "'Oh, but he is.'"

Sixteen

The messengers left Jerusalem urgently, and two days later the information had reached all the heralds in the land. But in spite of all the efforts, promises, and threats, the people of Israel preferred to stay in their homes rather than participate in the coronation ceremony in Shechem. Our messengers relished describing to us the heartwarming desolation of Mount Gerizim, which stood devoid of people. The only sign that an important event was scheduled to take place there was the many containers of water scattered around the foot of the mountain.

"Very good," said Hadad, rubbing his hands together. "Not that I don't trust your people, but knowing that the audience will be from Ephraim makes me feel most calm."

"I've heard that huge crowds flocked to Solomon's funeral."

"Of course," said Hadad. "They wanted to confirm that he was dead with their own eyes."

I didn't want to spoil Hadad's mood, but I did share my worries honestly with Elisheba. What scared me most was the possibility that things would get out of my control. It was enough for one person in the audience to draw a knife, and the king's soldiers were liable take the opportunity to attack everyone in crowd with swords or even bows and arrows. Hadad marveled once again that there had never before been such a nonviolent overthrow of a ruler, but I knew that at the moment of truth my clean rebellion could very well abruptly become a bloodbath.

On the morning of the ceremony, I went to Shechem to meet the elders who had been staying there since our return from Jerusalem. I instructed them to arrive early at Mount Gerizim so that they would have time to speak with the few members of their tribes who did come and make sure that they all disarmed themselves. The rumor of my arrival spread quickly, and before long many people had crowded around me, having flocked to Shechem from all over Ephraim, as well as from the land of Benjamin, to accompany me and protect me.

When I arrived at Mount Gerizim, I found it much more crowded than I'd expected. Armed soldiers were standing everywhere, and their polished swords gleamed in the sun, filling me with dread. I wasn't able to wipe away the horrifying images of what might take place after Rehoboam insulted the people with the words Ithiel had put in his mouth. On the other hand, I also harbored the opposite fear, that Ithiel might not have managed to frustrate the elders' advice and that Rehoboam was about to announce a reduction of the tax burden and deliver a soft, pleasant speech that would make him the next king of Israel.

The heralds announced the arrival of the crown prince, Rehoboam son of Solomon. The trumpets blew loudly, and the stony-faced crowd watched the royal procession climbing up the mountain. I had to admit, it was a spectacular sight. At the head of the procession rode horsemen decked out in magnificent uniforms; behind it, pretty girls in colorful silk dresses were dancing and singing; and in the middle was Rehoboam, sitting in an open chariot of gold, being pulled by six teams of horses, and he was waving his hand in all directions, a large smile spread across his face. On one side of him sat an older woman—his mother, I gathered, Naamah the Ammonite—and on his other side, I could see a beautiful young woman.

"His beloved wife, Maakah daughter of Absalom," one of the Shiloh gang members whispered in disgust. "I wonder what his grandfather would have said."

"He's already got dozens of wives," someone else commented, "and he isn't even king yet."

"A pathetic collection," added a third. "Nothing like his father's."

His words took me back to the comparison that Rehoboam was about to make between himself and his father, and I started to have cold feet at the thought of what was about to take place.

The open golden chariot pulled up right beside me, and the members of Rehoboam's family slowly got down from it and took the stage. They were followed by two soldiers who held between them a shiny tray that carried a vial of oil. The prophet Shemaiah, the last to arrive, took the oil from them and held it up high. Instead of cheering with joy, the crowd booed, but the ruckus died down the moment Rehoboam stepped out of the chariot and began climbing the steps to the stage. I looked over at the many ministers standing across from me and noticed Adoram staring back. It was impossible not to recognize that familiar narrowing of the eyes.

The trumpets sounded again, and this time they were joined by a long, ear-splitting blast from seven rams' horns. Rehoboam stopped in the center of the stage, facing the crowd. I assumed that he was about to speak, but instead he immediately got down on his knees, supported on either side by the two soldiers, and before I started moving, the prophet Shemaiah was already standing behind his back. I burst onto the stage at the very last second. The crowd gasped in surprise, but a moment later cries of joy began to ring out from all directions. I raised my hand in a signal that they should quiet down, and I looked down at Rehoboam and said in a forceful tone, "Rehoboam son of Solomon, a week ago I came to Jerusalem with the elders of all the tribes and gave you our demand. You cannot rule over us before we receive your answer."

He got up onto his feet, spread them apart, and put his hands on his hips with a flourish, asking derisively, "What is your request?"

I turned to face the people, and then after a few seconds I turned back to him, speaking the words slowly and emphatically, **"Your father put a heavy yoke on us, but now lighten the harsh labor and the heavy yoke he put on us, and we will serve you."**

Rehoboam took a deep breath and let it out with a quiet whistle through his pursed lips. Then he straightened his back, placed his hand on his loins, and called out:

"My little finger shall be thicker than my father's loins.

"My father made your yoke heavy,

"And I will add to your yoke.

"My father also chastised you with whips,

"But I will chastise you with scorpions."

Naamah the Ammonite raced toward the chief herald, who was standing agape at the foot of the stage, but before she got to him, Rehoboam called angrily, "Repeat what I said!" The herald looked around helplessly and said nothing. "Repeat what I said!" Rehoboam yelled. "That's an order!"

"'My little finger . . . ,'" the herald mumbled, but he couldn't go on.

Rehoboam approached him and loomed over him at the edge of the stage. "My little finger shall be thicker than my father's loins," he said.

"'My little finger shall be thicker than my father's loins,'" the herald repeated in a strangled voice.

"'My little finger shall be thicker than my father's loins,'" the other heralds, who were scattered across the mountain, repeated one after the other.

"My father made your yoke heavy, and I will add to your yoke," said Rehoboam.

"'My father made your yoke heavy, and I will add to your yoke,'" the heralds called.

"My father also chastised you with whips, but I will chastise you with scorpions," said Rehoboam.

"'My father also chastised you with whips, but I will chastise you with scorpions,'" the heralds called.

⤷⤶

The audience listened to all this in silence. Their restrained reaction disappointed me but also, in an odd sort of way, calmed me. I understood that our plan had failed. Apparently, the statements we'd put in Rehoboam's mouth weren't as insulting and outrageous as we'd thought. In another moment, the prophet would anoint his forehead with the oil and crown him the next king of Israel.

Suddenly a terrible, bloodcurdling roar tore through the sky. In the blink of an eye, the once silent crowd had turned into a herd of wild animals and was now storming the stage with clenched fists, screams of rage, and faces twisted with hate. **"We have no share in David!"** they screamed. **"And no part in Jesse's son! Every man to his tent, Israel!"**

A few seconds went by before I understood what was happening, and then, without any planning or forethought, I ran toward Rehoboam, placing myself between him and the crowd. I don't know how I wasn't injured, but I suppose the people recognized me in time.

"Do not shed blood!" I shouted. "No one is to be killed today!"

I led Rehoboam to the chariot, protecting him with my body. He tried to get on, but his knees buckled, and I had to support him with both my hands. The people watched me with pursed lips, wordlessly clearing a path for me. I ran alongside the chariot down the mountainside until I was sure we were out of harm's way. As I climbed back up, I heard up above me the ominous sounds of a cascade of stones. I quickened my stride, going as fast as I could, and I prayed that it was still possible to prevent the worst.

At the top of the mountain I saw an overturned, shattered chariot with no horses, and on top of it lay the body of a man, drenched in blood, his head and arms on the ground and his feet stuck between the steps, as though he had been trying to jump for his life. The sight was so revolting that I could barely stop myself from throwing up.

I regained control of myself and took a closer look at the body. I couldn't recognize the mangled face, but I recognized the clothing right away.

It was Adoram.

⚜

When I returned home that night and recounted the events of the day to Elisheba and Hadad, I kept going back to that terrible moment when I stood over Adoram's battered body and realized that my prayer had not been answered.

"No one before you has ever managed to overthrow a king with only one casualty," Elisheba consoled me.

"And not just any casualty," Hadad added, "but the most deserving casualty. You have to admit, there isn't a better casualty than him."

"I was hoping there would be no casualties at all," I said.

Hadad patted me on the shoulder and repeated his words of encouragement once more: "The worst is behind us."

And I believed him.

Seventeen

The message reached Hadad two days before my coronation ceremony. Our house was quite festive by then. Miriam was trying on her new silk dress, which had been made especially for the occasion. She spun around dizzily, trying to make the hem fly up, while Bilhah clapped with pleasure and Elisheba muttered to herself that the dress looked too fancy. In the other room, Benaiah was having a loud argument with Nadab and Abijah about the size of the crowd that could be expected to attend the ceremony. The boys thought that only the tribes of Rachel would make the effort to travel to Mount Gerizim twice in ten days, while the other tribes, especially the tribes of Leah, would stay in their own lands and give me their allegiance only after my reign was secure. But Benaiah argued vehemently that he was absolutely certain the elders would keep their promises and bring with them respectable delegations from all the tribes of Israel.

I sat in my room, trying not to listen to what was going on around me and instead focusing on the speech I was supposed to give before I was anointed. There were so many things I wanted to tell my people, and I was having trouble deciding what to focus on and what to leave out. It was clear to me that the subject of the taxes would be at the center of my speech, but what about the freeing of Edom and Aram? Was it a good idea to talk about the high price that the nation of Israel had been forced to pay in order to hold on to the countries David had conquered? Hadad had composed a good slogan for me—"Aram for the Arameans, Ammon for the Ammonites, Edom for the Edomites, and the Land of Israel for the Hebrews"—but perhaps that was best saved for another opportunity?

I began putting together a gentler slogan. The words were already on the tip of my tongue when I suddenly heard a piercing scream outside. I was momentarily startled, but when everything became quiet again, I figured that it must have been just some small matter and tried to get back to the line of thinking that had been cut off. Then, before I could even reconstruct a single word, Hadad burst into my room. I glanced at him quickly and felt my heart turn to stone.

"Ithiel," he said.

"No," I whispered. A moment later, I began begging, "No! No! No!"

"Rehoboam took revenge upon him for his misleading advice," choked Hadad. "He hanged his body on—"

"No!" I cried. "I don't want to hear it."

I have no memory of what happened next, but within an hour, maybe more, I found myself prostrate on the floor, my cheeks scratched and my forehead bleeding.

"O my brother, Ithiel!" I called out. "My brother, my brother Ithiel! If only I had died instead of you—O Ithiel, my brother, my brother!"

The joy in our house turned into grief. My family and friends tiptoed around, crying along with me in their hearts but at the same time trying to gather their strength so that they could comfort me. But I wouldn't be comforted. I cradled my face in my hands and cried ceaselessly. "O my brother, Ithiel, my brother, my brother, Ithiel!"

My keening continued through the evening, the night, and the next morning, and it hadn't stopped even by noon. I don't know what would have happened if Elisheba hadn't gotten me up out of my mourning by force. No one other than her dared to defy me, not even Hadad, who'd been the one who taught me how to overcome any kind of pain.

"Get up, wash yourself, and eat some bread!" she said. "You need to be at your best when you appear before the nation tomorrow."

I looked up at her, appalled. "Do you still believe I'll be king?"

Her look of shock made me whisper the words I didn't dare speak out loud: "I am not worthy of being king of Israel. I killed my best friend."

She became terribly upset and began to cry. "Don't talk that way!"

"It's the truth. If I hadn't saved Rehoboam, Ithiel would be alive now."

I left her there sobbing and ran outside to the thicket. My eyes were puffy, and my vision was blurred. It took me a few moments to realize I was standing before Ahijah the Shilonite. I tried to get away from him, but he was faster than me and gripped my arm.

"A king must have the ability to overcome his grief," he said. "Your emotions are no longer yours alone. They belong to the entire people."

That was too much. The wild predator of my youth burst out of me all at once. I yanked my arm out of his hand sharply and shoved him back into one of the trees. I attacked him, shaking his shoulders savagely and screaming with all my might, "Ithiel is dead because of you! You prophesied that he wouldn't succeed in his attempt to join the tribe of Judah to my kingdom. God killed him just so that your prophecy could come true!"

The warmth radiated off of him into my skin. I tried to hate him, but I couldn't.

"Ithiel was God's messenger," Ahijah said softly. "He frustrated the elders' advice and paved the way for your coronation."

"Then why did God kill him?" I cried. "Why does God kill His messengers?"

Ahijah shrugged and sighed deeply. "'As the heavens are higher than the earth, so are my ways higher than your ways, and my thoughts than your thoughts.'"

The rage that was pent up inside me didn't abate, but now it was focused solely on the One who did not bother to explain His motives even to His prophets. "And now what?" I went on shouting. "Now there's no one left to prevent a war of brother against brother between Judah and Israel. Is that what God wants?"

"No," Ahijah said confidently. "God won't allow his sons to fight one another."

Along with my burst of bitter laughter, I was choking back tears. "In that case, go to Rehoboam and tell him that God forbids him from going to war against the tribes that have left him. I'm sure he will give you his wholehearted attention, especially in light of the fact that you are my prophet."

"The word of God will reach Rehoboam through the prophet Shemaiah."

"And what if Shemaiah actually encourages him to go to war?"

"Shemaiah is my student."

"That's impossible. He is from the tribe of Judah."

"I train students of prophecy from all the tribes of Israel. Shemaiah will obey me and will tell Rehoboam whatever words I put in his mouth."

The stabbing pain in my heart was unbearable. "Tell God to find another king to lead His people."

"He has chosen you."

I breathed deeply and whispered, "I cannot become king. I'm guilty of the death of Ithiel son of Adonijah."

Ahijah closed his eyes and was silent for many long minutes. "You made the same mistake King Saul made," he said at last. "He was too merciful. That was his one weakness. He wasn't willing to hurt the people who undermined his reign, and he didn't stop the vicious people who stole the crown from him in time. His compassion brought disaster upon the people of Israel. Because of his compassion, they lost a king in whom even his most bitter rivals could find no fault."

My shoulders trembled. I hung my head and was silent.

"Remember this lesson, Jeroboam," Ahijah said, raising his voice. "One who takes mercy upon the cruel will end up being cruel to the merciful. Do not repeat your great-grandfather's mistakes."

He began walking toward the house, and I dragged myself behind him without a word. When we walked inside, everyone looked over at us expectantly. Nobody spoke.

"You will make a good king," Ahijah said, fixing his pure eyes on me. "The best king the nation of Israel will ever have. Even better than your great-grandfather."

⌘

A noise woke me up in the middle of the night, only moments after I had finally fallen asleep. I sat up with my back against the wall and looked all around in confusion. The pain in my heart was so palpable that for a moment I thought someone was stabbing me in between the ribs. It took several minutes before I recalled the tragedy that had turned my life upside down, and I felt myself falling into a dark abyss. I wanted to tell Elisheba that there was no way I could stand before my people today and ask for their allegiance, but she jumped out of bed before I could even open my mouth and ran outside. Through the door, I could hear an excited hubbub outside, but I couldn't summon the strength to get up onto my feet to see for myself whether they were the sounds of joy or of sorrow. I flopped back down on the bed, pulled the blanket up over my ears, and tried to sink into oblivion.

Hadad's loud voice interrupted my apparent reverie. "There hasn't been anything like this since Mount Sinai!" he bellowed in my ear.

I sat back up and looked at him without comprehension. His strong arms crushed me excitedly, as if we hadn't seen each other in many years.

"Mount Gerizim is filled to capacity, and the crowds continue to arrive in droves. All the tribes are coming. Yes, you heard me, even the tribes of Leah. The people of Israel are coming to your coronation ceremony in huge numbers—men and women, old and young. It's going to be the second exodus from Egypt. If the flow doesn't stop, the crowd will fill the space all the way to Mount Ebal. And then what will we do? How can we ensure that everyone sees the stage?"

I thought to myself that, until two days ago, this news would have made me happy, but now it left me practically indifferent.

Hadad read my thoughts. "Be happy!" he begged. "Your people want you to rejoice with them. You mustn't let them down."

"I can't," I whispered.

Hadad's eyes flooded with tears. "Years ago, Ithiel told you he was willing to sacrifice his life for you. Do you want his sacrifice to have been in vain?"

"I'll do what I'm required to do, but you can't force me to be happy."

He cast down his eyes in disappointment.

I felt searing pangs of guilt and tried to change the subject. "Have you prepared enough water?"

"The people are willing to die of thirst for you."

"This is not the time for jokes, Hadad."

"You act as if you don't trust me."

"I never said that."

"I took charge of organizing the ceremony, so please have faith in me that everything is going as it should."

"You said yourself that no one expected so many people to come."

"I ordered more water containers. There may not be enough to wash the dust of the road off our feet, but no one will go thirsty."

"And what about bread?"

"There was no bread during the exodus from Egypt, either."

"But there were unleavened cakes."

"So, this time we have figs and raisins. That's all I could get. The people of Ephraim are emptying their winter fruit stores for the pilgrims."

I regretted my aggressive tone but didn't know how to ask for his forgiveness. "There's no way I can free Edom," I said, working hard to put an amused smile on my face. "That's all I need, for you to go run your kingdom with Genubath and leave me alone to fend for myself."

He laughed. I wanted to laugh with him, but my tears returned abruptly. Thinking about the person who'd promised to remain at my side and help me run the affairs of the kingdom made my loss more tangible than it had ever been. What was it that I'd said to Miriam? Aside from my family, there are two people I love more than anyone else in the world. Now I only had one left.

I got up from the bed and hugged him. "I'm sorry, Hadad," I whispered. "I don't know what came over me. The grief turned me into someone else."

"Don't worry about it. I love you in any shape or form."

"That's my trouble. People love me too much."

Hadad raised his eyebrows. "Trouble?"

Until then, I'd never dared to talk about my agonizing doubts with anyone, not even Elisheba. I didn't want to upset the people dearest to me, the ones who followed me devotedly and believed that I would make a good king. But grief had weakened my once-great self-control and caused me to reveal my most secret misgivings to Hadad.

"Yes, Hadad, it's serious trouble. There's something about me that makes people love me and try to please me. When I was young, this power that I had amazed me, but as I got older that amazement turned into guilt, shame, and fear. I'm held in much greater esteem than I truly deserve, and I'm afraid that eventually my people will discover the fraud and be angry that I pretended to be someone I'm not. I have so many shortcomings that I don't know where to begin. You're familiar with my fits of rage, but trust me, that's only a small part of the black tar that bubbles inside me. So what if I'm the great-grandson of King Saul? That doesn't make me fit to be king. Even my success as Ephraim's tax commissioner doesn't guarantee anything. Serving as a tax commissioner and being a king are two completely different roles. Lately, I've been feeling that inside this big body there is nothing but a frightened and insecure baby, and all I want to do is scream out to people, 'Please, don't let your eyes deceive you—choose a more suitable king for yourselves!' But it's too late. Crowds of people are already thronging to my coronation ceremony."

Hadad said nothing for quite a while. Then he went over to the window, pulled open the curtain, and looked up. The first light of dawn had painted the sky gray. "It's cloudy today," he said. "I hope the first rainfall doesn't surprise us. The audience will disappear on us in the middle of the ceremony."

The sour taste of disappointment rose up in my throat. Here I was, revealing my deepest secrets to him, sharing things with him that I hadn't even told my wife, and all he's interested in is the first rainfall that may or may not come today. I sat on the edge of the bed and hung my head. He came over and sat down beside me. I stiffened my back in preparation for the coming slap, but instead I felt a caress.

"When Ahijah prophesied that you would be the best king Israel will ever have, I thought that he was saying nothing new." His loud, pounding voice was suddenly soft and slow. "I was wrong. Only now do I truly understand his prophecy. I can only hope that my Genubath will feel the same way you do before his coronation. I can only hope."

Eighteen

The blue silk dress, which had been made to my precise specifications, was the only thing that could dull the stabbing pain in my heart a bit. My eyes couldn't get their fill of looking at it.

"We have to go," Hadad urged me on, "especially if you still want to stop by the lepers' cave."

"*Want to?* I won't go to Mount Gerizim unless we do."

"Your threats have no effect on us. No one takes them seriously anymore. People say you're the second Moses? You're much worse. Moses didn't want to be the leader, that much is true, but after God reproached him, he accepted the position and stopped making trouble."

I wrapped the dress in a linen cloth and went out to the chariot that was waiting just outside the thicket. I had insisted on a simple chariot with a single team of horses, no more. I didn't even allow them to attach golden bells to it. The disappointed Hadad had argued passionately that people had made great efforts to travel to the coronation from far away in order to see the splendor of royalty up close. They had simple wooden chariots near home. He said it was bad enough that I'd stated in advance that I wasn't willing to move into a palace, and I didn't need to upset them further with some ugly wagon.

In the end, I agreed to compromise on olive branches and pomegranates, which were piled up on the roof and wrapped around the windows, giving the chariot a festive appearance. I also tried to resist the large number of horsemen assigned to escort us, but Hadad stated firmly that the subject was not up for debate since it was an issue that affected my security and that of my family. Nadab and Abijah took after me, and they squeezed into their seats modestly, but Miriam demonstrated her joy at the large crowds that had lined the roads waiting for us by sticking half her body out the window before we could stop her. "They like my new hairstyle," she remarked proudly. "I wish you'd let me wear jewelry. People want to see their princess with a crown on her head."

"You aren't a princess yet." Bilhah laughed.

She patted me on the back with her small hand. "Father, today they are going to put a golden crown on your head?"

"Yes, my daughter."

"And when you're king, will you let me wear a golden crown, too?"

"We'll see."

When we reached the cave, I took the wrapped-up dress with me and instructed Ahijah and Hadad to come with me. Nadab tried to persuade me to let him join in the visit to see Grandmother, too, but after Elisheba whispered something in his ear he grew quiet and looked at me with excitement.

⚜

Here is the cave I first saw thirty-three years ago. It hasn't changed at all—the same wide threshold, the same spacious hall, the same incense torches, the same colorful rugs on the floor and walls, the same long corridor leading to the small cell.

I draw the curtain and look at her. She is sitting in the torchlight and raises her covered face to look up at me. Her two eyes blaze at me from behind the mask. I approach her and place the linen-wrapped package in her lap. She opens it with her gloved fingers, and her body stiffens at the sight of the soft silk.

"What is this, Jeroboam?"

"This is the dress you will wear at my coronation ceremony. Grandmother told me that blue was your favorite color, and hers as well." I can hear Hadad clearing his throat behind me, but my voice remains strong and steady.

"Put it on, Mother!"

Silence prevails. The three of us stand frozen in place, watching her. She shakes her head. "The cave is my home. There are crooked things that cannot be straightened. When will you learn to accept that, Jeroboam?"

"If I were willing to accept that, I wouldn't be a king today."

She removes the mask from her head. A tiny, sad smile sprouts at the corners of her mouth. "You'll be a king to your subjects, but to me you'll always be the little baby I was forced to abandon on the day he was born."

I examine the wrinkles of her resolute face with astonishment and know I'll never encounter such supreme courage ever again—there is no way, not even on the battlefield.

"I want you to be by my side today, Mother."

"It isn't possible."

"You've never been by my side at any stage of my life—not when my baby teeth came in, not when I took my first steps, not when I fell out of the trees in the thicket, not when I left my childhood home, not when I returned to it, not when I got married, and not even when my children were born. But now, Mother, now I need you more than I have ever needed you. Put on that dress and come be by my side at the coronation ceremony."

"My heart accompanied you every step of the way throughout your life, and it will continue to accompany you until I take my final breath."

"I want all of you."

"I . . ." She tries to say something, but she stops.

Not one of us dares to move or to speak.

"I . . ." She leaves the sentence hanging in midair, hesitates, and finally finishes it with a sigh, "I can't, Jeroboam."

"It's been over forty years," I say dully. "The people who wanted me dead are no longer alive."

"But others have taken their place."

"Those who have taken their place will pursue me anyway. They see me as an enemy because of what I am, not because of my ancestors."

"If they find out that you are Saul's great-grandson they'll pursue you with many times the determination, and not just you, but all of your descendants, forever."

I kneel down and bury my face in her lap, feeling her hands in my hair and on the back of my neck, then I get up, turn my back on her, and head toward the door.

"Go to Mount Gerizim," I tell Ahijah and Hadad as I leave. "Stand on the stage, and tell the people of Israel that they have no king."

They look at me wide-eyed but then follow me out wordlessly. When we are already outside the cell, I suddenly hear a choked voice calling from inside.

"Jeroboam!"

Then louder, "Come back to me, my child!"

I pull aside the curtain again and stand in the doorway. She slowly raises her head up to face me. "I'll come with you, Jeroboam, but on one condition."

The powerful shaking of my legs threatens my balance. I grab on to some stones in the wall and wait for her to continue.

"On the condition that you never reveal your identity. No one can know that you are the great-grandson of Saul."

I feel as if I'm being stoned. "No!" I whisper, then yell: "My mask is coming off today as well!"

"We must both go on wearing our masks," she says.

"I want everyone to know who my ancestors were."

"Your ancestors prefer to remain anonymous, as long as it allows your children and grandchildren to live without a malevolent sword constantly looming over their heads."

"The moment I agreed to be king, I consigned my descendants to live under the shadow of that threat. The least I can do for them is to allow them and their descendants to take pride in their roots. In a short time from now, I will stand on the stage and declare before the entire nation that I am the son of Nebat, the grandson of Michal, and the great-grandson of King Saul."

Before she can open her mouth, Ahijah the Shilonite steps forward and stands at her side. "Your deeds and the stories that will be told about you will attest to your origins more than any explicit declaration. Future generations will know who your ancestors were."

"I don't understand."

Behind me, Hadad huffs impatiently. "You need to spell it out for him," he tells Ahijah. "Give him a clear, simple example."

"For example," Ahijah says, thinking out loud, "for example, the story about the tearing of my new cloak in the field. Future generations will see right away that I was correcting the wicked story that the scribes of Judah made up about Samuel and Saul."

"So?"

"You really don't understand?" Ahijah says in surprise. "Who am I in that story?"

"You're the heir of Samuel," Hadad answers for me. "A prophet, an Ephraimite, a Shilonite, and wearing a torn garment. Just like him."

Ahijah looks at me. "And who are you in the story?"

"You're the heir of Saul," Hadad explains patiently. "What's not to understand?"

"Don't include the story of the tearing of the robe in our book of chronicles," Mother interjects. "It's too obvious."

Hadad waves his hand dismissively. "Don't worry. These stories will be written in code. Only the best and the brightest will be able to decipher them."

Her brow furrows in concern, but after a moment, she gets up on her feet and spreads out the dress, holding it up in front of her face. "I hope I still remember how to wear such soft fabric."

We wait for her behind the curtain, and before she finishes getting dressed I yell out from the other side, "But under no circumstances will I yield on Father's name!"

"We mustn't—" she starts to say.

"No, Mother," I cut her off. "I've been waiting forty years for that name."

Nineteen

My mother climbs into the saddle and sits up straight, chin raised. The few rays of sunlight that are able to penetrate the clouds caress her bare face, deepening the many wrinkles that the years have etched into it. The soft silk dress she is wearing hugs her narrow waist and casts blue reflections onto her gray hair. She squints in the light, but her hands grip the reins with confidence, as if it hasn't been over forty years since she'd last ridden in the open air.

My family watches her wide-eyed through the windows of the chariot. Bilhah and Elisheba burst into tears, while Miriam claps gaily. "What a lovely dress you have, Grandmother! It's so much nicer than that black robe you wear in the cave."

"Why isn't she riding with us in the chariot?" wonders Abijah.

"She wants to feel the sunlight on her face," Nadab answers in a loud voice, trying to hide the lump in his throat.

I climb onto another horse, which one of the horsemen has vacated, and ride beside her down the mountainside to the outskirts of Zeredah. Hadad and Ahijah are riding their horses at the head of the procession; my family rides in the chariot at the rear; and the horsemen still surround us from all directions. As we cross Zeredah, my stomach clenches uneasily. The crowds that had just recently filled the streets have gone to Mount Gerizim, and not a soul is left in the town.

⊸◦⊱

Before we enter Shechem, we suddenly hear the sounds of a massive number of people, the likes of which we've never heard before, and as if from within a dream, huge crowds of people appear in front of us, shouting incomprehensibly, waving flags, blowing rams' horns, singing, making music, and drumming. They are everywhere—in the streets, in the squares, in the yards of the houses, and on the rooftops. Children are riding on their fathers' shoulders, mothers hold their infants in the air, and one old man is jumping in front of our horsemen with a young boy and pointing at me with his trembling hands. "Look, my grandson, take a good look at this handsome man. That's our king." Someone else leaps in front of me with a little girl in his arms. "This is the festival of our redemption. You will remember it for the rest of your life, and you'll recount it to your children, your grandchildren, and your great-grandchildren, generation after generation, forever."

I recover from the chills that run down my neck and ask Hadad why the people of Shechem are waiting in the town rather than on Mount Gerizim. He glances at me with a teary look in his eyes and lifts up his face to the mountains. "These aren't the locals. The crowds have filled Mount Gerizim, reached all the way to Mount Ebal, and are overflowing throughout the entire area. Even the great valley to the east is filled to capacity."

"Six hundred thousand," Ahijah whispers loudly. "Just like at Mount Sinai."

I float dreamily up to the mountaintop, and I hear the raging babble of voices all at once become the clear sound of harps playing a thrilling melody, to which six hundred thousand souls add their sound, singing together as one:

> **You love righteousness and hate wickedness;**
> **Therefore God, your God, has set you above your companions**
> **By anointing you with the oil of joy.**
> **You are the most excellent of men**
> **And your lips have been anointed with grace,**
> **Since God has blessed you forever.**

And all of a sudden, in the middle of the song, as I stand upon the stage facing the people, a hard rain begins to pour down on us. Mother opens her mouth to the sky and gulps down the raindrops, her face beaming. But the other members of my family look around in despair.

"All is lost," Hadad mumbles. "They'll all be running away from here in a moment."

But the crowd does not run to seek shelter. Instead, they raise their arms up to the sky and scream joyously. The rain lasts quite a few minutes, and they go on frolicking the whole time in the winter's first rainfall, which drenches their hair and their beards and their clothes, and which turns the earth into puddles of mud.

And when the rain is over, just as suddenly as it began, and tiny rays of sun peek out shyly through the clouds to caress the wet people, I realize that the speech I've prepared will not be spoken—not here, not now—and that a different speech will be given instead, one that I didn't even know existed until a moment ago. And immediately, with a nod of my head, I signal the heralds who are standing at attention at the sides of the stage, and the crowd quiets down, waiting expectantly to hear what I have to say.

"My brothers, my loved ones, people of Israel," I say, my voice growing stronger from moment to moment. "This blessed first rainfall, which has just now poured down upon us, reminds me of another first rainfall long in the past, one that poured down upon Zeredah thirty-three years ago, on the fifteenth day of the eighth month, on the precise day that the tribe of Ephraim celebrates its Festival of Rain. I was an eight-and-a-half-year-old boy back then, and I will never forget that first rainfall as long as I live."

I wait for the many heralds scattered all around to have a chance to repeat what I have said, and I glance quickly at Mother. Her face turns pale in fear, and I give her a reassuring smile, as if signaling her not to worry, and go on with my speech.

"Girls in green dresses danced on the muddy ground, women brought out sweet fruit and fresh pastries, and we all sang and danced and rejoiced and thanked our God for bringing that year's first rainfall on the very day of our festival."

I am quiet for a moment and turn to face Mount Ebal. "And then," my voice grows louder, "at the height of the festivities, a company of soldiers burst into Zeredah."

Even from where I am standing, I can hear the crowd stop breathing. The people are standing completely still before me, crowded and attentive, frozen in a stony hush, as if they are not living people at all, but rather lifeless statues.

"They tore the tablecloths off the tables, trampled our food and wine with their horses' hooves, and threatened to severely punish whoever dared to participate in the festivities."

A ghostly hush envelops me, the utter silence of a crowd holding its collective breath.

"My brothers, my loved ones, my people, on this day, thirty-three years after that company of soldiers ruined the Festival of Rain in Zeredah, I hereby proclaim the restoration of the ancient festivals of all the tribes of Israel. God loves the holidays of all of us: the rain festival of Ephraim, the fire festival of Manasseh, the dairy festival of Benjamin, the sun festival of Dan, the rainbow festival of Naphtali, the shearing festival of Simeon, the fertility festival of Reuben, the fish festival of Zebulun, the oil festival of Asher, the moon festival of Issachar, and the wine festival of Gad. And God also loves the ingathering festival of Judah, just as He loves the holidays of every other tribe—no less, but also no more. We will all continue to celebrate the Festival of Freedom, the Festival of Harvest, and the Festival of Booths, the three major holidays of Israel, while each tribe will celebrate its own holidays separately, as our ancestors did before us. These separate holidays do not harm our unity as a nation."

My voice is swallowed up by the great roar that rises from the people standing before me, and after a few seconds, when the herald's calls have reached all the surrounding areas, one thunderous roar erupts from the city of Shechem, from Mount Ebal, and from the great valley. Long minutes pass before I am able to speak again.

"God loves all the tribes and wishes to live in all of our lands, not only in the land of a single tribe. Build temples for our God, people of Israel! God wants our temples. Build them to your hearts' desire, but remember: our God does not wish to dwell in houses of cedar covered in gold, but in simple, modest temples, just like the Tabernacle that the Israelites built for Him in the wilderness. God likes His priests humble, too. Not every firstborn is fit to be a priest. Appoint to His service only the humble and modest boys who, despite being firstborns, have hearts that are not proud and eyes that are not haughty. The Levites and the descendants of Aaron the Priest will instruct our firstborns in the work of the temples, and they will perform the holy service alongside them, just as Moses commanded us in his Torah. The different tribes will place their own symbols in the doorways of the temples they build in their own lands, for God loves the symbols of all of the tribes of Israel: the calf of Ephraim, the wild ox of Manasseh, the wolf of Benjamin, the ship of Zebulun, the snake of Dan, the olive tree of Asher, the sun and moon of Issachar, the troop of Gad, the doe of Naphtali, the mandrake of Reuben, and the wall of Simeon. And God also loves the lion of Judah, just as he loves the symbols of the other tribes—no less, but also no more."

Laughter starts to erupt in front of the stage, rolls down Mount Gerizim, goes on to the city of Shechem and through the valley, and rises in rapid waves up Mount Ebal. Six hundred thousand people are laughing all around me in a great din. I want to join in their laughter, but a detailed picture of my beloved brother from Judah suddenly appears before my eyes, and I am choking back my tears.

"I am directing this call from the top of Mount Gerizim to the mountains of Judah," I say, my voice cracking. "My brothers, my loved ones, people of Judah, do not split off from us. Return to us, and we will be one people and one kingdom together, just as God promised our patriarchs. Let us all renew the covenant of the Torah that was made on our behalf by Moses in the wilderness and by Joshua in Shechem. Let us reestablish the united Kingdom of Israel, founded on our behalf by King Saul."

The roar of the crowd allows me to weep without being heard. Only Elisheba and Mother notice that I am crying. Their cheeks are shaking along with me.

A moment later, the roar turns into a song, and the enormous crowd sways in place to the sounds of drums and cymbals, as if it is being buffeted by the waves of the sea:

He was king over Jeshurun,
When the leaders of the people assembled,
Along with the tribes of Israel.
The law that Moses gave us,
The possession of the assembly of Jacob.
Joshua made a covenant for the people,
And there at Shechem he reaffirmed for them decrees and laws.

When the singing ends, I manage to steady my voice and conclude my speech with an oath:

"My brothers, my loved ones, people of Israel, God redeemed us from the house of bondage in Egypt so that we could be free. This day is the day of our exodus from slavery to freedom. I proclaim liberty throughout the land, and I swear to preserve your freedom and to lead you with devotion and with love."

Ahijah the Shilonite steps up to the stage and stands behind me. The crowd watches in silence. Two soldiers follow him to the stage and hand him a copper tray that carries a vial of oil and a crown of gold. I kneel down and close my eyes.

The gentle fingers of the prophet anoint my forehead with the oil and lay the crown upon my head. I hear his call from behind me, "Long live Jeroboam, King—"

But right away, before the heralds can repeat the words, I lift up my face to him and stop him mid-sentence. Startled, he brings his head close to me, and I whisper the words directly into his ear. He shakes his head from side to side, and I nod up and down. Then he shakes again and I nod again, twice and three times, until I become angry and say to him in a commanding voice, "That's an order!"

He sighs and rephrases his call of coronation. The heralds standing near the stage say nothing for a long moment, and then hesitantly, as if internalizing the strange name, they scream out the call to the heralds positioned far away. The call rolls along, spreading in all directions, but the crowd does not repeat it. Complete silence prevails all around. The entire world is a deafening hush.

And then, all at once, a naked, wordless growl slices through the air, followed by six hundred thousand throats erupting all together in one great cry, which rises up, spreads out, and covers the skies of the land:

"Long live Jeroboam son of Nebat, King of Israel!"